KNIGHT OF THE REALM

Calard realised that many of the Norscans had fled not directly away from the Bretonnians, but rather had moved off to the sides, pushing into the ranks of Norscans on the flanks. He turned his head from side to side in concern as he realised that none of the men he had faced appeared to be the heavily armoured Norscan elite that they had expected.

There was something very wrong here, he realised suddenly. His gaze was drawn upwards as the shadowy outline of the reportedly haunted, towering motte at the end of the valley hove into view.

Abruptly, there came a sound like a mountain falling, and a comet trailing hellish red flames shot up into the air from the top of the steep-sided hillock. It soared up high into the sky and Calard followed its trajectory skyward, mouth gaping wide in shock and wonder. Then the roaring comet reached the top of its arc and began to descend towards the ground; towards the charging Bretonnians.

By the same author

WARHAMMER

MARK OF CHAOS

EMPIRE IN CHAOS

KNIGHT ERRANT

WARHAMMER 40,000

DARK APOSTLE

DARK DISCIPLE

A WARHAMMER NOVEL

KNIGHT OF THE REALM

ANTHONY REYNOLDS

For my mates in Blighty. Miss you heaps... but not the weather.

A BLACK LIBRARY PUBLICATION

First published in Great Britain in 2009 by
BL Publishing,
Games Workshop Ltd.,
Willow Road, Nottingham,
NG7 2WS, UK

10 9 8 7 6 5 4 3 2 1

Cover illustration by Alex Boyd
Map by Nuala Kinrade.

A CIP record for this book is available from the British Library.

ISBN 13: 978 1 84416 695 4
ISBN 10: 1 84416 695 3

Printed in the UK by CPI Bookmarque, Croydon, CR0 4TD

THIS IS A dark age, a bloody age, an age of daemons and of sorcery. It is an age of battle and death, and of the world's ending. Amidst all of the fire, flame and fury it is a time, too, of mighty heroes, of bold deeds and great courage.

IN THE WEST of the Old World lies Bretonnia, a fabled land of magic and chivalry. It is also a land of honour and virtue, where noble knights of the realm keep their domains safe as their peasants till the fields, where knights errant strive to win their spurs in battle and where questing knights venture in search of the most holy of artefacts – the grail. For it is said to sup from this most holy chalice a knight will become more than just a hero, he will become a saint.

UPON HIS THRONE in the city of Couronne sits King Louen Leoncoeur, just ruler of Bretonnia and its greatest champion. By the will of the Lady of the Lake, beneficent deity of all Bretonnia, by lance and sword, are the lands of the king kept safe from greenskins and the mutant beastmen of the darkling forests, from malicious daemons and the walking dead.

AS THE TIME of battle draws ever nearer, Bretonnia will need its heroes like never before.

Bretonnia
The Battles of Gilles the Uniter
Cityport or Walled Town
Major Castles
The Wasteland
Couronne
L'Anguille
Lyonesse
Previous border of Mousillon and Lyonesse
Pale Sisters
Marienburg
Forest of Arden
Artois
Gisoreux
The Empire
Montfort
Mousillon
River Grismerie
Bastonne
Axe Bite Pass
Parravon
Great Ocean
Bordeleaux
Forest of Chalons
The Massif Orcal
Aquitaine
Brionne
Quenelles
Forest of Loren
River Brienne
Carcassonne
The Vaults

PROLOGUE

THE GLOW OF embers cast a hellish light through the tent, and ribbons of acrid smoke coiled around the seated figure. Threatening shadows surrounded him, whispering hatefully, and the seer's eyes snapped open.

Barking a curse of warding, the seer upended a bowl of warm blood onto the glowing coals. It boiled and spat and the murderous shadows retreated into the darkest recesses of the tent, banished. A moment later and the seer was alone, seated cross-legged before the hissing embers.

His upper body was naked, and a crisscrossing network of scars covered his sinewy, taut flesh, interspersed with talismanic tattoos and ritual piercings. Bones, flint runes and sticks were bound within his thick mane of dark hair, and his tattooed lips parted in a smile, exposing teeth that had been filed to points.

'At last,' he said.

The seer surged upright, pulling thick furs around his shoulders and snatching up his goat-skulled staff.

Throwing aside the heavy flap of his tent, he stepped out into the roaring gale.

The snow was knee deep, and he leant into the wind as he stamped his way through the Skaeling village of Strovengaard. Snow and ice billowed around him, and he could see little, merely vague shadows suggesting the tents and structures of the village. It mattered not; he could have walked blindfolded through the village without tripping or making a false step.

Climbing the icy stairs of the longhouse, hunched against the fury of the gale, the seer slammed the iron-shod butt of his staff against a pair of grand double doors. They were carved with stylised images of warriors and daemons, surrounded by spiralling designs that seemed to writhe with movement, but the seer was wise enough not to be ensnared by their tricks.

The doors opened a crack before their guardian recognised who it was that sought entrance and the doors were thrown wide. The seer strode inside, snow blasting in around him, and the portals were slammed shut.

It was stiflingly hot inside and stank of sweat and charred meat. The feast was in full flow, and the general hubbub rose to the rafters as the favoured warriors of the tribe, the huskarls, ate and drank, laughed and fought.

Each member of this warrior elite was a battle-scarred veteran that had proven himself time and time again before his peers, his lord and the gods themselves. They were giants among men, fierce, proud and volatile, each one marked in some way by the Great Powers, and yet even through their haze of drunkenness, they instinctively gave way as the shaman stalked amongst them.

The seer stood barely to the shoulder of any of the huskarls, but they parted before him like the ocean before the prow of a dragonship. None caught his eye, and conversations silenced as he passed. Even the massive warhounds of the tribe, stalking around the periphery of the feast, cowered before him, whimpering and snarling.

One pair of eyes did not lower, and the seer threw a glance towards the squat, inhuman figure seated in a dim corner of the hall. He saw malice and hatred in those stony eyes, and returned the glare briefly. How he would love to cut the heart from that one and devour it before life faded from the stunted bastard's eyes.

Dragging his gaze away from the dark dwarf, the seer continued to make his way through the press of warriors. An icy trickle ran down the back of his neck as the snow and ice upon his furs and hair began to melt. The butt of his staff slammed into the sawdust covered floor with every step.

Against the far wall was a raised platform, upon which a dozen people feasted, seated at a long table perpendicular to the others in the room, allowing them an unobstructed view across the hall. The wall behind this table was hung with weapons, shields, severed heads, skulls and beast pelts of all description. They were all trophies won by the lord of the tribe, their high jarl, in the decades since he had come to power; the day that he had hacked his father's head from his shoulders and claimed his ascendancy.

As a seer of the Skaelings, he had no need to bow to any man or beast, and yet as he reached the bottom of the dais he dropped to one knee and lowered his head. His jarl was more than just a chieftain to him, for he had welcomed him into his home, clothed and fed him, and taught him the ways of the Skaeling Norscans. To the seer, his jarl was a father in all but name and blood.

'Rise, Bjarki,' the Skaeling chieftain said, his voice deep and sonorous.

The seer lifted his head to look upon his adopted father, his eyes shining with savage anticipation.

High Jarl Egil Styrbjorn sat brooding upon a wooden throne carved to resemble a twin-headed dragon, its clawed forelimbs forming the armrests and its unfurled wings the high back. He was a massive man, tall and powerfully built despite his years. Bjarki could feel the touch of the gods upon the high jarl as a tingle upon his flesh and a dull buzzing in the base of his skull. Both his beard and long, dark blond hair were streaked with silver, though his icy grey eyes still blazed with strength and vigour.

Flanking him were his wives and daughters. His youngest wife, the personification of Norscan beauty itself – tall, proud, and strong – was leaning against her husband, her bosom pressed against one of his powerful arms. His youngest child was no more than a babe; his eldest was already past child-bearing years. Not that such a thing had been put to the test – no Skaeling chieftain would allow a daughter to marry until he had a son to carry his name.

'I have seen her, my jarl,' said Bjarki, a slight smile curling at the seer's tattooed lips.

All eyes turned towards him, and the dull murmur of conversation died.

'I have seen her in a blood-vision,' said the seer, 'delivered by the gods themselves.'

Styrbjorn's wives and daughters traded glances, and the Skaeling chieftain leant forward ever so slightly.

'Speak plainly, little bear,' said Styrbjorn.

'I have seen the one who will birth you a son,' said the Skaeling seer.

The only sound was the crackling of flames and the dull howl of the wind outside.

'Where?' growled Styrbjorn.

'Across the sea, in the land of the southern horsemen. *Bretonnia.*'

CHAPTER ONE

Boughs creaked and groaned overhead, and an icy wind whispered through the trees like a dying breath. Thorned twigs scratched at Elisabet's arms as she pushed through the tangle of brambles and branches, drawing blood.

The hem of her dress was tattered and stained, and strands of unruly hair had escaped their binding, pulled loose by snagging branches.

The wild forest resisted Elisabet's every step, and she began to imagine that there was a malicious sentience within it, a darkly verdant will that lurked at its heart, thwarting her attempts to penetrate its borders.

She shivered at the thought, realising that there was a certain truth in the notion; all the whispered stories she had heard said that the crone Haegtesse *did* exert some measure of power over the woods. That power ensured those who meant her harm, or those whom she did not wish to receive, were turned around, finding themselves walking back towards the edge of the woods instead of into them. It was for this reason that Haegtesse had not hung from the gallows decades, or indeed a century, earlier. In truth, many had come to believe that she was nothing more than a local superstition, a story told to scare children into behaving.

Elisabet, however, knew that the crone Haegtesse was no myth, for she had visited her once before. Long had she cursed that day, and a wretched sob rocked her slender frame.

She hardly knew why she sought out the hag again now. Was it shame that brought her back to the place that had started it all? Her resentment, her anger, her self-loathing?

Where else had she to go, she thought bitterly? She was outcast, her life forfeit.

Again she saw her beloved Calard's face, a mask of horror and disgust.

A twinge of bitterness stabbed through her. It had all been for *him*. How could he not see that?

In truth, Elisabet didn't know why she came here. It felt like she was being drawn here, and she had no power to resist this siren call. It was as if an invisible leash was fastened around her neck, dragging her inexorably back to the crone's cave.

Elisabet's foot caught between a pair of twisted roots resembling sinewy arms, and she winced as her ankle twisted beneath her. She fell awkwardly, hands burying themselves in the rich leaf litter. Insects and worms writhed across her skin. Horrified, she pulled herself free of the contorted roots and scrambled to her feet.

Her eyes widened as she came face to face with the doll-totem. She was certain that it had not been there just a moment before.

It dangled less than two feet in front of her face, and she staggered back from it, her large, dark-rimmed eyes wide.

It hung from a low bough, like a corpse swinging slowly from a gibbet, a crude representation of a woman, crafted of wood, bone and hair and strung together with half-rotted sinew. It stunk like rancid meat, and Elisabet covered her nose and mouth. What looked like dried blood was daubed upon the totem's chest, in between its malformed breasts, and strings of beads, shells and knucklebones hung from its cruciform, spread-eagled arms and legs. Its fingers and toes were twigs and it wore a frayed skirt of dried grass and thorns.

Its face was framed by dark, human-looking hair that crawled with lice. Skin, possibly human and dark with age, had been stretched across a lump of wood crudely carved in the shape of a human head, and Elisabet felt her stomach lurch as she saw maggots squirming beneath. A wide slash filled with human and animal teeth represented the doll-totem's mouth, and holes had been burnt for eyes. Rotten acorns stood in for eyeballs, and two further slits in the skin represented nostrils. Bloated flies crawled in and out of these gashes. The face seemed to leer at her, and Elisabet tried to stem the panic rising within her as it swung back and forth, creaking, in front of her.

Keeping her distance, Elisabet edged past the doll-totem. She saw more of them, the low branches hanging with dozens of the vile things, each one a horrific mockery of humanity. Some had twisted horns sprouting from their heads, and others were blackened with fire. Some had rusted nails hammered into their eyes, while others had disgusting, unrecognisable lumps of flesh hung around their necks like scarves, some with scraps of fur and skin still attached.

Keeping her gaze resolutely forward, Elisabet followed the twisting path. At last she came upon the cave. A moaning wind emerged from within, bringing with it the sickly scent of rot and decay.

The giant husk of a tree loomed overhead, its twisted roots spread out beneath it, slick with blood-like sap. This ancient tree had grown atop a rocky outcrop, its thick roots cracking the stone and framing the cave entrance like mighty pillars. The slim fissure was dark.

A raven sat above the cave entrance, its head cocked to the side as it glared at Elisabet with one yellow eye. It cawed, the sound ugly and harsh, and a whisper emerged from within the cave, carried to Elisabet's ears on the breath of a foetid wind.

'Come, child...'

Elisabet shivered, unsure if the words had been real or imagined. An inner voice was screaming for her to turn and run, to flee this horrid place, but she could not. The invisible leash tugged at her, impelling her onwards.

The black feathered raven stared down at her, and she felt the hatred and hunger of the carrion eater wash over her. She flinched as it took flight, crying raucously, and it flapped off into the darkness.

The pull upon her grew more insistent, and the last fragments of her resistance were stripped away. With a sob, she entered the cave.

Elisabet stretched her hands out to either side, fingertips brushing the cold, wet rock. After a dozen hesitant steps into darkness the tunnel turned to the right, leaving the daylight behind, and the dim glow of candles could be seen flickering across the walls in front. She saw that the stone had been carved into daemonic forms, capering horned figures, naked succubi and scaled, dog-faced warriors engaged in all manner of horrific debauchery, and she quickly averted her gaze.

The cave opened up before her. Its extent was hidden in darkness, but the candles, thick and squat and exuding reeking, black smoke, illuminated its centre. Roots from the tree above reached down into the cave like the arms of corpses. Less wholesome things hung there too: skinned hares dripping blood, twitching rodents and bats impaled on hooks, and dozens of doll-totems, grinning at her as they slowly turned.

Seated cross-legged upon a rotten pallet of straw and matted fur beneath these macabre ornaments was the crone, Haegtesse.

Her head was bowed, and unruly, matted grey hair hung over her face, obscuring it like a mortuary veil. Her withered, skeletal body was draped in dank cloth, and she clutched a doll in her claw-like hands.

'Come closer, my child,' said Haegtesse.

Elisabet wanted to run, but her own free will was of no consequence. Involuntarily, she began moving towards the hag. She felt like a player's marionette, her legs moving to the whim of another.

'No,' she whispered, tears running down her cheeks, even as she did as Haegtesse bid her.

'Do not fight it,' said the crone. 'It will be easier for you if you do not.'

With a gesture, the hag ordered Elisabet to sit down opposite her.

Elisabet was shaking her head, but found herself sitting cross-legged on the pallet opposite the crone.

'So young,' said Haegtesse, reaching forward with a withered claw of a hand to touch Elisabet's porcelain cheek.

'You made good use of the poison I gave you, then?' said Haegtesse.

Elisabet did not answer, but the hag did not seem to mind, muttering and chuckling to herself. Elisabet sat like a statue, unable to move anything but her eyes.

She flashed a glance down at the totem in the crone's lap. The doll's eyes were beetles, their legs kicking as they sought futilely to escape the pins that impaled them. The twig-hands of the doll were slick with blood, and fat flies crawled between its fingers.

'A good likeness, yes?' said the hag.

The witch laughed as understanding came to Elisabet.

The doll represented *her*.

The black hair stitched into the thing's head was hers. The tattered cloth that wrapped its body was a torn fragment of a dress she had discarded the previous winter. Who knew what other parts of the doll were connected to her? Nail clippings? Blood? What did it mean?

She tried to pull away as the crone reached for her, but she continued to sit as rigid as a statue, unable to move a muscle, nor so much as cry out.

There was a searing pain as Haegtesse pressed her fingertips to Elisabet's temples, and a feeling of vertigo overcame her. It felt as though the ground beneath her was shifting, and blinding agony stabbed in the back of her eyes.

From somewhere she heard the tortured wail of an animal in pain, and then she was falling, falling into darkness...

BENEATH THE SHADE of the tall, silver-barked beech trees, the hunters rode in a snaking line, two abreast. The mood of the nobles at the front of the party, carrying their stout, leaf-bladed boar spears, was sombre. Huge mastiffs, their powerful bodies armoured in thick plate, trotted alongside their masters.

Ranging out in front of the hunting party were dozens of peasants with snuffling dogs, scouring the forest for game. Unlike the armoured fighting dogs, these peasant runt-hounds were as scabby and wretched as those holding their leashes. Still, they had their uses. It was these half-starved animals that sought out the spoor of the great boars that roamed the Forest of Arden, and once discovered it was their duty to drive them back towards their noble masters for the kill.

Often, the runt-hounds and their peasant masters were gored to death by rampant boars or other less mundane beasts that dwelt within the wilds, but it mattered little. More important was that no damage was done to the mighty boars in the process; by law, only a noble was allowed to bring one down, and if it had already been injured by a foolish – and soon to be hung – peasant, then the honour of the kill was lessened.

Leading the hunt was a nobleman of middling years, Baron Lothgar of Artois. His face was a mask of irritation, and it was clear that his mood had infected those retainers and courtiers riding nearby. He wore a deep red tabard over his breastplate, and a silver boar's head was emblazoned upon his chest.

From further back along the procession of hunters came laughter, and the nobleman's expression darkened.

'Any game within a half a mile will be long gone,' he said in a low voice. 'Listen to them. They may as well be banging drums and singing the *Chanson de Folgar* at the top of their lungs.'

'His pedigree is sound, though, my lord,' said the knight at his side. 'A castellan, no less. He would make a fine match for Lady Madeleine. Without speaking out of turn, my lord, would it perhaps be wise not to allow your irritation to jeopardise this opportunity?'

The baron sighed. He knew the advice was sound, but he lived for the hunt. To have it ruined by disrespectful young knights made his choler rise. And he could not shake the nagging feeling that the young Garamont brothers were wasting his time.

He turned in the saddle to regard his guest, riding alongside his eldest unwed daughter, Madeleine.

Lothgar winced as he saw the young lord of Garamont drinking freely from the wineskin. The wine the young lord was swigging like water was a hundred and fifty years old, acquired for no small sum from fair Quenelles. Though it was Bordeleaux that was most famed for its vintages, the wines of Quenelles had a touch of the fey about them, grown near the Forest of Loren as they were, and were highly sought after by true connoisseurs.

Lord Calard, Castellan of Garamont, was a young man, no more than twenty-two years of age. He was not as tall as his brother, but was more powerfully built. His dark hair hung loose to his shoulders in the latest fashion. His wealth was obvious in the cut of his blue and red doublet, and his dragon rampant heraldry shone with silver. Indeed, the sword at his waist alone would have been worth more than half of Baron Lothgar's estates.

'He and his brother, along with his entourage, have been my guests for a week now, drinking my oldest wines and dining on my finest foods. Another week of this and I will be a pauper,' said Lothgar. 'I hope this proves worthwhile.'

'If Madeleine ensnares him then it will be, my lord.'

Baron Lothgar grunted in response, casting his gaze skywards.

'The weather is turning,' he said. 'and there is little chance of any sport here. The boar can wait another day. Let us return home.'

The knight nodded his head as he drew his steed to a halt. He signalled to one of the peasants trotting nearby, who lifted a horn to his lips and blew three sharp blasts.

'Let's hope that Lady Madeleine has been more successful in *her* hunt,' said Lothgar.

'IT WOULD APPEAR that the hunt is over, my lord castellan,' said Lady Madeleine.

A drunken cheer rose from the knights of Bastonne at the proclamation.

'About time,' said Lord Calard. 'We are in need of more drink, anyway.'

Lady Madeleine raised a delicately plucked eyebrow.

'You have not already consumed enough of my father's wine for one morning? I'd suggest that you were already drunk if it were not impertinent.'

'That would be impertinent indeed,' said Calard in a low voice, leaning towards Madeleine. 'But I am disappointed. I had hoped, amidst the confusion of the hunt, to have stolen some time with you alone, unchaperoned.'

'Now it is you who is being impertinent,' said Madeleine.

Calard stood in the saddle, and saw that Baron Lothgar was guiding his steed towards him. He dropped back into the saddle and gave Madeleine a wink.

'Care for a quick ride?' he said with a wicked gleam in his slightly glazed eyes. 'It is too fine a morning to return to your father's castle just yet.'

'Too fine a morning?' replied Madeleine, laughing. 'It's raining, you fool.'

'Nothing wrong with a bit of rain,' said Calard. He turned his steed in a tight circle, and it stamped its hooves, eager to run. 'Well?'

'My father will not be best pleased,' she said.

'And you? Would you be best pleased?'

Calard smiled as he saw the young lady shake her head slightly, exasperated with him. She sighed.

'Fine,' she said.

Calard kicked his horse into a gallop, and the two of them raced off through the trees, just as the baron was drawing near. Calard laughed out loud at the outraged look upon his host's face.

Calard had been away from Garamont for almost two weeks now. The pressures and demands of his new-found position niggled in the back of his mind, as much as he tried to ignore them.

He had a realm of his own to govern now, and was responsible for all who dwelt within it, peasant and noble. Levelling taxes and levies, resolving grievances, overseeing the proper usage of his realm's monies, negotiating alliances and border disputes with his neighbouring lords, ensuring his dues were paid to duke and king, maintaining order across his lands; all were his duty now to oversee. The amount of paperwork was unfathomable, the petty politicking and back-stabbing of his court exhausting. He had a newfound respect for his father, for he had never heard the old man complain, nor had he ever appeared to falter under the pressure. Indeed, Calard had never realised there *was* any particular pressure in the position.

'There is much work to be done here, my lord,' Folcard had said when Calard had informed him he would be attending the tournament in Lyonesse. 'I shall pen a polite refusal.'

'No,' Calard had said. 'I think a few weeks away will do me good. In my absence, I empower you to act on my behalf, Folcard. You are more suited to all this anyway.'

Calard was well aware that he was running away from his responsibilities, but he had pushed those thoughts to the back of his mind.

He and his companions had been on their way to the tourney when they had stopped in at Lothgar's estate a week earlier. The baron had welcomed them in, opening up his cellar and organising an impromptu feast, mistakenly believing that Calard was here to woo his daughter. In the week since, Calard had been happy to maintain the misunderstanding. They had time to kill before the tournament in Lyonesse began and besides, he was enjoying himself.

They rode for several minutes, weaving between the silver-skinned trunks of birch, and Calard was impressed with the skill of the lady's riding. Even at a full gallop, she remained elegant in her side-saddled position, courtesy in a large part to the double-pommelled saddle on which she sat. Such a saddle allowed ladies to ride at a gallop, and even to safely jump fences and fallen logs. Beneath her flowing dress, Madeleine's legs would be curled around the twin pommels, holding her tight against the horse's body.

At last they came upon a clearing, and the two of them reined in their steeds. Calard was laughing, and he swung his leg over his mount and dropped to the ground, using his boar-spear for balance. He staggered, and realised he was more drunk than he had thought. Madeleine laughed, and ramming the spear into the ground he stepped in close, his hands circling her slim waist.

He breathed in her scent as he lifted her from the saddle and placed her lightly on the ground. She did not resist as he pulled her close.

'So, when are you planning on asking my father, then?' she breathed.

'Asking your father what?' said Calard, distracted as he looked down into the impressive crevasse of her bosom.

'Why, for my hand in marriage, you fool.'

Calard blinked.

'What?' he said.

'You *were* going to ask my father for my hand?' she said, pulling away from him and fixing him with a steely look.

'Well?' she said, eyes hardening.

'Well...' said Calard.

Madeleine pushed away from him, a look of outrage on her face.

'You bastard,' she said.

From somewhere, Calard heard dogs barking, but in his drink-addled state, and with a furious young lady glaring at him, he barely registered the sound, nor what it portended. The ears of both horses suddenly flattened, and they began pawing at the ground, nostrils flaring.

'You are a drunkard fool, Calard of Garamont,' snapped Lady Madeleine. 'A boy, playing at being a man. I shall be telling my father forthwith that your intentions here have been anything but noble.'

The sound of dogs barking came ever closer, and Calard's eyes were drawn past Madeleine's shoulder. The horses whinnied in fear. Madeleine's voice seemed to fade away as he saw the undergrowth shudder, leaves and branches shaking.

'Are you even listening to me?' she said, but her voice had become just a distant drone.

A massive, furred shape burst from the trees, snorting and stamping. It was almost five feet tall at the shoulder, and its bulk was immense. Its fur rose in a sharp, matted ridge down its spine, and four tusks emerged from its slavering mouth, each easily two feet in length. Its beady, red-rimmed eyes were filled with rage. A second later and it was charging.

Calard hurled Lady Madeleine aside. She fell with a squeal of outrage to the muddy ground, and Calard reached for the spear embedded in the earth.

The immense boar, easily the largest such beast that Calard had ever clapped eyes on, came at him in a wild rush, hurtling across the clearing at great speed. Thick, ropey threads of spittle dripped from its maw as it bore down on him, and Calard spun the spear up in front of him. The beast must have been ten times his weight.

Jamming the butt of the spear down into the ground, Calard stamped one foot down hard onto it, setting it as best he could. The bladed tip he lifted, and he tensed his body as the immense beast hurled itself at him, intending to rip him from groin to neck with its tusks.

The spear took the boar in its chest, and the force of its impact drove it deep into its flesh. It felt to Calard like he had been struck by a falling mountain, and he was hurled backwards, falling to his back as the boar's momentum carried it over him.

The stink of the beast was terrible, and hot blood gushed across his face. It came down on top of him, its weight all but crushing the life from his body. The creature was not dead, and it struggled to right itself, slipping in the mud and its own blood. It snorted, swinging its head around to gore him, but trapped underneath the beast as he was, he was mercifully out of its reach, and it merely gouged out several great rents in the earth.

He heard the pounding of horses' hooves nearby, and heard dogs barking and growling furiously. He gasped as the great boar staggered to its feet, one hoofed leg almost crushing his hip, and he tried to roll to the side. The boar swung its head violently, and he heard a pitiful yelp as a dog was sent flying.

Calard rolled from beneath the mighty beast as a spear rammed down into its shoulder, and a pair of armoured boarhounds leapt on it, jaws snapping. Calard's spear was still embedded deep in its chest, and blood was pumping from the wound. Another spear was driven into the boar, striking deep behind its left shoulder blade. The tip of the spear found its heart, and it slumped to the ground, still fighting. The huge, armoured dogs continued to worry at the beast as it died, until they were hauled off the immense carcass.

Calard was helped unsteadily to his feet. He put a hand to his head and saw blood on his fingers.

'Are you all right, my lord?' said a voice, but he couldn't focus on whom it was that had spoken.

'Fine,' he managed. Then he fell backwards, and hit the ground hard.

Suddenly, everything changed.

Calard didn't hear the harsh words spoken between father and daughter, or the concern in the voice of his cousins, Huebald, Baldemund and Tassilo. He didn't see his companions as they swung from their saddles to come to his aid. It was as if as soon as he struck the ground he was transported to a different place, a different time.

Dark clouds rushed across the skyline with unnatural speed, as if hours were passing in the blink of an eye. The light faded, until it was as dark as twilight, throwing the surrounding forest into gloom. The temperature plummeted, and he began to shiver uncontrollably. His breath fogged the air in front of his face, and splinters of frost began to form across his armour.

A thick, cloying fog rose around him, and Calard looked around for any sign of his companions. He could see nothing. He was alone, utterly alone.

The undergrowth beneath him began to writhe like a living creature, and he cried out, but the rising fog deadened all sound. Ivy and grass coiled around his hands and boots, crawling over his leggings and curling around his arms. He fought to rise from the ground, but the plant-life tightened around him, pinning him in place.

A ghostly figure began to materialise within the fog, and Calard ceased his struggles, his eyes widening. He heard the snort of a destrier, and as the apparition solidified, he saw that it rode the largest warhorse he had ever seen.

An overpowering, earthy smell filled his nostrils. It was not an unpleasant scent, but was strong and heady, a mix of sap, moist earth, rotting vegetation, oak and fir.

The rider was armoured from head to toe in archaic plate. Coiling ivy bedecked this armour, and a thick plume of leaves erupted from the crown of his helmet. The greenery covering the apparition's armour was in constant movement, constant growth. Fresh leaves unfurled, new life bursting forth. Within heartbeats, these young leaves matured and grew wide, before starting to wither and yellow. Then they fell from its armour, and the mesmerising cycle began anew.

From within the darkness behind the eye-slits of its helmet burnt a pair of furious, glowing orbs, exuding a ghostly green light, and Calard felt his body shudder involuntarily with terror as they fixed on him.

Calard fought against the plants restraining him, thrashing and pulling against their restrictive grasp, desperate to get away. The grass, ivy and roots merely tightened their grip, and whipping strands of ground creepers wrapped themselves around his neck, constricting his breath.

The immense destrier stamped its hooves and snorted, exhaling great billowing clouds of steam. The apparition slowly drew its sword.

That sword, ancient and terrible, was covered with intricate spiralling engravings, and an icy fog fell from the blade. The knight levelled the point of the sword towards Calard, and he felt a freezing chill emanating from the blade.

Calard's breath was coming in short, sharp gasps as he stared up at the knight looming above him, expecting to be cut down at any moment. The supernatural figure exuded a raw, elemental power, a kingly majesty that was at once terrible and awesome. Its glowing green eyes glared down at him balefully and he felt its terrible rage wash over him like the untamed fury of a storm.

The knight muscled its immense steed closer, black hooves slamming into the ground scant inches from Calard. The mighty beast tossed its head, and he felt its hot breath on his face.

Face me, coward.

Calard reeled backwards as the stabbing pain of the unnatural voice pierced his mind.

Face me! it pulsed again, and he cried out.

'I can't!' he cried. How could he fight against this supremely powerful, mystical warrior, him with his hands bound by whipping cords of ivy, roots and grass?

How can you hope to best me, if you cannot even best yourself?

'Help me!' cried Calard, though to whom he cried to, he couldn't say.

Coward!

The power and malice in the words stabbed at him, and Calard cried out, closing his eyes tightly. He heard the mournful sound of the apparition's blade humming through the air, and he clenched his eyes tighter, waiting for the blow to fall.

'Just do it!' he bellowed.

'Do what, my lord?' said a concerned voice.

Calard opened his eyes, and found himself staring into his cousin Tassilo's concerned face.

'Tell me what you would have me do, my lord, and I will gladly do as you wish,' said the knight.

Calard turned his wild gaze from Tassilo, kneeling over him, and saw his other companions, Huebald and Baldemund, standing nearby, looking worried. A light rain was falling, but it was bright, despite the thick canopy created by the tall beech trees. The unearthly chill was gone, and of the apparition, there was no sign.

'Are you all right, my lord?' said Baldemund.

Calard nodded, though he immediately regretted it as shooting pain lanced through his head.

'I'm fine,' he said. 'Stupid of me, to have fallen. I'm fine, really.'

All sense of drunkenness had left him, though his head was pounding and there was a horrible taste in his mouth.

His hands were still shaking as Tassilo helped him to his feet.

'You gave us a terrible shock,' said the young knight with some relief. 'I thought you'd lost your senses there for a moment. One of the boar's hooves must have struck you in the head. It bled a lot, but the wound isn't deep.'

Calard mumbled something about the drink, and wiped a hand across his face. He waved away Tassilo, and pulled himself back into the saddle.

'Baron Lothgar? Lady Madeleine?' he said.

'Gone,' said Huebald. 'I don't think they are best pleased with you.'

'No?' said Calard, still somewhat woozy.

'I think the lady's words were something along the lines of *"I'd sooner marry the boar than that Bastonnian pig"*,' said Tassilo, smirking.

'You were thinking of marrying her?' said Baldemund.

'Of course not,' said Calard, looking around. 'Where's the boar?'

'The baron's peasants took it,' said Huebald.

'Was it as big as I remember?'

'Bigger,' said Tassilo, smiling.

'Come,' said Huebald. 'I'd say it was past time that we were making our way back. I think it wise for us to collect our gear and be on our way before the baron decides to gift it to the poor.'

Calard's mind was drifting back to the glowing eyes of the apparition. The Green Knight… It had been the same for months now, the vision. It haunted his dreams, and only strong drink seemed to keep it at bay.

Calard dragged his thoughts back to the present.

'Yes, I fear we have outstayed our welcome,' he said. 'Just let us hope that my brother has done nothing in our absence to bring further dishonour upon our host.'

He had a sinking feeling that was not going to be the case.

'GET UP!'

Bertelis tried to ignore the voice, and rolled over in the sumptuous bed, throwing an arm across his eyes.

Clothes – *his* clothes he realised – were thrown at him, and he groaned.

'Come back to bed,' he said, reaching out with a hand, his eyes still closed.

'Get up, you fool!' the girl said again, her voice filled with panic. Bertelis lowered his arm and propped himself up on the mattress, his gaze lingering on the girl frantically dressing herself at the foot of the bed.

Lady Celeste, Baron Lothgar's younger daughter, was a beauty and no mistake, petite and perfectly formed in all the right places. He watched the delicate curve of her back as she struggled to pull on her dress. Her fair hair was pinned up, but errant strands hung loose down her pale shoulders. He smiled, enjoying the view as she bent over to retrieve one of her slippers. Articles of clothing were strewn across the room, having been cast aside in the heat of passion the night before.

Celeste saw his grin and her eyes flashed with a mixture of panic and amusement.

'Get up, you fool!' she said again. 'My father is on his way here, now!'

The grin dropped from Bertelis's face and he hauled the sweat-soaked sheets aside, the threat of discovery galvanising him into action. Naked, he leapt to his feet.

'What is he doing back so early? I thought the hunt was meant to take all day?' said Bertelis.

'It was,' said Lady Celeste. She threw open the wooden shutters of her window and leant out.

'Oh, Lady above, he is already on his way up,' she wailed. 'I'll be disowned!'

Celeste raced around her room, throwing discarded undergarments into a basket in the corner of the room. She heaved a padded blanket off the floor and with a sharp whip, made it settle over her bed.

Bertelis was standing there uselessly, still naked, holding his bundle of clothes in front of him. Struggling to drag her wayward blonde hair into order, Celeste ran to the door and peered out. Bertelis made to follow her, but she pulled back abruptly, hearing footsteps and her father's voice. She slammed the door, panicking.

'He's here!' she said, eyes darting around the room. 'Lady, preserve me!'

Her gaze settled on the window. Following her gaze, Bertelis began shaking his head.

'No. No!' he said, even as Celeste began pushing him. He ducked and picked up his bundle of clothes as he was shoved towards the arched window.

'What are you doing?' he said, half laughing. 'It's got to be a fifty foot drop!'

'More,' said Celeste, still pushing him towards the window. She gave him another solid shove.

'There's a ledge,' she said. 'Now go!'

A cold wind whipped at Bertelis's back, and he glanced over his shoulder, seeing the cobbled courtyard far below.

There was a knock on her door.

'He's here!' Celeste wailed.

Bertelis turned around on the spot, so that he had his back to the room. The ledge was not even a foot wide.

Lady Celeste slammed the shutters of her window closed, almost knocking Bertelis down into the courtyard, stranding him on the sill. For a moment he teetered on the edge before regaining his balance. The cold air made goose-bumps rise all over his body.

Fearing what would happen if Lord Lothgar were to open the windows wide only to come face to face with his naked buttocks, he shimmied to the side, pressing himself up against the cold stone wall, his clothes bundled in front of him.

Looking down he saw his brother Calard riding into the courtyard below, accompanied by his retainers and vassals, returning from the hunt. He saw Tassilo's upturned face, saw the young man's mouth gape open.

Calard's gaze settled on Bertelis, seventy-five feet above the courtyard. Bertelis grinned, and raised a hand in greeting.

'WELL, THAT WENT well,' said Calard.

The five knights of Garamont, accompanied by some thirty-odd men-at-arms wearing the red and blue of Calard's heraldry, were around four miles from Baron Lothgar's castle. The rain was getting heavier, and the sun was dipping low.

'Who would have thought Baron Lothgar would have known such... colourful... language,' said Bertelis.

'Not I,' said Calard.

'I think my ears are still ringing.'

'Still, I would imagine any father would have a few choice words to say if they found a naked man on his daughter's windowsill,' said Calard.

'And if his other daughter had just been turned down by said man's older brother,' piped in Tassilo.

'True,' said Bertelis. 'I didn't quite realise she was *that* young.'

'Or that we had drunk quite so much of his cellar,' said Calard.

'Live and learn, eh?'

'Indeed,' said Calard.

Laughing, the brothers led their entourage away from their host's lands, heading north-west.

For a moment it was like old times between the two, the tension and distance that had grown up between the two brothers temporarily forgotten.

Such a respite was not to last.

* * *

Elisabet awoke to pain. She ached all over, and it felt as though there was a weight pressed against her chest, making breathing difficult. She was lying on her side, with her legs drawn up to her chest. Her joints groaned as she struggled to push herself up. There was no strength in her arms, and every movement brought with it fresh agonies.

She was still within the cave, she saw, though her vision was hazy and vague. Candles still burnt around her, giving off their sickly stink, but Elisabet was alone – of Haegtesse there was no sign.

The hateful doll-totem of herself lay on the pallet, grinning up at her mockingly.

Feeling the witch's control over her gone, she tried to push herself to her feet, to run from this horrific place, but her vision swam and her legs had no strength, and she collapsed in a sprawled heap. Wheezing, her heart hammering weakly against her ribcage, she sobbed.

What had been done to her?

It was then that she looked at her own hands. They were wasted, the skin loose and covered in liver spots. Her fingers ended in yellow, cracked nails. She saw that the hair hanging before her eyes was grey, and she could feel the lice against her flaking scalp. Looking down at herself, she saw that her youthful, supple body was gone, replaced with the cancerous, ancient and skeletal form of Haegtesse.

A groan of horror clawed its way up from her age ravaged, half-collapsed lungs, passing her toothless, bloody gums and emerging as a croaking wail.

Outside, Haegtesse heard the desolate cry, and smiled. She ran her hands over her stolen body, feeling the pleasing contradiction of softness and firmness, the tautness and fleeting elasticity of youthful skin. She breathed in deeply, rejoicing in her clear vision and the strength she felt in her limbs.

With a smile, she walked away from the cave, leaving her wasted, dying husk behind her. It had served its purpose these past ninety years. Now she had need of this body, young, untainted and fertile.

The brambles and thorns parted before her, and she began walking to the north.

CHAPTER TWO

BERTELIS'S ARMS FELT like leaden weights and his breath was coming in short, sharp gasps, but he pushed through his exhaustion and launched another attack.

Feinting with a strike to the head, he rolled his wrist and whipped his sword around in a low, disembowelling slash. His opponent took the attack on his shield and launched a strike of his own, his blade hissing through the air. Bertelis deflected the blade, letting it glance off his black and red shield, throwing the other knight slightly off balance. Not giving the man a chance to recover, Bertelis launched into a series of swift attacks, his blade cutting left and right, forcing his opponent backwards, defending frantically.

Stepping in close, Bertelis slammed his shield into his opponent. The knight grimaced and staggered back. His rear foot, supporting the majority of his weight, slipped in mud, and he dropped to one knee. In an instant, Bertelis's sword tip was at his throat.

'I concede,' said the defeated knight, Huebald, blinking rain out of his eyes.

None of the cousins felt any shame at being bested by their younger kinsman. Bertelis had always been talented with the blade but had never been one to dedicate himself to training. That had all changed since the death of Gunthar.

Gunthar, the old weapon master of Garamont, had taught both Bertelis and Calard in the arts of swordplay and the joust since the day they could walk. He had been one of the finest swordsmen in all of Bastonne in his day, and he had been wounded in a duel six months earlier, a duel that he had fought in lieu of Calard. Though he had defeated his opponent, Gunthar had in turn been badly injured. His wound had festered, and the only chance would have been to have his leg amputated, though even then his chance of surviving was slim. Refusing to suffer such an ignominious fate – for what good was a knight that could not even sit in the saddle? – Gunthar had given his life defending Bertelis, standing over him and protecting him while he was incapacitated. He had taken a dozen or more enemies with him before he finally fell, a hero, pierced by a score of blades.

The old weapon master had given his life that Bertelis might live, and that was something that the younger Garamont brother had found hard to accept. In the months since, he had dedicated himself to his training to an almost obsessive extent.

Bertelis removed his blade from his cousin's throat, his chest heaving with exertion. Still he allowed himself no rest, and turned to face his other two cousins.

'Come,' he said, nodding to Tassilo. Slender and quick, the youngest of his cousins was a skilful swordsman and Bertelis enjoyed sparring with him.

'Enough, brother,' said a voice.

Bertelis turned to regard Calard, who was emerging, dishevelled, from his red and blue tent. His face was heavy with stubble, and his dark hair was unruly, hanging around his shoulders. He was dressed in the same clothes he had been wearing the night before, and even from here, Bertelis could smell the reek of alcohol on him.

'Decided to grace us with your presence?' said Bertelis, sheathing his sword.

'Couldn't really sleep with the racket you lot were making, could I?' replied Calard.

'It's almost midday, brother,' said Bertelis. 'We were meant to strike the camp at dawn.'

'Water,' ordered Calard, sending servants scurrying. He was handed a goblet of water, and drank deeply.

'Midday?' said Calard, squinting up at the overcast sky.

'That's right,' said Bertelis.

Calard's bleary gaze wandered around the clearing.

'Training again?' he said.

'No, I've been milking cattle,' snapped Bertelis. 'Yes, I've been training, for all the good that it will do. At this rate we are not going to arrive at the tournament in time to take part anyway.'

'The tournament's what, a week away? That's plenty of time.'

'It is two days away, brother,' said Bertelis. He turned away, muttering under his breath, a look of disgust on his face.

Calard's expression darkened.

'Don't turn you back on me, brother,' he snarled.

Bertelis turned back towards him.

'How can I serve you, *my lord Garamont*?' he said, giving a mocking bow.

Feeling the eyes and ears of his knights and peasants all around, Calard bit back his angry retort. He fixed his younger half-brother with an angry stare.

'Come here,' he said through gritted teeth, lifting the tent flap and gesturing inside. 'I would speak with you alone.'

Seeing the shared glances between his knights, Calard felt his rage build.

'Strike the camp,' he ordered. 'We leave within the hour.'

CALARD POURED A goblet of wine and offered it to his brother. Bertelis refused, as he knew he would. The wine was worth a small fortune, being one of Bordeleaux's finer exports, and rather than have it go to waste, he drained the goblet. As an afterthought, he poured himself a second.

'Don't ever talk to me like that again in front of our cousins,' said Calard. 'Our father would never have stood for such disrespect. He'd have had you flogged for such insolence.'

'Our father is dead,' said Bertelis. 'You didn't save him, remember?'

The colour drained from Calard's face.

It had been less than six months since the death of Lord Lutheure, killed by a hateful creature of Chaos. Castle Garamont had been overrun and Calard, accompanied by the revered Grail Knight Reolus and a lance of loyal knights, had raced to save it from destruction. Even travelling the fey paths of the Lady of the Lake, led upon those mystical secret ways by his sister, the Damsel Anara, and travelling many hundreds of miles in the blink of an eye, he had been unable to save his father.

The true horror of the event had been two-fold. One, that Lutheure was already dying, his body withered and wracked by poison delivered by Calard's beloved, the

Lady Elisabet of Marlemont. And two, that Lutheure's killer, a horrifying creature that was truly neither man nor beast, was none other than the castellan's own mutated son, driven and obsessed to slay its own father. The same blood that flowed in its veins flowed through Calard's, and the horror and disgust of that knowledge haunted his dreams.

Tainted blood.

That was what Calard knew his knights whispered behind his back, and yet he did not silence them. Indeed, he feared it was the truth.

'You think he would have lived had you been there?' said Calard, his eyes haunted.

'We'll never know,' said Bertelis.

'Maybe you could have saved him,' admitted Calard. 'But you were *not* there; your injuries are only now fully healed.'

'As I said, we'll never know.'

Calard stared into his brother's accusing eyes, seeing the anger simmering there, and he sighed. Taking his goblet of wine, he sank onto a divan, his shoulders slumped.

'What is wrong with you these days?' he said, not looking at Bertelis. 'Where is all this anger coming from? Is it because of father's death? Is it because of me?'

Bertelis's hands were clenched into fists.

'What's wrong with *me*? Take a look at yourself. You've been drunk for months, neglecting your responsibilities... you don't even know what day it is.'

'I didn't ask for our father to die.' snapped Calard. 'I didn't ask to become the lord of Garamont.'

He looked up at his brother.

'Is that what this is about? You want to be the lord of Garamont, Bertelis? I'll abdicate. I don't want these responsibilities. You can have them.'

'That is not what I want and you know it,' said Bertelis.

'I'm sure your mother would be most displeased to hear you say that,' said Calard.

'Leave her out this,' growled Bertelis.

'I thought you'd be the last person to lecture me,' said Calard, taking another swig of his wine. 'You used to be different. All you do is train these days. You never used to be so... obsessed.'

'Would that I had paid more attention to Gunthar,' said Bertelis.

For a moment, there was silence.

'You've changed, brother,' said Calard, at last.

'Yes, I have,' said Bertelis. 'Maybe it is about time that you did, too.'

Calard placed his goblet on a side table and hung his head in his hands. His half-brother and he had always been the closest of friends. He had believed that he would always be able to rely on Bertelis, no matter what. How had things gone so wrong?

Everything had changed with the death of their father. Calard's whole world had been shattered. He was blood-brother to a mutant monstrosity. His beloved had been exposed as a would-be murderer. Attempts had been made on his life, and he had accused – falsely, it seemed – his step-mother, the Lady Calisse, Bertelis's mother. And he had been thrust into a position of great authority and responsibility that he was nowhere near ready for.

Coming back to the present, his head still in his hands, Calard sighed.

'There is truth in your words, brother,' he said. 'And I am sorry for mentioning the Lady Calisse.'

In a way, Calard felt sorry for his brother, for he knew that the Lady Calisse spouted her poison in his ear at every occasion.

Bertelis folded his arms and shifted his feet.

'You are under a lot of pressure,' he said. 'I do not envy you.'

Calard smiled, though his eyes were hollow and empty.

'Is it really two days until the tournament?'

'It is,' said Bertelis.

Calard swore.

'Two weeks we've been away from Garamont then,' he said, shaking his head. 'Folcard is going to kill me.'

THOUGH WELL INTO her middling years, Bertelis's mother, the haughty and proud Lady Calisse, was a strikingly handsome woman still, and as she laughed, the years dropped away from her.

In her prime, Calisse had been a renowned beauty, and before she had wed Lutheure of Garamont, a score of knights from all over Bretonnia had paid her suit, competing for her hand. Elegant and imperious, she was reclining on a velvet chaise longue within castle Garamont, her diaphanous silk dress flowing around her.

'It was *you* who tried to have him killed,' she said in a soft voice, her eyes gleaming with deadly amusement. 'I knew it!'

The chamberlain of Garamont, Folcard, stood in the doorway, tall and gaunt, like a looming vulture waiting for its prey to die. His face was long and severe, and his nose was hooked. He had the look of one who had been sucking on lemons, and deep frown lines were permanently etched on his face.

'Keep your voice down,' Folcard said.

'Oh, calm yourself,' said Calisse with a dismissive wave of a hand heavy with rings. 'I sent all the servants away that we might speak freely.'

For more than six decades Folcard had served the Garamont line, overseeing the day to day running of the castle and its estate with a rod of iron. He was the terror of the servants, an exacting and harsh master, but he was nevertheless widely respected for he was himself no slouch, even at his age, and put in more work than any of those who served under him.

Castle Garamont and its line was Folcard's life, utterly and completely, and his devotion could not be questioned. Which was why Calisse was so amused to have finally worked out that it was he who had tried to have Calard murdered while engaged in Bordeleaux the previous autumn.

Folcard glared at her, making no attempt to hide his disdain for her, though she was long past caring what the old chamberlain thought of her.

'It was Tanebourc, wasn't it?' said Calisse. 'He was the one that you coerced into doing your dirty work?'

'Your lover?' snapped Folcard. Calisse stared at him blankly.

'Yes, I knew that you were being unfaithful,' said Folcard. 'Your adulteries started soon after Bertelis was born, if I am not mistaken?'

'Was that how you got to him? You blackmailed him into doing what you wanted, threatening to tell Lutheure that he was bedding me if he didn't do as you wished?'

'Something like that,' said Folcard.

'If you knew of my… infidelity these last twenty years, why did you never speak of them to my husband?'

'*I* am a loyal servant of Garamont,' said Folcard coldly. '*I* would never have done anything to bring dishonour upon my lord.'

Calisse laughed, the sound cold and unfriendly, but filled with genuine humour.

'But you would happily have your lord's son murdered?' she said. 'It is a curious sort of honour you follow, my dear chamberlain.'

'The Lady Yvette of Bordeleaux was tainted,' spat Folcard. 'Touched in the head. Corrupted. She ensorcelled Lutheure, ensnaring him and clouding his judgement.'

Lady Calisse's expression hardened. Always she had felt as though she were in the shadow of her husband's first wife. Always it felt to her as if her husband had judged her, weighing her against his first partner. He would never allow so much as a bad word spoken of her in his presence, and Calisse had been forced to endure having a painting of the woman stare at her across the great hall for her entire marriage.

'She frequently suffered fits,' continued Folcard. 'She would fall to the ground, her limbs shaking and foam frothing from her mouth. It was clear to everyone but Lutheure that she was... *unclean*. When she gave birth to Calard, everything seemed to be in order. There was no obvious corruption in him, and I prayed to the Lady that his blood was pure. All seemed well, and indeed even Yvette's fits became infrequent. When she became pregnant again, Lutheure was ecstatic. She gave birth to a daughter; Anara. Truly, in all the days that were to come later, I never saw him happier than at that moment.'

Calisse bristled, but Folcard continued on, lost in the past.

'But it did not last long. The midwives refused to hold the baby girl. She was no more than weeks old, but they said that they could hear the babe's voice in their minds. There was something terribly wrong with Anara, and in the years that followed, it became clear that she shared her mother's curse. She was of the fey; touched in the head, abnormal. She would hug a kitten to her chest, and cry out in horror as its heart stopped beating. She would stroke one of Lutheure's hounds, only for its eyes to start bleeding; as much as she cried, it would be dead within the day. She would see things that had not yet come to pass. She could hear people's thoughts. Everyone hated her, and worse, she could read the hatred in their hearts. There was much relief in the court when the Enchantress took her away.'

Lady Calisse shifted uncomfortably. Though Anara was now a young woman, a holy damsel of the Lady no less, their brief meeting had left Calisse terrified.

'But still worse was to come, and it was this that proved Yvette's blood was truly cursed. Once again, she was heavy with child, though this time the pregnancy was difficult. She travelled to Bordeleaux, to be near her mother for the birth, which was long and bloody. She birthed an abomination. I will not dwell on it, for you saw the foul creature with your own eyes. I curse the day that it was allowed to live. Yvette hurled herself to her death in horror and shame.'

'Would that she had courage to have done so a decade earlier,' said Calisse. 'She might have spared all of us the horror of her foul get. But what relevance does this lesson in the sordid Garamont family history have?'

'Calard might appear wholesome and untainted, but the same blood that runs in the veins of his freak sister, the same foetid blood that ran through the veins of the abomination, runs in his own. By his bloodline, that of cursed Yvette, he is tainted. I love Garamont more than life itself, and I will not stand by and see its line devolve. Who is to say that were Calard to sire an heir, that son would not be a debased bestial fiend? No, I cannot allow such a chance. Thus, for the good of the line of Garamont, Calard must die.'

Calisse wore a look of repugnance on her face. She could not fault Folcard's logic, nor even his twisted loyalty. Her own desires were far more straightforward; she merely wanted to see her own son succeed her husband, not her stepson.

'It would seem that we are in accord,' said Calisse. 'We both want to see Bertelis become castellan.'

'That would seem to be the case,' said Folcard, somewhat reluctantly.

'Then, what do you propose we do about it?'

'Things are already in hand, Lady Calisse,' said Folcard.

'Ah,' said Calisse. 'I should have expected as much. You are so very efficient, aren't you, Folcard?'

'I do my best, lady,' his hawk-like eyes glinting. 'Now if that is all, I will return to my duties.'

'Fine,' said Calisse, dismissing him with a languid gesture.

With barely a sound, the stick-thin chamberlain backed off into the darkness and was gone.

She plucked herself a heavy, blood-red grape from the bowl at her side, and popped it into her mouth.

'Very fine indeed,' said Calisse to herself.

CHAPTER THREE

THE PEASANTS WERE clustered behind the dry stone wall, cowering against the wind and rain, pressed together for warmth. There was almost a score of them, and while they had tried to make a fire their kindling was soaked through and would not take. They had at last given up, and were now shivering beneath their rotting shared blankets, each lost in his or her own bleak thoughts.

There were only a handful of them; the last pilgrims of a living saint, the hallowed grail knight Reolus of Quenelles.

Once they had followed their glorious idol wherever he went, traipsing across the countryside and proclaiming his brilliance to whoever would listen. They had gloried in the magnificence of just being near him, and they had eagerly performed any mundane tasks that they thought might ingratiate themselves into his favour: collecting wood for his fire, delivering him fresh game, lovingly polishing his boots with their spit if he left them outside his tent.

They had worshipped the ground Reolus walked on – literally – for it was clear for all to see that the blessing of the Lady was upon him. He had drunk from the sacred grail of the goddess, and the power of the Lady infused him. The grail knight was, in their minds, the holiest, most devout paladin in all of Bretonnia, and perhaps just by being close to him, they might themselves share in a sliver of his blessed glory.

They had not clapped eyes on the object of their devotion for almost two seasons. They had accompanied him to Bordeleaux, there to fight the foul greenskins and beasts of the forest. Some forty-odd pilgrims had fallen in those battles, but they had done so gladly, hoping that in death they might be noticed by their idol. Nevertheless, once victory had been attained, the grail knight had entered a sacred copse of trees and never come out. In the blink of an eye, he had travelled across Bretonnia, leaving his pilgrims lost and in despair.

Immediately, they had set out to find him. Their journey had taken them hundreds of miles as they chased rumours of where he had been. They were run out of villages and pelted with stones, and several of their comrades had hung from the gallows for crossing the land of a Bordelen lord. They had entered Bastonne, for that is where they had been told he had travelled, but there they learnt that he had headed north, into Gisoreux.

The pilgrims had been forced to scrounge food where they could, and more of their number had hung when they were caught poaching on the estates of a Gisoren noble lady. In truth, it had been lucky that any of them had escaped. Then they had backtracked into Bastonne, having missed their lord by less than a day, but a week later they had lost his trail. A bear had killed two more of their number when they had tried to take shelter within a cave, and another had starved to death only days earlier. They had stripped his body and left him in a ditch, donning his clothes in an attempt to stave off the cold. Winter was closing in, and their predicament was only going to worsen. They were now in central Bastonne, and had no idea in which direction they should go to seek their lord and master.

Still, devout and full of faith that they would be reunited with the living saint, they continued to carry with them a varied melange of sacred objects: a broken shoe that Reolus had once worn, a gourd from whence he had drunk, a bone with meat still clinging to it, long rancid and filled with wriggling maggots, that he had chewed once and discarded, along with a host of other holy artefacts.

Several of the pilgrims wore scraps of royal blue cloth edged in silver, torn from Reolus's discarded tunics, tabards and cloaks. The most holy of these fabrics bore a good sized portion of Reolus's sacred heraldry – a silver unicorn upon a field of blue – and this was worn proudly upon the chest of Chlod, the leader of the pilgrims, a hunchbacked peasant with a lopsided face.

An opportunistic liar, murderer and thief, Chlod had bullied and lied his way to become the leader of the pilgrims, not out of any sense of actual faith or devotion, but for purely selfish reasons. As the abbot of this ragtag group, he had the pick of any food and scraps that they managed to scrounge, and he enjoyed ordering the others around. He had only joined the pilgrims in the first place as a means of hiding from retribution after he had been one of a handful of peasants hired to kill a nobleman. The murder of the young knight – Calard of Garamont – had failed, and while the other peasants had been caught, tortured and hung, Chlod had managed to avoid the clutches of the yeomanry.

Chlod was currently having the crown of his head shaved to the scalp by another of the pilgrims, a thick-bodied woman covered in mud and faeces. Her tongue jutted from the corner of her mouth as she concentrated. A rat poked its head out from the neck of Chlod's shirt, twitching its whiskers. Momentarily distracted, the woman's hand slipped, and she sliced his scalp with her rusted blade.

'Stupid woman,' said Chlod, turning and thumping her in the face with a meaty fist. She fell backwards with a cry, shielding her face from further assault. Chlod touched a hand to his head. He winced, and his fingers came away bloody. There were still several clumps of hair clinging to his shaved crown, but he decided that he didn't want the woman coming near him with her knife again today.

Several of the pilgrims were eyeing his rat, licking their lips, and he shoved the creature back under his clothing, glaring at them.

'You ain't eating him,' he growled. 'You can eat each other first.'

'Lord Reolus the holy will deliver sustenance into our hands,' said a toothless pilgrim, his eyes filled with passion and belief.

'Wish he'd do it soon,' muttered Chlod.

One of the peasants stood up, stretching his back. He squinted through the rain for a moment, looking back along the muddy road on the other side of the low, stone wall behind which his companions cowered. His eyes widened, and he dropped to the ground behind the wall.

'Someone's coming!' he said in loud whisper.

The pilgrims shrunk further under their grimy blankets, as if trying to disappear beneath them.

'Who?' said Chlod.

'Don't know,' came the reply.

'Is it a patrol?'

'Don't know!' said the pilgrim, in a belligerent voice.

'Shh!'

'Don't know,' repeated the pilgrim, quieter this time.

'Well, find out, then,' said Chlod, in a bullish stage whisper, a heavy, spiked club clenched in his hands.

The pilgrim turned around and warily poked his head up over the top of the wall. He looked around for a moment, then ducked back down.

'It's a woman,' he said. 'A lady.'

'A lady?' said Chlod, his brows drawing together. Curious, he scrambled around, shuffling awkwardly, and squinted over the wall.

She was walking along the road towards them, her head lowered as the rain lashed at her. She wore a long purple dress that clung to her body, completely soaked through as it was, and despite the fact that its hems were tattered and dragged in the mud, the material was clearly rich. Chlod imagined the rings that the lady undoubtedly wore on her fingers, the earrings that would pierce her lobes and quickly calculated what price he might be able to get for her hair. He licked his lips.

His eyes scanned the area around the lady, for what lady of renown would travel by herself, especially in such weather? As much as he tried, however, he could spy no guards accompanying her, no knights, no servants.

'Looks like Reolus delivered,' he said with a feral, lopsided grin.

The other peasants were peering over the wall now too.

'You think she might have some food to spare?' said the thick-limbed, female pilgrim.

'I think that the price we'd get for her dress alone would keep us fed for a year,' said Chlod, not taking his eye off his prize.

'But... she's a lady,' exclaimed another of the pilgrims, a stick-thin man of middling years with a gaunt face.

'We'd all hang if we so much as looked at her funny,' said another.

'There ain't no one around to see what happens,' said Chlod. 'And besides – if we don't get nothing to eat soon, how will we be able to serve our lord Reolus? Won't be much good to him dead.'

'But... she's a lady!' said the gaunt faced pilgrim.

Chlod pulled his predatory gaze away from the noblewoman, and glared at the speaker.

'How many ladies you know what wander around in the rain and the mist, all on their lonesome? She's a wanton, and no mistake,' he said. 'That's probably why Reolus sent her to us – Bretonnia'd be better off without her.'

'You really think Reolus would want us to rob her, Chlod?' said the gaunt faced man, his eyes wide.

The hunchbacked pilgrim nodded his head solemnly.

'I think it's our duty, as his holy pilgrims, to do so,' he said.

Chlod couldn't care less what Reolus might wish for him to do. All he cared about was his own skin. Murdering a noblewoman didn't bother him in the slightest, so long as he got away with it. He'd done worse.

He risked a glance over the wall again and saw the lady was no more than twenty paces away. Her path would take her close to the wall. Her dark, sodden hair was loose, and obscured her face. Gesturing for silence, he pointed for three of his companions to crawl back along the wall some way. He gritted his teeth in frustration at the racket they made, but glancing through a hole in the wall, he saw that the lady was still coming, seemingly oblivious to the danger.

When she was no more than a few yards off, Chlod leapt to his feet.

'Now!' he shouted, and with some difficulty, he clambered over the wall. His club foot clipped its top, dislodging a few stones, and he fell flat on his face. Righting himself quickly, he hobbled out into the roadway brandishing his spiked club, leering at the young lady before him, who had stopped moving as soon as he appeared. Had his intentions not been murderous, his appearance might well have been comical.

Three others leapt out onto the road behind the lady, brandishing broken swords, cudgels and knives, and he felt the reassuring presence of another behind him.

The woman was young, barely out of her teens. Had she been of low birth she would already have spawned half a dozen youngsters and her back would be bent from working in the fields, but this was a noblewoman. She had no need to work, and her back was straight, her skin as flawless as alabaster, and Chlod grinned as he saw the flash of silver on her fingers.

'Don't move, now, young miss, and you won't come to no harm,' he lied, his fingers tense on the haft of his club.

He edged towards her, moving slowly as if not to frighten her, and the other pilgrims closed in silently. She was like a rabbit cornered by hounds.

The young lady though, it seemed, had no intention of running. Indeed, she showed not the slightest hint of fear, which made Chlod uneasy. This was not how the rabbit was meant to act. His eyes passed her, trying to spot her guards, but the road was clear. From beneath her lank hair, he saw the lady's lips begin to move as she began to mouth something under her breath.

'Take her!' he barked, hefting his spiked club in both hands, intending to brain her with the brutal weapon and be done with it.

'I think not,' said the girl. There was something strange about her voice, and it gave the pilgrims pause.

Chlod saw one of her eyes then, wide and malicious, staring out from behind rain-slick strands of black hair. He thought he saw shadows moving in the periphery of his vision, but he could not drag his gaze away from the horrifying stare of the girl. Unholy power beyond the ken of simple folk lurked there. In her terrifying, black eyes, he saw an ancient soul long condemned to darkness.

Too late he realised his error. This was no defenceless noblewoman. This was something else entirely, something ancient and vile.

The girl's mouth continued to move, incanting softly.

Shadows shifted with malevolent purpose around him. He felt a chill as one of the shades passed by him, and the pilgrim behind him toppled face first into the mud without a sound, blood bursting from his eyes, ears and nose.

The shadows closed in, and Chlod knew that his end had come. He could hear them whispering to him, their insane, indecipherable voices filled with hatred and an unquenchable hunger.

'Wait,' said the girl, her voice making his skin crawl. The shadows paused, hissing angrily.

Chlod just stared at the girl-witch, his eyes wide in horror. She smiled from beneath her wild nest of hair. It was not a pleasant smile.

'You'd like to serve me, wouldn't you?' she said.

Chlod threw himself into the mud before her.

* * *

THE SILVER MOON of Mannslieb was high overhead when Calard and his companions finally crested a rise and saw the tournament camp laid out before them. The night was bitterly cold as winter drew in, but the sounds of laughter and music, and the smell of roasting venison and boar warmed their spirits.

They had crossed over the border of Artois the previous evening, passing into the lands of Lyonesse, on the north-western coast of Bretonnia. They had ridden through the night, stopping only briefly for a few hours rest before pushing on. The previous night had been the same, and everyone was saddle-weary and drained. Still, they were here now, and the tournament proper was not due to commence until first light the next morn.

Tournaments were encouraged by king and duke in times of relative peace as a means of keeping the knights of Bretonnia battle-ready and their skills sharp. While the southern lands of Carcassone and Brionne were currently at war, besieged by a plague of verminous skaven emerging from beneath the Vaults, and the north of Quenelles was being subjected to bloody attacks from a clan of ogres descending from the Massif Orcals, much of Bretonnia was currently untouched by war on any scale large enough for the call to reach L'Anguille, Lyonesse or Artois, hence this tourney.

Many of the nobles present would have arrived a week ago or more – or at least sent their servants ahead of them, in order to claim the best site for their tents – and though there would already have been countless individual bouts, jousts and many drunken nights of feasting, it was for tomorrow's event that the gathering had met. It was the highlight of the week's entertainment, and judging from the number of tents pitched across the lowlands, it would be one of particularly impressive scale.

Calard and his entourage rode down towards the jubilant encampment, scanning the pennants flying atop the tents for those of friends and relatives. While the vast majority of knights present were from Lyonesse, Artois and L'Anguille – the place chosen for the tournament was near the border of all three lands, after all – there was on display heraldry proclaiming that some of the participants were from more distant lands: Gisoreux, Couronne, Bordeleaux and Montfort. There was even one knight from war-torn Carcassonne, far to the south.

'There,' said Bertelis, spying what it was they had all been looking for; heraldry declaring that other knights of Bastonne were present.

Calard and his entourage turned their steeds towards the Bastonnian contingent, and he ordered his servants on ahead to find a suitable location to pitch their tents. The peasants were exhausted, for they had not even had the chance of rest that the knights had, busy as they were preparing food for their masters and taking care of their horses, but they knew better than to voice any resentment.

Without complaint, they kicked their heavy draught horses on ahead, laden with tents, foodstuffs, chests of clothes and anything else that their lords might need to make their lives more comfortable while away from home.

'Montcadas,' said Bertelis brightly, standing in the saddle to get a better view of the flapping heraldry.

Calard saw the Bastonnian baron's heraldry too, and he smiled. They had fought alongside the baron in the campaign in Bordeleaux two seasons past, when Calard and Bertelis, as Knights Errant, had ridden to Bordeleaux to engage a massive greenskin army. In the ensuing war, the Bretonnians became embroiled with a further enemy

– the beastmen. During those bloody times, Montcadas had left an impression on both of the brothers. As fierce as a bear and almost as hirsute, Baron Montcadas had taken the young brothers under his wing, earning their respect and admiration.

The smile dropped from Calard's face as he saw a tent near the baron's; it was white and flew a pennant with a blood-red dragon motif in its centre.

'Looks like the vermin have come out for the tournament as well,' said Bertelis.

'Maloric,' spat Calard.

For generations there had been a blood fued between the Garamont and Sangasse families. Three years Calard's senior, Maloric was the young earl and heir of Sangasse, and had been his rival and enemy since birth. Calard and Maloric had fought alongside each other in the Bordeleaux campaign, though their antagonism had resulted in Gunthar's mortal injury, and despite Maloric's assistance in the defence of Castle Garamont against the horrific half-human beasts of the forest, the hatred between the two remained strong. If anything, it had intensified since Calard had inherited the mantle of castellan; Maloric had seen first-hand the twisted creature that had been Calard's brother, and had spread the word around the courts of both enemy and friend of the Garamonts' shame.

'Maybe in the tournament tomorrow I will have a chance to put the weasel on his arse,' said Bertelis.

'I pray that one of us does,' agreed Calard.

'Come!' said Tassilo. 'Tis a night for revelry! For dance, for drink, and pretty faces!'

'Never mind their faces,' said Baldemund, 'I'm more interested in what else they've got to offer.'

Long tables packed with feasting nobles were positioned at the centre of the encampment, surrounded by heaving pavilions. From within these vast tents came sounds of merriment – and the clash of swords.

'We might not be too late to enter the duels,' said Bertelis. 'Care to enter, brother?'

'You go,' said Calard. 'I'm going to try and find Montcadas. I haven't seen him since…'

He didn't need to finish the sentence; Bertelis knew of what he spoke. Calard turned in the saddle and flicked a gold coin towards Tassilo, who caught it deftly.

'If the duels are not yet done, put this on my brother,' Calard ordered. His cousin nodded.

'Might enter myself,' said Tassilo with a smile.

Calard flicked him another coin.

'Put this on your opponent,' he said with a smile.

While Bertelis and Tassilo moved off towards the largest of the pavilions, accompanied by a quartet of peasants to act as their squires, Calard and his other companions dismounted, handing their reins to waiting servants.

'Make sure they are brushed down, fed and watered,' said Calard, not even deigning to look at the peasants to whom he spoke. 'The night is cold – see that they are well blanketed.'

'Now to find Montcadas,' he said. Succulent aromas reached his nose; he could smell roasting meat, as well as frying onion and garlic sauces, and his stomach grumbled loudly.

'But first,' he said, 'let us eat.'

Hunger was not a sensation familiar to many Bretonnian nobles, and the three knights were salivating as they picked their way through the crowd.

'GARAMONT!' BOOMED A deep voice, and Calard looked up from his meal of stuffed quail and venison to see the heavy-set figure of Baron Montcadas marching towards him. The baron was shorter than Calard, but what he lacked in height he made up for in width. A patch bearing the fleur-de-lys covered his left eye, and vivid scars covered the left side of his face. A wide grin split his thick beard, and as Calard pushed himself upright, the baron swept him into a crushing embrace.

'Good to see you, my boy!' said Montcadas, releasing him and slapping him hard on the shoulder. By the rosy tint of the baron's nose he guessed that the baron had been enjoying the vintages on offer.

'It is good to see you too, baron,' said Calard. 'You know my cousins?'

The two knights bowed to the baron, who nodded his head in response, before turning his attention back on Calard.

'A knight of the realm now, eh? And a castellan, no less.'

'I'd have fallen in my first battle had it not been for you,' said Calard.

'Ah, don't be daft, boy,' said Montcadas, though Calard could tell that his words had pleased the baron.

Montcadas's expression darkened, and he lowered his voice.

'I was grieved to hear of the death of your father. A good man, Lutheure,' he said. 'I am sorry for your loss.'

Calard nodded his head and smiled his thanks.

Montcadas took a step back from him, casting a critical gaze over the young lord of Garamont.

'You are not looking your best, boy,' said Montcadas. 'What's Folcard been feeding you?'

'I am not sleeping well,' admitted Calard.

Montacadas regarded Calard thoughtfully.

'There is a lot of pressure that comes with becoming the head of a noble family,' said Montcadas in a low voice. 'There is no shame in feeling out of your depth at first.'

'Am I so transparent?' replied Calard.

'You've a good head on your shoulders. You'll do fine,' said Montcadas.

'Were that it were so simple,' said Calard.

'Of course it is not as simple as that, but don't make the mistake of trying to complicate things. You're new to your role. You'll make a few mistakes, but everyone does. Learn from them and don't dwell on the past.'

'I'll try, baron,' said Calard, and despite himself, he felt his mood lift for the first time in months.

'The fates have not been kind to you of late, boy, and that's the Lady's truth. But it's what you do under such circumstances that will be your making,' said Montcadas, unusually serious. 'Or your downfall,' the baron added, shrugging. 'It's up to you now. But don't forget that you have friends and allies on your side.'

'I appreciate it, baron,' said Calard.

He saw an attractive young lady moving through the crowd towards them, being led by the hand by a young boy, no more than six summers old. The boy was wearing an exquisite, miniature suit of armour. Seeing their approach, Montcadas smiled, his previous seriousness evaporating.

'What you need is a wife,' he said, his voice booming. 'If you think running a realm is hard, try being married. It'll put things in perspective. And speaking of which, allow me to introduce you to my sister's youngest, the Lady Josephine.'

'Uncle!' she said in exasperation, shaking her head. Then she curtsied, gazing appraisingly at Calard for a moment before lowering her eyes as a good lady was taught.

'My lady,' said Calard, bowing.

'Lord Calard,' said Josephine, a smile in her self-assured voice, 'it is my pleasure to introduce you to your second cousin once removed, young Sir Orlando of Bordeleaux.'

Calard looked down at the boy, then towards Montcadas questioningly.

'Young Orlando here is the son of your mother's niece, Calard,' he said in a soft voice. 'They are close family friends of my house. I was, after all, the one who introduced your mother to your father.'

'I never knew,' said Calard, before turning his attention back to the boy, who was staring up at him curiously.

He dropped to one knee to be on a level with the boy.

'It is an honour to meet you, Sir Orlando,' he said, bowing his head solemnly.

The boy bowed in return, his face a serious mask of concentration. The boy's attention was suddenly drawn away from Calard, and his jaw dropped.

'Look!' he cried, pointing into the sky.

There were gasps and exclamations of wonder from the nobles around them, and Calard stood, looking up into the night sky to see what Orlando has spotted.

Angling down through the clouds, moonlight shimmering like silver upon their flanks and feathered wings, was a flock of winged horses. Fully armoured knights rode in their saddles, and they circled down towards the ground in graceful arcs.

'Pegasus knights!' cried Orlando, his voice full of excitement and wonder.

One of the knights pulled away from the others, leaning back in the saddle as his steed furled its wings tight against its body. It dropped towards the ground like a diving hawk, gaining speed with every passing moment. At the last second it spread its wings and scores of nobles ducked involuntarily as the pegasus swept down low, passing just overhead.

Peasants scrambled out of the way as the pegasus landed, silver-shod hooves striking the earth. It slowed its pace and halted, tossing its head.

The pegasus was larger than any destrier, and must have been pushing twenty hands tall at the shoulder. They were known to be aggressive, and though they looked noble and angelic in countenance, Calard knew that they could be unpredictable and dangerous when the mood took them, and would wilfully stomp a man to death if provoked. Nevertheless, amongst the Bretonnian nobility they were highly sought after steeds, fierce and loyal if raised from a foal, and eager to bear a knight into the thickest fray.

It was said that vast flocks of pegasus could be seen soaring the mountain peaks above the tiered city of Parravon, though Calard had never journeyed so far east to see if such tales were true. It was from those stocks that the majority of the pegasus seen within Bretonnia were bred. Such creatures did not come cheap, however, and those who rode them were amongst the wealthiest knights of all Bretonnia. Nor was purchasing a pegasus foal any guarantee that the beast would bond with its intended rider and accept him, and few were willing to risk the investment – one did not wish to be two hundred feet in the air before discovering that your mount had taken a dislike to you. No amount of wealth could protect you then.

The knight riding upon the snow-coloured beast wore a tabard of red and silver over plate shined to an almost painful degree, and he bore a silver pegasus motif upon his chest. The attention of every man and lady was upon him, and he tore his helmet from his head theatrically. Wavy blond hair dropped to his shoulders, and he flashed a winning smile to his audience as he slid from the saddle.

Spontaneous clapping erupted, and there were cheers. The knight lapped up the attention, bowing low.

Josephine's eyes shone as she looked upon the dashing knight.

Calard instantly disliked him.

'Who's this?' he said, unimpressed.

The knight was irritatingly good looking, and was instantly surrounded by a coterie of fawning supplicants, both men and women. He exchanged a brief word with several nobles, bowing to lords and placing a kiss upon the hand of half a dozen blushing ladies of particular beauty, wealth or social position.

'Laudethaire,' said Montcadas. 'Beloved of Parravon. Whatever else might be said about him, though, he's a damn good fighter.'

Laudethaire, his pegasus steed having been led away, swept by Calard and Montcadas with barely a glance, exuding scented perfumes. Over one shoulder he proudly wore a golden sash, which proclaimed him as the lord of the joust, having won the prestigious award earlier in the day.

He did a theatrical double-take when he saw Lady Josephine, and paused, a look of rapture on his face.

'Such beauty must surely make even the goddess envious,' he said, taking her hand. He maintained eye contact with her as he placed a kiss upon her hand. 'Enchanted, my lady.'

Josephine curtsied, oblivious to the venomous looks she was receiving from dozens of women nearby. With a warm smile, Laudethaire moved on, and Calard was bustled by the devotees following in his wake. As the jostling crowd began to clear, he saw that the Lady Josephine had a slight blush to her cheeks.

His expression brightened as he saw a familiar figure pushing through the crowd.

'Here,' said Tassilo darkly, holding out a pouch bulging with coin.

Calard took his winnings.

'I take it by the bruises on your face that you did not win then, my friend?' he said.

'No,' said Tassilo, placing a hand gingerly to his cheek. 'But at least you benefited from my humbling.'

'Bertelis?'

'Through to the finals,' said Tassilo. 'His is the next bout. He's facing the knight who defeated me – Merovech of Arlons.'

'Never heard of him,' said Calard.

'I hadn't, either,' said Tassilo. 'But the man is a devil with the blade.'

TIERED SEATING HAD been erected around the sides of the pavilion, from where hundreds of nobles watched the progression of bouts on display in relative comfort. They sat on down-filled cushions, and servants wound through their ranks, keeping goblets topped up and bearing platters of extravagant and exotic sweetmeats: jellied eels, ox tongues, liver pate, jaguar's earlobes, quails' eggs. The most wealthy and influential of these lords and ladies occupied private booths swathed in velvet and hanging with their personal and family heraldry.

Calard saw Lord Orderic, the host of this tourney, seated within the grandest of these booths. An immensely fat noble of considerable wealth and influence, Lord Orderic was drunk and clearly enjoying himself. He had boar fat dripping down his face, and he wore a lascivious grin as he slipped a pudgy hand up the dress of a serving girl.

'This way,' said Baron Montcadas. 'I have a booth.'

The bear-like Bastonnian lord trundled through the crowd, leading Lady Josephine by the arm. Young

Orlando held onto Josephine's free hand, staring around him in wide-eyed excitement. Calard, walking behind, found himself staring at Josephine's slender waist and the sway of her hips beneath her midnight blue slip.

A collective groan of empathetic pain rose from the audience as, down in the roped-off area in the centre of the tent, a broad-shouldered knight suffered a heavy blow to the head, wrenching his plumed helmet out of shape. Honourably, his opponent stepped away from him, allowing his seconds to rush forward and help the knight free of his damaged helmet. Polite applause greeted this act of chivalry, and the knight lifted his visor, smiling and saluting the audience while his opponent had a bandage quickly wrapped around his bleeding head. Several flowers were thrown in the knight's direction from blushing young ladies, who turned away giggling to each other when the knight bowed in their direction.

Montcadas led them into his private booth, and they took their seats overlooking the spectacle. Orlando stood on his seat in order to see over the wooden balustrade in front.

The wounded knight's seconds left the duelling floor, and the bout recommenced. It was over quickly, when the unwounded knight slipped on one of the flowers that had been tossed towards him. He stumbled, and his opponent struck him a mighty blow to his shoulder that knocked him to the ground. With a sword-tip at his throat, the knight was forced to concede, though his face was thunderous.

Trumpets blared and the crowd cheered and hollered. As the two knights left the competition floor, a troupe of players danced and cartwheeled in to entertain the crowd before the next bout commenced. One of them, a woman with greasepaint on her face, held up a flaming brand, and spitting out a mouthful of combustible oil, sent a burst of flame roaring into the air, like the breath of a dragon. Bizarrely, jugglers tossed dried and desiccated frogs into the air, keeping a dozen or more aloft at any one time, and the crowd laughed at the clownish expressions on the faces of a band of stunted men the size of children, who were dressed up like miniature knights and riding pigs. These 'knights' charged around the arena, waving wooden swords and clinging desperately to their steeds.

One of the swine took fright as the fire breather blew another burst of flame into the air, and the pig dove into the crowd, squealing wildly, while its miniature rider held on for dear life. Two more of the diminutive 'knights' came together, and a blow from one of them sent the other rolling off the back of his own swine, which garnered a cheer from the crowd.

'There he is,' said Tassilo, pointing.

Calard saw his brother on the edge of the arena, rolling his arms as he stretched out his muscles. Bertelis's heraldry, a silver dragon on a black and red field, was displayed on an unfurled banner held aloft by one of Garamont's yeomen. Calard yelled out, but his voice was lost in the crowd.

Another of the hog-knights was knocked from his saddle as his steed charged into one of the jugglers, and another cheer rose from the crowd. One of the rider's legs got caught in the rope that served as reins, and he was dragged around the arena on his back, much to the amusement of the crowd and his fellows. Orlando's giggling was contagious, and Calard found himself chuckling along with him.

At last trumpets sounded and the arena was cleared, the hog-knights being herded off to the side by the jugglers. One of the pigs had to be physically picked up by a strongman, and carried squealing back to its enclosure.

'Round eighteen!' bellowed a fat crier, his voice carrying out across the expansive pavilion. 'Betwixt Sir Bertelis of Garamont, Bastonne,' he roared, gesturing towards the young knight, 'and Sir Merovech of Arlons!'

Calard and his companions bellowed their support, stamping their feet and thumping the balustrade.

Bertelis smiled and waved to the crowd, turning around on the spot, before pulling on his helmet. The yeomen clustered around him helped strap his shield onto his left arm and he strode out into the centre of the floor.

His opponent, Merovech, walked out to meet him. Bertelis was one of the tallest knights of Garamont, yet Merovech was taller still, and he walked forward with a languid, relaxed grace that spoke of immense self-confidence. He moved as if his armour was a second skin.

That armour was of an archaic, old fashioned style, fluted and with serrated barbs at its edges, and for a moment Calard was reminded of the armour of the Green Knight, who continued to haunt his dreams. But no, this armour was quite different, though he suspected they were fashioned in a similar, bygone age – or at least Merovech's armour had been crafted with such ancient designs in mind. Armour styles were constantly in flux across Bretonnia, with fashion changing as frequently as the seasons, and while most knights would look down upon one who could not afford to keep up with the latest trends, there was not a single derisive comment or disdainful look cast towards Merovech.

His armour was of such dark steel that it was almost black, and he wore a spotless tabard of pure white over it. He carried no shield, but bore a pair of blades strapped at his side. He bore no heraldry other than a simple black fleur-de-lys, an ancient symbol that reflected purity and devotion.

That symbol was carried by most nobles in some form or other, both knight and lady. Whether it was worn as a silver pendant around the neck, engraved on a knight's armour, or woven into a maiden's undergarments as a symbol of her chastity, it was a symbol of ancient and holy significance. It was said to represent the lily, the sacred flower of Bretonnia. In the old tales, hundreds of lilies reputedly burst into flower under the full silver moon when the Lady of the Lake first appeared to Gilles le Breton, in the age of heroes long past.

The first knight to be given the honour of bearing the fleur-de-lys as his personal heraldry had been Landuin – the finest of all of Gilles's Holy Companions. The fairest, most skilful and noble knight ever to have walked the Old World, Landuin hailed from the realm of Mousillon, which was at that time the envy of its neighbours. Landuin's tale was one of tragedy and betrayal, however, one from which his reputation, and that of his realm, was never to recover. 'Those dwelling at the loftiest of heights have the furthest to fall,' was an infamous line from *The Death of Gilles le Breton*, referring to Landuin's fall from grace.

Repressing a shudder at merely thinking of the cursed realm of Mousillon, Calard dragged himself back to the present.

Merovech's helmet was crafted to resemble a snarling dragon, and the tall knight saluted Bertelis graciously as the crier and seconds cleared the arena. Bertelis returned the salute, and the two stepped away from each other, awaiting the signal for them to commence.

'For Garamont!' roared Calard, thumping his hands on the banister.

Brass horns hanging with pennants were raised to lips and they blew a resounding staccato.

Bertelis drew his sword and cut the air in front of him with a few practise swings. Merovech drew the larger of the two blades scabbarded at his waist, a sword of beautiful design. Most knights would have been forced to use the weapon with two hands, such was its size and weight.

The crier raised his hands into the air, silencing the horns.

'Commence!' he roared, going red in the face before trotting backwards out of the way.

Calard leant forward, watching intently as the bout began.

The pair of knights stalked around each other.

Stepping forward with the speed of a striking serpent, Bertelis was the first to make a move, whipping his sword in towards his opponent's chest. His footwork was precise, his strike perfectly balanced. Merovech turned it aside with the minimum of effort, and feinted a riposte.

The two knights continued to stalk around each other, Bertelis launching the occasional testing strike, which Merovech would deflect with the barest turn of his wrist, but Calard could see that neither knight had revealed their full speed or power.

Bertelis launched another attack, an overhead strike. As Merovech's blade rose to deflect it, Bertelis rolled his wrist, flicking his sword towards his opponent's neck. It was a blindingly fast shift of direction, one that had caught Calard out on more than one occasion, but Merovech avoided it easily.

Again and again it looked like Bertelis was going to score a hit upon the taller knight, only for Merovech's sword to turn the blow aside at the last moment, scant inches from striking home. Calard could see his brother getting increasingly frustrated, but where in the past this might have led him to attack furiously, leaving himself open for counterattack, he now channelled his emotions, using his anger to add strength and focus to his blows.

He launched a blinding series of strikes, attacking high and low. As Merovech side-stepped, Bertelis spun around on the spot, his blade slicing through the air towards his opponent's neck. It was a perfectly executed strike, and one that Bertelis had clearly set up. Merovech swayed backwards at the last second and Bertelis's sword missed him by less than an inch.

Stepping back, Merovech saluted Bertelis for a move well performed, and drew his second blade, a shortsword that he wielded in his left hand to complement the one held in his right. He twirled the blades before him, and stepped forward to engage Bertelis.

The twin blades formed blurring arcs and the audience sat in silence, spellbound. Bertelis backed away steadily, desperately fending off the attacks coming at him from every angle. There was no time for him to even consider launching a counterattack of his own, and it took all his skill and concentration merely to keep his enemy's blades from his neck.

Merovech swatted Bertelis's blade to the side with his shortsword, and a spin of his other sword sent Bertelis's blade sailing into the air. It spun end over end and sank point first into the ground. The move had been so fast that Calard had barely seen what had happened, but he applauded as Merovech stepped back to allow Bertelis to retrieve his weapon in order to allow the bout to continue.

'He's good,' he said grudgingly.

Saluting each other, the knights came together again. The bout lasted only a few more heartbeats. Bertelis saw an opening, and lunged forward, the tip of his blade striking for his opponent's heart. Belatedly he realised that Merovech had lured him into the strike.

Bertelis's sword was battered to the side and Merovech's twin blades crossed, slipping through the gap between Bertelis's helmet and breastplate, and as they touched the chainmail coif protecting his neck, they stopped. Had the blow been followed through, Calard had no doubt that his brother's head would now be lying on the ground, such was the near perfect execution of the killing move.

Thunderous applause broke out across the pavilion, and Calard joined in, shaking his head at the skill of the unknown knight. The only knight he had ever seen to rival his skill was the revered grail knight, Reolus.

Merovech saluted Bertelis once more, before sheathing his swords and pulling the helmet from his head. His face was as white as virgin snow. His hair too was devoid of colour and it fell halfway down his back, as straight as a blade.

Bertelis looked furious with himself, but Merovech leant in to him, speaking words unheard by any other.

Bertelis's heraldry was pulled down from the boards positioned at either end of the duelling grounds. The heraldry of eight more knights, including Merovech's, remained; these were the finalists, and they would duel to become the overall winner and be awarded the scarlet sash that would proclaim them as lord of the sword. Calard had no doubt that Merovech would be wearing that winner's sash come the end of the evening.

'How did he not win the joust?' said Calard.

'He did not compete,' replied Tassilo. 'He only came into camp after dusk.'

Calard drained his goblet, his mind drifting back to his nagging responsibilities, knowing that the time to return to Garamont drew near. He lifted his empty goblet again, waving it impatiently. As it was being filled, he cast a look along the length of the booth.

Lady Josephine was leaning forward in her seat, smiling and laughing with someone on the other side of the balustrade. Leaning forward to see who it was, Calard's expression darkened. His long time rival and foe, Maloric of Sangasse, was standing on the tier below the box, smiling and chatting.

Feeling eyes upon him, the rakishly handsome Sangasse nobleman glanced in Calard's direction, and though he maintained his smile, his eyes hardened. He said something to Josephine, and they both laughed lightly, and Calard's free hand clenched on his sword hilt.

Maloric placed a lingering kiss upon Josephine's hand before he moved off. He nodded his head respectfully to Montcadas as he passed, and his eyes glinted with sardonic amusement as he glanced up at Calard.

'I see that your brother lost, Garamont,' he said, his voice thick with derision. 'What a surprise. Doing Bastonne proud.'

'Keep walking, Sangasse,' snapped Tassilo.

'Tighten your dog's leash, Garamont,' said Maloric, managing somehow to look down his nose at Calard and his companions, even though he was positioned on a lower tier. 'Its yapping is wearisome.'

'Piss off, Sangasse,' growled Calard, his face an angry red.

Maloric leant in, peering at Calard's face, and he chuckled.

'Drunk again, I see. It's becoming rather frequent, from what I hear. I also hear that the new lord of Garamont is unfit to rule his own household, let alone his realm, and that his elderly chamberlain is forced to run it for him. Such a sad state of affairs,' he said, shaking his head in mock remorse.

'Go to hell, Sangasse,' said Calard, 'or I'll call you out here and now. You have no swordsman to hide behind this time.'

'And you no old man,' replied Maloric. 'But I would take no pleasure in killing a drunkard, even one with a bloodline as cursed as yours. Come for me when you're sober, perhaps.'

'Is there a problem, Sangasse?' boomed Montcadas.

'No problem,' replied Maloric. 'Though, methinks Lord Garamont here has had enough wine for one evening.'

The Sangasse noble turned on his heel to leave, and the glass in Calard's hand shattered.

Maloric looked back over his shoulder, laughing.

'Are you all right, cousin?' said Tassilo, concern in his voice.

'Fine,' snapped Calard.

CHAPTER FOUR

The wooden cup slipped from Rolan's hand, falling to the stone floor and spilling its contents. He came awake with a start at the sudden noise, his entire body jerking violently. He was still dressed, and seated in the sole rickety wooden chair before the fireplace, and he blinked dimly as he heard the cup rolling across the uneven floor.

It was deathly cold in his small hovel, and dark, and he scowled into his fireplace, pulling his lice-ridden blanket further around his shoulders. An icy wind clawed through the cracks in the walls, and his breath fogged the air in front of his face. Clutching his blanket around him like a cloak, he knelt down in front of the hearth, his knees cracking alarmingly. He picked up the rusted scythe-head leaning against the wall and poked at the lump of peat in the centre of the fireplace. Smoke was still rising from within the fibrous hunk of bog mud, and embers glowed and crackled as he poked at it.

Leaning close, he blew steadily until tongues of flame licked up its sides.

Rolan stood up with a groan, stretching his back out. His joints ached; winter was fast approaching, and he was not looking forward to it. He had lived on the island of Landri his whole life, and recognised the signs that the approaching season would be long and harsh. There were literally thousands of islets that made up the archipelago off the north-west coast of Bretonnia, though the vast majority of them were uninhabited and barren. Landri was one of the furthest from the mainland, and was large enough to maintain a steady, if small, population.

Outside, the wind had picked up, and he heard his sheep bleating frantically.

'Bloody foxes', said Rolan. Throwing off his blanket, he stood up and moved to the door.

'Come, dog,' he said.

Hauling the door open with both hands – its leather hinges were long rotted and useless – he braced himself against the icy wind that swirled in around him.

'Dog!' he said. 'Come!'

On her belly, the sheepdog backed away further under the table, its tail between its legs and its head between its paws, whimpering.

'Stay there and let your master catch his death out here alone then,' muttered Rolan.

Rolan stepped out into the night and hauled the door closed behind him. As an afterthought he grabbed the rusted pitchfork leaning against the wall of his hovel. Mannslieb was full overhead, but the silver moon was obscured behind a thick bank of clouds, making the night darker than it ought to have been.

His hovel was located on the northern point of Landri, positioned high on the grassy headland and staring out into the dark wasteland that was the ocean. All was darkness across the water, and the roar of the swell was loud. Immense sheer cliffs dropped down onto sharp rocks jutting like knife-points from the turbulent waters. The sea crashed relentlessly against the base of these cliffs, battering the headland with primal force, day in, day out.

Rolan's closest neighbour was more than a mile away, and it was a good three miles to Landri village and the abbey around which the mainstay population of the island was clustered.

Rolan could see his flock only dimly in the gloom, pale shapes clustered in a tight conglomeration in the corner of their stone-walled enclosure that backed up against his hovel. The shaggy-coated animals were pushing and shoving at each other, desperate not to be on the edge of the flock, and several were scrabbling frantically to leap the low walls.

Clucking his tongue reassuringly, Rolan swung the gate into the enclosure open, and stepped into the muddy, churned up yard. These sheep were his life, literally; if harm was to come to them, it was he that would suffer for it. His lord was not a forgiving man.

He stomped through the mud, using his pitchfork as a walking stick, and started to count his livestock. As far as he could tell, they were all accounted for, and they seemed to calm a little in his presence.

The wind changed abruptly, and a smell carried to Rolan's nostrils. It was a wet, bestial odour, like rancid meat, sweat and urine; the stink of a predator.

His flock went berserk, bleating madly, fighting each other to escape their enclosure, trying futilely to clamber over the dry-stone wall. Rolan spun around, bringing his pitchfork up before him, eyes wide.

At first he thought it was an animal, massive and shaggy and horned. It clambered over the wall on the opposite side of the enclosure, dislodging several stones that would have taken two men to lift. Then he saw the long handled axe held in its hand, and he realised it was a man, albeit one of immense stature, who was wearing the pelt of some great beast across his shoulders and a horned helmet on his head.

Rolan was not a tall man, and long years of work, solitude and malnutrition had further shrunk his shoulders and stooped his back. The stranger towered over him, seeming to grow with every quiet step he took towards him, and Rolan suspected that even his lord would have been dwarfed by him. Nevertheless, Rolan was no coward.

'Back with you, devil,' Rolan said, jabbing the air with his pitchfork,

The interloper laughed then, a barking, harsh sound. The clouds parted briefly, and Rolan saw the stranger more clearly, and a cold fear gripped his heart. *Norscan...*

Prayers to Manann were made daily, and weighted effigies of sacrifice were thrown into his ocean depths by the peasants on holy days each year, in the hope that the god of the sea would protect the island's fishermen, and smash the ships of any Norscan raiders. It seemed that these devotions had not been enough to abate Manann this year.

There were scores of watchtowers and keeps scattered through the archipelago, each equipped with a pyre that needed just a spark to ignite it. Those beacons, once lit, could be seen for miles all around, giving advance warning of the approach of any enemies. Why had none of them been lit?

Rolan saw more of the raiders now. They were circling around the sides of his hovel, dark and be-horned shadows moving with silent, deadly intent, like hunting pack animals, like wolves closing in on the kill. Rolan turned and ran.

He rounded his hovel only to see another of the immense, fur-cloaked Norscans slam a heavy, iron-shod boot into the door, smashing it to splinters.

Spinning, Rolan made to run to the south, over the wind-swept moorlands towards the village, but he froze as he saw the glow of fire in the distance. The village was burning.

There came a tortured yelp from inside his hovel as the raiders found Rolan's loyal sheepdog. His limbs were quivering now, and he backed away towards the cliff edge as the Norscan closed in around him. He felt the open expanse behind him, and he glanced down towards the crashing breakers far below.

In the bay that swung around to the west of the headland on which he stood, a score of ships could be seen. These were not the fishing boats used by the Bretonnian fishermen, nor even the multi-tiered greatships of the fleets of Couronne and Bordeleaux that he had glimpsed on occasion in the distance. No, these were Norscan longships, equipped with square sails and banks of oars that propelled them at formidable speed through the oceans. A brazen idol projected forth from the prow of each of these vessels, twisted representations of gods and daemons, and immense spiked rams sliced beneath the water-line. Black shark fins cut through the waves in the wake of the longships.

Larger ships, with two, three or even four banks of oars remained in the deeper water offshore, while the smaller longships rode the waves onto the beach, like killer whales hurling themselves onto land to snatch at seals basking there.

A dozen longships had already been dragged up onto the beach, and in the moment before the clouds once again obscured the view, Rolan could see scores of Norscan butchers making their way up the twisting paths from the beachhead.

Eyes wild, Rolan spun back towards the half dozen giants closing in around him, brandishing his pitchfork. It looked useless next to the heavy, spiked and bladed weapons of the raiders, and he doubted that he would be able to even land a blow before the end came for him.

Stories of the bloody sacrifices performed by these northern monsters came back to him, stories of still beating hearts ripped from chests, and all manner of agonising tortures performed on their victims before the release of death was granted. He took another step backwards, and felt the edge of the cliff beneath his heels.

He glanced down again. Better to be dashed upon those rocks than be butchered in the name of some infernal daemon-god. The pitchfork dropped from his fingers, spinning end over end towards the jutting rocks below. With a shuddering breath, Rolan closed his eyes and stepped backwards into open space.

A mailed fist grabbed him by his shirt front. Feet dangling out over the cliff-face, Rolan gasped. He was hurled to the ground away from the cliff's edge, tossed through the air one-handed as if he weighed no more than a newborn lamb. There he cowered, shaking like a leaf in a storm, looking up at the Norscans with wide, wild eyes. One of them grabbed him by his hair and hauled him roughly to his feet. With the haft of his axe, another then struck the back of his legs hard, breaking the bones and forcing him to his knees.

Rolan cried out as his head was reefed backwards. His eyes bulged as an axe was buried in his throat.

Overhead, the gods rumbled their approval.

* * *

High Jarl Egil Styrbjorn placed one heavy boot on the prostrate, dying priestess and yanked the blade of his axe free. Splintered ribs protruded from the chest wound, blood bubbling around them. The dying woman's eyes were wide, her mouth open in silent agony, but the jarl gave her no further notice – just another weakling southerner, a pitiful wretch that he earned no honour from slaying. Spinning an axe around in each hand, he continued up the steps towards the abbey's smashed doors, leaving the woman to die, alone and ignored.

The axes that the Skaeling warlord wielded were ancient, hellforged weapons, heavy with infernal magicks, their blades shaped in the likeness of wolf heads. A gleaming blood-red ruby was inset into the hafts of the axes, representing the eyes of the great wolves, and they blazed with inner fire. The axes were named Garmr and Gormr, in honour of the great wolves that accompany Kharnath on his bloody hunts across the heavens. They were holy artefacts of the Skaelings, handed down through the generations.

The air was rich with smoke and the sounds of butchery – the screams of the dying, the clash of weapons, the roaring of his men. At the top of the stairs, Styrbjorn paused, looking back towards the sea.

The burning enemy township grew like a malignant tumour around the abbey. Scattered pockets of resistance remained, but the enemy were weak, and Styrbjorn felt no particular desire to join the slaughter. These were not worthy foes, not like the Graelings, the Vargs, or any other Norscan tribes, nor the Kvelligs and Tahmaks of the Kurgan. The slant-eyed Hung tribesmen too were enemies that you could be proud to fight and kill, men that knew not the meaning of fear or panic.

But these soft-bellied southerners, they were hardly men at all. Few stood even to the Norscan's shoulders, and they were as weak in spirit as they were in body. Almost universally, it seemed, they were a race of malformed runts; pathetic, wretched and honourless. Any one of them would have been killed at birth had he been born of a Skaeling woman, for any mother would have been shamed to bear such a stunted wretch. Only the ruling class had any backbone at all, and even they would have been regarded as lesser men had they been born into any Norscan tribe.

Scores of longships could be seen in the harbour of the burning township, though it was only a fraction of the fleet that had accompanied him from Norsca. Fully half of his ships had beached unseen on the north side of the island, and their warriors had closed in on this town under the cover of darkness. When the first of his longships had been seen approaching the town, the terrified inhabitants found that their escape was already cut off from behind. None had been spared – not man, woman or child. Even the dogs of the enemy were butchered like vermin. Bands of his warriors still roamed the town, hunting down the last survivors. Some dragged screaming women by the hair from burning buildings, to be used and slaughtered in the name of the true gods, while others ransacked the more wealthy structures for plunder.

Even as he watched he saw more of the enemy cut down by his men, smashed from their feet by axe, sword and spear. He saw heads hewn from shoulders and lifted high into the air for the gods to see, before being rammed onto spikes or hung from belts. He saw weeping, terrified men have their throats slashed before being kicked face down into the streets and spat upon for their cowardice. He saw shaggy-furred warhounds worrying at the bodies of the fallen, tearing apart flesh and crushing bone with their powerful jaws.

Styrbjorn whistled sharply and two of the hounds lifted their blood-smeared snouts from the belly of their latest kill.

The warhounds, brothers of the same litter, were massive beasts the size of small ponies. Their back legs and flanks were scaled like a lizard, the skin tough and leathery. Their heavy shoulders, forelegs and heads were covered in thick black fur. Bony spurs ran down their backs, and tusks like those of a boar jutted from their toothy maws. Around their necks were thick, spiked collars, and Styrbjorn's rune was branded into their flesh. They slunk away from their kill, growling and swinging their heavy heads from side to side, and a curt command from Styrbjorn brought them loping towards him.

Flanked by the warhounds, Jarl Styrbjorn stalked inside the abbey. Its doors had been smashed off their hinges and lay in splinters, and he stepped over bodies sprawled across the floor. The stink of blood made his eyes dilate and his heart beat a little quicker. It was clear to Styrbjorn that many people had fled here to the abbey for protection. The notion that any god would offer succour to those who cowered from their enemies rather than fight them was laughable.

Guttural laughter accompanied a cry of agony that echoed through the interior of the abbey and Styrbjorn strode down the central aisle towards its origin. A cluster of his elite huskarl warriors were gathered on the dais at the head of the abbey, surrounding a figure sprawled on the floor. Encased in ornate armour of Chaos, these warriors had the mark of the gods about them, a palpable aura that made the skin tingle. Still, Styrbjorn was god-touched himself, and he wore the favour of his warlike deities like a cloak.

Styrbjorn's huskarls stepped aside, bowing their heads, and he saw that the figure that occupied their attentions was an elderly woman, perhaps someone of holy significance. She was garbed in a long green dress, and a silver amulet resembling a three-petalled flower hung from a fine chain around her neck.

Bjarki, the Skaeling seer, stood before the holy woman, clutching a curved sacrificial blade. He was grinning.

Blood was streaming down the woman's cheeks. Her eyes had been cut out, Styrbjorn saw. Her fingers and thumbs had been hacked off as well, and she groped around her blindly, leaving bloody smears on the stone floor.

Bjarki had long been in the jarl's ear, urging him to strike against the lands of the southern horsemen, the lands called Bretonnia in the indecipherable southern tongue. Long had the seer desired to see wreck and ruin come to these lands, and his excitement that his dreams of devastation were now starting to come to fruition was abundantly clear.

Almost twenty years ago, Styrbjorn had been aboard the longship that had come across the tiny fishing coracle, adrift in the middle of the sea that divided Norsca from the southern lands. There had been two people aboard that tiny boat – an old man, and a young boy no more than six winters old. From their dress and the indecipherable babble that they spoke it was clear that they were southerners, and knowing the currents of the seas in that region as well as any living man, Styrbjorn knew that they had come from Bretonnia.

Laughing, Styrbjorn had nailed the old man to the mast of his longship, and a similar fate would have befallen the boy, had the Norscans not seen the witchlight in his eyes. Defiant and unafraid, the small boy stood his ground, his fists clenched as he stared down the longship full of Norscans, and every Skaeling there could see as clear as day that the boy was god-touched.

Impressed with his bravery in the face of death, the Norscans had instantly dubbed the boy *Bjarki* – 'little bear' in the Skaeling dialect. Styrbjorn had taken the child into his household, feeding and clothing him and teaching him the ways of the Norse. He had taught him how to hunt sabretusk and blood-bear, to kill with axe and blade, to honour the gods with your actions and taught him the meaning of pride and honour.

The boy never talked of why he was adrift on a coracle accompanied by no one but an old bondsman, and Styrbjorn never pressed him. It was clear that the child had renounced any ties to his birth land and embraced the way of the Skaeling wholeheartedly. That he harboured a burning hatred for Bretonnia was obvious, and Styrbjorn encouraged this emotion, knowing that it would fuel the youngster's growing strength.

It mattered not at all that Bjarki was not of Norse blood – the power of the gods was with him, and no tribesman would be foolish enough to incur the wrath of the gods by doing him harm.

Styrbjorn's seer at that time, old Skaelabran, had been a withered ancient who had all but despaired of finding a successor. For a decade the old seer clung to life as he taught the secret ways to the young Bjarki, and many were the scars and beatings that the youngster endured under his harsh tutorship.

When Bjarki had been with the Skaelings a little over a year he had first voiced his desire to see Bretonnia burn. Four times Styrbjorn had raided its coastlines during Bjarki's childhood, and the boy had raged and stamped his feet when he had not been allowed to accompany him, to witness the slaughter first-hand. Styrbjorn was impressed with the youngster's enthusiasm, but his decision would not be changed. Bjarki was much smaller than the Skaeling boys his age, and Styrbjorn would not risk incurring the wrath of the gods by taking him on a raid before he was ready for it.

It was not old age and senility that eventually did for old Skaelabran. Little more than a skeletal husk held together by bitterness and diabolic will, his life was finally ended with a knife thrust to the heart, care of his young apprentice. Having learnt all he could, Bjarki saw no further use for the vicious old Norscan. It had been a proud day for Styrbjorn, who regarded Bjarki as his blood-kin.

The seasons flowed into each other and the years turned, and for the last five years Bjarki had accompanied Styrbjorn on his raids. Those had been fruitful years of plenty, and much wealth and favour had been garnered in raids against the Empire, the Kurgan and other Norse tribes. Much of their successes had been attributed to Bjarki, and Styrbjorn was past the point of feeling any jealousy or anger when these whispers reached his ears. Still, in that time Styrbjorn had not chosen to pitch himself against the Bretonnians.

'Only a foolish hunter returns to the same hunting ground every day,' he remembered his grandfather telling him. 'A wise hunter varies his hunts, so as not to hunt any one of his prey-flocks to extinction.'

He remembered the words well, and after a half-decade of raiding the Bretonnian coastlines every season, he had then directed his men elsewhere for a further five years, allowing the Bretonnians to grow weak and complacent.

The tortured priestess on the ground – for Styrbjorn was certain now that she was a holy woman – looked up at him, despite her lack of eyes, and he felt certain that she perceived him. She began to talk, spouting a stream of garbled nonsense that he knew was directed at him in particular.

'What does she say?'the jarl asked.

Bjarki licked his lips, his eyes filled with bloodlust and hunger.

'She says that we defile this place with our presence,' said the seer, smirking. 'That the Lady will strike us down.'

'The Lady?' questioned Styrbjorn, nodding his head towards a pristine marble statue at the rear of the dais.

Bjarki turned his head towards the statue and gave a curt nod.

'The patron goddess of this land,' he said. He spat towards the statue. 'A minor deity of little true power.'

Styrbjorn knelt down before the woman on the floor. She could not see him, but recoiled from his closeness. It was not something that Styrbjorn was unfamiliar with – there were few even amongst the Skåelings who were able to remain close to him for long without experiencing discomfort, even pain. The eyes of the gods were on him, and just to be in his vicinity was to catch a measure of their gaze. Those of particular weakness were even known to fall to the ground in his presence, their bodies becoming instantly warped and altered as the gods gifted them the blessing of change.

The tortured priestess tried to grasp the totemic amulet around her neck, but without fingers, the movement was pathetic and useless, making Styrbjorn smile. He reached out and closed his own large hand around the amulet, ignoring the pain it caused and the stink of burning flesh. With a sharp yank, he broke the chain, and hurled the offending amulet away from him.

The priestess tried to pull away, her face a grimace of loathing, but he reached down and grabbed her by the throat, his fingers almost encircling her neck. It was like the neck of a swan, delicate and fragile, and it would take no more than a twist to end her life. Exerting little effort, he dragged her towards him, so that her face was no more than a foot from his own.

'Before you perish, know that your death shall not be meaningless. The lord of skulls shall feast on your heart and drink of your blood, woman. And know that in the times of Darkness that will soon come to engulf the world, the gods themselves will walk the lands, leading their legions in the battle to end all battles. And in those End Times, great Kharnath will cut down your Lady, hacking her head from her shoulders and great shall be the lamentation. Your goddess will perish – she knows this. And now you too know the truth.'

It didn't matter to him that she could not understand his words; he could see that they pained her, and that was all that he wished.

Sobbing and babbling, Styrbjorn allowed her to pull away from him as he rose back to his full height.

'Do with her what you will,' he said to his men, and stepped past them, moving towards the statue of the goddess. Styrbjorn shook his head derisively. If this was who they prayed to, then no wonder they were weak. This was no god to be feared and respected; not like the gods of the north.

The goddess was tall and slender, with flowing hair entwined with ivy and leaves. In her hands she bore a chalice. Tears ran down her cheeks, dripping rhythmically into the goblet, and Styrbjorn touched a finger to her face. The tears appeared to be real, pooling in eyes that were far too expressive to be carved of mere marble.

Behind the Skaeling jarl, the agonised cries of the priestess faded into a strangled, gargling sound, and he knew that Bjarki had slashed her throat. Still staring into the statue's eyes, he saw that the salty tears of the goddess suddenly turned red. She wept blood tears for her defiled priestess, and Styrbjorn chuckled.

Turning back towards his warriors, Styrbjorn held out his hand.

'Give me your hammer,' he ordered one of his huskarls, who immediately handed over the massive double-handed weapon to his lord. Indeed, had Styrbjorn calmly ordered him to kill himself, or any of his comrades, the man would have done so without a second thought. Styrbjorn smiled. It was good to have such devotion.

The Norscan chieftain was in good spirits as he swung the hammer around in a powerful arc. The blow smashed the goddess's head from her shoulders. Stepping forward, Styrbjorn slammed the flat of his foot into the statue's midsection, tipping it backwards. It broke in two as it struck the back wall, and he swung the hammer again, shattering goblets and chalices carefully arrayed along the ledges set into the walls to smithereens.

'Will you not strike me down?' Styrbjorn sneered down at face of the goddess, whose head had rolled so that it had come to rest looking up at him, blood tears still trickling from its eyes.

Nothing happened, and he smirked, shaking his head.

How could he respect a people whose very god was not worthy of respect?

IT WAS THREE hours later, and the sky was lightening with the approaching dawn. Styrbjorn sat upon his throne, which had been brought up from his longship and placed upon the dais where the statue of the Bretonnian goddess had once stood.

Impaled figures surrounded him. Not all were dead, and many twitched and moaned as they slid further down the spikes. Only cowards faced such a death – warriors who stood and fought, even weakling southern warriors such as they had encountered, were given honourable deaths, killed by the blade and the axe. Those who fled in panic and cowardice, who soiled themselves in fear, or dropped their weapons mid-battle – they were given no such respect.

Bjarki squatted at his feet, a savage grin on his blood-smeared face. The shaman had enjoyed the night's work, though Styrbjorn sensed this bloodletting had merely whetted his appetite.

The pews that had filled the abbey had been smashed apart and piled atop each other, and a fierce blaze now roared in the middle of the floor, the flames licking up towards the rafters high overhead. The stained glass images of the enemy goddess had been smashed out, and hundreds of corpses had been nailed into the stone walls; their bodies stripped and their flesh used as parchments, the runic symbols of the Norse gods had been carved into their skin.

The fires were being stoked with oil and wood, and severed heads were thrown into the searing heart of the blazing pyres. Hair frizzled and burst into flames, and skin and flesh melted from skulls like butter. Inside, brains and tongues bubbled and broiled under the intense heat, and lower jaws fell away from the skulls as muscles and tendons were rendered to ash. Finally, all that would be left would be blackened, ash-covered skulls, and once the fires had died down they would be dragged from the embers and arranged into piles, in honour of Styrbjorn and great Kharnath, the skull-taker.

'Why do we linger here, manling?' snarled a voice like rocks grinding against each other, and Styrbjorn turned from staring into the flames to regard the craggy face of Zumarah.

The dwarf stood no taller than a Norscan boy of ten years, though he was almost as broad as he was tall. His chest was immense, and his thick limbs were easily as strong as any Norscan's. The fire of hatred burnt in the dwarf's deep set eyes, and a double row of lumps protruded from beneath the flesh along the ridge of his brow. Styrbjorn did not know if those studded growths had been implanted beneath the flesh, or whether they were gifts of the gods. The pair of tusks that rose from his lower jaw, however, were certainly evidence of the gods' touch. The dwarf's skin was tough and stony, the texture of rough granite and a deep, ruddy colour, and a thick beard, as black as coal and bound into a dozen tight, ringletted coils wound with meteoric iron hung down past his waist.

'We linger here because I wish it, dwarf,' said Styrbjorn.

'You promised me slaves, Norscan,' growled Zumarah, 'and I would have them. So far I have seen none.'

'These ones were promised to the gods,' said Styrbjorn, gesturing to the impaled figures arrayed around the edge of the dais. Those still living cried out for death, but no one harkened to their pleas. 'And I would not seek to anger the gods by denying them, for you or any other mortal. Be patient, Zumarah – tonight was just a skirmish; the real battle will come soon. You shall have what you were promised.'

'My services do not come freely, Norscan,' snarled Zumarah, 'nor do they come cheaply. And *Ereshkigal-Namtar* hungers.'

'Your... daemon-construct shall feed soon. I have given you my word, dwarf-kin, and the word of a Skaeling jarl is not given lightly. Your geld shall be honoured.'

The dwarf snarled, setting his feet solidly and glaring up at the seated jarl. Hatred and vitriol oozed from the dwarf's every pore.

'Do not think to cheat me out of my dues, manling,' growled Zumarah.

The greed of the dark dwarfs was unlike anything Styrbjorn had ever experienced. It was beyond passion, beyond desire. It was more akin to a burning *need*, a desperate compulsion for acquiring wealth and slaves far beyond what they could ever need. Still, it mattered little. The daemon-construct that Zumarah had crafted and bound to his will was a weapon of awesome power and destruction. He had first seen its power in action against the Aesgars, and it had levelled their fort in moments. The destruction it had wrought was wondrous and terrible.

'The rest of my fleet is two days behind us,' said Styrbjorn. 'We wait here until their arrival before we push onto the mainland.'

'You have such little faith in the strength of your warriors that you must wait for reinforcements?' sneered Zumarah.

Bjarki hissed, exposing his sharply filed teeth and rattled a bone-charm threateningly. The dwarf looked at the Skaeling seer with a look of derision and contempt.

'You think I fear your curses, bane-spinner?' snarled the dwarf. 'Stay your tongue or I'll rip it out.'

Bjarki leapt to his feet, his face flushing with anger, but Styrbjorn laid a hand of his shoulder, keeping him from lashing out.

'Two days, we wait here,' said Styrbjorn. 'This is my decision, and there is to be no discussion. The gods caused the seas to rise in anger, and the ships bearing my tuskers have been delayed; I wish to see how these *Bretonnians* fare against such beasts, and will not attack without them.'

The dwarf regarded the jarl defiantly, refusing to be cowed by the big Norscan chieftain. The stony-faced creature's beard split into a grin.

'We understand each other, you and I,' said the dwarf. 'This is good. Two days.'

With that, Zumarah turned and strode away from the jarl, his short legs and heavy build giving him an oddly rolling gait.

'Why did you hold me back?' spat Bjarki. 'He deserves the blessings of the Pox Father's touch for the way he spoke to you, my jarl.'

'Is it for my honour that you would call down Grandfather Nurgleth's attentions, or your own?' said Styrbjorn.

Bjarki, still quivering with barely suppressed rage, flashed an angry glance towards him, witch-light sparking.

'It is always for your honour, my jarl,' he said.

'You feel that I need your help, or that of anyone else, to protect my honour, Bjarki?' said Styrbjorn, his voice low and dangerous.

The seer licked his lips.

'Of course not, my jarl,' said the seer finally.

'Good,' said Styrbjorn, and his eyes took on a lustful, eager light. 'Now tell me, the woman who shall bear my son – she is coming to us even now, you say?'

'She is making her way towards the crow-fields,' confirmed Bjarki. 'There, the gods have decreed that you shall win a proud victory over the weakling horsemen. Great will be the slaughter. Great will be the lamentation of their women. Your consort-bride will arrive on the eve of battle, and your son shall be conceived under the green moon, after victory has been won.'

Styrbjorn smiled. A son! He had waited so long for one of his women to bear him a son to succeed him, but long had that eluded him. Thirteen daughters his wives and consorts had borne him, but no son. Indeed, two of them accompanied him now, sword-maidens of commensurate skill, easily the match for any of his warriors.

'You hear that, daughters?' he said. 'Soon you will have a brother, and then you will be free to wed!'

Fraygerd and Hrefna were born of different mothers, but that they were sisters was obvious. Both shared their father's tall stature and noble countenance. Both had long, straight hair the colour of sand, though Fraygerd wore hers bound in tails while Hrefna's hung loose and wild. A little more than a year separated the two – they were nineteen and seventeen respectively – and though Fraygerd was the taller and stronger of the pair, Hrefna's fiery nature more than made up for that deficiency on the field of battle.

'I've yet to meet the man who I would deem worthy of marriage,' said Hrefna, and Styrbjorn smiled. He turned back towards his seer, who was staring at the two girls with undisguised desire, for all that they stood more than a foot taller than him.

'Tell me where she is now.'

The seer nodded, and knelt cross-legged on the floor. With one hand he drew his knife, and slashed it across his palm, which was crisscrossed with a mass of scars. Blood welled and muttering an incantation under his breath the seer wiped his knife clean on the matted furs wrapped around his shoulders before sheathing the blade. Clenching his fist and holding it above him, he threw his head back and allowed the drips to fall onto his face, splashing onto his tattooed lips, his cheeks and falling upon both eyelids.

Bjarki began to rock slightly, still muttering an incantation. The taut muscles of his arms and torso, covered in ritualised scars and ink, began to twitch as his spirit soared. God-touched as he was, Styrbjorn felt the vicious little shaman's spirit pull clear of its mortal flesh; it felt like a cold breath on his skin as the seer's soul-spirit brushed by him and was gone.

Moments later, he felt the shaman return, and Bjarki gave a shuddering breath as he slammed back into his body.

'Well?'

'She's five day's walk south of the crow-fields.'

'She has an armed guard?'

'No,' said Bjarki, wiping away the blood that was dripping from one of his nostrils. 'She has a measure of power of her own.'

'She is alone?' said Styrbjorn, concern in his voice.

'A group of wretches accompany her. She is using them for her blood-magic. They are armed, but they are not warriors. But she does not need them for protection, my jarl – as I said, she does not need protecting.'

Styrbjorn was unconvinced.

'I want you to go to her, Bjarki. I will not risk anything befalling her before the consummation. Kveldulf,' he ordered, gesturing towards one his warriors nearby, a bow-legged, broad-shoulder Skaeling with a nose that had clearly been broken a dozen times. The warrior stepped forward and dropped to one knee. 'You and your horsemen will accompany Bjarki to the mainland.'

'As you wish it, my jarl,' said Kveldulf.

'Find her, and protect her, Bjarki,' ordered Styrbjorn. 'Bring her to me. I'll see you at the crow fields – that is where the battle is to take place, yes?'

'That is what I have read in the entrails, my jarl,' said Bjarki, bowing his head. Standing, he nodded to Kveldulf. 'Ready your horsemen, warrior. We sail within the hour.'

[illegible] of th [illegible]

Leading the charge of th [illegible]

[illegible] departure that [illegible] the knights of [illegible]

would fight [illegible] si [illegible]

CHAPTER FIVE

Calard's head wasn't pounding yet; that would come later. Cursing himself for having agreed to take part in the day's event, he grimaced as he accepted a lance handed to him.

The sun could not pierce the thick banks of cloud overhead, for which Calard was thankful – he didn't think he could have dealt with direct sunlight stabbing into his eyes. Drinking deeply from a waterskin, he swished the cooling liquid around his mouth. Bertelis was riding alongside him and though he said nothing Calard could feel his brother's silent rebuke.

'Keep tight, and don't break formation,' said Montcadas, ahead of them.

The baron, being the most senior of the contingent from Bastonne, had assumed command, and would be leading the charge of their formation. It had been the baron's decision that all the knights of Bastonne would fight as one single lance formation, much to

Calard's chagrin, for it meant that Maloric and his Sangasse lapdogs would be fighting at his side. He had hoped to face his rival from opposite ends of the field, but the baron had scuppered any such ideas the night before. Indeed, had it not been for that proclamation, Calard would certainly not have drunk quite so much as he had – at least that was what he told himself at any rate.

'Think you can manage to stay in the saddle until the start without throwing up, Garamont?' sneered Maloric.

'If I'm sick, I'll make sure it's in your direction,' muttered Calard.

'Can we stop this line of conversation, please?' groaned Tassilo. The young knight was positively green in the face from overindulgence.

'And for the love of the Lady stay downwind,' snapped Maloric. 'I can smell the wine on you from here.'

'Don't disgrace me today,' snarled Bertelis under his breath to Calard, leaning in close, and he bit his tongue not to snap back an angry retort.

'Let's show these uptight bastards how the knights of Bastonne fight!' roared Montcadas, and the nobles around Calard and Tassilo lifted their lances high with a cheer.

'Does he need to be so loud?' groaned Tassilo.

'You'll feel better to be up and moving about soon,' said Calard, though there was little conviction in his voice.

Abruptly, Tassilo lost his battle with his insides, and he leant over in the saddle and vomited loudly. Maloric turned away in disgust, while Huebald and Baldemund chuckled and instantly began ribbing the young knight for his lack of drinking constitution. Bertelis said nothing and merely stared straight ahead, the muscles in his jaw twitching. Calard himself was breathing deeply.

A scabby peasant dog dodged between the legs of the horses and began to lap at Tassilo's vomit, and Calard felt his stomach heave. A sharp horn echoed across the field and Calard willed himself not to be ill, holding onto his lance tightly.

The knights began to move, walking forwards to the cheers of the crowd in the stands. Heralds hollered the names of the knights in turn as they moved forward, accompanied by further cheers and shouts, amid much banner-waving and fanfare. Horns blared, and drums beat out regular tattoos as the knights moved into position opposite each other across the open field.

The field had been well chosen, for it was broad and flat. It slid off to the south-west, where it became marshy and boggy, but was otherwise well drained, and though its grass would still doubtless be completely churned up by mid-afternoon, it would not become the muddy quagmire that had been the fields of several tournaments he had taken part in. One such tournament the previous spring, at Glaston, had been an utter debacle. By its conclusion, it had been impossible to discern who was ally and who was opponent, for everyone was caked head to toe in clinging black mud that obscured their heraldry and colours. The event had been called off after more than two dozen deaths, most suffered when destriers had broken limbs in the sinking mud and thrown their riders.

Gunthar had always taught him that the location of a battle was as important for victory as any other factor, often more so even than the quality of the combatants. He had told Calard stories of castles held by half a dozen peasants against endless hordes of greenskins, and of entire armies of knights being slaughtered by lowborn archers because of a poorly chosen battlefield, situated with a sinking marsh across its centre.

This was a prime location for an even contest that favoured neither side, and as he cantered his destrier into position he looked across the field. The sides had been evenly split, with roughly six hundred knights gathered on each end of the tournament field. Double that number of peasants were gathered behind their masters, though they would take no direct part in the event. They were there as support for their lords, to attend to the fallen, to supply fresh lances and water on each turn.

This was not a florid, theatrical joust. This was a true test, the closest that one could come to true warfare during times of peace. The dukes and even the king himself were known to compete in these events on occasion, often in disguise so as not to receive any particular quarter from their opponents, and more than one knight had been honoured for having proved a worthy opponent to these luminaries.

In essence, this was a battle as any other battle, mortal or otherwise. The knights, ranked up in tight formation, would charge across the field at each other in an attempt to strike their opponents from the saddle. Those unwilling or unable to continue retired, aided or carried from the field by their retainers if necessary, and so the tournament continued. Having made a pass, the knights would wheel around and their formations would regroup for another charge. So it would continue until one side was declared the winner. More often than not, the battle would rage through the morning, and horns would blare, announcing a cease to the event, and the combatants would eat and drink and have any injuries tended. Then, another horn would sound, and the battle would recommence. Usually, a victor was declared before mid-afternoon, but it was not unheard of for battles to rage long into the afternoon and into dusk if no clear winner could be seen.

Serious injuries were commonplace, and death was an accepted part of every tourney. Even those with the smallest turnout would be lucky not to have at least one death during the day's event, but this was but a part of what made the tournaments what they were. If there was no risk, then the tourney would be a poor training ground for the rigours of real battle.

'The enemy have refused to quit the field!' bellowed a crier, yelling the traditional phrase at the top of his lungs. 'In the Lady's name, our honour demands that we clear the field of their presence!'

A great cheer rose from the gathered knights, and Calard heard Tassilo groan. He smiled. He was still not feeling great, but the fresh air and light mist of rain that had begun to fall was making him feel eminently better than he had when he had first risen. He might even make it through without losing the contents of his stomach, he thought.

'For Bastonne!' roared Montcadas.

The knights began to edge forwards, nudging their steeds into a walk, and Calard slammed down the visor on his helmet. That walk turned into a trot, and the knightly formations began angling towards each other across the field. Several smaller detachments of knights errant kicked their steeds forward on the flanks, galloping out to take up flanking positions against their opponents while their comrades advanced more slowly.

The first strike was between two of these smaller detachments of young knights errant, who, eager to get to grips with the 'enemy' had charged headlong across the field towards each other from outset.

Cheers rose as a dozen knights were struck from the saddle, falling hard onto the earth.

Montcadas, riding at the tip of the wedge of Bastonnian knights, urged his steed into a canter, and the others did likewise, keeping their formation tight. Lances were held in the vertical position, and for a moment it seemed strange to Calard that the baron had a lance in his hand too, rather than his usual spiked morning star. Still, such a weapon would have been inappropriately deadly for a tourney. As it was, tourney lances were not nearly as lethal as war lances, blunted and crafted to break more easily with far less likelihood of skewering the victim. They were capable of delivering a powerful blow, easily enough to break bones and send a knight pitching from the saddle, but usually not enough to penetrate armour or impale.

Calard felt the familiar thrill as the speed of the knights picked up, and the ground began to thunder beneath the pounding of hooves. Great sods of earth were torn up as twelve hundred knights drew towards each other, gauging the moment to lower lances and kick their horses into the gallop.

'CHARGE!' ROARED MONTCADAS, kicking his spurs into his steed's flanks. As one the Bastonnians swiftly lowered their lances and their destriers leaped forwards to meet the foe head-on and at full pace.

The knights of Bastonne and Lyonesse struck each other at full gallop, and the power of the two forces coming together was bone-shattering. Even muffled by his helmet the sound was tremendous, with men shouting and bellowing, horses screaming, hooves pounding the ground like an avalanche. Lances cracked sharply like dry tinder as they broke upon shield and breastplate, and metal struck metal as horses and knights smashed into each other.

Adjusting his bodyweight for the strike, Calard expertly guided his lance-tip towards the chest of a knight with a snarling lion upon his helmet crest. Intent on his own strike, the knight was not prepared for the blow, and Calard rose in the saddle as he struck, putting the full weight of his armoured body and the momentum of his horse behind the blow. The strike was nigh on perfect, and it struck the knight just below the heart, lifting him from the saddle even as Calard's lance shattered into splinters.

The Lyonesse knight pitched backwards to fall amidst the flailing hooves, and Calard was rocked backwards in the saddle by the force of the impact, which jarred up his arm and shoulder, numbing it. A lance speared towards him, and he turned his shield at the last moment as he reeled, forcing it to skid off the shield's surface without breaking.

Splinters of wood spattered off his helmet as more lances were broken. As he thundered past the knight, he slammed the weighted, counterbalanced end of his splintered lance into a knight's helmet. The man did not fall, but he slid sideways in the saddle as his balance was thrown, and Calard saw Maloric's already broken lance smash him to the ground.

Abruptly, there was nothing in front of Calard but open ground, as the two wedges of knights rode clear of each other. Throwing his shattered lance to the ground, Calard turned in the saddle, smiling, as he heard his brother Bertelis alongside him whoop with unashamed joy. Around six of his comrades had fallen in the exchange, but more than ten of the Lyonesse knights were down.

The knights rode across the field to where their opponents had begun the charge, where hundreds of peasants were arrayed, holding out fresh lances. Others were racing across the field either on foot or upon the backs of thick-limbed draught horses, dodging between charging lance formations, to attend to fallen nobles and lords. Already dozens of knights were being stretchered off the field with broken arms and legs, and the screams of horribly injured horses were cut short as their throats were mercifully slashed.

'Tassilo?' asked Calard, not seeing his cousin.

Huebald lifted his visor and shook his head, rolling his eyes.

'He practically threw himself onto a lance,' he said. 'I think he just wanted a lie down.'

Calard laughed out loud, feeling the last hint of his hangover dissipate like fog under a rising sun.

'Baron?' said Bertelis sharply, cutting through the jovial chatter.

Montcadas was slumped in the saddle, and Calard's smile dropped from his face. He swung from his horse and dropped to the ground, running to the baron's side, as the big man pitched sideward.

Calard caught him, but the baron was a huge man, and his armour easily doubled his weight. Maloric was at his side a moment later, and together the two of them lowered the big man to the ground, the blood-feud between them momentarily forgotten.

A shattered lance was embedded in the baron's chest, having punched through his breastplate. It was on the opposite side than his heart, thankfully, but blood was bubbling up through the rent metal, staining the light-coloured timber of the lance a deep red. A tourney lance should not have been able to penetrate a breastplate, but it had been known to happen on occasion, usually when the blunted tip of the lance had already been broken off.

The baron was roaring through gritted teeth like a wounded bear.

'Get a surgeon here, now!' bellowed someone.

Calard was staring at the wound, realising that the lance tip had pierced one of the baron's lungs, and knowing that he would likely begin drowning in his own blood shortly if nothing was done. Nevertheless, the shock of seeing the injury had frozen him into inaction, and he stared numbly at the blood foam bubbling from the wound. Unaffected by Calard's immobility, Maloric pulled the baron's helmet from his head.

The Sangasse nobleman hissed, and Baldemund, standing behind them, swore under his breath. The baron was still roaring in pain, his jaw gritted so tight that Calard feared he would shatter a tooth.

A splinter of wood four inches long had pierced Montcadas's right eye – his sole remaining eye. Blood was streaming down his cheek and soaking his silver-flecked beard. Instantly, Calard understood what had happened. When the lance that had pierced Montcadas's chest had shattered, one of the long splinters of wood had shot upwards, slipping through the visor-slit of the baron's helmet and sunk into his eye.

'Pull it out, Lady damn it,' roared Montcadas.

'Don't touch it,' Huebald advised. 'Pulling it out might do more damage.'

The baron reached for the sliver of wood and Calard was shaken out of his stupor, grabbing Montcadas's gauntleted hand before the older knight could rip the offending splinter from his eye. The baron roared in agony and rage, fighting against the hands holding him down, desperate to tear the shard of lance-wood from his eye.

'More damage?' Baldemund muttered under his breath. 'The man won't see again, mark my words.'

Calard knew instinctively that his cousin spoke the truth. Montcadas was shaking his head from side to side in absolute agony. His eye was a pool of blood, and Calard winced just looking at the stiletto-sharp, red-soaked splinter protruding from the socket.

'Where's that damn surgeon!' bellowed Calard.

A blast of horns sounded in the distance, echoed by dozens of others back and forth across the tournament field. It was the signal to cease combat, and for a moment Calard thought that perhaps the competition was being called to a halt because of Montcadas's injury. He dismissed it straight away – even deaths rarely halted a tourney.

He heard men shouting in the distance, voices raised in concern and inquiry, but he paid them no mind.

A surgeon arrived, slipping his way through the knights crowded around Montcadas, and Calard was pushed aside. He stood up, feeling helpless and distraught.

More raised voices intruded on him and horns blared nearby. He turned towards Bertelis, who had turned away from Montcadas and was craning his head to see what was going on. The men all around were calling out in confusion, speaking in hurried tones as whispers spread like wildfire through the gathered knights.

'What is it?' said Calard.

'Yeoman outriders, wearing the colours of the Duke of Lyonesse,' said Bertelis.

'Lyonesse is under attack!' shouted one of the yeomen from horseback. 'The duke requests your aid! The enemy is upon us!'

'What enemy?' shouted Calard.

'Norscans!' came the reply.

CHAPTER SIX

Every movement was agony. Her joints throbbed with rheumatism and arthritis, and she became short of breath after hobbling no more than twenty paces. Her vision was hazy and indistinct, and the bright light hurt her eyes. She leant up against a barrel placed to the side of the muddy roadway through the hovel village to catch her breath.

Elisabet had left the crone's cave before dawn, desperately trying to make her way back to her home. Surely, she thought desperately, someone would be able to help her.

Elisabet was still gasping like a fish stranded on land when the rock hit her. It struck her on the cheek, splitting her aged skin, and weak, thin blood ran down her face. She cried out and raised her feeble arms up to protect herself as more rocks, lumps of manure and rotten vegetables rained down upon her.

'Witch! Witch! Witch!' shouted the voices of children, taunting her.

Elisabet covered her face protectively. A rotten marrow exploded as it hit the barrel beside her, spreading stinking foulness and writhing maggots. Another rock struck her, this time hitting her between her withered breasts, and there was a dry, wooden snap as a rib broke.

Crying out, she staggered to her feet and hobbled as fast as she could, trying to escape the relentless children. She slipped in the mud and fell.

'Witch! Witch! Witch!'

The children closed in around her, and several of the larger children began hitting her with sticks. Scabby dogs darted around the filth-encrusted youngsters, yapping excitedly, and Elisabet cowered, crying and wailing.

'Get away, you dirty little wretches!' bellowed a voice, and the old woman cried out in relief as the children scattered, shouting insults and laughing.

She lay crying in the mud and the manure, trying desperately to catch her breath and slow her heart that was fluttering like a bird's. Everything hurt. Vaguely she registered a group of men standing around her, but she didn't have the energy to lift herself up or to offer them thanks.

''Ware yourself, warden,' said one of them. 'That's the crone Haegtesse, that is.'

'Bollocks,' scoffed the warden.

'That's her all right,' said another. 'Old witch put a curse on my cousin, she did. I ain't touchin' her. She's got the evil eye.'

A shadow leant over her, and she cowered before it.

'That right, you old hag?' said a brutish voice.

She shook her head painfully, moaning.

'I asked you a question, witch,' said the warden, jabbing her with the butt of his halberd.

'No,' she managed.

'You callin' my man a liar? This good upstanding pillar of the community, here?' he said, jabbing her in the chest again with his halberd.

'No,' she whimpered. She crawled on hands and knees towards the man, scrabbling for him with claw-like hands. He stepped away from her reach.

Trying to reclaim some dignity, Elisabet climbed to her feet, straightened her back and lifted her chin to look upon the yeoman ruffians.

'Don't look 'er in the eye!' warned one of them, and they all took a wary step backwards.

Affecting an imperious tone, she addressed them.

'I am the Lady Elisabet of Marlemont, and I demand that you escort me to my father's estate immediately.'

For a second there was silence, and then the yeomen burst into laughter. The sound struck Elisabet like the stones that had been hurled against her moments earlier, battering her with equal force and she felt herself wither beneath the onslaught.

A name floated up from the back of her mind, and she realised that she recognised the voice of the warden. He was one of the peasant warriors that had accompanied her beloved Calard to the east six months previous, to fight the greenskins menacing Bordeleaux. Before he had left, he had done her a kindness, she remembered. What was his name? Perdi? Perlo?

'Perdo,' she said, pointing a finger towards him as she remembered. 'Warden Perdo.'

The warden stepped back from her with a sharp intake of breath.

'How do you know my name, hag?' the peasant yeoman demanded, his men shuffling nervously.

'You did me a kindness once. I was riding with Calard, returning from the western fields. A dog barked, startling my mare and she shied. I lost my balance for a moment, and dropped a scarf to the ground. You picked it up for me,' said Elisabet, the vision as clear in her mind as if it had been yesterday. 'I tried to stop him, but Calard's brother, Bertelis, cuffed you over the head for it. Said I'd never get the stink of your touch out of the silk. I am sorry for that. It was a noble gesture, and I never thanked you for it.'

Silence greeted her claim.

'Told you, Perdo. She's a witch,' muttered one of the men.

Elisabet made to speak again, but the warden stepped forwards and slapped her across the face with flat of his mailed hand. The blow stung her, loosening several rotten teeth and sent her sprawling back down into the mud.

'There weren't nobody there but myself, the lady, and the two young lords,' he snapped. 'Only way you could know that is if you really *are* a witch. Bind her! And gag her, so she don't bewitch us.'

Elisabet was shoved face-first into the mud, and her hands were trussed up painfully behind her back. She winced, trying to beg them to stop, to listen to her, but her head was reefed backwards and a twisted strip of stinking cloth was jammed into her bloody mouth, then tied around the back of her head. Her ankles were bound with biting cord, and she was lifted up roughly, like a prize pig being led to the blooding.

'Take 'er to the dungeons,' ordered the warden. 'She can rot down there until the chamberlain decides what to do with her.'

CHLOD LICKED HIS lips as he glanced fearfully towards the noblewoman seated before the glowing embers. Her arms were covered in blood up to her elbows, and her hair was matted and tangled. Her once fair dress was muddied and torn around its hems, and her face was streaked with grime and dirt.

The corpse of one of the pilgrims was spread-eagled out before the witch, chest ripped open and ribs splayed. She pawed through the innards, muttering under her breath, and lifted several organs to her nose. Some she merely sniffed, others she licked or nibbled. Chlod's stomach churned. Her hands dipped again into the viscera, hauling intestines out and slapping them down onto the flat of a rock, and she began poking through the mass of stinking guts.

The pilgrims huddled together in a miserable clump, their faces long and their eyes haunted. Some of them, like Chlod, were watching the woman's grisly work, while others had their eyes tightly closed, their heads turned resolutely away. Some cried softly to themselves, and one was muttering a prayer to Reolus, begging him to deliver them from this evil creature.

'Quiet,' snapped the witch, casting a hateful glance in their direction, and the pilgrims shrunk under her gaze.

Turning back towards her grisly work, the witch peered intently into the human entrails, poking at them with her long fingernails and delving amongst the glistening, ropey tract with her blood-slick, slender hands.

From within a big bag covered in matted fur, the woman pulled a vile doll, its body made from a twisted burl of wood and strands of dark hair stitched into its head. Its face was horrific, something from a nightmare, with the skin of some creature pulled taut across it and held in place with nails. Sharp animal teeth, perhaps from a wolf or a badger, protruded from its gash of a mouth, and its eyes were staring buttons on bone. What looked like tattoos had been painted onto the thing's lips. It was a hideous thing, and the witch stroked a bloody hand across its hair, smoothing it down in a horrible mimicry of child-like affection.

The witch nestled the doll amidst the entrails of the pilgrim, standing it upright so that it looked back at her from within its gory throne, and she began to chant, rocking back and forth and holding her bloody hands out before her.

The pilgrims murmured in fear, hugging each other tighter. There were only a handful of them left now. This was the second victim that the witch had taken for her vile practices. At least it was one less mouth to feed, Chlod thought.

He didn't have any idea what the witch's destination was, but she seemed to know where she was heading. She pushed them on relentlessly, heading in a steady north-westerly direction. She seemed to have a sixth-sense for avoiding trouble, and guided them around patrols of knights and men-at-arms, avoiding chattels, castles and peasant villages as if she could see the lay of the land from high above, like it was a map laid out before her.

Chlod felt a chill run down his spine. Frost began to form before his eyes, coating the low-hanging branches near the witch, making them droop low from the weight, and he saw a thin coating of ice appearing on the doll, crackling across its face like a creeping sickness.

The witch looked up into the empty space above the coals of her fire pit and smiled. Chlod wondered if she were demented, for there was nothing there, but she began to converse with the empty space as if it were a living and breathing person. He wondered if there *was* something there, something that he did not have the ability to perceive.

She was talking in a language that he did not understand, one that sounded harsh and guttural to his ears used to the soft and florid language of the Bretonnians. He had heard men of the Empire speaking their own tongue, and this language was something akin to that, though subtly different and perhaps not quite as hard on the ear as that loathsome tongue.

The one-sided exchange lasted for several minutes, until an accord seemed to be met, and the conversation ended. The icy chill departed, and Chlod began rubbing his hands together, trying to restore the circulation in his fat, sausage-like digits.

One by one, the pilgrims drifted into a restless sleep. Chlod remained awake the longest, watching the witch as she continued to poke through the grisly remains of his erstwhile comrade until his eyes started to droop. He hadn't slept in several days, and when oblivion finally came upon him, sneaking up like a phantom in the dark, he slept like a dead man, neither moving, nor dreaming.

THE SEVERED HEADS hanging from the saddle and traces of Bjarki's pony bounced up and down as he galloped across the dark landscape. For three nights he had been back in the lands of his birth. They had ridden hard through the nights, moving without pause from dusk till dawn. The Skaeling ponies were hardy beasts, and though Bretonnian warhorses would easily outpace them over short distances, they were capable of maintaining their pace for hours on end without rest. After three nights of ceaseless travel, Bjarki and the band of riders moving with him had covered hundreds of miles, but their steeds showed no sign of tiring. They lay low during the daylight hours.

A dark, insatiable hunger gnawed within Bjarki. For long years he had waited for his chance to avenge himself against the society that had turned its back upon him, and now that his time for vengeance had come he found himself drunk with the desire for bloodshed.

Being back in Bretonnia brought all his old memories resurfacing. With the return of this knowledge, his fury and hatred increased tenfold.

Had he stayed on at his father's wealthy castle-estate, no more than three days ride from where he now was, then the Enchantress would have come to claim him sooner or later. Such was the way of things in Bretonnia. In this land, those born with the gift – 'fey-touched' as the Bretonnians would say – were regarded with outright fear and suspicion. The Enchantress scoured the countryside for children with the witch-sight, for those who had the gift of premonition and who could instinctively tap into the breath of the gods that flowed down from the north. These children she gathered to her, taking them from their families who attempted to forget that they had ever been born. Perhaps one girl in every hundred taken would return a decade or more later as a handmaiden of the Lady, one of her damsels, schooled in the mystical arts; boys that were taken were never seen again.

Even as a child he had heard a myriad of possible fates for these sons of Bretonnia stolen from their families. Some said that they were abandoned in the middle of the dark wildwoods of the realms, left to fend for themselves against the beasts that dwelled there. Some even said that that was what beastmen were – the boy-children abandoned by the Enchantress and altered by her magic. Others said that they were spirited away to the Lady's fair isle, there to live in perpetual states of childhood, doomed never to grow up, and to serve forever as pageboys and servants. Some even whispered that it was the sacrifice of these children that kept the seasons turning, and that if the practise were ever to cease, that Bretonnia would become entrapped in an eternal, never-ending winter.

Such would have been his fate. In a society raised to abhor those with his talents, he had no place. His parents hated and feared him, and even as a toddler he had come to despise them for it, taking pleasure in making them feel awkward when guests paid visits, antagonising them whenever he could.

In the witching hours of one mid-autumn night, he had been woken by his elderly caretaker, and hurried from his father's castle. Scared, and not knowing what was happening, he remained silent as he was led down the empty winding streets towards the harbour. A boat was waiting for them. Terrified and shivering he had somehow fallen asleep.

When he had awoken it was just before dawn and land was only a vague, misty shape on the horizon. Wide eyed and pale, he'd been given food and water, and the old man tried to calm him. The Enchantress was coming, he'd said. Doubtless his parents would have been relieved to have had him taken off their hands, but this old man, fearful of what would become of his young charge, had taken it upon himself to save the boy. The old fool.

It had been the will of the gods that the Norscans found him.

Bjarki licked his lips, tasting the blood upon them, rich and metallic. He was in his correct, allotted place, doing what it was the gods wished of him.

The woman who would bear his jarl a son was nothing more than a tool, he saw that now –a lure to bring the Skaelings to these lands. She was important – if it were not for her, his jarl would not have been tempted to attack the southlanders – but he was under no illusions about her real value. However, his lord would have no reason to keep his warriors here in Bretonnia if any harm came to her, and so he would protect her with his life.

She was close; he could almost taste the breath of the gods upon her.

Bjarki turned towards the minor Skaeling chieftain, Kveldulf. The man was a born horseman. He was awkward when moving on his own two feet – his legs were bow-legged and too short for his broad body – but in the saddle there were few Skaelings who could match him.

'Hurry,' he urged the chieftain. 'She is close – less than an hour ahead of us.'

The horseman nodded his head, making his beard, braided with tiny skulls, shiver like the charms Skaeling women used to protect their young from wind-borne daemons.

With a barked command he passed the word, and the twenty horsemen picked up their pace.

CHLOD WAS PISSING up against a tree when the marauders rode into camp. Hurriedly, he finished his business and dropped to the ground. He swore to himself. Why did these things always seem to happen when he was relieving himself?

There was a score of them, brutal looking savages dressed in outlandish furs and leathers, their heads covered in horned helmets. They were big men, and their arms and faces were covered in warpaint and tattoos. Many sported beards of blond hair, and they rode upon unarmoured, stocky horses. These were sturdier beasts than the warhorses of the nobility, smaller and more compact, with shaggier coats. Severed heads and hands hung from their saddles, and vile symbols had been daubed and branded into their flanks.

Chlod pressed low against the ground, his eyes wide and fearful as he peered around the thick roots of the tree at the intruders. It was still an hour or two before dawn, and had the urge to urinate not come upon him, he would undoubtedly have still been fast asleep.

The marauders stood motionless amongst the trees as they surveyed the camp. Chlod didn't know if he had been seen, but he dared not move for fear of drawing attention to himself.

As it was, the attention of the riders appeared to be focused upon the witch who stood to meet them.

One of the riders, a short, wiry figure with unruly dark hair and a massive cloak of spiked fur over his shoulders, dropped to the ground, stepping towards the witch, speaking the same language that Chlod had heard the witch talking earlier in the night. She answered him in the same language, and he gestured questioningly towards the sleeping pilgrims.

Hearing voices, one of them woke up and yawned. That yawn turned into a startled squeal as she saw the horsemen.

The witch shrugged her shoulders and the wiry one smiled, before swinging towards the pilgrims.

Chlod shrank back further between the roots of the tree as he saw the savage figure slide a handaxe from his belt, keeping his body between it and the pilgrims, so that they could not yet see it. The others were awake now, and they stared around them with wide eyes, visibly shaking. One of them cried out for Reolus to save them, but no avenging paladin of light appeared. Another waved a slipper that the Grail Knight had once worn at the horsemen, perhaps hoping that they were nothing more than apparitions and that by brandishing the holy artefact would banish them. It didn't.

The fur-cloaked individual slammed his handaxe into the neck of the slipper-wielder, who fell clutching at the wound, blood fountaining from between his fingers. Two of the pilgrims made a run for it, but these the horsemen struck down. An axe spun end over end and struck one of them in the back, and another of the marauders stood in the saddle and hurled a javelin that took the other pilgrim in the neck.

She fell no more than ten yards from Chlod's position, and for a moment he stared into her eyes as she looked right at him. The tip of the javelin, along with two feet of its length, was protruding from her throat and blood bubbled around it as she died, one hand reaching out for Chlod, who shrank back.

A horseman thundered across the clearing and ripped the javelin loose, and Chlod felt certain that he had been seen. He closed his eyes, but opened one a moment later when the fatal blow did not fall. The horseman had turned away from him, and looking past him, Chlod saw the last of his pilgrim companions butchered, head caved in by the wiry one's axe.

One of the horsemen moved forward, and the head of his steed lowered towards a bloodied body. The pony bit into the pilgrim's arm, tearing off a strip of flesh that it gulped down greedily, and Chlod felt his gorge rise as the other steeds stepped forward to graze on the corpses.

The axe-wielding savage spun suddenly, turning his gaze in Chlod's direction, eyes narrowing. It was clear that he could not see him in the gloom, but perhaps he sensed him there. Blood and brain matter dripped from his axe head, and he took a step in Chlod's direction.

A word from the witch halted him, and he spat a reply in her direction. He threw a quick, venomous glance in

Chlod's general direction, and then swung away with some reluctance. A horse was made available for the witch, and though the beast shied away from her, whinnying in fear, a barked word from the wiry man made it freeze. She climbed up into the saddle of the beast, whose ears were flat against its head and eyes were wide in panic.

Without a backwards glance, the witch rode away from the camp, accompanied by her newfound companions, leaving the bloodied corpses of the pilgrims in her wake.

Chlod lay motionless, petrified into immobility, as he listened to the sound of horses' hooves moving into the distance. He lay there long after the sound of the horses had faded. Not until the first weak rays of the early winter dawn turned night into day did he dare shift his position.

Shivering uncontrollably, he shuffled forward and began to rifle through the pockets and pouches of his dead comrades. He took what little foodstuffs and coin they had, and almost as an afterthought, he stripped them of all the artefacts of devotion.

Though the holy items had done little to protect them from the axes of the marauders, Chlod judged that he had little to lose by carrying them, and if perchance there was any remnant of sacred power within them, then he figured he might magnify their protection by bearing them all.

Half an hour later Chlod wandered out of the treeline, his pockets bulging. He wore a dented knightly helmet on his head, one that had been worn and discarded by Reolus a decade earlier, and a breastplate upon his chest that had been shorn almost completely in half by the dreaded cockatrice of Yoravale. He'd discarded his trusty spiked club, and now wore a sword on his hip, one once wielded by Reolus, though it had been tossed aside after its blade had been shattered two feet from its tip by a river troll at the Bridge of Tears. His malformed, hunch-backed body was wrapped in scraps of material from Reolus's personal standard, and he was beginning to feel good, upbeat even. Once again, he'd survived against the odds and come out, if not smelling of roses, at least better off than he had been an hour earlier.

A smug smile was smeared across his uneven face as he walked out onto the fields beyond the tree line.

In the distance he saw a wagon, loaded with produce, making its way along a pitted roadway.

Snow began to fall, but even that could do nothing to lessen Chlod's buoyant mood. Breaking into an awkward, loping jog, Chlod headed for the distant wagon.

CHAPTER SEVEN

The Bretonnian army was gathering strength as it moved northward. Each day, hundreds more knights and their respective entourages joined the march, answering the Duke of Lyonesse's call to war. Word was received that already Duke Adalhard had already engaged the Norscan vanguard on the fields of northern Lyonesse, fighting them to a standstill, but that while he was engaged, a far larger force had swung to the north-west, riding unopposed inland into hillier country.

From the reports of the yeomen outriders, it was understood that the Norscans had landed without warning some three days ride north of Castle Lyonesse and struck swiftly inland, burning everything in its path. The force was said to number in the tens of thousands.

It had pained Calard to leave Baron Montcadas behind. The grizzled, tough old fighter had been treated as best he could, and the field surgeons had been confident that he would recover well from the wound he had suffered in the chest, barring complications arising from infections. However, there had been nothing that could be done for the baron's eye. The splinter of lance that had embedded itself there had damaged it beyond repair. Having already lost his left eye in battle against the beastmen six months earlier, the baron was now blind, condemned to live out the rest of his life in darkness. Worse, it ensured that he was unable to fight for his duke and king, for what good was a blind knight in battle? How could he fulfil his sworn duty if he could not even defend himself, let alone the lands bequeathed to him by his lord?

Montcadas had put on a brave face, but Calard had seen through his bluster, recognising that he was fighting back a terrible black despair. In the care of the young Lady Josephine, and escorted by a cadre of retainers, he would even now be making his way back to Bastonne. Calard's young cousin Orlando had wanted to ride with them to war, and had sulked when he had been told in no uncertain terms that he would be riding back to Bastonne with the baron and Josephine. Calard had asked that they come visit him at Garamont upon his return and had fared them well, feeling a deep sense of pity for the baron.

Calard had seen the knight kill orcs and beastmen by the dozen. He'd seen him bash the brains out of twisted monstrosities twice his size, and seen him shrug off injuries that would have slain a lesser man. And yet, for all his resilience all it had taken was a random freak accident in a tourney to lay him low. The field surgeon had said he'd been lucky – had the splinter sunk an extra half inch it would have pierced the brain. In the baron's place, Calard wondered if he might have preferred that it had.

Word had been received that a Bretonnian army was moving in support from Couronne, dispatched at the king's behest, and it was said that it already crossed the Sannez and was pushing into the ancestral lands of L'Anguille. There, it was due to link with a substantial, if sluggishly marshalled army of that dukedom, and from there they would turn southward in the hope of halting the Norscans' progress inland.

There had been bad blood between Lyonesse and L'Anguille of late, border disputes and a rekindling of a long dormant feud, and it was said that this was the reason for Duke Taubert of L'Anguille's lack of urgency in coming to the aid of his neighbour. Apparently, he had raised a considerable army, but was holding it back, waiting to see if the Norscans turned towards his own lands. In the meantime, it seemed he was content to let them ravage the lands of his rival. Only when the force sent from Couronne entered his realm did he make any pretence of aiding Lyonesse.

The Norscans' goal remained unclear. Had they been just a raiding force intent on loot and slaughter, then doubtless they would have stuck close to the shore, for there were many settlements and towns dotted all along the north-west coastline. They might have sailed eastward towards the city of L'Anguille itself, with its famed lighthouse built long before the rise of the Bretonni, or sailed southward towards the bountiful lands of Bordeleaux, Aquitaine and Brionne.

Calard and his companions had left the tourney fields two and a half days ago, and ridden hard through the lands of Lyonesse. It was a fecund landscape, though more open than Bastonne, and almost oppressively flat. It was markedly colder here than it was in his homeland too, and cutting winds whipped across the fields from the distant coast.

Pulling fur-lined cloaks around them tightly to combat the ceaseless winds, utterly ignorant of the discomfort of the freezing Garamont men-at-arms struggling to keep up the relentless pace, the brothers allowed the drudgery and boredom of the ride to wash over them. It was too cold and the wind too loud for them to pass the time in conversation, and each was left alone with his thoughts.

Only at night, as they clustered around campfires, drinking wine and feasting on succulent venison and boar did they swap stories and boasts with the other knights with whom they travelled. Calard, his brother noted, drank only sparingly, and was mixing water with his wine.

Several of the Lyonessian knights had fought the Norscans before, and the brothers listened to their tales intently, seeking to learn all that they could of the foes they would be facing within days. It seemed that the sight of their dreaded longships appearing in the night to raid and burn was not uncommon along the Lyonesse coasts. From these warriors they learnt that the Norse were depraved, bloodthirsty barbarians that had sold their souls to Dark Powers, towering brutes of men, savage and fearless in battle. It was said that they had no concept of honour and were nothing more than merciless butchers, neither giving nor expecting mercy on the field of battle. It was also said that they murdered their own children, the ones deemed too small or weak to uphold the honour of the tribe, and that their lives were ones of constant struggle and warfare, against both rivals and the harsh landscape of Norsca itself, filled as it was with mutated, predatory beasts, never-ending winters and months on end of absolute darkness.

They heard tales of berserkers more animal than man, who foamed at the mouth and felt no pain as they hurled themselves at their foe, and of shaggy beasts that came down from the frozen mountainous lands of the barbarians to join battle. They heard tell of dark sorcerers who called down the curses of their bloodthirsty gods, and of daemons of blood and fire that stalked alongside the Norscans, flames billowing from their maws and their blades smoking with infernal runes.

What made them worse in Calard's mind was that they were, or at least had once been, men. These were not near-mindless, savage creatures like greenskins, whose nature it was to fight and kill, nor were they feral beasts of the forest whose base, uncontrollable urges and innate jealousy forced them to seek out humans to kill. No, these were men, thinking, rational men, who had chosen willingly to walk a path into damnation. They revelled in it.

Calard shuddered to think of how far they had allowed themselves to fall.

He was riding alongside his brother in silence, with his cousins Tassilo, Baldemund and Huebald nearby. Horizontal sleet slashed at them, and they were braced against biting wind, lost in their own misery. The other knights that paid fealty to Garamont rode behind them, and Calard's men-at-arms, bone-weary and half-frozen, marched and stumbled alongside, heads bowed. These peasants, bedecked in tabards of blue and red, bearing heavy polearms and shields freshly painted with Calard's dragon heraldry, were forced to stomp through the snowy, long grass alongside the road, which was occupied by the knights of the army.

One of the peasants stumbled, clearly exhausted. The man had wrapped a threadbare strip of cloth around his lower face in an attempt to keep warm, but he had no gloves, and he was shivering uncontrollably. He lurched into the roadway in front of Bertelis's steed, tripping over his broad-headed polearm, and the younger Garamont noble was forced to drag his steed's head to the side, pulling the destrier out of the way to avoid a collision. As he passed the man, Bertelis kicked him in the side of his pot helmet, knocking him to the ground.

Turning in his saddle, Bertelis glared angrily down at the man, pulling his mink-lined cloak close around his neck with one sheepskin lined glove. His gaze roved across the men-at-arms and settled on the yeoman in charge of the regiment, a thick-jawed, brutish man sporting a livid scar across his left cheek. His lips were blue, and his teeth were chattering.

'Discipline your man, yeoman,' Bertelis snapped. 'Had I not been wary, that one might have injured my horse. See that he suffers twenty lashings at the end of the day's march. And I want your entire regiment on a double-watch duty tonight in penitence for his failings.'

The yeoman warden bowed his head, accepting the punishment without complaint. Any word of defiance would only have made things worse for him and his men, and with a nod, he ordered the man who had stumbled lifted back to his feet, and the march continued.

'Lazy wretches,' said Bertelis as he turned away. Calard merely grunted in response.

Another half an hour passed in silence, until a shout came from up ahead. Peering through the blinding white gale, Calard saw Laudethaire and one of his pegasus knights descending through the clouds, fighting against the buffeting winds. The Parravonians had been ranging out ahead of the army, scouring the land below.

'Hope the bastard falls off,' remarked Bertelis as Laudethaire came swooping down to land.

'I'd pay to see that,' said Calard.

It was from the pegasus knights that the army had learnt of the movements of Duke Adalhard and his warriors, and of the army of Couronne and L'Anguille moving south-west to cut off the Norscans.

'I'm going to ride forward to hear what news he brings,' said Calard. 'I could do with moving, just to try and warm up a bit. I think my arse is frozen to the saddle. Coming with me?'

Bertelis nodded his head in response.

'Keep an eye on this lot,' said Calard to his cousins, nodding towards the men-at-arms stumbling alongside the road. 'Make sure they don't slacken off the pace.'

Kicking their steeds forward, the brothers pulled off the roadway and cantered up past line upon line of knights. Men-at-arms, wretched peasant bowmen and servants scurried out of their way like vermin fleeing before a lamp, but Calard paid them no mind – they may as well have been invisible to him. Towards the head of the column he rode, passing several hundred knights whom he had seen at the tourney, though he had been unable to spot the knight who had beaten Bertelis in the duel, Merovech of Arlons. He certainly would have been handy in the coming battle, for rarely had Calard seen a knight more skilful with the blade.

Horns blew, and the entire column came slowly to a halt.

Bertelis shook his head as many hundreds of peasants by the roadside slumped gratefully to the ground. Others quickly broke open wagons of food and drink, running lightly through the ranks of knights offering refreshments.

'It'll take an age to get them moving again now,' he said.

Cantering forward, they came upon a circle of knights that had gathered around Laudethaire to hear his report. The blond-haired knight, clearly enjoying the attention, was speaking to Orderic, the noble who had organised the tourney.

Calard and Bertelis nudged their horses forward until they were positioned just outside the inner circle of knights, and they strained forward to hear Laudethaire's words.

'They are riding ten miles ahead of us, my lord,' the Parravonian said, in answer to a question from Orderic.

'Who's he talking about?' Calard said to a nearby knight.

'Norse war party,' answered the man.

'They are riding hard, in order to rejoin their main force. They have with them a noblewoman of Bretonnia,' said Laudethaire, his voice carrying over the wind, and his gaze passing over the gathered knights theatrically.

Calard frowned, and several other knights voiced their outrage.

'A captive?' called one knight.

'I would presume so,' answered Laudethaire. 'I would have launched a rescue attempt, of course, but the cross winds would have made such an attack a foolish, suicidal endeavour. It is risk enough that my pegasus fly at all in these conditions.'

'Of course,' said Bertelis under his breath.

'She must be rescued,' announced Orderic. 'She is a noblewoman of Bretonnia. She cannot be allowed to suffer whatever loathsome fate awaits her at the hands of the savages. If we sent riders ahead, now, do you think they would reach the war party before it rejoins the full Norse army?'

'No,' said Laudethaire. 'But there is more. The enemy, it seems, has grown weary of running. They have set camp, and await us no more than half a day's ride to the north. It seems that a stage has been set for us to face the Norse in battle at last!'

A cheer rose from that pronouncement.

'And what of the army of Duke Adalhard?' said Calard, raising his voice so that he was heard. 'And of the forces of Couronne, and L'Anguille?'

Laudethaire looked through the crowd at Calard, assessing who it was that addressed him. His eyes flickered condescendingly over Calard's heraldry and bearing, a look of distaste on his handsome face. Clearly unimpressed, he turned away.

'The army of Lyonesse is making camp five miles from the Norscans' position,' he said finally. 'If you ride hard, you should make it there before daybreak.'

'And the knights of Couronne and L'Anguille?' said Calard, an irritated edge to his voice.

'They are a day and half away,' said Laudethaire, casting another condescending glance in his direction. 'Have I answered enough of your questions now, *Bastonne*?'

Calard felt his face redden as several knight chuckled, and he saw Bertelis reach for his sword. Calard reached out a hand to halt his brother.

'For now, yes, oh *Beloved of Parravon*,' said Calard in a mocking tone that raised more chuckles.

'Enjoy riding through the snow and the mud,' snapped Laudethaire, and with that, he spun his pegasus around, which snorted and stamped its hooves. It broke into a gallop, wings unfurling and beating hard as it soared up into the air.

'He will be sipping wine in the duke's camp within the hour, I'll wager,' said Bertelis, as he and Calard swung away from the disbanding gathering.

'Bastard.'

* * *

As night descended over northern Lyonesse like a shroud the Skaeling horsemen thundered into the Norscan encampment, Bjarki and Haegtesse riding at the fore. The shaggy coated Norscan ponies' flanks were lathered in sweat. Hounds snarled, and bondsmen and warriors moved out of the way respectfully, eyeing the witch desirously.

Haegtesse rode with her head held high, enjoying the stares. She had made herself more presentable for the lord of the Skaelings, braiding her hair into plaits and washing the blood and grime from her pale skin. A blood bear's pelt hung across her shoulders, the fur spiked and thick, and her totem-dolls hung from her delicate silver belt. To the Skaelings Haegtesse looked like some foreign princess, and they felt pride that this was to be the one who would bear their jarl a son. Pale, youthful, cold and beautiful, she drew many openly lustful looks and enthusiastic whoops from these men who had not had a woman in weeks, though those nearest to her lowered their eyes and backed away, feeling in their bones and their guts that she was powerfully god-touched.

Night was drawing in quickly, and the sky overhead was dark with movement. Tens of thousands of ravens and crows accompanied the Skaelings, hanging overhead like an impenetrable thundercloud, hungry and impatient for the slaughter to begin. These dense flocks of carrion eaters had accompanied the Norscans from their homeland, a black amorphous cloud of feathers and malicious will that had shadowed their longships, knowing that a feast of soft flesh would soon be theirs.

Less mundane beasts circled overhead, shadowy hissing creatures with leathery wings that snapped like canvas sails.

In the distance there was a trumpeting roar, and the ground shook as some beast of immense weight and power thrashed against its restraints. Laughter and the sounds of feasting warriors mingled with the sound of weapons being sharpened, of seers invoking the blessings of the Dark Gods. Those Norscans with more than a little beast in them, the ones known as the ulfwerener, howled up at the rising green moon, the eye of the gods, and the bestial sound was joined by the roars, growls and howls of many hundreds of the immense hounds that prowled the outskirts of the camp, seeking easy meat.

While her outwards appearance was one of youth and health, Haegtesse could already feel the malignant black cancers growing inside her, corrupting her newfound body from within. Already they were working their way insidiously through her liver and stomach, and their loathsome black touch was reaching towards her lungs. It was happening quicker now than she had experienced before – each new body that she claimed decayed quicker than the last, and it seemed that the process was speeding up exponentially. She doubted that this body, young and strong as it was, would last her longer than a handful of years, a decade at a push, before it was a little more than a rotting cadaver, toothless and haggard, having aged a dozen years with each passing season.

Much of her strength was currently being utilised to protect her womb from the malignant sickness spreading through her body, shielding it so as to ensure that she did not fall barren. Such a thing could not be allowed to come to pass – the daemon-child that she would bear the Skaeling jarl was the key to her immortality.

The Norscans had set their camp at the northern end of a sweeping valley ridged by steep sided hills. At the far end of the valley rose a hill that was not unlike an ancient burial mound, though of a scale that would only have been built for a king of great wealth and influence. No one knew how these mounds, or mottes as they were known locally to the Lyonessians who lived in their shadow, had come into existence. They seemed too regular in shape to have been naturally formed, so it was surmised that they had been built of human endeavour, but for what purpose remained unclear. Perhaps they *were* burial mounds, of the first Bretons tribesmen that had come to these lands, or perhaps they had been raised as defensive structures, with wooden hilltop forts constructed on top of them by even more ancient peoples long forgotten.

Whatever the case, the mottes dotted the landscape of northern Lyonesse. Most of them had castles built atop them, for they occupied powerful positions in the landscape, but this particular motte was said to be cursed, and no one had ever dared to raise a foundation upon it.

'Make way!' snarled Bjarki.

Passing by tens of hundreds of Skaeling warriors, all readying themselves for battle, the horsemen wended their way towards the motte at the far end of the valley.

Haegtesse's eyes shone is she stared up at the towering hillock. That was the place where the child must be conceived. She had read the portent in the eyes of the sacrifices she had lured into her woodland cave, seen it in the entrails of a dozen slaughtered swine and witnessed it in a score of prophetic dreams. Under the full moon, on the turn of the tide, the child must be conceived – not an hour later, nor an hour earlier. And while predicting the waxing and waning of the Chaos moon of Morrslieb was an impossibility, she knew with absolute certainty that the auspicious night was close. Two nights perhaps, maybe three, and the green moon would wax gibbous, passing as close to the surface of the world as it had for a decade and exerting its power upon those beneath its baleful gaze.

It was on such nights that the dead rose from the earth, when once sane family men brayed at the moon and slaughtered their sleeping families with hands that had turned to talons, and when the veil that separated the material world from the realms of Chaos was at its thinnest. Even those without the sight were able to perceive daemonic *things* straining to tear through the ethereal boundary that bound them, screaming into reality to rend and feed.

And it was under such a moon that the daemon-child would be conceived.

At the foot of the towering hillock they reined their steeds in. Simple tents of fur and crossed logs had been erected here, and totems hanging with skulls, severed heads and burnished icons of the Norscan gods had been hammered into the ground. The Skaeling jarl's huskarls lounged here, massive intimidating god-touched warriors bedecked in heavy armour and fur.

'Where is he?' demanded Bjarki.

Before the huskarls could answer, skin tent flaps were thrown aside and Styrbjorn emerged from his hastily erected residence to greet his bride. A pair of sword-maidens emerged behind him, and from the similarity they bore to the Skaeling lord, Haegtesse surmised these to be the jarl's daughters.

The Skaeling too had prepared himself for the meeting, and he looked every inch a warrior king.

He stood a head taller than any of his huskarls, and his broad shoulders were encased in thick plates of dark metal fashioned into the likeness of snarling, tusked wolf heads. His broad chest was protected by a breastplate of ensorcelled dark iron, with the azure, unblinking eye of Tchar in its centre. Chainmail hung from his eight-pointed belt-buckle, and his legs were encased in spiked armour.

His thickly muscled arms were bare and covered with tattoos, and gold and bronze torcs were coiled around them. He was not wearing his war helmet, and his long, grey-streaked hair hung down his back. Over his shoulders he wore the shaggy pale fur of an ymgir, one of the snow yetis that stalked the mountains of Norsca.

The jarl's eyes, as pale as the eye of Tchar on his chest, settled hungrily on Haegtesse.

The witch smiled as she saw the Skaeling jarl, and slid languorously from the saddle.

Without speaking a word, the jarl swept her into a crushing embrace, pulling her hard up against him and drawing her into a powerful kiss. Haegtesse allowed herself to melt into his body, feeling his taut muscles and the invigorating touch of the gods on his tongue. She felt her desire for him strongly as her body responded to the towering Norscan, and was pleasantly surprised by the strength of her passion. It had been many decades since anyone had stirred her like this.

Breaking from the passionate kiss, the Skaeling hooked a powerful arm around her back and began to guide her forcefully towards his tent. It was obvious that he intended to have her there and then, to rut with her like an animal and slake his desire, but Haegtesse stopped him with a hand upon the chest.

'Not yet,' she said in the Skaeling dialect.

Standing up tall she came barely to the Norscan's chest, and her body was weak and fragile compared to the brutal power in his massive frame, and yet Styrbjorn froze beneath her touch. She could feel his lust raging within him, and she knew that he longed to drag her into his tent, screaming and fighting if needs be, but she realised that he could feel her power, and was respectful of it.

Such respect was a welcome thing after dwelling within Bretonnia this last century, where she was feared and despised. It was good to be back amongst those who understood her place in things. They were not Kurgans, but at least they paid homage to the true gods, even if they knew them by different names.

'What is wrong, woman?' said the Skaeling, his eyes flashing dangerously.

'Patience, jarl of the Skaelings,' Haegtesse said, playfully running a fingertip down the front of Styrbjorn's breastplate. 'The gods themselves have ordained this conception, but it must take place under strict ritual. Trust me and the son I bear you will be the greatest warrior your tribe has ever seen.'

The Norscan flicked a glance towards Bjarki, who nodded almost imperceptibly, and the jarl released Haegtesse.

'Fine,' he said.

'It must take place at the top of carrion hill,' said Haegtesse, gesturing up at the hill looming behind them, 'under the gaze of the gods. I will need eight of your strongest men for sacrifice.'

'They are yours,' said Styrbjorn without hesitation.

'Good,' said Haegtesse. 'I will take my leave, and prepare the site.'

When she had gone, the jarl slapped a meaty hand on Bjarki's shoulder, rocking the slighter man.

'She's the one,' enthused Styrbjorn, his eyes filled with passion and excitement. 'After all this time! A son!'

'Indeed, my jarl,' agreed Bjarki.

'And all this ritual is necessary?'

'It is, my jarl.'

Styrbjorn looked down at the seer curiously.

'What is it that bothers you, little bear? Are you not pleased that at last I shall father a son? Your position within the clan will not change, you know that.'

'I know, my lord. That is not what troubles me.'

'No? Then what? Speak, man.'

'I don't trust her, my jarl,' said Bjarki. 'What does she get out of this?'

'She will be the mother of the greatest Skaeling warrior ever to walk the earth. Is that not enough?'

'I don't know. Maybe.'

'She's a beauty as well, isn't she? And powerful. Just touching her made my flesh tingle.'

'She is a powerful blood-witch, it is true. But it would be wise for us to be wary of any trickery on her part. I'd suggest killing her as soon as the child is born.'

'After she bears me my son, you may do to her anything you like, little bear,' said Styrbjorn.

'Tomorrow, we will rout these southlander horsemen,' said the jarl, changing topic and gazing out along the valley. 'We will slaughter them all, and laugh as they beg for mercy. It will be a good day, little bear.'

'I have no doubt of that, my lord.'

'They are arrogant, these southlanders. They think we are nothing but mindless barbarians, like the slant-eyed Hung. They will underestimate us, expecting us to simply charge at them across the open ground.'

'There is honour to be had in such tactics,' said Bjarki. 'The blood god favours such a direct approach.'

'The skull-taker cares not whose blood it is that runs,' said Styrbjorn. 'Personally, I would rather it was their blood and not mine.'

'True enough,' said Bjarki.

Bjarki had lived alongside his jarl for long enough to know that the grizzled old warrior had devised a battle plan days earlier. He would have been labouring over the best way to defeat the southlander horsemen ever since he had announced the invasion, constantly refining and discarding plans as he concocted new and better ways of claiming victory.

He was a wily old wolf, Styrbjorn. That was the reason the jarl had ruled as long as he had. Normally, a chieftain of his age would have long since been supplanted by a younger, stronger aspiring champion, but Styrbjorn was cunning. He could outthink his younger rivals. It was a rare gift, and Bjarki looked forward to seeing what ploy the old wolf would employ against the southlanders.

'Their pride will be their downfall,' predicted Styrbjorn. 'And they will fall hard.'

CALARD AND THE other knights from the tournament rode into Duke Adalhard of Lyonesse's camp close to midnight, bone-weary, aching and cold. They had ridden ahead of the lowborn men-at-arms and archers, who were unable to keep up the pace. The footsloggers would likely not reach the camp before dawn.

Storm clouds were building overhead, blotting out the stars and the moons, and snow had been falling since nightfall. Already, it was several feet thick on the ground, and several inches were being added with every passing hour.

The camp was a hive of activity when they rode in, despite the late hour, with hundreds of flaming braziers lighting up the area like day. Thousands of peasants ran to and fro, busy on errands and mundane tasks, and a great many knights were already fully armoured and mounted up, in readiness for attack. From the northern outskirts of the camp, came shouts and the sound of weapons clashing, and it was clear that the Norscans were already launching probing attacks, testing the

Bretonnians' defences. It was obvious that few would be getting sleep this night.

Laudethaire made a special effort to come out and greet Calard and the other weary knights as they rode into camp, making a show of how rested he was, and Calard's mood darkened as he saw the smirk on the noble's face.

Garamont servants had ridden ahead and made tents and food ready for the brothers, and while they were hungry and the idea of a soft pallet was tempting, Calard and the other noble lords made their way towards the duke's pavilion, to present themselves to him before seeking sustenance and rest.

The duke was a man of middling years, a tall knight with dark, shoulder-length hair who wore an expression that showed he clearly did not suffer fools. He was garbed for war, and a fine red tabard bearing a silver lion-head design hung over his exquisite suit of plate. A cloak made from the pelt of a lion was swept over one shoulder, and seeing the skin of the mighty beast Calard was reminded of the tales of Gilles le Breton and his companions he had learnt at his father's knee.

Thierulf, closest friend and devoted ally of Gilles, harkened from the lands now known as Lyonesse, and it was said that when he was no more than a boy he slew a marauding lion with his bare hands. Skinning the beast and wrapping its still bloody fur around his body, Thierulf returned to his father's hill fort in triumph, and his legend was born. It was in honour of this great hero that the nobles of Lyonesse, particularly those who claimed descent from Thierulf's bloodline, incorporated a lion into their heraldry in some form or other.

Calard was instantly impressed with Duke Adalhard. The aura of authority around the man was palpable; this was a man who was used to being instantly obeyed, and yet it was obvious that he was a warrior first and foremost. He had no doubt that the duke would be leading the charge once battle was met; he had the air of one who would not shirk from battle.

'Lyonesse thanks you all for your swift response,' the duke said to the gathered, weary nobles. 'With your aid, we shall wipe the field of these barbarian invaders, and win a great victory on the morn. You've ridden hard, and I thank you for that. Get some rest – I'll need you fresh tomorrow.'

'On the morn, duke?' questioned one of the knights. 'Are not the Norscans already assailing us? Is not battle already underway?'

'There is no real strength behind their attacks,' said Duke Adalhard. 'It's all bluster. They are merely trying to keep us in a state of readiness and tension, to sap our strength before tomorrow – that is when the real battle will take place. Get some rest. My men will ensure that the attacks are nothing more than feints.'

The duke's gaze settled on Calard, and he reddened beneath the stern warrior's gaze. There were only fourteen dukes in all of Bretonnia, each ruling over one of the ancient dukedoms formed when Gilles le Breton unified the Bretonni tribes. As such, the Duke of Lyonesse was one of the most powerful individuals in all of Bretonnia, and Calard felt awed merely to be in his presence. He lowered his gaze as the duke's eyes narrowed.

Your bloodline is tainted.

Again he heard Maloric's voice, the words stinging him. Did the same corruption that had spawned his mutated, hateful beast-brother reside in him?

'It is Garamont, isn't it?' said the duke finally, snapping Calard from his doubts. He looked up, startled to have been picked out, and even more shocked that the duke knew his family.

'Yes, my lord,' he managed, and the duke nodded his head sagely.

Calard felt incredibly self-conscious as dozens of pairs of eyes turned towards him. Knights who had previously barely registered his presence now looked at him with newfound respect. Just being recognised by the duke had clearly raised him in their esteem.

'I knew your old weapon master, Gunthar,' said Duke Adalhard of Lyonesse. 'A good man. Best swordsman I ever met. I was saddened to hear of his passing.'

'Thank you, lord,' said Calard. 'Not a day goes past that I do not miss his presence.'

Calard breathed out and wiped a hand across his brow as the duke's attention shifted away from him.

The snow continued to fall as preparations for the next day's battle were made, and with the sounds of Norscan war drums, horns and shouts echoing through the night, Calard finally allowed himself to succumb to his exhaustion. Half an hour after meeting the duke, he fell into a fitful sleep in his tent, dreaming of blood and fire, haunted by howling warriors with the faces of wolves. Inevitably, his dreams shifted, and again he faced the ethereal, terrifying apparition of the Green Knight.

Again he was powerless, stricken with paralysing fear before the ghostly spectre. It loomed before him, brandishing its dolorous blade, surrounded by coiling fog.

'Face me!' the Green Knight taunted, and Calard awoke lathered in sweat.

It was dark, still an hour or so before dawn. He had been asleep for no more than an hour. Nevertheless, Calard pushed himself from his pallet; he would get no further sleep this night.

CHAPTER EIGHT

THE SNOW HAD continued to fall throughout the night, and the landscape was blanketed in a thick, unspoiled layer of white. Within an hour the blood of thousands would be splashed across it, the battlefield churned into a quagmire of slush and mud, but for now it was pristine and virginal.

The early morning sun was hidden behind thick clouds. Not a sound rose from the Bretonnian battle line other than the snap of standards blowing in the wind and the occasional whinny of horses. Peasants held the reins of their lords' steeds as the knights knelt in the snow, heads bowed as they prayed to the Lady of the Lake, invoking her protection in the coming battle.

Relentless drumming could be heard from the Norse lines, a mile and a half further along the valley, but the sound was muffled by the worsening storm. The howl of wind muted all other sound, and swirling eddies of snow ensured that the enemy were indistinct and hazy in the distance.

Such a blizzard was unnatural, particularly so early into winter, and Calard wondered if there might not be some diabolic sorcery at work.

His eyes were closed tightly and his lips moved silently as he beseeched the Lady for her protection. Warmth infused him as he whispered his prayer, dispelling the icy chill from his limbs, making him feel rested and strong. All doubt washed away as he felt the power of the goddess upon him, and he was confident that by day's end the Bretonnians would be victorious.

A horn sounded and Calard completed his ritual prayers, blinking his eyes as he came back to the present. Still feeling the warmth of the Lady's blessing within him, he mounted his armoured destrier and accepted a war lance as it was handed to him. Across the battle line, some ten-thousand other knights swung up into the saddle, all having prayed to receive the blessings of the goddess. Five times that number of peasants were ranked up in deep formations behind the knights. They had not prayed; the Lady of the Lake was a goddess of the nobility, and no peasant was allowed to worship her – not that she would answer them if they did. The idea that the goddess would care for the lowborn masses, who had no understanding of honour or chivalry, was laughable.

The valley was open and flat, almost two miles wide and clear of rocks and trees. It was the perfect horseman's battlefield, and it suited the Bretonnian way of doing battle to fight the enemy here. The sides of the valley rose up to hills, and although it was now completely obscured by the blizzard, Calard knew that a massive motte was located at the enemy's back.

As a predominately infantry army, one might have expected the Norscans to position themselves atop that motte, forcing the Bretonnians to assail them there, but it seemed that the Norse were eager for battle, and had marched forward to meet the Bretonnians head-on.

Already, yeomen outriders were riding those hills, ensuring that no enemy forces would outflank the Bretonnians. The weather was too severe to allow Laudethaire and his pegasus knights to overfly the enemy army, and the exact number and disposition of the enemy forces was vague. Nevertheless, it was clear that if one discounted the peasant men-at-arms and bowmen who were unreliable in battle at best and a liability at worst, the Norscans outnumbered the Bretonnians, but not by a substantial margin. Considering that the bulk of the Norscan army was on foot, and that most of them wore little in the way of armour, the odds were considered favourable.

From what little had been garnered by the yeomen scouts, the enemy were forming up in a wide advance, with a strong centre. It was there in the centre that the most heavily armoured warriors had been seen, and it was likely there that the enemy chieftain had positioned himself. Light cavalry had been seen ranging out on the flanks. The duke had positioned his knights accordingly. The enemy appeared to have little in the way of missile fire, and lacked the long pikes and spears that were the bane of knightly formations, and so the duke's plan was to hit them hard and fast, to ride them down in one concentrated charge that would rip the heart out of the enemy army.

The knights of Couronne and L'Anguille were still a day and a half's march to the north, but it seemed to Calard that trying to forestall battle until their arrival was unnecessary. Clearly the Duke of Lyonesse had come to the same conclusion, though Calard wondered how much of his decision had to do with his running feud with L'Anguille. For decades there had been tension between the two dukedoms, and border disputes and bloodshed between their nobles had become commonplace.

Muffled shouts could be heard on the wind, and banners were dipped and waved as orders were passed. In response, several thousand lightly armoured peasant bowmen ran lightly forward on the flanks of the knightly formations, and the mounted yeomen on the extreme left wing began cantering out wide.

The bowmen trotted through the snow ahead of the main battle line and Calard swore. He was freezing, and he just wished the battle would commence so he could get moving and warm up. Despite all his best efforts, snow had seeped through the joints of his armour and melted, soaking the padding against his skin and making his limbs shiver uncontrollably.

'Come on,' he said. A trickle of melted snow slid down the back of his neck, and he grimaced in discomfort. He brushed snow from his shoulders, feeling the chill through his gauntlets, and kicked away the ice that had formed on his stirrups.

Muffled drums echoed in the distance, and Calard felt a brief flicker of trepidation as he heard wolves howling above the gale. Monstrous, trumpeting horns blared in the distance, and Calard briefly pondered the size of the instruments needed to make such a sound. The crisp, clear sound of Bretonnian horns blared, signalling the advance.

'At last,' murmured Calard.

The knights began to move at the command, walking their steeds forward through the snow while tens of thousands of men-at-arms marched behind.

Duke Adalhard was situated in the centre of the army, surrounded by his most senior knights, all bedecked in the finest armour that money could buy. The duke's standard bearer held aloft the famous banner of Lyonesse, an embroidered, four hundred year old tapestry depicting the hero Thierulf, wearing his trademark lion pelt, standing atop a pile of dead greenskins, his head surrounded by a halo of light. It was a revered artefact rumoured to have the hair of elven princesses woven into its design, and it was said that no army fighting under it had ever lost.

The knights of Bastonne had once again formed up together, though it left a bad taste in Calard's mouth to be forced to fight alongside Maloric and his Sangasse lapdogs. Despite his lack of sleep, Calard's mind felt more focused that it had done in months – most likely due to his refusal to partake in any wine since the abandonment of the tourney, four days earlier. His senses were as alert as they had ever been; perhaps a blessing of the goddess. He vowed that he would outdo Maloric this day.

All across the field, scores of knightly formations moved forwards through the storm, standard bearers straining against the wind to keep their banners upright. Horses snorted and stamped their hooves impatiently as the icy winds blasted, driving snow against them. Calard patted the neck of his destrier, murmuring soothing words that were swallowed by the gale.

Out ahead, the peasant bowmen took up positions on the flanks, angling their lines up against those of the enemy in the far distance. Under the barking orders of villeins and yeomen, and with more than a few cuffs to the backs of heads of the more dull-witted of the inbred sots, the bowmen set themselves, planting arrows point first into the ground in front of them. They did not draw yet, for while the enemy would have been at the extreme of their range under normal circumstances, the blizzard and blustering winds were such that firing at anything more than half the regular longbow range would have been pointless.

Calard had his visor down to keep the biting wind off his face, and he squinted through the blizzard, trying to see the enemy. They were nothing more than vague shadows in the distance now, and as blasts of wind and snow whipped across the valley, they were almost completely obscured. Calard prayed that the scouts had been correct in their appraisal of the Norse battle lines, for by the time they got close enough to see the enemy lines clearly it would be far too late to alter the battle plan.

Nevertheless, Calard knew that there were few forces in the entire world that could stand against a concentrated Bretonnian heavy cavalry charge, and he had little doubt that today would once again reassert the dominance of the Bretonnian knight. Even if this vile weather *was* some sorcery of the enemy, it would avail them little. The snow was certainly not deep enough to hamper the powerful destriers they rode, and the centre of the valley dropped away slightly to either side, ensuring that the deeper snow drifts were located off to the flanks, far from the action that would be taking place in the centre of the field.

All ten-thousand knights were moving forwards now, the entire noble contingent of the army bar some four hundred knights that were being held back as a tactical reserve. One mighty charge, concentrated at the enemy's centre, and the battle would be as good as over. The knights out on the wings would ride forward as if they were going to assault the flanks of the enemy, before angling inwards once the enemy had no time to react to the change of direction, and they would smash into the centre along with the bulk of the Lyonessian force.

It was a simple plan, but one that many Bretonnian generals had used to good effect on dozens of battlefields.

Calard and the other knights of Bastonne were located towards the right of the centre, formed up behind an uninspired but wealthy and influential knight of their lands, Lord Sigibold, who was the most senior knight of their party since Baron Montcadas had been forced to leave them. He was a capable warrior, though Calard recognised that he was a poor leader of men, and it had been with some reticence that the knights of Garamont had fallen in behind him.

Calard's cousin Tassilo had summed the man up well when he described him as 'deeply average in all regards.' No one disliked the man, but no one really liked him either, and it was clear for all to see that he was far out of his depth.

Still, Calard doubted that even Lord Sigibold could possibly make a mess of leading the Bastonnians today. All the knights of Bastonne were seasoned warriors, and while Calard and Bertelis were the knights with the least experience of them all, they were far from the eager young knights errant that they had been a year earlier.

Horn blasts sounded, and the knights all along the battle line urged their steeds into a canter. They passed by the bowmen on each flank, kicking up powder as the destriers' momentum began to increase.

Dark, low clouds hung over the Norscan army and it seemed to Calard that they were somehow unnatural; they were too dark, too low, and they seemed to shift and pulse like a living creature, their shape in constant fluctuation.

Pushing the thought aside, he concentrated on making sure he kept tight with the knights around him, and as their pace increased, the knights seamlessly formed the wedged lance formation that had proven so deadly against the enemies of Bretonnia for so many centuries. Deadly and with the full weight of armoured men and horses behind it, the lance formation was able to punch through the most resilient defences and drive deep into formations, dividing them and sending men scattering. Indeed, many times all it took was for an army to see the Bretonnians thundering towards them en masse to send them fleeing the battlefield; it was a brave – or foolish – man who willingly stood in front of a charging knight, let alone an entire army of them. Such an outcome was unlikely this day though, Calard judged. Nothing he had heard about the Norscans made him think that the notion of turning tail and fleeing in the face of their enemies would even cross their barbarian minds.

The snow muffled the sound of the thundering hooves, and again Calard thought he heard the sound of wolves howling, though it was impossible to pinpoint where the sound was coming from.

A regiment of knights errant out to the right, impetuous and hungry for glory, lowered their lances and kicked their steeds into a gallop, breaking ranks and pushing ahead of the battle line. Calard knew instinctively that they had launched the charge too early, and that their steeds would be struggling by the time they struck home.

For many of those young knights, some of whom might have been as young as fifteen, this would be their first and last taste of battle. Every battle was dangerous, of course – even tourneys had no small amount of risk involved – but it was a knight's first foray into battle that was so often his last.

It was the way of battle, Gunthar had taught him. The first to die in any battle were the most inexperienced, the weakest, the poorest warriors, the unlucky, those too young to be fighting, or those too old and slow. Most of these died in the first clash, and it was then that the real fighting would begin. This factor was even more emphasised in a siege, Gunthar had told him. In the first days of a siege, the weak were picked off one by one until only the most veteran, hardened warriors were left on either side. It was brutal and it was savage, and many good men were lost in the opening skirmishes, but it was the way of things, in the same way that the wolf picked off the weakest in the herd, and the runt of the litter invariably died when the hardship of winter descended.

Calard could see the enemy moving now, could hear their drums pounding out a savage rhythm as they began loping through the knee-high snow towards the wall of knights bearing down on them.

Glancing out along the line to the right, he could see barbarous, lightly armoured horsemen bearing down on the yeomen riders out there, who were firing their bows from the saddle.

Clouds of arrows fired by the foot archers further back darkened the sky, arcing over the knights' heads before descending into the enemy ranks that were now running full pelt towards the knights, screaming war cries that could be heard only vaguely, as if they were coming from a great distance. The depth of the enemy ranks could still not be gauged due to the gusting snows, but Calard saw hundreds of men stumble and fall as the arrows slammed down amongst them, driving through furs into heathen flesh and muscle, punching through horned iron helmets to pierce skulls. Shields were lifted up high as hundreds more arrows sliced down through the gale, but it did not slow the Norscans.

From amongst the barbarian lines, black iron chains were released, and hundreds of shaggy-furred hounds were set loose. Slavering and howling, they bounded ahead of the Norscans, kicking up clouds of snow powder in their eagerness to close the distance. They were immense beasts, and many of them bore the mark of mutation and corruption. Some had boar-like tusks curling from their maws, while others had two heads or serpentine tails that ended in snapping snake heads.

They bounded through the snow towards the impetuous knights errant out in front, Norscan hound and Bretonnian knight hurtling towards each other at full speed. One warhound, a massive beast with hindquarters striped in alternating bands of orange and black, leapt into the air and ripped the first knight from the saddle, massive jaws clamped around his head. Then the rest of the knights and hounds struck each other, coming together with colossal force.

A dozen monstrous hounds were skewered on lances, and several more were bowled over by the flailing hooves of the mighty destriers, bones shattered. Young knights were dragged down into the snow, yanked from their saddles as jaws locked around legs and torsos, wrenching plate mail out of shape. Calard saw a destrier stumble and fall, screaming horribly as a warhound bore it to the ground, jaws gripping its neck, and the unfortunate knight in the saddle of the mauled horse was ripped apart as three snarling hounds leapt upon him.

The knights errant charge had completely stalled now, their impetus lost, and those young knights still in the saddle were slashing down at the hounds with swords and lance-butts. One of the beasts was struck in the spine, and its hind legs gave way beneath it. Still snarling and snapping, the beast was killed as hooves caved in its skull.

Seeing that the young knights were getting the better of the warhounds, the rest of the Bretonnian army flowed around the melee, keeping their momentum going as they bore down on the Norscans.

They were around two hundred yards from the barbarians, and horns blared suddenly. As one the wall of Bretonnian knights spurred on their steeds, breaking into a thundering gallop.

Ten-thousand lances lowered, and a roaring cry rose from the lips of the knights.

'For Bastonne!' roared Calard, and dug his spurs into his steed's side once again, urging the stallion on.

His heart was racing. There was something breathtaking about being part of a massed charge, and it never failed to fill Calard with excitement.

He could see the enemy more clearly now; hulking brutes bedecked in furs and hefting brutal looking axes, blades and spiked maces.

The barbarians' charge faltered, individual warriors slowing as the wall of knights thundered towards them. Calard felt the thrill of victory wash through him. The enemy were men after all. They were not daemons or monsters, but merely men – men that knew fear.

The howls of wolves echoed from the flanks, but Calard ignored the sounds, intent on the enemy in front of him.

The flush of imminent victory spurred the Bretonnians on, and they hurtled towards the Norscans, lances lowered.

The battle would not last long at all, thought Calard. Overhead, a sound like thunder shook the heavens.

A DARK RED, spitting light shot up through the blizzard and exploded overhead.

'That's the signal,' snarled Zumarah to his dark kin, his eyes gleaming. He spoke in his native tongue, a guttural language not unlike the sound of gears grinding and rocks being crushed.

The Chaos dwarf gazed adoringly at *Ereshkigal-Namtar,* his beloved and priceless daemon-construct.

Zumarah had personally overseen its creation in the nightmarish hellforges deep below the scorched surface of Zarr-Naggrund. For over fifty years he had slaved over its construction, barely allowing himself or his slave-crews any rest so consumed was he in his obsessive work. Thousands of slaves had perished during its forging. These ones had their life fluids drained from their bodies, their bones and gristle ground to powder, and this viscous mix was added to the alloys, tempering them and dyeing the metal of the great beast a ruddy, blood-bronze.

Upon the completion of the physical, inert form of the infernal machine, he had been present for fifty days and fifty nights of ritual and ceremony as great Hashut's high priests infused it with the eternal daemon-twins. *Ereshkigal* and *Namtar* had been the true names of these malicious daemons of blood, rage and industry, and they had struggled hard against their bindings, screaming and roaring as they strained to break their bonds and rip the high priests, and Zumarah, apart from the inside out. Nevertheless, their struggles had been in vain, and they had now been caged within his daemon-construct for over a decade.

Its construction was a thing of beauty, and Zumarah felt a jealous pride as he looked upon *Ereshkigal-Namtar's* exalted form.

It was the size of a small house, standing almost fifteen feet tall and some twenty feet long, and weighed more than a fully laden Norse dragonship. Indeed, transporting the infernal machine across the seas had not been an easy task, but one that, if the Norscan's word could be valued, would be worth his while.

Ereshkigal-Namtar had not accepted its imprisonment, and still it strained against its bonds. Steam rose from its brazen body, and runes that glowed with heat shimmered across its form. Ensorcelled chains, each link the size of a man's head, bound the daemon engine, connected to its blood-bronze body and pounded deep into the ground to hold it in place. Chunks of shiny black volcanic rock engraved with runes of power were hammered into its sides, and these runes glowed like lava as they exerted their power of containment upon the twin daemons locked inside the machine.

The bulk of the engine's weight was borne upon a pair of immense, spiked wheels, each taller than an ogre, and filled with hundreds of intricate, interconnected cogs and wheels that were in constant motion. The barrel of the engine's gaping, tooth-filled maw, which was wide enough to swallow a horse with ease, was rimmed with more runes of binding, and the stink of sulphur, blood and death rose from within.

The brass flanks of the daemon engine rippled with movement as the daemons struggled vainly to escape, and a myriad of gargoyle-like faces pressed forth from within, each one more horrific than the last as they snarled and reached for Zumarah.

The stony-skinned dwarf laughed at them.

'Ready *Ereshkigal-Namtar* for firing,' he growled over his shoulder to his two kinsmen.

Belonging of a lower caste level than he, these two Chaos dwarfs wore but simple masks of metal over their faces rather than the tall helmets of the nobility, and heavy aprons of leather, with strips of metal woven into them, protected their squat bodies from the heat of their daemon-machine charge. They bowed their heads to their forgemaster, and moved forwards to align the cog-runes for firing.

Hellcannon the Norscans had called his beloved daemon engine. Zumarah liked the name. It was appropriate, and fitted well.

A dozen black orc slaves with heads bowed in dog-like submission squatted near the engine, their powerful bodies covered in scars and burns. As Zumarah's kinsmen aligned the cog-runes, the heat from *Ereshkigal-Namtar* increased exponentially as its power grew, and the black orcs whimpered, turning their heads away. Creatures sorcerously bred for servitude by the high priests of Hashut in ages long past, each of the black orcs wore a collar of iron around their necks. Thick chains connected each of these collars, and just like the daemon-engine that they tended, the ends of this chain had been hammered into the ground.

Zumarah turned towards the battlefield below, and although it was all but completely obscured from view by the roaring blizzard, he knew that his estimations of the distance and trajectory were accurate.

He grinned to himself, his eyes blazing with hatred and his tusks pressing against the stony flesh of his cheeks as he imagined the carnage about to be unleashed.

'Fire,' he growled.

THE NORSCANS' ADVANCE had completely stalled, and some of them were even now turning around, pushing back against those behind in their panic. They were already breaking and running and the Bretonnians were still a little over a hundred yards from their lines. This is going to be an absolute rout, Calard thought.

The entire Norscan centre turned tail and fled in the face of the Bretonnian charge. It was hard to see exactly what was going on, thanks to the blinding gale of snow and ice particles, but it was clear that the Norscan centre had almost completely dissolved.

Again he heard roars and howls off to the flanks, and this time he thought he heard something else reach his ears on the wind; men screaming in pain and terror. He glanced to the east, but could see little, though he thought he saw vague shapes, animalistic and furred in the blizzard, and knights turning around in confusion and panic.

The sight was alarming, but there was little that he could do but concentrate on his own duty, and he dragged his attention back to the front and centre. Besides, even if the Norscans were somehow overwhelming the Bretonnian flanks, their entire centre had been all but routed.

Seeing the enemy running before them, the Bretonnian war horns blared, and the army of Lyonesse swept forward into the gap.

The knights at the forefront of the charge caught up with the Norscans, many of whom, seeing that they were about to be overrun, turned and hurled themselves at the knights, swinging their axes murderously. These ones were hacked down where they stood, lances smashing them from their feet and impaling them.

The Bastonnians thundered into the breach in the Norscan line, and Calard lined up a fleeing man with his lance. The man spun towards the charging horsemen, but Calard's lance took him in the chest before he could swing his axe, driving through his ribcage and punching out his back. The lance was wrenched from Calard's hand and he slid the blade of Garamont from its inlaid scabbard, the ancient heirloom gleaming coldly.

More Norscans were run down, and Calard struck a blow upon the head of one of the barbarians, cracking the skull.

Calard realised that many of the Norscans had fled not directly away from the Bretonnians, but rather had moved off to the sides, pushing into the ranks of Norscans on the flanks. He turned his head from side to side in concern as he realised that none of the men he had faced appeared to be the heavily armoured Norscan elite that they had expected.

There was something very wrong here, he realised suddenly. His gaze was drawn upwards as the shadowy outline of the reportedly haunted, towering motte at the end of the valley hove into view.

Abruptly, there came a sound like a mountain falling, and a comet trailing hellish red flames shot up into the air from the top of the steep-sided hillock. It soared up high and Calard followed its trajectory skyward, mouth gaping wide in shock and wonder. Then the roaring comet reached the top of its arc and began to descend towards the ground; towards the charging Bretonnians.

'Lady protect us,' Calard breathed as the roiling inferno came screaming down towards the valley floor, and he heard shouts of panic and fear spread through the ranks.

Calard was thrown from the saddle as the missile smashed down amongst the knights fifty feet to his left, making the ground shudder beneath the impact, and the sounds of horses and men roaring in agony rose to the heavens, louder even than the screaming winds. The heatwave of the blast burnt Calard's lungs, and he gasped as, even at this distance, his plate armour heated up to an uncomfortable level.

Those knights closer in to the blast were cooked alive inside their armour, their flesh bursting into flames along with tabards, banners and horseflesh. A circle over fifty yards in diameter was scorched into the ground, ice and snow instantly turning to steam. Hundreds died in that first barrage, their flesh igniting beneath the intense heat, their blood boiling within their veins.

Those directly under the impact of the fireball were unrecognisable, nothing more than charred, twisted corpses that still burned fiercely. So intense were the unnaturally burning, vivid red flames that plate armour ran like quicksilver, dripping onto the ground in flaming, hissing blobs.

Hooves flashed near Calard's head as he pushed himself to his knees, horses screaming and bucking in terror all around. The stink of cooked flesh made him gag, and he staggered unsteadily to his feet as knights fought to regain control over their horses. Spying the precious blade of Garamont on the ground a few feet distant, he leapt for it, uncaring of the danger, and closing his hand around the hilt, he sheathed it.

'Calard!' bawled a voice, and he looked around to see Bertelis. Dodging through the chaos of terrified animals, he reached his brother, grabbed onto his saddle as he caught his breath, standing close so as to lessen the chance of getting trampled or kicked.

'What in the name of the Lady was that?' Bertelis shouted. Calard merely shook his head in response.

'Sigibold?' he shouted.

'Dead,' replied Bertelis.

Calard spied a horse with no rider nearby, its ears flat against its head and its eyes wide in terror. He lurched towards the beast, making a grab for its reins. Securing them, he swung himself up into the saddle. The terrified animal reared, but Calard would not be unsaddled again, and the animal quickly began to calm down under his firm control. Calard cast a quick glance around him, appraising the situation.

Duke Adalhard, thankfully, had not been engulfed in the blast, and Calard could see him and the majority of his army of knights still charging up the centre, intent on running down the few fleeing Norscans that could still be seen there. From his position, it was obvious that the Norscans were merely leading the Bretonnian duke further into their midst. He caught a glimpse of massive warriors bedecked in black iron closing in from the flanks, giants of men with horned helmets and snow-covered furs over their shoulders that were stalking towards the Bretonnians in their thousands, encircling them.

The Bretonnians had been duped into charging the centre, Calard realised, which had given way before them with little resistance. It had been a simple, well executed ploy, and Calard felt despair as he realised that in all likelihood no knights would ride away from this battle alive. Now the hammer blow was about to fall, and the Norscans were going to close in on either side, like wolves.

No, Calard corrected, seeing further as the wind suddenly dropped. The first hammer blow had already fallen.

He saw thousands of corpses strewn across the snow out on the flanks, bodies that had literally been torn apart.

Even as he stared despairingly out towards the flanks, he saw figures bursting from snow drifts, powder and snow exploding upwards as they leapt from their concealment and fell upon the knights and peasants out on the army's edge. Calard heard their war cries as they laid into the Bretonnian flank, tearing through rank after rank, their axes reaping a bloody toll, hacking men apart without mercy.

'This is a massacre,' said Calard, turning his horse to survey the battlefield all around. The surviving knights of Bastonne were milling around in confusion. No one was taking command. In every direction Calard saw thousands of Norscans marching through the blizzard towards them. In the rear, seeing the enemy closing in, the men-at-arms and peasant bowmen took flight, hurling weapons to the ground and quitting the field.

Seeing the rout, Bertelis swore and jerked on his reins, bringing his nervous steed back under control.

'We die here, then,' Bertelis shouted over the roar of the wind. 'We'll take as many of these whoreson bastards as we can with us.'

'No,' shouted Calard, shaking his head. 'We have to pull back. There is no victory to be had here!'

'Coward!' shouted a voice, and Calard spun to see Maloric. 'You'd bring dishonour upon the knights of Bastonne by fleeing like peasants?'

Some four hundred yards ahead, another fiery comet of death roared down through blizzard, and though its impact was hidden in the gusting snow-flurries, the ground shook beneath them as it struck home, and screams could be heard dimly from within the snowstorm.

'This battle is lost!' bellowed Calard. 'What good will more deaths do? Alive, we can seek vengeance!'

'The battle is not over yet!' snarled Maloric. 'Knights of Bastonne! To me!'

Calard cursed, but the milling knights rallied to the call, dragging themselves into order, and Maloric raised his voice to address them.

'We must ride to the aid of the Duke of Lyonesse!' bellowed Maloric, raising his sword into the air. 'It is our duty as the king's knights! Are you with me?'

Muted cries of affirmation answered the Sangasse noble, though Calard remained silent, his face dark. The wind changed direction suddenly, and Calard could see the Norscans closing in, thousands upon thousands of them – they appeared to be in no particular hurry.

'I'll not follow a Sangasse dog,' snarled Tassilo.

'Then be branded a coward and a traitor,' retorted Maloric, loud enough for all to hear, and the nobles affiliated with Garamont bristled in anger. Tassilo brandished his sword, but Calard halted him with a barked order.

'The king would wish us to ride to his brother duke's aid!' roared Maloric, infuriated by the reticence of Calard and his knights. 'We ride now, with or without you, Garamont!'

Calard's cousins looked to him to make his decision. He could feel Bertelis's gaze upon him, and he knew that his brother wanted to fight, even if that meant following the Sangasse noble. His every instinct told him that it was folly, but reluctantly, Calard nodded.

'Fine,' he said.

As one the Bastonnians broke into a gallop, charging into the snowstorm after the duke and the bulk of his army, riding hard. They could see little, though Calard knew the enemy were near at hand, and he felt certain that this ride was doomed.

They came upon the army of Lyonesse abruptly as the winds shifted, and they saw that the entire force of knights was engaged in a desperate battle. A hectic melee was underway, with the full force of the duke's knights engaged on three sides. Clearly, the Norscans had turned to face the Bretonnians, picking this place to make their stand, and they had stood up to the duke's charge. Doubtless the casualties had been many, but they had absorbed the charge, and the Bretonnians' flanks were now completely overrun. The slaughter was terrible, with countless hundreds of knights already ripped from their saddles and butchered.

With a shout, Maloric ordered the knights of Bastonne forwards, spearing towards the heart of the melee. More Norse were appearing out of the snowstorm, and Calard knew that they were completely surrounded. And still worse was to befall the Bretonnians, for the Norscan chieftain had one final surprise.

The ground began to shudder and reverberate as if shook by an earthquake and monstrous trumpeting lifted above the roar of the wind, the same sounds that Calard had heard before battle had commenced. It was akin to the blare of massive horns, but Calard could not begin to fathom the size of the instruments needed to create such a din.

He didn't have to wait long to discover what it was that made the sounds, and what he saw made his blood run cold.

From out of the blizzard's whitewash came three massive shapes, pounding forwards through the snow and ice, the ground reverberating with every titanic footfall of the monsters.

They were giant, shaggy-hided beasts, each as tall as a castle wall. They had huge trunks of muscle extending from their wide heads, and one of them raised this prehensile limb to the heavens and again the terrifying trumpeting sound echoed across the battlefield. The immense beasts were quadrupeds, with large flapping, dark furred ears and beady eyes filled with burning rage, and each had four immense tusks that curved down to the ground.

Atop the backs of these monsters were strapped immense howdahs of timber, their sides draped with furs and leathers and dotted with shields, and within these structures were dozens of warriors.

The Norscans battling the Bretonnians hurled themselves aside, though many of them were too slow or too far lost in their own battle frenzy. The beasts thundered forwards, smashing into Norscan and knight alike with titanic force, sending men and horses flying through the air with each great sweep of their heads. Tusks skewered destriers and riders alike, blood spraying in all directions, and massive trunks wrapped themselves around men, crushing ribs and limbs before hurling them into the blizzard, arms and legs flailing. Still others were crushed into nothingness, trampled beneath immense stamping hooves that flattened them completely – armour, bone and all.

Hundreds of knights were slaughtered as the trio of behemoths smashed through the knights with the elemental force of a thunderbolt, and many more were killed by the javelins and axes hurled by the Norscans riding within the howdah towers. Lances and swords dug into the legs of the shaggy-furred beasts but it was like striking rock, and weapons were jarred from numbed hands. These attacks were little more than pinpricks to the mighty beasts, who seemed not to feel any pain.

The army of Lyonesse, already struggling to survive being engaged on three sides by the brutal Norscan warriors was utterly shattered by the appearance of these three monstrous beasts. Merely the stink of them, thick and unpleasant, was enough to drive horses mad with terror, and panic spread across the entire battle line. The heart of the Bretonnian army was smashed apart, the immense mammoths thundering through the ranks of knights with impunity, killing everything that came near them. Hundreds of noble knights of Bretonnia were left as unrecognisable smears of blood trampled into the ground, and countless more were killed as they were smashed through the air by swinging tusks, or hacked apart by the bloodthirsty warriors who descended on the panicked knights in a fury, axes smashing men from saddles and cleaving the legs from beneath proud destriers driven mad with fear.

The banner of Lyonesse fell and was trampled underfoot. Tens of thousands of black-feathered carrion birds were descending from the skies, battling the winds in their eagerness to feast on the corpses, and Calard realised that what he had earlier taken for a storm cloud had actually been these feral birds, massing in their tens of thousands.

Calard saw what could only be the war-chieftain of the Norscans seated upon a high-backed throne atop the howdah-tower of one of the mammoths, a giant, grey-bearded warrior bedecked in dark metal, and he felt intense hatred that such a barbarian had caused the deaths of so many noble knights. His gaze flickered to the figure seated at the chieftain's feet, a woman of obvious beauty, and Calard felt his blood run cold.

Elisabet!

Knights were streaming from the field now, with no thought of honour or dignity, leaving their butchered comrades to lie where they fell. He could feel the displeasure of the goddess.

The duke fell, and panic rolled across the battle line.

The army of Lyonesse was routed.

CHAPTER NINE

It was nearing midnight and Styrbjorn stood amongst his huskarls in a wide ring atop the plateau of the steep sided hill. The battle had gone well, the horsemen army crushed, and he could feel the gods' approval. The scale of the bloodshed had fuelled his desire, and he stared hungrily at his writhing witch-consort, alone within the circle before him.

She wore nothing more than a light shift, which showed off the contours of her body to good effect. Her arms and legs were bare and she wore no shoes or slippers upon her feet, though she gave no indication that she felt the chill night air. Every inch of exposed skin, from the smooth flesh of her legs and arms to her face, was covered in ritualistic patterns and runes carved into her flesh by Bjarki's steady hand. These cuts were not deep, just enough to bring the blood to the surface, but they did nothing to mar her beauty. Indeed, to the jarl, they merely enhanced her allure, for the sight of blood always enhanced his desire.

His witch-consort had created a consecrated circle at the top of the wind-swept hill, and it was outside this that Styrbjorn's warriors were gathered. The edges of the circle were marked with gore-coloured powder from which a vague red smoke arose, together with a smell like bowels that had been opened by a sword thrust. Eight bodies – the warriors that Styrbjorn had handed over for sacrifice – were positioned equidistant around the circumference of the circle, each representing one of the eight points of the star of the true gods.

Each of the Skaeling warriors was nailed to an A-frame of timber propped up with a third hunk of lumber, their arms spread wide and their feet dangling two feet above the ground. Their skin had been flayed from their bodies and their chests had been ripped open, the ribs broken and splayed outwards to expose the organs within. Not all of them were dead, and those still living moaned wordlessly from mouths bereft of tongues, twitching as carrion birds pecked at their moist innards, jabbing sharp beaks into soft, living flesh. Their hearts, exposed to the elements, thumped erratically, and they thrashed their heads from side to side, trying vainly to stop the murderous crows and ravens from feasting on them.

Blood-smeared, foul smelling totem-dolls hung from the A-frames, turning slowly as the winds pushed at their bloated, repulsive forms. The closest of them was a representation of a child, or a baby. Blond hair lined with silver – his own, he realised dimly – was stitched into the babe's head. A pair of horns, perhaps hacked from the head of a goat, protruded from the babe's chin.

A raven landed on the head of this doll before realising that it was an unstable roost and flapping off, cawing loudly, sending the totem-doll swinging wildly.

Skull-headed braziers burnt foul herbs and roots, embers glowing brightly as the icy winds howled.

Three fifteen foot tree-trunks stripped of their branches leant against each other in the centre of the circle, tied together with barbed chain, forming a crude tent structure with no sides. The excess length of the chain hung down in the centre of the structure, and another totem-doll hung there, the rusted hook emerging from its back passed through one of the links, so that it hung some four feet above the ground, spinning slowly.

The ground beneath the doll was spread with furs, and it was upon these that Styrbjorn's witch-consort lay, writhing and moaning softly, speaking in the daemon tongue. Her eyes were hazy and indistinct, and she ran her hands over her body in ways that made Styrbjorn's heart rate quicken. The hallucinogenic smoke from the braziers was having an effect on him as well, and he could see the insubstantial shades of daemons cavorting around his witch-consort, caressing and stroking her flesh. His desire for her was strong; all he wanted to do was step forward into the circle and take her.

'Not yet,' said Bjarki, at his side, as if hearing his lustful thoughts. 'The conception must take place at the exact right moment.'

'And how long will that be?' said the Skaeling jarl, his voice husky.

As if the gods were giving him their own answer, the wind suddenly picked up, making the embers in the braziers glow brightly. Like the breath of the gods themselves, it swirled around the circle in an anticlockwise direction. Under the effects of the mind-altering smoke, Styrbjorn saw elemental daemons and spirits howling within that wind. Faces snarled at him, and clawed hands reached out towards him. The wind intensified, and he saw more creatures in the flash of movement whipping around him, skinless winged beasts with reptilian faces, naked women with bird-like talons in place of hands and feet, and monstrosities with mouths filled with rotting fangs and worms. Styrbjorn smiled deliriously as the daemons of the air whipped around him, scratching at his flesh and tugging at his braided beard.

The wind began to lift, rising high into the sky above the circle, and the clouds themselves began to rotate, slowly at first, then faster, and faster. Soon the sky resembled one of the great whirlpools that sometimes appeared to threaten his dragonships off the coast of Norsca, a swiftly spinning maelstrom centred directly overhead. A patch of open sky appeared in the centre of the swirling clouds, and Styrbjorn's breath caught in his throat as he glimpsed the immense green eye of the gods peering through the clouds down at him.

The clouds were ripped aside by the force of the swirling winds and Styrbjorn could see that the green moon was hanging low and full, directly overhead. His flesh tingled as the green light bathed him in its glow, and he heard the moans of his witch-consort escalate. In his drug-addled state he imagined that the moon was literally a great eye, its pupil slitted like a serpent's. He could feel the malevolence flowing down from that eye in waves, and he smiled drunkenly; the gods themselves had manifested to witness the conception. Truly, his son would be blessed by the gods indeed!

Licking his lips, he looked down at his shaman.

'Now?' he said, his voice rough and bestial.

The wiry seer, an expression of rapture on his face, nodded his head.

Styrbjorn shrugged off his furs and stepped over the blood-powder marking the circle. Billowing smoke rose from the powder as he passed the barrier, and he felt more than saw the shadow-daemons within the circle rise up to challenge him, surrounding him, hissing malevolently. Shadows of movement flickered in the corner of his vision as they jabbed at him with insubstantial talons, but he heard them hiss in pain and recoil, even as he felt their icy claws numb his flesh.

Then Styrbjorn felt delicate, warm hands against his flesh and he forgot the daemonic shades, forgot that he was surrounded by his entourage of onlooking huskarls, forgot that the gods themselves stared down from the heavens. He gazed upon his witch-consort, the one who would bear him a son, and she pressed a goblet into his hands, brimming with a potent smelling brew. He drained it in one draught, throwing his head back and closing his eyes. It burnt as it washed down his throat, and he marvelled as he opened his eyes, for all the colours he perceived seemed brighter than they had done before, swimming before him with almost painful brilliance.

All of his senses were heightened to levels that Styrbjorn could never have imagined possible as the potent brew began to take effect. The overload of sensation was staggering. He tossed the goblet aside, eyes focused on the woman writhing on the ground before him.

The witch gazed up at him with eyes that had turned completely black and licked her lips. Taking him by the hand, she drew him into her embrace, and under the unblinking eye of the gods overhead, a daemon-son was conceived.

SCORES OF BIRDS took flight, filling the air with the flapping of wings and panicked cries, shattering the peace of the forest glade. Tiny glowing sprites with flickering, insubstantial wings darted away, disappearing in an instant as if they had never been.

The majestic equine beast that had a moment before been drinking from the still pond lifted its head. Its flanks glowed like moonlight and the single horn that rose from its forehead gleamed with pearlescent brilliance. It regarded its mistress with deep, soulful eyes.

Morgiana opened her almond-shaped eyes and turned to regard the noble creature.

'You felt it too, then,' she said, her voice soft and musical. The unicorn stamped one of its forelegs into the ground, and tossed its head.

Horrific images of fire and death still lingered in her eyes, and she shuddered at the brutality her prescience had foreshadowed. She saw again the as yet unborn child, daemonic eyes ablaze with the promise of savagery. She saw him as a young man, flames wreathing his horned head, the coastal cities of Bretonnia in ruins and the oceans filled to the burning horizon with tens of thousands of Norscan longships. The screams of the endless lines of innocents being led to the sacrifice made her wince, and she saw mountains of skulls piled high beneath the turbulent heavens. She heard children weeping, and the stink of burning flesh still lingered in the back of her throat.

Morgiana folded her long, slender legs beneath her as she sat up. She moved with unearthly grace, her every movement languid, her every gesture effortless. She carried herself like a queen, yet no queen of Bretonnia had ever wielded such power as was hers to command.

No higher authority existed in all of Bretonnia than the Fay Enchantress, save the divine. The power to dethrone kings was hers to command; only the goddess could call Morgiana to question.

A priceless hand mirror hung from the golden girdle encircling her slender waist, and she lifted the potent artefact up in front of her. Her own, flawless image stared back at her coldly. Her hair was bound up within an elaborate headdress of the latest Bretonnian courtly fashion, and her ageless, regal face was pale.

The Enchantress blew lightly upon the mirror. Hoar-frost began to form upon the intricate silverwork of its frame, and her reflection misted over as if a sudden, impenetrable fog surrounded her.

Shapes began to form in the mirror, hazy like a dream at first, but slowly solidifying into recognisable human forms; a pale, dark haired young lady, her head thrown back in rapture and a powerful warrior kissing her neck.

The young damsel opened her eyes and stared out of the mirror directly at the Enchantress. Her suitor continued his affections, oblivious to their distant observer.

Morgiana reached a hand towards the image of the girl in the mirror, eyes locked with those of the dark haired young woman. Her finger tips touched the surface of the looking glass, which was as cold as ice, and sank within. The mirror's surface was as yielding as water, and ripples made the vision of the damsel and her lover shimmer as Morgiana's hand sank within it.

She placed her fingertips upon the young damsel's head. Morgiana felt the damsel shudder as she sent the vision of what might come to pass if the daemon-child lived into her mind. It was over in a second, and the Enchantress pulled her hand back. It was numb with cold, but she ignored the discomfort.

'What would you have me do, mistress?' said the vision of the girl in the mirror. Her lover tensed and lifted his head, looking around for who it was she talked to.

'Bring the child to me,' Anara the Enchantress whispered. Her gaze flickered to the broad, strong features of the damsel's lover. 'Take Reolus with you. His sword will be needed.'

'It shall be as you wish, my mistress,' replied Anara.

Then the vision in the mirror faded, and the Enchantress stared at her own reflection. There was a hint of sadness in her eyes.

'I'm sorry, Anara,' she whispered.

THE GOBLET THAT the jarl had drained and hurled away from him had rolled to the edge of the circle of blood-dust surrounding the intertwined couple. Smoke rose from where the liquid seeped from the vessel, and Bjarki knelt down before it. His jarl and the witch were in the throes of passion within the circle but Bjarki paid them no heed, concentrating on the goblet. Lifting it carefully, so as not to disturb the ritual circle, he raised it to his nose, sniffing. Frowning, he touched a finger to the small amount of liquid still contained within and licked it.

All manner of herbs and roots could be tasted within, as well as the essence of certain dream-inducing mushrooms that he was familiar with. But behind all that, there was a bitter taste that he recognised, though he could not put his finger on what it was. Bjarki furrowed his brow and stood, pushing through the circle of enthralled, drug-addled huskarls, trying to identify the substance in his mind.

Bjarki stalked down to the bottom of the hill, the witch-consort's banshee screams of pleasure ringing out across the lowlands. Muttering to himself, he entered his tent, wracking his mind for the source of the herb or root that he had tasted in the brew. Herbs, roots and the innards of animals and men hung from cords strung above his head, and he flicked through them, hoping that something would jog his memory.

Finding nothing, he squatted on the floor and began to tear open his saddlebags, untying leather thongs and rolling out bundles of leather within which were hundreds of small pockets, each containing a neatly wrapped bundle of leather and fur, tied up with dried sinew and horsehair. Within each package was a rare ingredient, either gathered by Bjarki or one of his predecessors or traded from the lands of the Kurgan, the Hung or the southlanders, or lands even further afield; the hot forests of the lizard-people many months' sail to the south-west, the realm of the Dragon King in the east beyond the great wall, or from the lands of sand and dust-daemons to the south.

Norse runes were burnt into the leather of these packages, telling him what was contained within each – some he had never opened, having never had the need. He flicked through his precious collection with growing irritation, cursing.

Bjarki finally gave up, angry and frustrated, and he threw himself down onto his furs.

It came to him just as he started to drift off to sleep.

'Whorlroot,' he said to himself. 'The devious bitch.'

The witch had dissolved a large amount of the deadly root in his jarl's draught, concealing its taste within the hallucinogenic brew's potent flavour. In small doses, if taken regularly, Bjarki knew that the root would slowly kill a man, wasting his muscles and eating him away from the inside. It was a cunning way to do away with an enemy if obvious hostility needed to be avoided, so long as one could slip the root powder into a draught regularly enough without causing suspicion, for its symptoms were akin to many wasting sicknesses, and only one particularly skilled in herb-lore would ever detect it. Taken in the quantity that the witch had slipped into Styrbjorn's draught, it would cause the victim to fall into a deep sleep from which he would not wake – unless a draught to countermand its effects was imbibed. Thankfully, such an antidote was relatively simple.

Quickly, Bjarki began tearing open his pouches and grinding up roots, praying to the great gods of the Skaelings that he was not too late.

Haegtesse opened her eyes with a start as she felt a sharp kick from within her belly. The cold light of dawn penetrated weakly through the low hanging cloud cover, and fresh snow blanketed the top of the hill, but with her naked body wrapped in the thick furs strewn within the ritual circle atop the hill, she felt the chill only on her cheeks.

Her hands ventured down over her stomach, which had been firm and flat only hours earlier, marvelling at the considerable bump there now. Her flesh was taut and stretched, bulging with new life. She felt the daemon-child within her kick again, more forcefully this time, and she gasped. She could hear the child's as yet unformed thoughts flowing through her mind like an incoherent whisper, confused and jumbled yet pulsing with staggering intensity. Such power!

The gods of Chaos had clearly blessed the union, and she judged that she would come to term within the month. She felt a flicker of unease as she considered how powerful the boy would be by the time she gave birth. He was already so strong, though his power was as yet unfocused and vague. Once he gained mastery over it, he would be horrifyingly potent. He would – if he lived – command power that she could not hope to comprehend.

She sat up with some awkwardness, unused to the weight of the child within her. She clutched the furs around her and glanced down at the figure of the Skaeling jarl. He had rolled away from her, and was wrapped in furs, so that she could not see his face. She did not hear his breathing. She was almost sorry to have killed him; he had been a fine lover.

Nevertheless, his death had been necessary – he would never have stood by and allowed her to do what it was she intended. She would leave this stinking Norscan camp concealed in the shadow of Dark Magic and birth the child in the wilderness, alone. It would be a simple matter to befuddle the minds of any sentries, and yet she didn't even think that would be necessary; the Skaeling warriors had celebrated their victory long into the night, and few warriors would be yet awake.

Again the child kicked within her, and she gasped.

By the time the daemon-child reached five years of age he would be capable of things that had taken her half a dozen lifetimes to master, and she doubted that she would be able to overcome him. But as a newborn? He might have power, but he would not yet know how to control it, nor have the self-awareness necessary to protect himself from her. And he would be dead long before he mastered his gods-blessed power.

She stroked her belly lovingly.

'A month's time, and the gods will hear your birth screams,' she whispered. 'And then you will die – by my knife – and I shall live forever.'

'I don't think so,' said a voice in her ear.

She started in alarm and spun around to see Jarl Styrbjorn staring at her, his eyes as cold as ice. How could this be? He had drained enough of the draught to kill one of his immense tuskers!

She began to mouth an incantation that would summon her guardian daemon-shades to her and rip Styrbjorn's soul to shreds, but the jarl backhanded her hard across the side of the face and she fell with a cry. She hadn't even seen the blow coming, and the pain was intense. Stars flashed before her eyes and she could already feel the bruise rising.

'Kurgan bitch,' growled Styrbjorn. 'You think I'd let you harm my son? You think you could kill *me*?'

Haegtesse couldn't talk, still dazed by the sledgehammer blow that the Skaeling jarl had struck her. She tried to get away from him, scrabbling frantically on hands and knees, but he grabbed her by the hair and hauled her head back, exposing her throat. She was powerless against his strength, and for a second she thought he was going to kill her.

As Styrbjorn held her immobile, a horrific device of black iron was lowered over her head by another set of hands. The Skaeling seer, she realised dimly. Of course – he must have been the one to realise what it was Styrbjorn had drunk, and concocted its antidote. Damn him!

The device the seer carried was a helmet-like cage, and it stank of blood as it was lowered over her head. She saw that runes of the Dark Tongue were engraved upon its bands, and she struggled violently, screeching like an animal as she tried to avoid having it locked in place.

Styrbjorn struck her again then, a blow that rattled her brain and left her almost insensible. The brank was fastened around her head. Inward facing spikes carved deep gouges in her flesh, and she winced. The front of the headpiece was hinged, and as its door was pushed closed and locked, a spiked metal tongue depressor was forced into her mouth. It pierced the flesh of her cheeks and tongue and bit deep into the roof of her mouth. She almost choked on her own blood as it filled her throat.

Her arms were wrenched painfully behind her back and bound tightly with cord. The Skaeling seer, Bjarki, squatted in front of her, grinning, and her eyes flashed with hatred. Yet without the power of speech and with her hands bound, she was as helpless as a newborn.

'Whorlroot,' said Bjarki, still grinning. 'Clever. It was a close thing – another half an hour and the father of your unborn child would have been worm-food.'

Jarl Styrbjorn stood up, stretched his arms, and shouted for his armour.

'Bring her,' he said, gesturing to the clearly pregnant, bound figure of Haegtesse. 'We make for the coast.'

'Tell us another story?' begged one of the peasants, a plea which was echoed by a dozen others crowding around inside the hovel, hot with sweat and the heat of the open fire.

Chlod, stuffing his mouth with hard bread dunked in stew, grinned, wiping hot gravy from his chin. He waved a hand, and one of the peasants that made up his audience handed him a clay jug of cheap wine, which he swigged from.

The peasants were looking at Chlod expectantly, and he was relishing being the centre of attention as he spoke of the holy feats of the grail knight, Reolus.

Chlod had arrived at Lyonesse, upon the rocky north-east coast, some two days earlier, borne upon the back of a wagon laden with produce, and had been enjoying its hospitality ever since. To his audience, he was a dashing adventurer, a heroic pilgrim seeking his master, and they happily fed and watered him in exchange for his tales.

'One more story, then,' he said, smacking his lips.

It didn't get much better than this, he thought, with a smile. He should be able to work this charade here for at least another few weeks. He shoved half a biscuit down his shirtfront for his rat, and then, with his audience hanging on his every word, he began another fanciful tale about how he, a lowly peasant pilgrim, saved the life of the holy paladin Reolus.

CHAPTER TEN

THE WAVES POUNDED relentlessly against the white stone of the castle walls, the crashing of the surf sending deep, sonorous booms echoing through its halls. Sprays of foam and icy water exploded up the sheer sides of the fortress, reaching for the battlements. Snow was falling from dark clouds overhead and while it was only early afternoon, it was as dark as twilight.

Calard stood upon the north-west wall, braving the elements as he stared darkly out towards the horizon. He could taste the salt spray upon his lips, and snow gusted through the crenulations, billowing around him and chilling his flesh.

It had been three weeks since the catastrophic defeat of the army of Lyonesse, three weeks since he had been forced to flee like a peasant from the wrath of the Norscan whoresons. He had felt the Lady's displeasure as he and the other knights of Bastonne had fled the field, pursued by the howling hordes of Chaos.

The slaughter had been terrible, and above it all the Norscan chieftain had watched from atop his throne upon the back of the immense tusker, laughing as the monstrous beast smashed men and horses out of its path with every swing of its heavy head.

He shuddered as he thought again of the violent trumpeting of the monsters as they rampaged through the ranks of the proud knights, stomping and slaughtering everything in their path. They seemed inured to pain, ignoring scores of lances imbedded in their tree-trunk legs, and barely seeming to register the flashing swords that hacked at them. Calard felt his despair grow. What could a man do to fight such beasts? What could an *army* do to fight them?

Calard clenched his hand into a fist and struck the cold stone of the battlements, compacting the snow settling there.

He thought of the Lady Elisabet, the lady whom he had given his heart only to be cruelly betrayed. She had been the last person he had expected to see in the midst of that chaotic battle, a prisoner sat at the Norscan warlord's feet upon the back of the mighty beast.

Again he saw Elisabet's large tearful eyes as she tried to get close to him, just after he had learnt of her murderous plot to kill his father, the castellan of Garamont. He saw again the hurt, the pain, and the desperation – the love – in her expression, and it felt like a cold claw clutched at his heart. He had believed that he would wed Elisabet within a year of his return home from Bordeleaux, and had even gone so far as to meticulously plan how he was going to ask for her hand.

He hated her. She had shattered his dreams. She had poisoned his father, turning him into a withered skeleton, old before his time. And he hated himself for the fact that there was a part of him that loved her still.

She was out there, he thought, staring off into the distance, a captive of the brutal Norscan warlord. His anger rose just imagining what horrors she was being subjected to by the Norse chieftain, by his men. No matter what she had done, she didn't deserve that.

Staring intently at the horizon, seeing the storm clouds rolling in from the north and the flash of lightning in the distance, he swore. He felt so helpless. She was probably in Norsca by now; if she was still alive at all.

The battle had ended in butchery, and the scale of it filled him with loathing and disgust; the enemy were nothing more than bestial savages. He had seen knights hacked limb from limb by frenzied Norsemen long after there had been any honour left in the fight. He had seen blond-haired marauders tear out the throats of knights with their bare teeth. He saw hulking, black-armoured barbarians bedecked in furs matted with congealed blood slaughtering the injured, beheading them with mighty sweeps of their broad-bladed axes. None were given mercy or clemency. Even the steeds of unhorsed knights were hacked apart by axe and sword, giant mutated hounds savaging them and tearing great chunks of meat from their flanks.

The Duke of Lyonesse had been carried clear of the slaughter, though the famed banner of Lyonesse was lost, trampled into the mud. Miraculously, the duke was still alive; he'd merely been knocked unconscious by a blow to his head. The Lady had clearly intervened on his behalf, protecting him from worse hurt. He was hastily borne away from the battlefield, his closest coterie of knights escorting him swiftly for Castle Lyonesse in the west, upon the walls of which Calard now stood.

After their victory, the Norse army had struck for the coast, driving hard. For a week Calard and those surviving knights that had not accompanied the duke had dogged the progress of the barbarians, but there were less than fifteen hundred survivors of the ten thousand knights that had fought in the battle, and they could do little to threaten them.

They had engaged in running battles with the outriders of the Norscans but these were nothing more than skirmishes for they had not the numbers to force the Norscans into a decisive battle. They had not even the strength of numbers to stop the Norscans from sacking a dozen villages and small hamlets as they rampaged back towards the coast, and the mood of the Bretonnian camp had been grim.

By the time the knights of Couronne had caught up with the remnants of the shattered Lyonessian army, half of the Norscan army had already put to sea. The relief force had been pitifully small, however, for the majority of the knights despatched had turned back as soon as it was clear that the Norscans were not seeking to penetrate deeper into Bretonnia. Only the younger knights errant, those desperate to prove their worth, had continued their ride from Couronne.

He had been surprised to see a familiar face amongst the knights, however; none other than the foreigner Dieter Weschler, a nobleman of the Empire that Calard had fought alongside six months earlier. The man's appearance was, if anything, even more fastidious and outlandish to those attuned to Bretonnian sensibilities than Calard remembered; all puffy sleeves, tights, ostentatious plumes and lacquered black steel.

Dieter was, it turned out, now the Empire's ambassador to Bretonnia, though he confided in Calard that he was growing tired of the king's court, with all its intrigue and back-stabbing. He had leapt at the opportunity to ride forth and do battle, and he saw that doing so was an opportunity to further strengthen the relations between Bretonnia and the Empire.

However, as pleased as Calard was to see his old comrade in arms, he was furious to learn that the entire relief force that had set out from L'Anguille had turned back once it had established that the enemy no longer threatened their own border.

Nevertheless, fighting alongside Dieter, Calard and the remaining knights had made a good account for themselves in a daring attack against the last of the Norscans boarding their longships, yet the battle had little relevance; the enemy warlord – and Elisabet – had already departed Bretonnian shores.

In impotent rage Calard had stood upon the snow-covered beach, surrounded by dead and dying Bretonnians and Norscans, and watched as the last longships pulled away into the distance. It had been a grim journey from there to Castle Lyonesse, a day to the south, and Calard and the other Bastonnian knights had ridden in silence, escorting the injured. For two nights they had been the guests of the Duke of Lyonesse within his island fortress – one of the most impressive and defensible castles in Bretonnia.

It was located just off the north-west coast of Lyonesse, some four hundred yards from the mainland.

Calard heard someone climb to the top of the stairs behind him, but did not bother to turn to greet them. In silence Bertelis moved to his side and leant against the battlements, gazing out to sea.

The brothers stood in silence, listening to the pounding of the surf as snow billowed around them. Only a week earlier neither of them had seen the ocean, and Calard had dreamt of the day when he would since he was a child, but this was not how he had imagined it. He had envisaged blue-green waters sparkling with reflected light and filled with an abundance of life, not the unyielding fury of this isolating wasteland of black, icy water.

'Do we return to Garamont then, brother?' said Bertelis finally, his voice low.

Calard sighed. He had no wish to return to his ancestral home and face his responsibilities, but he could not continue to shirk his duties, he knew.

And as much as he hated to admit it, there was nothing that could be done now to save Lady Elisabet. She was gone, as were the Norscans, across the seas.

'Yes,' he said at last. 'It is time to return home. Ready the men.'

Bertelis nodded and turned to leave when a fanfare of horns began to sound. Calard frowned.

'What's this?' he said.

They could see men running towards the east gate, and they heard shouts of excitement and awe. The gates were opened, and the portcullis raised, and again long fluted horns blared.

'Must be someone important,' said Bertelis, and the brothers began descending the walls quickly, with no further discussion, joining the crowds that were thronging towards the east gate.

REOLUS, HOLY GRAIL knight of the Lady and the epitome of knightly perfection, rode alongside a damsel of the Lady through the rapturous crowd, his head held high.

It seemed that the clouds parted momentarily as the illustrious pair entered Castle Lyonesse amid a fanfare of excitement, and rays of sunlight shone down upon them.

Reolus rode upon a powerful, jet-black destrier that was easily twenty hands high, while the damsel rode without a saddle upon a smaller dappled grey. The grail knight carried aloft his gleaming silver lance, the famous Arandyal, and bore his helmet under his other arm. His face was expressionless, his features strong and ageless.

The grail knight wore a flowing tabard of regal blue over his gleaming armour, its edges embroidered with silver thread. The damsel wore a filmy purple dress, and her hair was bound up in an elaborate headdress, her face obscured by a silken veil.

A thick cloak, its inside lined with softest mink fur, hung from Reolus's shoulders, and a golden clasp in the shape of the Lady's holy chalice was fastened upon his chest. Only those who had supped from the grail were allowed to wear such emblems, those who had come face to face with the goddess herself and been found worthy. The grail knights were the most respected individuals in all of Bretonnia, paragons of virtue and honour who were beyond reproach.

Calard's breath caught in his throat as he gazed upon the hallowed warrior once again. A palpable holy aura shimmered around Reolus, and his eyes gleamed with the Lady's power.

The Duke of Lyonesse was amongst those that spilled out to witness the grail knight's entrance to his castle, and he bowed low before Reolus and the damsel of the Lady. Calard and Bertelis pushed through the crowd to hear his words.

'Lord Reolus and Lady Damsel, I am honoured,' said Duke Adalhard. 'What is mine is yours; I will have apartments readied for you immediately. We shall feast this night in your honour!'

Reolus raised a hand, and the cheering that had erupted at the duke's announcement simmered down.

'Your hospitality does you proud, my lord duke,' said Reolus. 'However, I fear there are more pressing matters at hand. The Norscans.'

'The Norscans have left,' said the duke with a frown.

'No,' said the damsel, and Calard jerked as if he had been struck, as he recognised the voice as that of his sister, Anara.

'No, my lady?' questioned Duke Adalhard.

'The Norscans have *not* left Bretonnian lands,' said Anara, her voice vague and ethereal. 'They are encamped thirty miles westward. They have defiled the temple of the Blessed Lady upon the Isle of Landri, and slaughtered all its priestesses. I can hear their souls crying out in fear even now, denied their eternal rest.'

'The Lady Elisabet?' called out Calard, pushing to the front of the crowd, and he blushed as he felt hundreds of pairs of eyes turn to focus upon him. Anara regarded him as if he were a stranger, with no hint of recognition in her eyes.

'She is there,' said Anara finally, 'and it is the will of the Lady that she be reclaimed from the Norscan infidels.'

CHAPTER ELEVEN

Calard shivered as the icy wind whipped across the exposed top of the keep. The pegasus stamped their hooves, clearly unimpressed, and the knights of Parravon stroked their necks, whispering quietly to placate the powerful steeds. They looked as unhappy as their mounts with the arrangement, and Calard felt a knot in his stomach at the prospect of riding one of the temperamental beasts.

'Mount up,' said Laudethaire.

Calard grimaced as Bertelis gave him an excited smile and pulled himself smoothly into the saddle. The pegasus snorted and reared instantly, unfurling and beating its wings violently in protest at its unfamiliar rider, but Bertelis stayed in the saddle, grinning like a madman, and brought it under control with a firm yank on the reins. Its ears were still flat against its head, and it quivered in anger, but it began to settle as its owner grabbed it by the bridle and talked to it in a firm, calm voice.

Reolus was already astride his mount, as stoic as ever, and his pegasus seemed content and relaxed beneath him. Anara ran a hand along the length of the pegasus she was to ride and it knelt before her, much to the amazement of the Parravonian knights, allowing her to step into the saddle in a dignified manner. She barely seemed to register the strangeness of the situation, lost as she was in an animated discussion with herself.

Calard gazed at the pegasus that he was to ride and felt his mouth go dry, though he did not for a moment regret insisting that he be part of the rescue. The Parravonians had been resistant, but Reolus had backed Calard's wish, and his word brooked no argument, even when Bertelis demanded that he too accompany the war-party.

The winged steed was a magnificent beast, larger than a Bretonnian warhorse and as white as virgin snow. Its mane was thick, a mix of feathers and hair, and its powerful wings were held tight against its body, furled like an eagle's. It flashed him an angry look, steam billowing from its flared nostrils, and he swallowed.

'Frightened, Garamont?' said Maloric smugly from the back of his own pegasus.

Calard flashed the Sangasse noble a dark look. He still could not believe that the grail knight Reolus had suggested he accompany them; couldn't the grail knight see that he was nothing but a treacherous dog?

'Mount her just like a horse,' advised the knight holding the pegasus's reins. 'Get your feet in the stirrups quickly and hold on tight, as she won't like being ridden by a stranger.'

Calard nodded, blushing as he felt the eyes of his companions upon him, and gripping the pommel with one hand, he placed his left foot in the stirrup and hauled himself into the saddle. The pegasus bucked, throwing its head around violently, and spun on the spot. Calard had ridden since before he could walk, and was well used to breaking in rebellious steeds, but never had he ridden a beast as large and powerful as this, and he struggled to bring her back under his control.

She reared, unfurling and beating her wings, sending snow gusting in eddies before her, and Calard felt himself half-kicked out of the saddle as the pegasus reared and bucked again.

'Whoa!' shouted Calard in what he hoped was a firm, authoritative voice, and using his whole body weight and the strength in his arm, he pulled the pegasus's head to the right, simultaneously using his right leg to disengage its hind quarters, robbing it of its strength. It snorted and pulled against him, but could do nothing against his practised one rein stop, and it began to calm down as it realised its rider was not inexperienced.

'Damage her mouth and you will be paying restitution, Bastonne,' said the Parravonian knight haughtily.

'And what restitution will you pay if she throws me into the ocean?' muttered Calard in reply.

Having brought the pegasus under control, at least temporarily, Calard looked out over Castle Lyonesse and its surrounds, trying to ignore the knotting of his stomach. He breathed out evenly, trying to slow his rapidly beating heart.

The keep on which they stood rose higher than any of the castle walls, allowing a clear view across the island fortress and the surrounding sea. It truly was an impressive defensive structure, and though Calard felt there was a good amount of pride involved in the duke's claim that it would never fall by force, he could well believe that fully manned and well provisioned, the castle could hold against an enemy besieger for many months, possibly even years.

Its walls were high and thick, and towers topped with immense trebuchets were built at strategic points along its lengths, each one offering good vantage for archers to fire down upon anyone trying to scale the sheers walls on either side. Even the smallest of these towers was easily three times the height of any of the towers of Castle Garamont – indeed, the entirety of Castle Garamont could be completely enclosed within Castle Lyonesse ten times over.

From his high vantage point, Calard looked over the tightly packed buildings huddled within the castle walls below the keep towards Lyonesse harbour. A dozen ships were anchored in the calm waters of the protected cove, inside the protection of the walls. After the keep itself, the massive gatehouse that covered the entrance to the harbour was the most defensible part of the stronghold. That arched gateway was of such scale that the largest ships of the Bretonnian fleet would be able to sail through it into the harbour with room to spare, passing beneath the most immense portcullis Calard had ever seen.

When that portcullis was lowered, he heard tell from the proud local knights, its weight forced a second portcullis to rise from the rock beneath the water like a counterbalance. These two black iron gates, one falling and one rising, would meet a few yards under the water, forming an impenetrable barrier.

Calard's eyes drifted away from the harbour towards the temple of Manann, positioned on top of the rocky cliffs at the southern tip of the island. He could see the statue of the sea-god staring out to the open sea atop the circular temple, trident in hand and flanked by bizarre beasts that were half lion, half fish.

Though the Lady of the Lake was the official patron deity of the Bretonnian nobility, it was a fool that would not pay his respect to the lord of the ocean when travelling upon – or over – his domain. Calard had already left an offering of gold at that temple earlier that day; the idea of falling from the back of a pegasus into the ocean filled him with dread. He knew that if such a thing occurred, the weight of his armour would ensure he sank like a stone. The mere thought of the deep sea beasts that Manann ruled, the unnamed, blind and pallid horrors said to dwell upon the abyssal ocean floor made him shudder with horror. He hoped that his offering would see him safely back onto solid land.

'How long will it take to reach the island the Norse have desecrated?' asked Reolus.

'An hour, with favourable winds,' replied Laudethaire.

'May the Lady protect you all,' said Tassilo. He stood with the rest of Calard's cousins, Baldemund and Huebald, looking concerned.

Calard nodded and pulled on the reins as his steed began to become agitated.

'It is time that we were gone,' said Reolus, and is if understanding the grail knight's words, his pegasus stretched its broad, feathered wings, first to one side then the other, like an eagle readying for the hunt.

Cold fear knotted Calard's stomach again, though as no one else seemed to be showing any sign of unease, he tried to hide it.

'I've always wanted to fly,' said Bertelis. For a moment he looked again like the excitable young boy he had once been, his eyes alight with adventure, rather than the rather serious, solemn young man he had become since their return from Bordeleaux. Calard felt none of his exuberance, and was clutching his reins tightly, his jaw clenched so hard it hurt.

'For the glory of Parravon, the Lady and the King!' bellowed Laudethaire, raising his lance high.

'For the glory of Laudethaire, more like,' said Maloric under his breath, and had he not been in a mild panic, Calard would have grinned despite himself.

'To the air!' cried Laudethaire, and urged his steed towards the edge of the battlements.

'Lady protect me,' muttered Calard as the other pegasus broke into a gallop towards the edge of the keep. The animal beneath him wanted to join them, and with a flick of the reins and a kick he urged it forward.

The pegasus in front leaped the battlements, wings beating powerfully. Then Calard's own steed was at the crenulations and he roared wordlessly as it launched into the air.

There was a moment of weightlessness and Calard felt his stomach rise up into his chest. The sheer walls of the keep fell away and suddenly there was nothing between him and the ground a hundred yards below but air. For a sickening moment he was certain that he was about to plunge to his death.

Then the pegasus beat its wings and they rose into the air, his steed tucking its forelegs beneath it like a leaping horse. With no prompting from Calard, who was concentrating on not falling to his death, the pegasus swooped into a banking turn behind the other knights, soaring around the keep. The rush of the wind made Calard's eyes water, and he gaped at the sheer drop below him, clutching at the pommel as he stared in uncomprehending horror down at the buildings at the base of the keep, far below.

They swung around to the west and dipped down towards the wall. Flying past one of the great towers that guarded the approach from the western seas, Calard dimly heard people cheering and saw waving banners, but he was too busy trying to stay in the saddle to pay them any attention. The pegasus briefly furled its wings, and Calard let out an uncontrolled groan as they hurtled down towards the ground for a moment. Swooping down low over the western wall, he saw men-at-arm sentries waving up at them. His eyes goggled as he saw the waves crashing against the jagged rocks far below and then they were out over the ocean, with nothing beneath them but the icy depths, leaving Castle Lyonesse behind them.

Calard realised that he had been holding his breath, and he let it out slowly, trying to relax. The winds buffeted them, making the pegasus rise and fall in the air unpredictably. Nothing could be seen out in front but the open ocean and storm clouds, with the occasional jagged spear of rock rising from the black water, and Calard cursed.

He heard a shout, and turned his head to see Bertelis waving at him exuberantly. Calard ignored him, and turned his head forwards again, staring resolutely out to sea, clinging to the reins with grim determination.

'An hour,' he muttered to himself. Right now that seemed like an eternity.

THE PEGASUS BANKED and began to circle down through the clouds. Calard was frozen, and his whole body was aching – he had found it impossible to relax in the saddle knowing that he was hundreds of feet above the ocean. He could see nothing through the dank clouds; they might have been a thousand feet up or a dozen.

A gap appeared in the clouds below, and for a brief moment he saw the island that the Norscan had claimed, far below. Calard saw countless figures moving in the light of thousands of fires far below. They looked tiny and insignificant from his vantage, but he knew from experience that each of those figures was a fearless warrior, standing almost a head taller than any Bretonnian. Low fog hung over the ocean, but he could see thousands of longships that had been pulled up upon the beaches of the island. His rage grew as he looked upon the defiled ruin of the chapel to the Lady upon the southern tip of the island.

That chapel seemed to be the focus of the Norscan's revelry, and he heard drunken shouts, roars and booming laughter echoing up from it. It had been gutted by fire, and its roof had caved inwards in several sections, allowing the billowing snow to fall within.

Then the clouds closed in, concealing his view and their approach. Like a flock of birds flying together in an arrowhead-like formation, the pegasus swooped down through the clouds, with Laudethaire at its apex. Calard had no idea how the knight was navigating their progress, but he seemed to know where he was headed. They dropped further through the clouds, Calard leaning back in the saddle as the angle of descent increased, and he felt that they must surely hit the ground or the ocean at any moment.

They broke through the low hanging clouds again, and Calard saw that they had dropped perhaps a hundred and fifty feet. The open ocean was now beneath them, partially concealed in thick fog. Laudethaire had clearly guided them out to sea, so as to approach the island from an unseen quarter.

Calard swore as his pegasus dived, and he hung on grimly. The pegasus dropped like a stone as it entered the thick bank of fog. It swooped low, hooves trailing in the icy water as it followed Laudethaire's lead towards the rocky cliffs in front of them.

The swell was immense, and Calard's pegasus lifted them higher with a powerful beat of its wings as a towering wave threatened to engulf them. The beast tossed its head in pleasure as the wind whipped sea-spray off the top of the waves into them.

'Stupid beast,' spluttered Calard, spitting sea water from his mouth.

The flight of pegasus banked to the east, gliding silently through the fog, heading for a rocky cove. There were no longships beached here, for blade-like rocks pierced the waters on approach to the small bay, making navigating it safely impossible. Thankfully, there were no Norscans in sight – this was clearly an unoccupied area of the island. On the headland, Calard could see the defiled chapel of the Lady, lit daemonically from within by fires.

The flight of pegasus glided into the cove, and they hit the ground running. Calard dragged his steed to a halt. Swinging a leg over the saddle, he dropped to the ground. His legs were shaky, but it felt good to have solid ground beneath him, and he let out a ragged breath.

'Didn't fall off then, Garamont?' asked Maloric from nearby. Calard was pleased to see that for all the cockiness in his voice, the Sangasse noble looked pale and worn – clearly the flight had taken its toll on him as well.

'Sorry to disappoint,' said Calard through lips that were numb with cold.

In a low voice, Laudethaire indicated that two of his Parravonian kin would take the pegasus to the skies, so as to avoid risk of their discovery.

'What if we need them in a hurry?' asked Bertelis.

'They will be near,' said Laudethaire, looking briefly at the younger of the Garamont nobles as if he were a bug.

'Does anyone else think that the Norscans might not just stand idly by while we walk into their camp and take Elisabet?' said Maloric.

'Scared, Maloric?' said Calard in an acidic tone.

'Just not stupid,' he shot back. 'I care for her too, Garamont.'

'She'd not give you the time of day, Sangasse,' said Calard, his voice rising as hatred and jealousy reared within him. In Bordeleaux just before the war against the beasts of the wildwood, Maloric and he had exchanged heated words regarding Elisabet. Maloric had claimed that the token of affection he wore on his arm had been a gift from her, and Calard had reacted angrily, discounting his words as those of a viper. Still, even then, he had suspected the Sangasse noble spoke true.

'Stay your tongues,' said Reolus, his voice low and firm.

Calard fell instantly silent, ashamed to have been admonished by the holy paladin.

'The Lady's power shall conceal our approach,' said Anara, her voice vague and ethereal as she stared around at things that the others could not perceive. 'We shall be as ghosts, spirits passing unseen through the night.'

Calard shuddered, and swapped an uneasy glance with Bertelis.

'Do not speak,' said Anara softly. 'Do not make sudden movements. Do not draw your weapons. Any of these things will break the spirit-walk and that will be the death of us all.'

The knights, other than Reolus, regarded the slight figure of Anara warily, but they nodded their heads in understanding. Each of them regarded the damsel with a mixture of reverence, suspicion and fear, for her ways were strange and unearthly, and yet undoubtedly divinely inspired.

As the pegasus took to the air, angling out over the sea and disappearing into the fog, Anara began to incant. Calard could not understand her words, but it made the hair on the back of his neck stand on end, and he could taste an oddly metallic tang in the air. Anara's eyes rolled back in her head and she threw her arms out to either side, palms held up to the heavens as she continued to speak in that soft, unnatural voice.

Calard felt his skin prickle, and a wave of intense cold passed through him, making him shiver involuntarily. Ice crystals began to form on his armour, and his breath misted the air in front of his face. Thick fog rolled up off the water and began to surround the knights, who looked around them in unease. The biting chill permeated deeper into Calard's body, making his joints ache and every breath painful, and the forming ice threatened to lock up the joints of his armour. His hands and feet were numb, and he could feel that numbness creeping up his limbs and into his body.

It was suddenly hard to keep his eyes open. All he wanted to do was to lie down and let oblivion take him.

Blinking against the urge, Calard looked around at Bertelis, who was pale and drawn, his eyes haunted. The fog continued to build around them, rising to engulf them completely, and Calard felt the icy touch reach his heart. He gasped.

This was what death must feel like, he thought. To lie down and give in to it was so tempting. He could forget the pressing responsibilities that he felt unworthy to bear. He could forget about his doubts as to his own purity. All he had to do was close his eyes, and nothing would matter.

Do not, thundered his sister's voice in his mind, making him start with its sheer power. *Give in and you will be lost forever in this place, neither alive nor truly dead.*

Calard's drooping eyes flicked open, and he focused on his sister's face. She gave no indication of having spoken to him, still engrossed in her incantation, with her head thrown back.

Lost in this place, Calard thought, confused. Where are we?

He was not surprised when Anara answered him, still speaking directly into his mind.

We are in between, she said, *in the shadow realm. This is neither the world of the dead nor the world of the living.*

Calard looked around him. His surroundings had not changed, though the fog obscured them. No, he realised, that was not quite correct. The landscape around him *had* changed, but he had not noticed it at first, blurry and indistinct, as it was in the thick fog. The surrounds were devoid of all colour, he realised, cast in shades of grey, like the vague memory of a dream.

Come, said Anara into his mind, and this time he realised that she must have been speaking to everyone. With the grail knight Reolus at her side, his eyes shining with holy light, Anara stepped forward. The fog parted before her like a peasant rabble before a queen, and the knights fell in behind.

They walked in silence, and indeed every sound seemed to be muffled, as if they were hearing them from a great distance. The pounding of the waves, deafening only minutes before, now sounded faint and even the howling of the wind seemed distant. Calard frowned as he realised that he could not feel the touch of the wind at all, and though he was chilled to the core of his being, he could not feel the snow upon his face. Indeed, those flakes of snow being carried into him by the wind that he could not feel were not settling on any of them, he realised. He reached out to catch one of the snowflakes; it passed right through his hand, as if it were nothing more than an image, with no physical form at all.

'What…' he began before he remembered Anara's warning not to speak. He saw by his brother's expression that he too was trying to understand what was happening, and as they climbed steadily up from the beachhead, Calard realised that nothing around them seemed real; everything was like a dream.

The hillside itself was shadowy, with no colour to it at all. The rocks and low shrubs clinging to the hillside were vague and indistinct, like after-images that were not really there at all. Calard reached out to a strand of tall grass as he passed it, but his hand passed through the colourless ghost image.

Gazing up towards the defiled chapel, Calard saw that it too appeared as a slightly distorted shadow image, and even the light of the fires burning within had no colour to them – they merely burnt bright white.

Abruptly a pair of Norscan appeared, rounding a stand of rocks just ahead, heading directly towards them, moving down towards the cove, axes in hand. They were no more than a dozen yards away and could not fail to notice the group of knights in their path. Curiously, he could see a glowing sphere of light in the centre of the Norscans' chests.

Calard's hand flashed to his sword but a hand stopped him. Anger surged as he saw that it was Maloric's, and in that moment all he wanted to do was cut the Sangasse noble down. How dare he lay hands upon him!

Maloric shook his head and nodded further up the line. Calard glanced up the hill, seeing that the Norscans were making no aggressive moves towards them – indeed it looked as if they had not noticed them at all, though they were now less than half a dozen paces away. His eyes were drawn again to the glowing light in the centre of each Norscan's chest. The glow was coming from *within* them.

Calard felt a chill as the Norscans' eyes passed over him, looking *through* him. He saw also that the two warriors were vaguely transparent and he realised that just as everything else in this shadow-realm, they were as ghosts. Or perhaps, he thought, it was himself and his companions who were the ghosts here.

The larger of the Norscans, a hulking warrior that loomed over them all, was clearly irritated, and he and his companion were bickering in their brutish tongue, though it sounded like their voices came to his ears from a long way away. The smaller man was pointing down at the cove, and Calard guessed that he had heard or seen something of the Bretonnians' arrival. They are probably sentries, he thought.

Anara and Reolus gave the pair no mind and continued to climb up the shale-strewn path, and the Norscans walked straight through them. The ghost images continued on, still bickering, and Calard flinched as they walked through him. He felt nothing except a momentarily flicker of warmth as the glowing centre in the middle of the Norscan's chests touched him in passing.

Marvelling at the powers wielded by his sister, Calard and the knights topped the shale path and found themselves looking down upon the Norscans' camp. Tens of thousands of warriors were picketed in the snow, their tents dotting the landscape as far as the eye could see. The hills rolled out before them, and Calard saw endless campfires surrounded by marauders who were eating, drinking and fighting.

Every one of them had a burning sphere of light in their breast, and he saw that some were brighter than others. A couple of the warriors, perhaps one or two in every thousand, had fires that burnt with such white-hot intensity that it hurt his eyes to look upon them.

An altercation between two clearly inebriated warriors escalated, cheered on by their comrades, and one of them buried his axe in the other's neck. Blood rendered black in Calard's monotone vision sprayed out across the snow, and with another blow the head was severed from the warrior's shoulders. The victor hefted the head of his opponent high into the air, but this was not what Calard was focusing on. His eyes had been drawn to the soul-light of the defeated Norscan. He watched as the sphere flickered and grew faint before blinking out completely, like a candle snuffed out.

Quickly, whispered Anara, and the knights followed as the damsel and the grail knight led the way up towards the headland, towards the imposing chapel positioned there.

They moved through the Norscan camp, walking straight through tents and warriors like ghosts. An immense warhound lifted its head at their passing, growling, but a drunken Norscan kicked the beast into silence.

They walked straight through cooking fires on which animals and men were spitted, feeling nothing as they passed through the flames.

In the distance they could hear the trumpeting of the shaggy mammoths that had wreaked such havoc against the army of Lyonesse, though where those beasts were caged or picketed, Calard knew not.

Everywhere he looked, Calard saw vile evidence of the Norscans' brutality. Bodies were impaled on spears driven into the earth, their skin stripped from their muscles and loathsome symbols carved and branded into their flesh. Warriors were stretching the flayed skins of men across their shields and massive pauldrons, daubing their breastplates and faces with blood.

Warriors that seemed more beast than men hunkered down over the butchered carcasses of animals, ripping them apart with hands and teeth in the manner of dogs, growling at anyone that came near.

They passed near a warrior whose soul-light burnt with particularly fierce intensity. The hulking Norscan was bedecked head to toe in black armour, and a single twisting horn sprouted from his helmet. A pair of serrated swords were crossed upon his back, each blade covered in glowing runes of dark power, and a forked tongue darted from his mouth as if he were tasting the air as Anara steered them past him. He stood up, sniffing, searching for them, but his eyes, which Calard saw were as black as pitch, passed over them without focussing – clearly even with his daemon-given powers he could still not see them.

Every instinct screamed for Calard to draw his sword and attack these vile, heathen barbarians. Their very presence was an affront to the goddess, and he was quivering with hatred as they picked their way through the enemy encampment. These were the ones who had butchered so many honourable knights three weeks earlier, and he dearly wished to enact the Lady's vengeance upon them.

They climbed in a direct line towards the defiled chapel at the top of the headland. Bloody standards made from the flensed skin of his kinsmen were rammed into the earth outside the temple, and they fluttered and waved in a strong wind that he could not feel. The ornate stained glass windows of the chapel had been smashed, and he saw that young women wearing the garb of temple novices had been nailed to the walls, the symbols of the profane deities of the Norscans carved into their foreheads and their eyes plucked from their sockets by the carrion birds that perched on every available roost. There were tens of thousands of the crows and ravens, and they squabbled and fought for positions out of the wind.

She is near, came Anara's voice.

If Anara felt any outrage at the wrong done to the temple of her patron deity, she gave no outward sign. The doors of the temple had been smashed inwards with colossal force, hinges ripped completely from the wall, and the bodies of innocents were strewn around, nigh on unrecognisable as having once been men and women. Most of them had been half-consumed by carrion birds and warhounds.

Reolus made to climb the steps and enter the temple, but Anara stopped him with a hand upon his arm, and proceeded to walk around the outside of the temple, heading for its rear.

Dim sounds of revelry could be heard coming from within as the knights followed the damsel's lead.

They were high up on the headland here, with sheer cliffs that fell away into the ocean far below. Calard jerked in shock as there was a dim crash and a man fell through him to land at his feet, an axe embedded in his back, amid a shower of glass. Calard stepped away from the man as he tried to rise then fell forward, dying, his soul-fire flickering.

Calard continued on after the others, rounding the rear of the temple. What he saw made him recoil in horror.

A circle of eight thick wooden pylons had been driven into the ground, their fire-blackened lengths daubed with infernal symbols. They were hazy and indistinct, as was everything in this cursed shadow-land. Affixed to each pole was a chain. The eight lengths of chain met in the centre of the circle, where they were welded to a thick collar of metal encircling the neck of a young woman.

The woman was heavily pregnant, and a black iron brank was locked around her head like a cage. The device was akin to the scolds' bridles that were sometimes used to punish gossiping or argumentative peasant women, but this one filled Calard with loathing, for there was something deeply unnatural about it. Shadows writhed around it like living things, and it was engraved with vile runes that burnt with fiery intensity, binding the woman as powerfully as the brank itself.

A crude awning – a heavy canvas sail of a Norscan longship, Calard realised – had been strung up over the woman, giving her a modicum of protection from the elements, and fires burnt outside the circle. Furs were strewn beneath her, but the tension of the chains ensured that the woman was unable to lie down upon them – the best she could manage was to sit slumped, her head lolling forward, with the chains keeping her in an upright position. To treat anyone with such disregard made Calard feel sick to the pit of his stomach, but to do so to a pregnant young lady was beyond reason.

A score of armed guards stood around the circle, talking amongst themselves, backs to the fires to ensure they maintained their night-sight, but Calard paid them no mind, his eyes focusing on the slumped form of the pregnant woman. Even shadowy and ghostlike as she was, with her face obscured by the repulsive brank locked around her skull, he realised that there was something sickeningly familiar about her.

'Elisabet,' he breathed in horror.

The ghostlike figures of the closest sentries snapped to attention as he spoke aloud, their heads turning in his direction.

One of them muttered something under his breath, staring straight at Calard and making a warding motion with one hand. Calard reached for his blade, his hand closing around its ornate hilt.

The other sentries were hefting shields and weapons, gazing around them warily. As if awoken by the sudden tension of her captors, the imprisoned figure of Elisabet moaned and lifted her head, the chains attached to her neck clinking.

'In the Lady's name,' breathed Calard in horror, taking an involuntary step forwards.

One of the sentries barked a word in the harsh Norscan language, and made to lift a horn to his lips and sound a warning that would bring the entire Norse army running.

Reolus was suddenly in motion. He drew his sacred sword, Durendyal, and in this shadowy in-between realm it blazed with ethereal flames. Similar flames seemed to burst into life from the grail knight's eyes, burning with the fury of the goddess, and the Norscans fell back from him, terror written on their faces at the ghostly apparition taking shape before them.

Then the grail knight cut down the first sentry, his blade first hacking through the Norscan's horn just as it touched the warrior's lips and slicing cleanly through the man's head, carving through teeth, skull and brain matter with the ease of a hot knife cutting through pig-fat. Before the top half of the man's head had slid away from the rest of this body, Reolus had stepped past the warrior and killed another two men, his blade sliding through the muscled torso of one and the other dying instantly as Reolus skewered his head-on the length of his sacred blade. He moved with such sublime grace and speed that no one had even made a move, and three men were already dead.

'Take them!' roared Reolus, and Calard tore the blade of Garamont from his scabbard, leaping towards an axe-wielding ghost. He saw that his own sword too was glowing faintly, and his vision shimmered before him as he stepped out of the realm of shadows and back into reality.

Sensation returned to Calard in a flood, almost stunning him with their vibrancy. The sound of battle around him was loud, and he felt the biting wind tugging at his cloak, felt the heat of the fires nearby. He smelt blood and death, and he plunged his sword into the throat of the Norscan before the hulking warrior could react to his sudden appearance. The warrior's ice-blue eyes widened as the blade slid through his flesh and severed his spine, blood bubbling up from the fatal wound.

Laudethaire and Maloric hacked down another pair of the sentries, and as Calard kicked the Norscan off his blade, he saw Bertelis sunder the skull of another, his blade carving down through the man's head. Reolus spun through the melee, a living avatar of the Lady, killing and dismembering with every pass of his blade.

All the guards were dead in seconds, and Calard ran to Elisabet's side. She had stood at the sound of battle, and he could see her eyes wide as she stared around her through the bars of her imprisoning headgear. He looked down at her distended, pregnant belly, his mind reeling. How was this possible? When last he had seen her, no more than three weeks earlier, she had been as slim as ever, a petite girl.

Calard looked helplessly at the chains that bound Elisabet, having no idea how to release her from their bondage, but Anara was at his side suddenly. She placed her hands upon the seamless iron collar around Elisabet's neck. Speaking a single word, there was a flash of light and then the collar fell away.

Now that the chains no longer held her upright, Elisabet slumped forwards, and Calard caught her lightly in his arms.

'There is powerful sorcery at work here,' said Reolus as he looked down upon the brank enclosing Elisabet's head.

'Get it off her,' said Calard.

'I shall try,' said Anara, and she placed her hands upon the cage of black iron, closing her eyes. Smoke began to rise from under her palms, and Calard gagged as the smell of burning flesh filled his nostrils. Elisabet, unable to speak because of the iron gag of the brank, moaned in distress, and Calard held her strangely unfamiliar body tightly against him.

'Brother... Did you?' asked Bertelis, staring at Elisabet's pregnant form.

Calard shook his head in response.

The horrible runes engraved upon the iron bars of the brank blazed a deep red, and Calard saw beads of sweat begin to run down Anara's face and her brow crease in pain. Smoke and the stink of burning flesh continued to rise from the damsel's hands, and the runes binding the ironwork burned ever brighter. At last there came a sound like the cracking of ice, and the ironwork broke, falling away from Elisabet's head and dropping to the ground, the skin of Anara's palms still attached.

Anara fell backwards in a swoon, her hands blistered and raw as if she had grasped a red-hot poker from the coals. Reolus lowered her gently to the ground, and Calard looked down into Elisabet's face.

She was looking up at him with a smile that made his blood run cold, and as he stared into her eyes, they turned as black as night, as if ink had been dropped into her irises and was spreading rapidly to cover the entire surface of her orbs.

Calard released her, recoiling as if he had suddenly found himself embracing a cadaver.

'You're not Elisabet...' he groaned.

'No, I'm not,' said the thing that wore Elisabet's body. Then it began to speak in a tongue that made Calard's stomach clench in horror, and maddening, horned shadows rose up around him. He heard malignant whispering in his ears, and his sword dropped from numb fingers.

Then he felt insubstantial talons pierce his flesh and he gasped in agony and fell to his knees.

CHAPTER TWELVE

THE INTERIOR OF the despoiled chapel was filled with wood smoke and the smells of sweat and cooking meat, and the sounds of drunken revelry rose to the rafters. Warriors shouted, clinked drinking horns and laughed as a young skald recounted the gore-soaked adventures of Knut the Bloody, a Skaeling berserker who had fought alongside the ever-chosen Asavar Kul.

This revered hero had taken part in the sacking of the Kislevite city of Praag two hundred years earlier, before, glutted with blood, he ventured northward, journeying into the heart of the god-touched lands there where dreams and nightmares become reality. The Skaelings were enjoying the tale, roaring their approval as the skald re-enacted a battle fought between Knut and a mighty bloodthirster of Kharnath that ended with him breaking the back of the monster over his knee, and the powers that be granting him daemonhood and eternal life as a reward for his tenacity.

In one corner of the chapel a fight was underway. More warriors were sent sprawling and tables overflowing with food and drink were sent smashing to the stone floor as a massive, bearded huskarl laid around him in a drunken fury. He had already sent one man crashing through a stained glass window, an axe buried in his back, and half a dozen others were strewn around him, bloody and broken. Another was felled, bellowing as the huskarl shattered his forearm with a hammer-blow of his fist.

Styrbjorn reclined in his throne atop the stepped dais at the end of the chapel, only half listening to the ranting Chaos dwarf, Zumarah, who was speaking angrily, standing one step from the top of the dais, spitting his words out as he addressed the Skaeling jarl.

'...promised me slaves, manling,' the dwarf was saying. 'And here we sit on this Hashut-forsaken rock, doing nothing!'

'Patience, Zumarah,' said Styrbjorn, waving away the words of the infuriated dwarf. 'Once the witch bears my son, then we shall take the fight back to the southlanders.'

'You speak lies and poison, manling,' said Zumarah, placing a foot on the top of the dais. Styrbjorn's warhounds were instantly on their feet, baring their teeth and snarling at the dwarf. Unfazed, the dwarf merely snarled back at them, though he did not move any closer to the Skaeling jarl. Styrbjorn barked a command, and his warhounds dropped to their haunches, tails between their legs, though their unblinking eyes remained fixed on Zumarah.

'Once the bitch spawns the child, you will be taking it back to Skaeling lands, mark my words,' said the dwarf. 'If you do not deliver on your promise to me, I shall take my slaves from amongst your own people, starting with your bitch daughters.'

The shield-maidens Fraygerd and Hrefna, standing to either side of their father's throne, bristled. Hrefna half-drew her sword from her scabbard, her face twisted in anger. The dwarf, standing only half the height of the tall, blonde warrior woman but easily three times her weight, snarled and reached for the double-headed axe strapped to his back.

'Let me cut his heart from his chest and offer it to mighty Kharnath, father,' spoke Hrefna.

Styrbjorn held up a hand to forestall any violence, and cast an amused glance at the dwarf.

'It's a foolish individual who insults a Skaeling woman, Zumarah,' he said. 'Their fury is far deadlier than any man's.'

'And it's a dead man who thinks he can swindle a dawi, manling,' snarled the dwarf.

Bjarki was seated cross-legged at Styrbjorn's feet, head down as he listened to the conversations occurring around him, and he smiled to himself. In truth, he agreed with the dwarf's sentiment; Styrbjorn was growing soft. He had believed that the Skaeling jarl would stay on in Bretonnia after the great victory at the crow fields, carving a swathe of destruction across the length and breadth of his hated birth land, and he had longed to be a part of the slaughter of the people who had turned their back on him. Long had he dreamed of returning to his father's estate and killing everyone there. He had not expected the jarl to flee like a frightened child to this island sanctuary to see his son birthed in solace, stalling Bjarki's blood-dreams of vengeance.

'Your son should be born surrounded by death!' Bjarki had argued with Styrbjorn the day after the victory. 'The first sounds he hears should be the din of battle; the screams of the dying, the roar of the victor, the clash of steel and the rending of flesh!'

Styrbjorn had grabbed him around the throat, his face flushing in anger and his eyes glinting with the gods' favour.

'Who is jarl here? Remember your place, little bear.'

Styrbjorn had shoved him away, and Bjarki's hand had leaped to the welts around his throat. He was not used to such treatment. As wiry and tautly muscled as he was, he was still slight of frame and puny next to the hulking Skaelings – and Styrbjorn was larger even than any of his chosen huskarls – but few would dare incur the wrath of the gods by laying a hand upon one of their chosen representatives.

Before he could snarl a curse, Styrbjorn had levelled one meaty finger at him.

'Don't go against me in this, Bjarki,' the jarl had warned in a dangerous voice. 'You are like a son to me, but I will not risk my blood-son by staying here in this foreign land.'

Bjarki knew that many of the Skaeling warriors were unhappy with the decision to leave the southlander's lands, and he had heard whispers of malcontent amongst the chieftains that had sworn themselves to Styrbjorn. In truth, if he did announce that he was sailing back to Norsca after the birth of the daemon-child, the seer would not be at all surprised if a leadership challenge arose, and that Styrbjorn was forced to fight to maintain the dominance he had held these past decades.

Bjarki came back to the present, his head snapping up as he felt the sundering of the rune-magic binding the witch, Haegtesse.

'The witch!' he snarled, leaping to his feet, interrupting the bickering between the dwarf and the Skaelings. 'She's free!'

Styrbjorn rose instantly from his throne, snatching up the twin axes, Garmr and Gormr.

'With me!' he roared deafeningly, his god-touched voice booming through the chapel. All activity ceased instantly, the young skald freezing mid-sentence, and giving pause to the bearded huskarl, who was holding another man by the scruff of the neck, fist poised to cave in his face.

Then the jarl was racing through the chapel, smashing men out of his way in his hurry, warhounds at his heels, and he angled towards a side-door leading out to the rear. Bjarki darted forward in the wake of his jarl, flanked by Styrbjorn's daughters, and every warrior present followed a second later, swords and axes bared.

IT FELT LIKE blades of ice were being driven into his flesh, and Calard gasped in agony as they pushed towards his heart. He'd never felt such pain in his life, and his eyes were wide as he tried to focus on the face of the shadow-creature before him.

It was no more solid than a firelight shadow, and he could see straight through it, though the impression of a blank, featureless face could be vaguely discerned. It turned its head on the side and leant in close to him, staring intently at him as if intrigued by the pain it was inflicting. He groaned in excruciating torment as the shadow's talons encircled his heart. He knew that it could kill him at any moment; all it had to do was clench its hand and his heart would burst like an over-ripe melon under a hammer.

The nightmarish shade seemed to be savouring his torture; he saw its outline shudder as if in the throes of pleasure as it fed upon his pain, and heard its whispering hisses increase in excitement. He stared in horror as it lifted its other hand towards his face, needle-like talons of black smoke poised to ram into his brain. He could do nothing against it, paralysed in agony and terror.

The creature's hissing stopped abruptly and it swung its strangely ovoid, blank face away from Calard, as if it had heard a sound. Reolus's blade, gleaming like quicksilver, sliced through its insubstantial cranium, and it emitted a horrible, wailing screech as its head came apart.

Calard gasped and fell forward as the shade pulled its talons from his flesh, its long limbs contorting as it reeled in agony. Its shadowy head was in two halves, each hanging loose from its shoulders, and for a second Calard thought he was going insane, for a second image flickered before his eyes, superimposed upon the outline of the shade.

It was a skinless, horrific thing and it writhed in agony as a substance like oily smoke rose from its split head. It had no eyes or nose, just a lipless mouth filled with tiny, serrated teeth. The daemon emitted a chattering wail that might have been pain, and thrashed around as if in the midst of a fit. Calard saw the image for only a fraction of a second before the daemon was once more as insubstantial as a shadow, but he knew that he had glimpsed the creature's true form.

Then it was gone, dissipating into smoke, leaving behind it a stench akin to rotting, foetid meat. Dimly, Calard heard the frantic cries of his fellow knights, and Bertelis gasped in pain.

Calard's chest was numb where the daemon's talons had pushed through his flesh but feeling had returned to his fingers and he swept up his fallen sword as he leaped to his feet. Shadows danced all around, and he saw one of them rising up between him and Bertelis, who was trying to keep it at bay with sweeps of his sword as he backed away. Calard, looking through the shadowy daemon, could see his brother's face contorted in horror.

The daemon glided forwards and he saw Bertelis's sword pass clear through its body. It had no visible effect on the shade, which loomed over him with taloned arms raised high, ready to plunge them down into his body. Calard cried out and threw himself forward, and he slashed the blade of Garamont through the insubstantial creature's body.

Its whispers turned into wails and it swung towards him, oily smoke coiling from its wound. It lashed out with one long, taloned arm, and again Calard saw it as it truly was for a fraction of second. The exposed muscles of its skinless arm glistened wetly, and sharp, curving bone protruded six inches from the bloody flesh of its fingertips. Calard leapt back from its strike and struck with his blade, which was gleaming with silver light. He severed the daemon's arm at the elbow and it wailed again. He cleaved his sword through its neck with his return strike. It felt like he struck nothing more solid than air, but the daemon dissipated into the night, leaving a rancid stink behind it.

Two of Laudethaire's Parravonians were down, twitching and writhing, and Calard saw a third slump to the ground as one of the shadow daemons plunged its talons into his head. He saw the man twitching horribly, blood running from his nose and his tongue lolling from the side of his mouth. His eyes rolled back in his head, and he went into violent convulsions, arms and legs rigid and his back arching unnaturally.

Horrifyingly, the dying man seemed to attract the interest of the daemons, which bent over him, their heads lowered so that they were only an inch from the faces of the convulsing man, as if utterly fascinated by the spectacle, forgetting everything else that was going on around them. Several of the daemons crowded around each dying man, completely absorbed as they thrashed out their last moments of life.

Laudethaire slashed furiously with his own blade, and two of the shadows disappeared into coiling smoke. Calard saw Maloric backing away from another pair of the daemons that materialised out of nowhere, his face pale as his sword passed harmlessly through them. Bertelis swore as he slashed his own blade through the head of another creature, to no effect.

'Stay with me,' said Calard, keeping the creatures at bay with the ancestral sword of Garamont, which was said to have been blessed by the Lady of the Lake. He had always thought that was just a story, but now he believed it. The shadow-wraiths were wary of the glittering blade, and they kept their distance now, chattering and whispering.

Now with some space around him, Calard cast his gaze around the circle.

Anara was picking herself up from the ground, leaning upon her white staff, her eyes locked onto the... *thing* resembling Elisabet. Calard cried out as a trio of shadows darted towards his sister, but he needn't have bothered. As they descended on her, ethereal claws raised, the damsel whispered a word and slammed the butt of her staff into the ground. A sphere of light flashed into existence, completely enclosing her, blinding and crackling with power. Two of the daemons were caught in the blast, and they were instantly rendered to smoke. The third recoiled away, only to be cut in half by a flick of Reolus's gleaming sword, which he was wielding in two hands with consummate skill.

The grail knight, his eyes blazing with fey power, was closing on the witch, who was cackling maniacally. From over her shoulders and under her outstretched arms dozens of shadow-wraiths were flying forwards at the holy paladin, hurling themselves into his path as the witch backed away towards the cliff edge.

Reolus hacked his blade around him in a blinding dance as he stepped forwards, his body angled as if he was battling against a gale. Scores of shadow daemons flew against him, intangible clawed hands reaching to impale him but he carved through them, in constant motion, slicing his way towards the witch.

Calard gasped as he felt frozen knife talons plunge into his leg, and the entire limb went numb. Bertelis cried out, but there was nothing he could do against the revenants, and Calard knew that he would have died then and there had it not been for Laudethaire, who sliced his own gleaming blade through the back of the shade looming up before him. It screamed in torment as its body dissipated into the air.

With a nod of thanks, Calard spun around, his blade leaving a trailing arc of light through the air as he forced another shade back. He saw Maloric surrounded, and the Sangasse nobleman lifted his shield before him as one of the phantoms struck at him. It was a futile gesture, for its taloned arm merely passed through it, and Maloric cried out.

For a moment, Calard's rival looked straight at him, looking *through* his attacker, and Calard saw the desperation in the knight's eyes. Calard knew that Maloric was too proud to cry for help from the likes of him, and as a silent communication passed between the two rivals, he saw the flare of hatred in the Sangasse noble's eyes.

He doesn't expect me to go to his aid, Calard realised, and again he felt a contradiction of emotions: mild satisfaction in knowing that Maloric was about to die; a twinge of dishonour that the Sangasse expected him to do nothing.

Another revenant rose up behind Maloric. The Sangasse earl did not register this new threat, and he was unprepared as the shade readied to plunge its knife-like claws into his head.

Everything seemed to be happening in slow motion. Dimly, he heard Norse war cries and realised that they had been discovered. They would be overrun in moments, but that didn't seem to matter at this instant. Calard's entire world shrunk; all he saw was his mortal enemy about to be cut down.

Then everything was moving quickly again.

Calard roared a cry of warning and leapt forwards. His blade struck one of the daemons standing in his path, which dispersed into amorphous, stinking smoke, its true form flashing before his eyes momentarily. Maloric, perhaps thinking that Calard was going to strike him down next, lifted his shield protectively and drew his sword back, ready to plunge it into Calard's neck, unaware of the danger behind him.

The shade rearing up behind Maloric struck, and Calard threw himself forwards to intervene. Even as insubstantial, shadow-talons stabbed down towards the Sangasse earl's helmet, Calard thrust his gleaming sword over Maloric's shoulder, impaling the daemon.

For a second he saw its blind, skinless face spitted on his sword tip before it disappeared.

Maloric's sword was just inches from Calard's throat, his eyes were wide in shock. Calard swung away from him to engage the other darting shadows surrounding them both.

Laudethaire lifted a curving, silver horn to his lips and blasted a long note upon it, before turning to face the onslaught of Norscans closing in on them. More of his companions had been overwhelmed now, for their weapons were useless against the daemons. Clusters of the shadowy daemons still lingered over their twitching bodies, heads lowered over them in fascination, chittering excitedly.

Reolus was continuing to battle against a veritable flood of daemons. They had completely surrounded him, stabbing and slashing. It was impossible to discern how many of them there were, for their forms blurred together into one, nightmarish twisting fury, spinning around the grail knight and almost completely obscuring him from sight.

Calard dragged his gaze away as again he heard the roar of enemies made of flesh and blood. A tide of Norscans was racing towards them, axes and spears raised. At their fore was a massive beast of a man whom he recognised as their war leader, a seven foot tall giant with grey-streaked hair and beard. He wielded an axe in each hand and his face was a mask of rage.

A pair of giant warhounds raced out in front, outpacing their master as they headed directly for Calard, but the warlord barked a command, pointing towards the witch. They changed direction instantly, heading towards the heavily pregnant noblewoman, who was still backing away towards the edge of the headland.

Laudethaire blew another note on his silver horn, and cutting through the shadowy body of another daemon, he swung to face the onslaught of Norscans.

Anara was shouting words that Calard could not understand. He realised that she had been incanting for some time, and as she reached a crescendo she slammed her staff into the ground again. A blast of light and wind radiated out around her, exploding outwards with colossal force.

Calard was thrown to the ground, half blinded, but as he blinked his eyes and struggled to his knees, he saw that the last of the daemons were gone.

The witch too seemed to have been stunned by the sheer power that Anara had unleashed, but she recovered quickly. Calard felt sick to the pit of his stomach as he saw the features of his Elisabet twisted by hatred and evil as she stared at Anara, and he felt the witch gathering her power.

Lightning crackled in her black eyes, but before she had a chance to unleash it, one of the giant Norscan warhounds struck her, bowling her over and jaws clamping around one of her arms. There was the sickening sound of bones crunching as the beast bit down hard, and the witch screamed in agony, her concentration shattered. The second hound leaped on her, biting into her thigh and shaking its head from side to side, throwing her to the ground like a rag doll.

Then the Norscans were upon them. The giant enemy war leader claimed the first kill, cleaving his axe through the body of one of the Parravonians, the huge weapon shearing through plate armour, flesh, ribs and spinal column, and blood splattered everyone nearby. The knight fell, hacked completely in two through the chest.

An axe arced for Calard's head, and he managed to turn it aside with a frantic swipe of his blade, though the force of the blow jarred his arm. A spear-tip screeched a line across his helmet, and he lashed out with his sword blindly. A solid boot slammed into his chest, knocking him backwards to the ground.

A wild-haired Norscan leapt on his chest, straddling him. This one was not nearly as large as the others, and his hair and eyes were dark where the others were generally flaxen-haired and pale-eyed. Still, for all that he seemed possibly even more savage than his comrades, with a crazed look in his eyes that was somehow akin to the unnatural light he sometimes saw in Anara's eye, and he wondered if this could be some feral Norscan sorcerer or priest. His tautly muscled chest was covered in tattoos, and he wore thick, matted furs over his shoulders. Calard's eyes focused on the serpentine dagger the Norscan lifted up in both hands, blade angled downwards, ready to be plunged into his neck. He fought him, struggling to throw the manic Norscan off him, but to no avail.

A shield smashed into the Norscan's face, breaking his nose and knocking him off Calard's chest, and Bertelis stepped in front of his brother, defending him as he scrambled back to his feet.

Another of the Parravonians was hacked down by the Norse warlord, split from crown to sternum, and another had his head shorn from his shoulders by the thick-bladed sword of a black-armoured bear of a man who looked incredibly drunk.

The enraged gaze of the warlord was fixed behind the knights desperately forming a defensive circle against the Norscans surrounding them, and Calard risked a glance behind him to see what was happening. Only feet from the edge of the headland, he saw Reolus kick one of the warhounds away from Elisabet. The animal scrabbled frantically, but went over the edge, yelping as it fell a hundred feet onto the rocks below. The grail knight impaled the other beast with a downward strike of his blade, plunging it down with both hands like a huge dagger. The sword was driven through the warhound's thickly muscled neck, pinning it to the ground as it died, thrashing and snarling, hot blood pooling beneath it.

Calard heard the Norse chieftain roar in fury as he launched himself towards the grail knight, barging his own warriors out of the way in his haste.

The witch-Elisabet, one hand clutching her distended belly, was trying to regain her feet. One arm was a floppy, blood-smeared ruin, but there was still power in her, and she inhaled sharply, electricity crackling in her eyes.

Again Laudethaire blew a note on his silver horn, and the air behind the witch was suddenly filled with beating wings and flailing hooves as a white, equine shape soared up from the edge of the cliff, a knight in its saddle. The witch spun around and extended one hand towards the pegasus, and arcs of contorting energy leapt from her fingertips to strike the beast in the chest.

It screamed as its flesh withered and atrophied beneath the coruscating dark energy, as if all the moisture in its body was suddenly drawn out. It muscles shrivelled and its skin shrank. In a heartbeat its ribs were protruding like those of a month old corpse, and its head was little more than a skull covered in a taut layer of dried skin, shrivelled eyes lolling in empty sockets.

Bones snapped like dry twigs, unable to hold the pegasus's own bodyweight, and the noble beast toppled out of the air as its wings snapped with audible cracks. It hit the ground and all four legs were instantly broken. Desiccated, but somehow still alive, the pegasus toppled backwards over the cliff's edge, taking its rider with it.

The witch spun back towards Anara, but the damsel thrust the point of her staff forward, striking her squarely between the eyes. The blow felled the witch instantly, and she slumped to the ground, unconscious.

More pegasus rose up from over the edge of the headland, and they swooped down into the frantic melee. They buffeted the Norscans with their powerful wings, breaking arms and knocking men back, their hooves caving in skulls. Only one of the beasts had a rider in the saddle, and that knight drove his lance through the body of a Norscan, impaling him.

'Mount! Mount!' shouted Laudethaire, leaping into the saddle of his own steed, which had cleared a space around its master. A hurled spear struck him in the shoulder, driving up underneath his pauldron and embedding deep in his body, and he rocked backwards, gasping in agony.

Bertelis took a heavy blow on his shield that bent it out of shape, though his lightning riposte slashed open his attacker's throat, and blood fountained from the fatal wound. He spun, and grabbing the saddle horn of a pegasus, he hauled himself up.

There was a rearing pegasus before Calard, keeping the Norscan temporarily at bay with its flashing hooves.

'What about Reolus and Anara?' shouted Calard, trying to see through the press of pegasus and men.

'They're fine,' shouted Laudethaire, wrenching the spear from his shoulder and hurling it away from him. 'Get in the saddle, Garamont!'

Calard stepped into the stirrups and was up in the saddle in an instant. A blade arced towards him and he met it with a blow of his own, the sound of steel on steel ringing out loudly. He hacked the blade down as the pegasus reared and flapped its wings, carving through a Norscan's helmet and skull.

Guiding his steed with his knees, Calard turned around, casting a wary eye around him.

A pegasus nearby went down, an axe carving its legs from beneath it, splashing its pristine white body with blood, and another knight was killed, dragged from the saddle by a frenzied warrior woman and hacked apart. The Norse had encircled them now; the brief respite that they had enjoyed with the arrival of the pegasus was now lost.

Laudethaire was already airborne, and the other pegasus were eager to fly, following his lead.

Another of the noble creatures was killed, an axe shattering its chest and it spilt its rider over its head as it ploughed into the ground, rolling on top of the knight and crushing the life from him.

Calard slashed down at a Norscan straining to grab his reins. He sliced the fingers from the marauder's hand, and narrowly avoided being struck from the saddle by a wildly aimed axe-strike.

'Go! Go!' he urged, kicking the pegasus hard, and it broke into a gallop, bowling Norscans out of the way, and then he was in the air. A spear sliced past his head, and he saw another of the pegasus fall screaming as it was struck by a hurled axe, the heavy weapon spinning end over end before breaking the beast's right wing.

As he rose into the air, he glanced around towards the headland. He saw Anara in the saddle of a pegasus, and Reolus climbing into the saddle of another, cradling the unconscious form of the witch that wore Elisabet's form.

Calard saw the enemy warlord launch himself towards Reolus, roaring in outrage. Anara was in his way, and her pegasus reared as the Norscan bore down on her, silver-shod hooves flashing as it rose into the air. The Norscan came on, undaunted by the power in the beast's limbs, and he grabbed it by its bridle, dragging it back down to earth in an inhuman display of strength. Even as he pulled the pegasus off balance, he slammed his axe into its neck, and blood sprayed.

Reolus's pegasus could not possibly carry three people, and Calard tugged frantically on the reins, dragging his steed's head around towards his sister. She had rolled clear of her dying mount, and was facing the towering Norscan looming before her.

Calard guided his pegasus down towards the warlord from behind, and his blade sliced through the air as they dipped low.

The Norscan sensed the attack coming and hurled himself to the side, throwing himself into a roll, avoiding Calard's blade by scant inches. The pegasus hit the ground running, and Calard reached towards Anara with one hand. They gripped each other's forearms, and the damsel swung up behind him. The powerful steed continued to gallop for a few steps before it leaped out over the edge of the cliff, and they soared into the updraft.

Calard glanced over his shoulder and saw Reolus, bearing the unconscious and pregnant body of Elisabet, launch into the air behind them. The massive Norscan chieftain standing on the cliff's edge roared in outrage, eyes blazing in fury.

Turning, Calard leant forward in the saddle and patted his pegasus mount on the neck.

BJARKI MOVED TO stand alongside Styrbjorn, wiping the blood of his broken nose from his face. The jarl stared in fury at the white shapes of the pegasus flying into the distance, heading eastward.

'I want her back, Bjarki,' Styrbjorn said. He looked down at the seer, his eyes blazing with the fire of the gods. 'If it means killing every single one of these southlander whoresons, I want her back.'

Bjarki smiled and licked his sharpened teeth in anticipation.

CHAPTER THIRTEEN

INSIDE THE WALLS of Castle Lyonesse, in the shadow of the looming keep, Chlod shivered and stood as straight as his hunched back allowed. The yeoman warden stalked up and down the ranks of peasants, scowling as he barked orders at them. Chlod had been one of the lucky ones – only a tiny fraction of the population that inhabited the township on the mainland had been allowed to make the crossing and take shelter within the castle walls.

The Norscans had appeared on the horizon at dawn and panic had spread like lice through a flophouse. The sails of countless longships could be seen in the distance, spread as far as the eye could see. Peasants in their tens of thousands had streamed to the docklands, desperate to board one of the barges that ferried between the town and the island fortress of the duke, just offshore.

In times of peace, those barges ran back and forth from the duke's castle half a dozen times a day, loaded with produce, servants and taxes. The ferry-masters had been serving their duke in such a manner for countless generations, and they knew their craft well. Only in the most turbulent of seas were they reluctant to make the crossing.

A growing, panicked mob of peasants had raced to the docks, fighting each other in desperation to get aboard the flat-bottomed vessels, but they had been met by a garrison of men-at-arms, who were determined not to let them pass. Scores were killed in the ensuing ruckus, but the crowds had been held at bay until a contingent of knights had arrived. The duke's knights had ridden into the crowd, killing scores before the remainder had scattered.

Only those who were judged able to fight had been allowed to make the crossing, for there was a finite amount of space within the castle walls; there was no hope of it providing shelter for everyone. Those deemed unable to aid in the defence of the castle – including women, children, the elderly and the infirm – had been advised by the duke's men-at-arms to abandon their homes and strike westward, to seek shelter in the villages a day's ride away. No escort was offered – every able man was going to be needed in the forthcoming siege.

One loudmouth peasant merchant, fat with self-righteousness, had berated the men-at-arms, shouting that it was the duke's duty to protect those who laboured in his service, those who paid him taxes. Chlod had backed away from the merchant, as had all the other peasants nearby, knowing what was to come. The obese man had been clubbed to the ground by the soldiers, leaving him a broken, bloody mess in the mud. No one else had voiced their displeasure after that. They knew better. They understood and accepted their lot in life, and did not voice such complaints; or at least not within earshot of the men-at-arms.

Chlod had heard a rumour that the famous knight Laudethaire, Beloved of Parravon, had conducted a daring raid against the Norse two nights ago and rescued a beautiful princess from the clutches of the barbarians. He had also heard that the story was being spread by individuals in the pay of the Parravonian knight, and while some might had said that was mere slander, Chlod could well believe it was true.

The story had sounded romantic and heroic in its increasingly exaggerated retellings the night before, but now that the consequences of it were becoming clear, Chlod dearly wished that the noblewoman had been left where she was. The nobility had never done anything for him but make his life a constant misery; it would be just his luck to die now because of one upper-class wench. All those who had not been allowed to seek shelter within the walls of Castle Lyonesse had probably been condemned to death – some ten thousand peasants, all told. He found it morbidly amusing, and not at all surprising, that the nobility would happily sacrifice so many for the life of one of their own.

Nevertheless, Chlod happily admitted to being a selfish individual, and he was just pleased that he had managed to be amongst those deemed sturdy enough to help in the defence of Castle Lyonesse. In truth, he had no desire to fight – he had been engaged in one of the noble's wars before, in Bordeleaux, and frankly it had scared the stuffing out of him – but he reckoned that he was safer within these stout walls than outside them.

His judgement had proven sound. Only hours after the longships had been sighted, the Norse had surrounded the island fortress, and hundreds of their ships had been beached on the mainland. From atop the walls, the Bretonnians had watched impotently as the township on the mainland was sacked. The ash from the burning town still filled the air, falling from the sky like a dark mimicry of snowflakes. They had watched as enemy outriders had galloped westward. Chlod expected few of the peasants that had abandoned the town would survive.

Several of the Norse ships had been sunk as the immense trebuchets atop the castle tower had loosed, giant counterweights propelling the arms of the war machines at great speed. Chunks of rock were hurled high into the air, and while most fell short, splashing down into the ocean, some of the longships had ventured within range and were smashed to tinder. The Bretonnians had cheered as the waters around these wrecks had turned into a bloody, churning froth as the Norscans were devoured by the sharks following in the wake of the ships, but the mood had soon turned sombre once more as the sheer scale of the Norscan force became apparent.

Just outside the range of the trebuchets, the Norscans formed an arcing blockade around the island fastness. Longships were lashed together, forming an impenetrable wall, and hundreds upon hundreds more were beached on the mainland. A few of the ships were unlike the others – large hulks with giant cages built into their decks, though what was held in those holds Chlod could not discern. Still, the trumpeting that issued from them as hundreds of Norscans strained to drag them up the beach had threatened to make his bowels loosen.

Barbarians swarmed through the burning streets of the town, and Chlod had seen thousands of them march off to the north and south. He had hoped that perhaps they were heading off to find easier pickings elsewhere, but his hopes were dashed when, hours later, the enemy began to return with freshly felled lumber. For ladders, battering rams and such, most likely.

All through the day the enemy had worked, and now that it was approaching dusk it seemed that they were readying themselves for their first attack against the castle. Chlod shivered again. He had hoped to have slunk off and found a place to hide by now, but no such opportunity had as yet presented itself. Patience, he thought to himself. In the confusion of battle it should be easy to disappear.

In truth, Chlod didn't expect there to be any such need, however. The walls of the castle were huge – indeed the fortress was the grandest structure that he had ever seen – he could not conceive of how the enemy could possibly tackle it.

Chlod was snapped out of his reverie as he heard the blare of a thousand horns sound.

'Right, this is it then, you scum!' shouted the yeoman warden who had been given the job of getting Chlod and the other untrained peasants into a semblance of a fighting force. The men around him, farmers, shopkeepers and merchants in the main, looked scared, holding their simple spears awkwardly. None of them had been given shields or armour. Few of them had ever held a weapon in their lives.

'Don't even think about making a run for it,' snarled the yeoman. 'I've passed the word amongst the men-at-arms that they are to kill anyone who does not stand and fight. Now get moving!'

Men-at-arms wearing white tabards with a red lion's head on their chests flanked the new recruits, and they jabbed them forward with their halberds. Chlod found himself herded along with the rest of the group he had been assigned to, passing through the streets inside the castle toward the eastern walls.

At the bottom of the walls he paused, squinting upwards. The stairway up the inside of the wall was steep and high, and there was no banister to stop anyone from falling if they made a misstep. He swallowed thickly.

'What's the matter with you?' barked one of the men-at-arms, giving Chlod a shove.

'Afraid of heights,' said Chlod.

The man-at-arms snorted, and cuffed him hard over the back of his head, making his teeth rattle.

'Get moving,' said the man, and Chlod begin the ascent, pressing himself hard up against the wall, keeping as far from the edge of the stairs as possible.

Finally, sweating and shaking, he reached the top of the towering wall. It was colder here, for there was no protection from the biting winds. Thousands of bowmen were already stood upon the walls, with bundles of arrows stacked against the battlements. Chlod pushed past them to look through the crenulations. What he saw took his breath away.

Night was falling rapidly, but the enemy could be clearly seen thanks to the fires still raging through the township on the mainland. More than a thousand longships, each one brimming with Norscans, were being rowed at speed towards the island.

Countless drums began to beat then, both from the land, the approaching ships and from aboard all the longships surrounding the castle, and tens of thousands of voices rose in a blood-curdling roar.

The siege of Lyonesse was about to begin.

Calard stood alongside Bertelis and the Empire ambassador, Dieter Weschler, as they surveyed the approaching Norscans from the top of the eastern gatehouse. Calard's cousins, Baldemund, Huebald and Tassilo stood nearby. The knights of Bastonne were all fully armoured in plate and chain, over which they wore their heraldic tabards and cloaks. They had the visors of their helmets raised, and each stood with their hands resting upon the pommel of their swords.

Dieter, in contrast, was dressed in the fashion of the Empire, which was frankly bizarre to the eyes of the Bretonnians. He wore a black lacquered breastplate, with a gold symbol of a twin-tailed comet upon it, the symbol of the barbarian hero the citizens of the Empire worshipped as their patron god. He wore knee high riding boots, bright blue tights and an outrageously prominent codpiece. The sleeves of his silk tunic were puffy and slashed, and extravagant dyed red feathers – griffon feathers he said – bobbed from the top of his black sallet helmet.

However, it was the Empire nobleman's weapons that drew the most disapproval from the Bretonnians. He wore a sheathed sabre – lighter and more flimsy than any Bretonnian sword – and had a pair of pistols holstered at his sides. Calard had seen Dieter use those weapons before, and though no Bretonnian noble would ever use a missile weapon anywhere outside of the hunt, he respected their killing power. Alone of the men gathered atop the gatehouse, Dieter was not paying attention to the Norse longships being rowed towards them. His whole focus was upon the weapon held reverently in his hands, a multi-barrelled handgun. He was oblivious to the looks of distaste of the knights around him as he lovingly stroked it.

'This,' said Dieter, speaking the Bretonnian tongue with a strong, harsh accent, 'is von Meinkopt's Whirling Cavalcade of Death.'

'That's nice,' said Bertelis mildly.

'Yes, she is beautiful, is she not?' said Dieter, spinning the barrels of the weapon. 'The repeater handgun – the epitome of superior Empire technology.'

Calard grunted, paying little attention. The Norse ships were almost within range of the trebuchets.

'You know that the engineers of Nuln have devised a carriageless horse?' continued Dieter. 'A mechanical, equine steed superior in every regard to a horse of flesh and blood. A marvel.'

That got Calard's attention, and he turned towards the Empire ambassador with a look of bafflement on his face, unsure if this was some strange joke that did not translate well. He shook his head, and turned back towards the enemy. The air was filled with the reverberation of thousands of drums, echoing in from all directions, making Calard think of the huffing beat of a forge's bellows; or perhaps the breathing and heartbeat of some infernal god.

'This is not a full scale assault,' said Tassilo. 'They will just be testing our strength.'

'Looks like a lot of them to me,' said Huebald.

'What is going on over there?' said Calard, peering past the approaching longships towards the mainland. There was a flurry of activity on a hill overlooking the beachhead claimed by the Norscans. He had already learnt that the Norscan warlord was no unthinking barbarian. The tactics he had used in defeating the army of Lyonesse spoke of a cunning strategist, and he was suspicious of what he was up to now.

'They're building something?' ventured Tassilo.

Dieter pulled out an extendable cylinder with glass at either end, and raised it to one eye. The Bretonnians swapped bemused glances behind his back, not having any idea what the eccentric Imperial envoy was doing.

'They are digging in,' said Dieter, removing the cylinder from his eye and replacing it back in its case without explanation.

'They are what?' said Tassilo.

'They are creating a defensive emplacement. It is common in my homeland. For...for...' Dieter waved his hand, trying to find the right word to use. '*Artillery*,' he said in Reikspiel, though the Bretonnians stared at him blankly. 'War machines. Cannon,' he said, finding no suitable Breton word.

'That's far out of range of our trebuchets,' said Calard, eyeing the distant construction of the emplacement with unease.

As if speaking the word for the giant stone throwers was the signal, the first of the trebuchets nearby fired.

The leather sling attached to the arm of the war machine whipped through the air, flinging the chunk of rock nestled within it spinning high into the sky. The peasants arrayed along the walls below gave a cheer, and a dozen trebuchets fired, hurling their missiles into the darkening sky.

The first rock scythed down through the air, smashing the mast of a longship and plunging through its rear deck, taking a dozen oarsmen with it. The ship instantly floundered, taking on water, and Norscans were sent reeling into the turbulent waters as their vessel began to sink. Great explosions of water marked the place where other rocks had missed their mark, but several more ships were sunk as their hulls were smashed to splinters, and scores of warriors were killed as the sharks cutting through the waters gorged themselves.

Still, the number of ships far outweighed those few that were sunk, and they sliced through the water at impressive speed, their dragon-headed prows smashing aside the timbers and warriors floating in the sea before them. Banks of oars rose and fell with perfect synchronicity as the Norscans heaved at them, pulling the longships swiftly through the ocean.

Several of the longships struck rocks and submerged reefs as they neared the island, ripping great rents in their hulls and dooming the warriors aboard. But for every longship that floundered, either struck by trebuchet fire or fatally damaged by the knife-like reefs below the surface, a score successfully ran the gauntlet.

The first longships ran aground, ploughing at speed into the soft sand that ran along the eastern bank of the island, and Norscans were instantly over the edge, leaping into the knee-deep waters and racing for the walls. Hundreds of arrows were loosed as knights and yeomen spread across the battlements shouted the order to fire. The first wave of Norscans onto the beach were scythed down, but more leaped onto the sand as longship after longship joined the fray.

Scores of hastily constructed ladders were carried up the beach by teams of fur-clad warriors. The air was thick with arrows, and hundreds more Norscans were cut down, but still on they came, mindless of the casualties they were suffering, stamping uncaring over their fallen comrades.

Dieter moved towards the gatehouse battlements, his repeater handgun loaded and clasped in his hands.

'Excuse me,' he said, but the peasant bowmen loosing their shafts through the crenulations did not hear his polite words.

Bertelis slapped a peasant archer across the back of the head as he was reaching for an arrow, and the man, an ugly brute with warts all over his face, mumbled an apology and shuffled aside, moving to a different firing position.

Dieter threw the young Garamont noble a dark look and nodded his thanks to the peasant, before stepping up and taking aim with his handgun.

A moment later there was a deafening boom and acrid smoke billowed from the weapon, which bucked in Dieter's hands violently. There was a clockwork clicking noise and the barrels rotated, and Dieter fired another shot. Again the barrels rotated, and he fired again. Each shot resulted in the death of an enemy, punching through breastplates and skulls with impressive force. The amount of smoke almost completely obscured the Empire ambassador, and Calard coughed. Dieter fired the last two barrels, though Calard doubted he could actually see a target now so thick was the smoke.

Blinking away the tears that the black powder brought to his eyes, Calard moved to the southern battlement of the gatehouse, looking along the long eastern wall.

Many hundreds of bowmen were positioned there, though as the first ladders were slammed against the walls, they moved back to allow the men-at-arms, knights and spear-armed peasants behind them to step forwards.

Polearms and spears pushed at the first ladders and several were knocked backwards, the Norscans already climbing them falling into their comrades swarming towards the walls behind them. Hundreds of arrows were fired from the towers and the gatehouse into the Norscans massing at the base of the walls. Men fell from ladders as arrows thudded into their bodies, though others ignored the shafts protruding from shoulders and necks and pushed on, climbing up towards the battlements.

Boiling oil and pitch was tipped over the edge of the walls, scalding flesh and searing upturned Norscan faces, making eyes run from sockets like melted fat. Still more longships ploughed into the soft sand of the western beach, though Calard saw that this was but a fraction of the Norscan's strength.

More ladders were hefted into position along the western wall below Calard's position on the gatehouse, and he saw the first enemy berserkers reach the battlements. They leapt over the walls, roaring incoherently, swinging axes and swords wildly.

Polearms were brought crashing down onto the horned helmets of some, killing them instantly. Spears stabbed others, but the Norscans appeared not to care about the wounds they took, and began laying about them with furious abandon. He saw a massive, near naked savage with three arrows protruding from his tattooed flesh take a sword thrust to the chest as he scrambled over the battlements, but even that didn't stop him. With foam spilling from his mouth, he hacked the head from a knight's shoulders, sending it flying down to the ground inside the castle walls, far below.

More Norscans pushed onto the wall, spilling into the gap formed by this berserk fiend, and Calard instantly saw the danger.

'With me!' he roared, drawing his sword and throwing himself down the stairs towards the breach.

A polearm slammed down onto one of the berserker's shoulders, making his arm go limp, but still he would not fall. He hacked his axe into the neck of one peasant, and kicked another off the wall. Calard barged his way through the men-at-arms and archers, running along the wall towards the immense Norscan, who he realised must have been over six and a half feet tall.

'For Bastonne!' Calard shouted.

Hearıng his cry, the Norscan spun around towards him, swinging his axe in a murderous arc. Calard ducked beneath the blow and rammed his sword up into the marauder's belly. Blood burst from the shocking wound, and his guts flopped out onto the stonework, accompanied by a repellent stink. The Norscan dropped his axe, bellowing in fury and pain, but still he did not die. He grabbed Calard around the neck and squeezed, and the squeal of metal being forced out of shape sounded sharply.

A sword hacked into the berserker's neck and he finally fell. Calard gasped, and nodding his thanks to his brother Bertelis, he ripped his sword free of the Norscan's gut. Other knights had also seen the breach, and had raced forwards from the other side, and the last of the Norscans that had made it over the wall were cut down.

He saw a pair of peasants struggling to push a ladder back away from the wall, and cursed their stupidity.

'Slide them to the side!' he shouted. The peasants stared at him stupidly, and he cursed again. Sheathing the blood-smeared blade of Garamont, Calard grabbed a broad-bladed polearm from the dead hands of a man-at-arms. The weapon had a vicious hook on the backside of the blade, normally used to drag knights from the saddle, and Calard hooked this around the top of the ladder.

'Help me!' he ordered, and a pair of peasants leaped forward to lend him their strength. Together, they dragged the ladder to the side. Just as a snarling Norscan appeared at the top of it, the ladder began to fall. The warrior leaped for the wall, grabbing it with one hand, but a mace pulverised his skull and he fell without a sound.

The falling ladder gained momentum as it tipped, striking another some yards away and knocking it sideward. Three ladders in all were sent smashing to the ground, taking scores of Norscans falling to their deaths.

The battle raged on for an hour, and Calard's sword arm felt like a leaden weight by the time he heard the Norscans sounding the retreat.

Thousands of the enemy had been slain, the dead littering the ground. Teams of peasants moved along the walls, clearing them of the dead. They killed any wounded Norscans they came across, though these were surprisingly few – the enemy tended to fight on until they were killed, pushing through the pain of horrendous injuries and forcing the Bretonnians to finish them with killing blows. The corpses of the Norscans were thrown unceremoniously over the walls. The Bretonnian peasants who had been killed in the first attack too were hefted over the walls.

The bodies of the knights who had fallen in the battle were carried reverently from the battlements and borne to the square down by the protected Lyonesse harbour. There they were gently placed upon pyres, their arms crossed over their chests. They were all fully armoured, and their shields were placed at their feet. They were cleaned of blood and gore as best they could, so that they looked like they were merely lying in repose. Those knights who had suffered particularly horrendous wounds were covered with their cloaks.

The entire castle was silent as the pyres were lit.

'This is just the beginning,' said Bertelis as the knights' bodies were consumed in the roaring fires.

Calard knew that it was going to get much worse.

CHAPTER FOURTEEN

WEARY AND SORE and still wearing his full battle gear, Calard knocked on the heavy oak door. The hallway was dark, lit only by flaming sconces set into alcoves every five yards. An icy wind blew in through the arched windows facing out to sea, making the flames flicker and dance, sending shadows cavorting madly across the stone walls.

The door was opened by a grim faced steward, who motioned for silence and ushered Calard inside. The murmur of voices involved in deep discussion came from within.

He stepped inside and the door was silently closed behind him. It was much warmer in here, with a pair of fireplaces on opposite walls burning fiercely. This was the Duke of Lyonesse's personal study, and Calard was overawed to be stood within it.

The ceiling was high, and paintings of the past dukes of Lyonesse lined the east and west walls. Some were standing in heroic poses, one foot placed upon the body of a vanquished foe, or upon a rocky outcrop and gazing into the distance. Others were riding mighty, rearing destriers, or doing battle with monstrous foes. All were suitably dramatic and incredibly lifelike. The dukes in the older portraits wore archaic styled armour and old-fashioned haircuts and clothes. Several elaborate suits of armour stood in-between these paintings.

The south wall was dominated by the stuffed and mounted heads of monsters and beasts hunted and killed by the various dukes. Calard saw the immense, wide-skulled head of a wyvern, the head of a stone troll, the brutish head of an orc warlord with skin so dark as to be almost black. Other creatures he did not even recognise; there was a snarling lizard creature with a bright red frill of skin around its neck, the head of a creature that vaguely resembled an ogre but with skin that looked like stone, and the head of a snarling, hateful looking beast with a thick black mane. That one might have been a manticore, Calard thought. There were the stuffed heads of giant boars and exotic, sabre-fanged cats, and a huge, humanoid skull that was easily ten times the size of a man's. Above them all was the head of a black dragon, its maw spread in a frozen, eternal roar.

A polite cough drew Calard's attention, and he reddened as he turned towards the north wall, realising that he had been gawping with all the slack-mouthed dignity of a peasant. A small gathering of knights stood around the fireplace, the ones that he had heard speaking in hushed tones as he entered, though they had fallen silent now and were looking towards him.

He bowed low to the group, his cheeks burning.

Calard's gaze was instantly drawn to Reolus. The grail knight dominated the room, radiating power and authority, and the others stood around him, their body language showing their deference. His face was broad and ageless, and he nodded almost imperceptibly to Calard in greeting, a slight smile on his lips, and the young lord of Garamont felt instantly more self-assured.

He did not know all of the knights standing with Reolus, though from their heraldry, ornate armour and rich clothing he recognised that they were important nobles of the Lyonessian court. It was likely that they were related to the duke either through birth or marriage. They were all easily a decade older than Calard, and were most likely the duke's most senior knights.

Maloric was there as well, and he flashed a dark look towards Calard, who smirked at him. If anything, Maloric's hatred of him had merely increased after he had saved the Sangasse noble's life on the Norscan occupied isle of Landri.

The Empire ambassador, Dieter Weschler, gave him a clipped bow. Everything about the man was neat, organised and precise, from his carefully waxed and curled moustache to every fold of his puffy sleeves. Even his movements were measured and efficient.

Laudethaire stood with them, affecting a dramatic pose with one hand upon the mantelpiece above the fire and his luxurious blond hair flowing past his shoulders. He eyed Calard with a look of disdain.

'Are you lost?' said Laudethaire, loudly.

Calard, taken aback, did not answer immediately.

'I... I, um,' he stuttered eventually.

'"I, um". Very insightful,' said Laudethaire. 'We are here awaiting the imminent arrival of the Duke of Lyonesse, so why don't you run along now and leave this to your betters, hmm?'

Calard reddened again and stumbled over his words as he tried to form a reply. He saw Maloric's face twitch in amusement, but Laudethaire had not yet finished.

'It's bad enough that we have one noble of Bastonne present,' said Laudethaire with a careless gesture towards Maloric, 'and I mean "noble" in the loosest possible sense of the word, but two?'

One of the knights of Lyonesse chuckled in amusement and the humour dropped from Maloric's face. Calard wanted the floor to open up and swallow him whole as he felt the eyes of everyone present boring into him.

'The young lord of Garamont came here at my request,' said Reolus, his voice quiet as he stared at the Parravonian pegasus knight. 'Are you calling my judgement into question, Laudethaire?'

To his credit, Laudethaire hardly baulked, his fear of causing the displeasure of a grail knight flashing only momentarily across his face.

'I jest,' he said smoothly, recovering instantly. 'And if my humour was misinterpreted, I offer my most humble apologies. The Parravonian wit is oft misunderstood.'

Laudethaire bowed low to Reolus. As he straightened, he flicked his long blond hair over his shoulder and flashed Calard a winning smile that did not reach his eyes.

'No insult was taken, I am sure,' he said.

'None at all,' mumbled Calard. Reolus winked at him behind Laudethaire's back.

Thankfully, the conversation the knights had been having before Calard had entered the room started up again, and the attention was taken off him. He moved towards the group, but stayed on the outer fringe, affecting an interested expression.

The discussion, which was mainly between the knights of Lyonesse and Laudethaire, went largely over Calard's head, and he had little to contribute. They were discussing inter-dukedom politics and court life, and Calard was amazed at the offhand way they spoke of the back-stabbing, machinations and duplicitous plotting that occurred between their various Bretonnian households. From the sounds of it, the politicking that took place in the royal court of Couronne was as deadly as any battlefield; more so in many ways, for at least on the battlefield you knew who your enemies were. To Calard it sounded vile, a poisonous viper's nest of intrigue and double-dealings. As lord of Garamont he knew that he would be forced to become involved at least in part in the politics of Bastonne, but he did not relish the thought of it at all. He did not believe he was even remotely suited for such duties.

'Montforte is a fool,' Laudethaire was saying, scathingly. 'He has lost much favour at court due to his heavy-handed approach in dealing with the trade issue. His decrees are restricting the flow of goods through the pass…'

'Axebite Pass?' said Dieter, his brow furrowed in concentration as he tried to keep up with the swift-flowing diatribe.

The valley known to the cartographers of the Empire as Axebite Pass was the largest and most accessible route between Bretonnia and Dieter's homeland. It cut through the giant peaks of the Grey Mountains that separated the two lands of men. At either end of the sheer-sided valley stood a mighty fortress, spanning the gap. On the Bretonnian side was Montforte; on the Empire side was Helmgart. Countless battles had been fought in the valley between the two impenetrable castles, for the peace between Bretonnia and the Empire was a fractious thing, and there had been blood spilt on numerous occasions.

Laudethaire looked at Dieter, as if weighing whether to even bother answering his question. Finally, he nodded once, and turned away to continue talking with the Bretonnian knights.

'His wife is the one with the brains, you know. Montforte has got rich thanks to her shrewd dealings. Abominable woman. She should have been born a man,' said Laudethaire.

'Or strangled at birth,' said one of the Lyonesse nobles, eliciting chuckles from his comrades.

A pair of double doors opposite those that Calard had entered through were thrown wide and conversation ceased. A thickset man dressed in courtly array stepped into the room.

'Lord Adalhard, Duke of Lyonesse, and the Damsel Anara!' he bellowed, far louder than was necessary, and stepped aside. The knights dropped to one knee, lowering their heads respectfully.

'Rise,' said a firm voice, and as he stood upright Calard saw the duke escorting his sister into the room, her forearm gently placed upon his. The duke was garbed for war. Anara's gaze floated lazily around the room, her eyes distant, as if she were seeing things that no one else could perceive.

'We don't know when the enemy will attack again, so let us get straight to the point,' said the duke, coming to a halt and casting his gaze around the gathered nobles. A manservant swiftly brought a chair to him, but he waved the man away. 'Casualties?'

A steward stepped forward, flipping open a leather-bound book.

'Nineteen knights of noble birth slain,' he said. 'Forty-two injured. Of those, nine will not fight again, and seven will require months of recovery time.'

'Peasants?' said the duke.

'Under two hundred,' said the steward.

'And rough estimates of the enemy losses?'

'Perhaps... eleven hundred,' guessed the steward.

'If we maintain those odds, my lord, then the enemy will surely have no chance of breaching our defences,' said one of the duke's knights, a massively overweight marquis with glittering rings on his fat fingers. 'We could hold them here for months on end, if not indefinitely, could we not?'

'It would be costly, Carabas,' said the duke. 'And who knows what L'Anguille is up to while we are occupied here. Invading my lands, no doubt. The man is a swine.'

'There is a way that the siege might be broken,' ventured another of the duke's knights, a stick thin, severe looking baron.

'Speak it then, Broussard,' said the duke.

'We give them what they want. We give them the girl.'

Calard's eyes widened and his jaw dropped.

'Pah!' scoffed the marquis, scowling at his compatriot. 'Castle Lyonesse has never been taken. We have nothing to fear from the likes of this barbarian rabble. Why should we deliver them what they want, like bullied children?'

'We have already underestimated them once,' said the duke, 'and we all know what happened as a result of that. I will not do so again.'

'But my lord... you cannot really believe that the castle could fall, surely?' said the marquis. 'It has stood for more than fifteen hundred years, and outlasted a dozen sieges.'

'It has, Carabas,' agreed the duke. 'But that does not answer the baron's question.' He looked around the room, and his gaze came to rest on Laudethaire. He raised his eyebrows questioningly. 'Well?'

'I swore an oath to protect those unable to protect themselves, my lord' said the knight loftily. 'I would rather die than break my word.'

'Nobly spoken,' said the duke. 'Though I feel there is a caveat coming...'

'You are as perceptive as you are honourable, my lord,' said Laudethaire with a bow. 'If it was known beyond any shadow of doubt that the lady that Lord Reolus and I rescued was indeed what she appears to be, there would be no contending what must be done. But I saw her wield unholy powers with mine own eyes. She is possessed. I say give the witch over to the Norse.'

The duke grunted noncommittally. He looked down at the ground thoughtfully for a moment, then lifted his gaze, switching between Maloric and Calard.

'And you two? I believe that both of you had some... attachment to the girl.'

Calard licked his lips, his mind spinning.

'I cared for Lady Elisabet of Marlemont, it is true,' said Maloric slowly. 'But I am not convinced that the *creature* that lies unconscious is her.'

'Anara? *Is* it Elisabet?' asked Calard, looking at his sister, who was talking to herself, acting out two sides of a hushed conversation. She did not seem to have heard the question, and several of the knights glanced at each other uneasily. She laughed to herself, and then scowled, and kept talking under her breath.

'Anara,' said Reolus, gently touching her on the arm. She snapped out of her double-sided conversation, looking vaguely startled, like someone forcibly woken from the middle of a dream. She smiled warmly at the grail knight, and for a moment she once again resembled the girl that Calard remembered.

'Your brother asked you a question,' said Reolus.

'Is it Elisabet?' said Calard as the damsel turned towards him with a questioning expression. 'Is it Elisabet that we brought back with us?'

'Yes,' said Anara solemnly. 'And no.'

Calard furrowed his brow.

'It is Elisabet's body,' elaborated the damsel, 'but she does not inhabit it.'

'Possessed, as I said,' said Laudethaire.

'I don't understand,' said Calard.

'Her body is a puppet,' giggled Anara, making spider-like motions with her hands, as if she were manipulating a marionette. 'She has no control over her strings. I thought at first she might be in there, imprisoned and helpless, a passenger with no control, but that's not so. She is... gone.'

'Gone?' said Calard.

'Gone,' said Anara.

'Can you expel this... presence... that has taken up residence within the girl's body?' asked Reolus.

'Yes,' said Anara.

'Elisabet will be herself again?' said Calard.

'Yes. No. Maybe,' said Anara, shrugging. Her eyes misted over. 'If she is alive, there is a good chance that she will return. It might happen instantly, or it may take years, or never. She may not be able to find her way back. She may be wandering the spirit-world, lost and blind, or she may already have passed through the veil into the realm of Morr. She might not *want* to come back.'

'It is worth the risk,' said Calard. Maloric nodded his head in agreement.

'Fine,' said Duke Adalhard. 'Do it. And if she does *not* return, then do we hand her over to the Norscans? Reolus, what do you say on the matter?'

'You know my answer. It is unthinkable to even consider handing a noblewoman of Bretonnia over to the likes of these Chaos worshippers. Even if she were to pass from the world when the exorcism takes place, she deserves better than to have her body handed over to the enemy. Were it to mean the death of every last knight of Lyonesse, I would answer the same,' said Reolus. 'As indeed would you, my lord.'

'I would,' nodded the duke. 'It's agreed then. Our fates are in the Lady's hands, and the courage of those defending this castle.'

'We have nothing to fear from these heathen savages, my lord,' said the Marquis of Carabas. Calard noted that this knight had not been present at the massacre some weeks earlier, and he shook his head at what he saw as his uninformed bravado.

'What's that noise?' said Laudethaire suddenly.

At first Calard heard nothing, then a distant sound like the roaring of a furnace could be discerned above the howling wind. And it was getting closer.

Horns blared in warning, and shouts of panic, fear and alarm echoed up from all over the castle. Then there was an almighty crash, like the rumble of thunder directly overhead, and the ground shook. Calard felt the floor reverberate, and the suits of armour arranged around the room clattered as the vibrations running up through the keep made them shudder. The reverberation made an ancient candelabra upon the mantelpiece jump forwards, and it would have smashed upon the floor had not Laudethaire caught it as it fell. He placed it back upon the mantelpiece as the reverberations subsided.

'Earthquake?' said Laudethaire.

'No,' said Reolus, shaking his head. 'The Norse.'

* * *

A SECOND FIREBALL was arcing through the air, daemonic fire trailing in its wake, as Calard burst out onto the top of the keep. He ran to the east-facing battlements, leaping up the stairs to the crenulations as other knights rushed up the stairs behind him, pushing gawping men-at-arms out of the way. Calard noted that it came from the location that they had identified earlier as the dug-in emplacement upon the beachhead. Shouts of panic could be heard from all over the castle.

The blazing comet lit up the sky, like a miniature sun screaming across the heavens, though the light it cast was a deep, malevolent red, tinging everything ruby with its daemonic glow. It roared like a dragon as it hurtled down towards the castle. The turbulent strait running between the island and the mainland was lit up, and Calard could see hundreds of longships ploughing through the water towards them. The second assault was about to begin.

'To arms!' shouted Calard, he raced back towards the stairway leading down through the keep.

Halfway down the spiralling, dark staircase, Calard was thrown against the wall, losing his footing as the ground shook beneath him; the fireball had clearly struck, and deep reverberations made the whole island shudder. He swore and pushed himself off the wall, and continued his mad dash down through the levels of the keep.

He was breathing hard as he reached the bottom of the spiralling stairway and ran out into the courtyard at the base of the keep. Men-at-arms were running towards the eastern wall, and Calard paused to catch his breath. Reolus and Dieter ran out into the courtyard behind him.

The sky was filled with a hideous roaring sound, and Calard shielded his eyes against the inferno as another fireball came screaming down towards the island. Even from this distance, Calard could feel the intense heat it radiated as it fell inexorably towards one of the immense towers looming above the eastern curtain wall. Calard looked on in horror.

Men were streaming away from the doomed tower, racing along the walls to either side of it and hurling themselves down the stairs leading from its lower levels to the inside courtyard. There was only one exit from the top of the tower, a steep spiralling staircase, and no doubt scores of men would be fighting to hurl themselves down it. Calard knew that none of them would survive.

The roaring inferno struck the top of the tower with colossal force, engulfing it in red fire. The entire castle trembled beneath the impact, and the top two levels of the tower were utterly demolished in an instant. Stone turned molten beneath the unnatural heat, running like syrup down the sheer sides of the walls, and tons of red-hot rock were sent flying in all directions.

Hundreds of men were consumed in the raging holocaust. Those standing exposed on top of the tower were killed instantly, flesh and bones burnt away to cinders even as the trebuchets were rendered into ash. The skin of those inside burst into flame, their lungs filled with scalding heat and fire as they breathed in. The top of the tower exploded like earthenware left too long in a kiln, stonework thrown out in all directions. The lucky ones were ripped apart in the detonation, heads and bodies crushed by hunks of superheated stone, but those that were not killed instantly were hurled into the air, their flesh burning as they plummeted hundreds of feet to their deaths.

Molten, burning chunks of rock crashed down into the buildings within the castle walls, smashing through shingled and thatched roofs, and a dozen of them were instantly ablaze.

The walls of Castle Lyonesse had stood resolute in the face of the restless dead of cursed Mousillon, and had repelled more than one large-scale assault by the dark elven kin from across the seas. They had withstood stones hurled by catapults, had defied battering rams, and even held firm against the cannons of the Empire navy. Yet even after just minutes of this barrage, it was clear that Castle Lyonesse was doomed unless the enemy artillery was neutralised.

A red-hot piece of stonework the size of a man's head spun end over end down towards Calard. He shouted a warning and dived to the side as it arced towards him. It took a peasant warden standing nearby squarely in the face, taking his head clean off.

There was an almighty crash, and Calard looked up to see the upper half of the tower, or at least the half which had not already been destroyed, collapse and fall, its structural integrity shattered. Once again the earth shook as hundreds of tons of stonework smashed to the ground, causing a great cloud of dust to rise.

'By the blood of the Breton,' swore Calard, seeing the terrible destruction that had been wrought.

'Not even the cannons of Nuln are so potent,' said Dieter, his face red from the exertion of racing down the stairs.

'If this continues, Lyonesse will be a molten ruin in hours,' said Reolus, his eyes blazing with rage.

The snap of timbers heralded the re-commencement of the firing of trebuchets. The Norscan longships were drawing close once again. Hundreds of knights and men-at-arms were racing towards the battlements of the curtain walls, and Calard was about to join them, to aid in the defence, when Reolus spoke once again.

'The enemy artillery must be silenced,' said the grail knight grimly.

'Laudethaire's knights?' said Calard, and Reolus shook his head.

'The Parravonians are too few.'

'What then?' said Calard, feeling a deep sense of foreboding and helplessness. 'They are out of range of the trebuchets. And it is not like we can sally forth and ride across the ocean.'

'This was not always an island,' Reolus said thoughtfully. 'Back in the times of Gilles le Breton, there was a sprawling township below this hill. It was the greatest city in Bretonnia, the envy of all, before it was drowned by Manann's wrath. The main entrance to the castle ran along a ridge – you can still see where that ridge is. It forms a causeway beneath the water,' he said.

Now that it was pointed out, Calard could vaguely recall seeing a cobbled road leading from the eastern gate into the ocean. He had thought nothing of it, but now that it was drawn to his attention, he could well imagine the sunken land beneath the waves, picturing the sprawling township in his mind's eye. He could well believe that a road had once run along the ridge from the towering wooden palisade of the castle that would have stood where Castle Lyonesse now did.

Another fireball roared into the air, and Calard dragged himself away from his musings.

He could not fathom what possible relevance the grail knight's random lesson in history had. And unless Reolus was proposing to swim across the strait, he saw no possible way of nullifying the enemy war machine, other than Laudethaire and his kin. He felt the grail knight's impenetrable gaze boring into him, and he shrank beneath it ever so slightly.

Reolus cocked his head to one side, his brow creasing, as if hearing a voice that Calard could not. The young lord of Garamont shuffled restlessly, his hand clenched around the hilt of his sword. Again he glanced towards the eastern walls, seeing the archers atop the battlements preparing to loose their arrows. Calard was impatient to join the defenders. He knew that his brother and his cousins were there, for he had left them there when his presence had been requested in the duke's chambers.

Barbarian horns and drums could be heard now, and Calard was about to abandon the grail knight and run towards the curtain wall when Reolus snapped out of his reverie.

'Get your steed saddled,' ordered the grail knight, swinging south towards the stables.

'What?' said Calard, his desire to fight alongside his brother urging him to run westward with all haste. 'Why?'

Reolus stopped and rounded on Calard, who quailed under his fierce glare. The grail knight seemed to shine with a potent light from within, his eyes blazing with holy fervour and Calard took an involuntary step backwards. What had possessed him to question the holy paladin?

He dropped to one knee, bowing his head, unable to hold Reolus's terrible gaze.

'I'm sorry, my lord,' he mumbled. 'It shall be as you command.'

Reolus merely nodded in response, before turning away from Calard and striding towards the stables. Calard had to jog to keep pace with the paladin.

A section of the eastern wall was struck by a fiery inferno as Calard jogged along behind Reolus, and screams of pain and fear echoed through the night as a fifty foot section exploded inwards, as if it were made of sodden timber, not thirty feet of solid rock. The war machine had struck high, taking off the top twenty feet of the high wall. A full breach had not been smashed through the immense barrier, but Calard had no doubt that the next shot would be recalculated to be more damaging still.

He looked back over his shoulder as he ran, and whispered a silent prayer to the Lady that Bertelis and his cousins were all right.

Scores of buildings were ablaze now, and while teams of peasants were running back and forth from the harbour, hefting barrels of water to throw over the raging inferno, Calard could tell that it was a useless endeavour; those buildings already burning were lost. All that could be done was to try to contain the blaze.

Amid the mayhem, Calard noticed that the grail knight had a scarf wrapped around his upper left arm – a token of affection, gifted by a noblewoman. He realised that he recognised the mauve, silk scarf as belonging to his sister.

'Your sister is far more powerful than you give her credit for,' said Reolus. 'By the Lady's grace, Lyonesse may yet survive the night.'

CHAPTER FIFTEEN

ANARA STOOD PRECARIOUSLY atop the battlements of the eastern gatehouse, arms lifted to the heavens and her head thrown back as she invoked the power of the Goddess. If she slipped, she would fall more than a hundred feet to her death, but she had no fear. Her black hair whipped around her wildly like the serpentine locks of a gorgon as the fierce winds buffeted her. She stood barefoot, unmindful of the ice and snow turning her toes blue, and her wispy, sheer dress fluttered around her like a shroud. Nothing mattered but the rush of power surging through her.

The men-at-arms stationed atop the gatehouse eyed her warily, making warding motions with their hands, for even they could feel the gathering energy being channelled through the damsel. Knights kissed tokens of the Lady as they felt the presence of the goddess manifesting within Anara.

Below her, the Norscan longships were just reaching the island, horn-helmed warriors leaping the gunwales into the shallows in their eagerness to take the walls. Thousands of arrows sliced through the night, cutting down the first wave of Norscans onto the beach, but as before, there were more enemies than archers, and countless hundreds of the northern barbarians, bellowing war cries and waving axes, were streaming towards the wall sections damaged by the devastating barrage.

The clouds roiled above as Anara continued to draw the winds of magic into her, and her limbs began to shudder. It threatened to consume her, and she clenched her hands into fists, but her concentration was solid, and a slight smile played at the corner of her lips as she slowly gained mastery over the power she was attempting to control.

Her eyes began to glow as if there was a light burning within her, and as she moved her lips, speaking in the language of the fey, blinding light billowed from her mouth. Wisps of ethereal fog rose from her skin, and her hair played out around her as if charged with static energy. The air crackled with intensity and an electric tang could be tasted upon the air.

Waves crashed furiously against the shore, and Norscan longships rose and fell as the swell intensified. Walls of water crashed over the sides of several, and one was smashed against the rocks as it was turned sideways by a towering wave, its hull splintering like matchwood. Men were dragged screaming into the icy waters which churned as frenzied sharks feasted, turning the waters red and the foam pink with blood.

Still Anara continued to call upon the power of the Lady, and a trickle of blood ran from one nostril. Her legs were quivering now, threatening to buckle, but no man stepped forward to support her, fearing that to do so would break her concentration, dooming them all. A thick fog began to form across the raging strait, hanging low over the water and growing thicker with every passing moment.

The ocean continued to heave, rising and falling with increasing fury. The Norse strained at the tillers of their longships, desperate to keep their vessels astern of the heaving surf, for if they were turned even slightly when a wave hit them they would be lost. Few civilisations were as skilful as the Norse at navigating treacherous seas but, even so, more longships were being overturned and smashed against the rocks as the surging ocean swell continued to build.

Within minutes, the unnatural fog surrounding the island fortress was so thick as to be utterly impenetrable, swallowing all sound. The shouts and roars of the Norse became dim and muted, and even the pounding of the waves was now faint. The fog rolled up the beach, obscuring the rocks and the Norse until it caressed the castle walls. Looking down from the battlements, it looked as though an ethereal ghost sea surrounded the fortress.

Dimly, Anara registered intense heat on her face as a roaring inferno screamed over her head, passing no more than twenty feet above her. The searing heat that radiated from the fireball made the snow and ice atop the castle gatehouse melt, and steam rose from Anara's clothes. The war machine's fiery missile came down inside the castle compound, fifty feet behind the gatehouse. It smashed down through the roof of a well-to-do inn, and the whole structure, and the stables and blacksmith attached to it, was instantly a hellish inferno.

Still the seas rose and the fog thickened, forming an impenetrable, heavy soup, and Anara pulled herself out of her incantation for the briefest of moments.

Now, she pulsed.

* * *

'Now!' roared Reolus, and the mighty, thirty-foot high doors of the gatehouse groaned open. The wall of fog beyond the gate rolled through the portal as it opened, creeping across the cobblestones like a living, amorphous beast. It coiled around the legs of the grail knight's destrier, making the paladin and his steed appear like some vengeful, holy manifestation; a supernatural avatar of the Lady's wrath. Calard shuddered, seeing again the Green Knight closing in on him, sword drawn, but he shook the disturbing vision off.

Anara's voice ghosted down from the top of the gatehouse overhead, musical and otherworldly. His flesh tingled and the hairs on the back of his neck stood on end as the air filled with expectant energy, and Calard lifted a devotional pendant carved in the likeness of the Lady to his lips, invoking her protection.

Calard could feel the blessing of the Lady upon Reolus, radiating from him like the heat from a forge. A vaguely shining aura surrounded the holy knight, a luminous glow that seemed emphasised by the fog billowing around him.

In one hand the grail knight held aloft his silver lance, Arandyal, its length shining with holy light; in his other hand he held its twin, the sacred sword Durendyal. Both holy weapons were of immense cultural significance, and even the lowliest inbred peasant had heard the tales of the terrible foes Reolus had vanquished with them.

The paladin's face was hidden behind the visor of his tall helm, topped with a gleaming heraldic unicorn of silver surrounded by a crown of lit candles, but his eyes blazed with the Lady's favour. His intricately-worked, ornate armour reflected the light of those candles and the roaring flames of the buildings burning within the castle walls. The silver edging of his regal blue tabard glowed.

Reolus's unicorn heraldry was emblazoned proudly upon his chest, the design mirrored on the flanks of his steed's matching caparison. That destrier was large, powerful and as black as pitch, and it bore the weight of Reolus and the heavy chain and plate barding beneath its flowing caparison effortlessly.

The thick, reinforced gates groaned fully open, and Reolus gestured forward with his blessed lance.

'To victory!' he roared, his voice infused with the power of the divine, filling the fifty knights gathered behind Reolus with fiery passion.

'To victory!' they echoed, and Calard's chest swelled with pride to be part of such an august company, to be riding behind such a holy knight.

As one they kicked their steeds forward, galloping out through the gates and into the fog beyond.

Calard could not see more than ten feet in front of him, but he felt no sense of fear or doubt as they thundered out of the castle, galloping directly towards the sea across the sand-swept cobbles on the ancient roadway. The Lady was with them, and they were led by one of her greatest champions – nothing in the world could stand against them.

They came upon the Norscans suddenly, and judging by the expressions on the barbarians' surprised faces, they must have appeared like ghostly apparitions, galloping out of the fog and led by a faintly glowing demigod of war, his helmet ringed with candles. Still, the Norscans were a warlike people not given to fear, and they responded with admirable courage, dropping ladders and leaping forward with axes raised, war cries on their lips. Yet for all their bravery they were smashed aside by the tight wedge of knights, crushed and broken beneath the hooves of the mighty destriers.

The causeway dipped as its angle increased and they ploughed through the fog towards the sea. Reolus did not slow his charge, and none of the knights riding behind him faltered. A voice in Calard's mind was urging him to pull his steed up, telling him it was utter foolishness to continue this mad ride through the fog and into the sea, but he grinned fiercely, rejoicing in the feeling of freedom that riding a warhorse at full gallop allowed.

A dragon-prowed longship appeared out the mist, driving a furrow through the sand off to the right of the causeway as it slammed into the beach. Calard saw Norscans leaping over the gunwales gaping in astonishment at the formation of knights riding at full gallop along the causeway towards the ocean, but then they were past them and Calard turned his attention back to the fore.

Impossibly, he heard Anara's voice in the fog all around him. Other voices joined hers, and Calard felt an aching pang in his heart at the beauty of the half-heard song.

The knights galloped down the causeway. It extended out into the strait further than the beach itself, and Calard could see the waves lashing the shore off to either side. The stones were slick with sea water beneath the hooves of the warhorses, and seaweed was clumped in stinking piles. Crabs as large as a man's head skittered sideward off the causeway, waving their oversized claws, their armoured shells covered in spikes.

Suddenly the ocean could be seen before them, dark and threatening. Black fins cut through the water no more than fifteen feet out, and yet on the knights galloped, guiding their steeds straight towards the sea. There was a great sucking sound from up ahead, and Calard saw the icy waters of the ocean surge away from the tip of the knightly formation, as if being drawn back to form an immense wave.

They rode forward for another dozen yards or so, and still the waters retreated before them. The causeway continued to descend at a steady angle, and he saw fish and eels flopping uselessly upon the ground, gasping for breath. He glanced to the side and saw the ruined corner of an ancient building protruding from the rock bed, the crumbling stone walls covered in weed and barnacles.

They were underneath the heavy fog that blanketed the sea then, and the path before them was suddenly clear. Calard took a sharp intake of breath as he saw the walls of water to either side of them as they continued to plough down the causeway, galloping deeper even as the waters continued to draw back away from them.

They drove a wedge through the ocean waters, which parted before them like enemy soldiers before the charge. The ruins of more buildings could be seen off to either side of what Calard realised must once have been a thriving thoroughfare. He gaped in astonishment at the sheer walls of water to either side of the lance of knights; it looked like they would come crashing down on top of them at any moment. There was nothing physical holding them back, but hold they did, and the knights galloped on, still riding downhill, moving ever onwards.

Finally the causeway levelled out and they were galloping along the flat. The sheer walls of water on either side were over thirty feet high here, towering cliffs that loomed over them threateningly. The sea spray washing over their edge was blinding, and Calard looked up, open-mouthed. The fog blanketing the ocean was falling over the edge towards them like a gaseous waterfall. So strange was the experience of looking up at the ocean from its floor, with the fog cascading over the walls of water, that Calard wondered if he might be dreaming.

All manner of hateful ocean-dwelling creature was stranded upon the ground around them, flopping back and forth impotently. He saw all sorts of fish, many of which had gaping mouths filled with razor-sharp teeth. He saw a shark easily three times the size of his horse, and it thrashed back and forth furiously. It was no natural beast, that, and he recognised the touch of Chaos upon it – dozens of grabbing tentacles surrounded its tooth-filled maw, and clusters of hate-filled eyes glared at him from the side of its broad head.

The bodies of Norscans were there too, the corpses of those that had been dragged to the ocean floor by the weight of their iron armour. Many of them were missing limbs and great chunks of flesh, clearly having been partially devoured by the sharks and whatever other flesh-eating creatures dwelt in the depths. Crabs swarmed over these bodies, obscuring them in a chittering blanket of chitin, tearing strips off their flesh with barbed claws.

Calard heard shouting overhead and glanced up to see the prow of a Norse longship balancing precariously on the edge of the oceanic cliffs. The raiders were frantically rowing backwards, trying to pull themselves back from the brink, but the ocean swell buffeted them, pushing them further over the edge. He urged his steed on, casting a nervous glance back up towards the teetering longship.

It tipped over the cliff of water and began to fall. Men tumbled from the ship, arms and legs flailing. Calard leant forward over the neck of his steed, kicking his heels into its flanks.

A Norscan fell on top of a knight behind him, knocking the Bretonnian from the saddle, and making his horse stumble. An oar smashed down onto the rump of another destrier, making its back legs give way and sending its rider flying. That knight plunged into the wall of water and was instantly set upon by the sharks lurking on the other side.

There was an almighty crash as the prow of the longship smashed down onto the ocean bed behind the knightly formation. The draconic figurehead ploughed into the causeway, and there was a sickening sound of splintering timbers as the weight of the ship crashed down behind it. Its mast broke, crushing a pair of knights at the back of the lance formation as it smashed down onto the rocky ocean floor.

Turning in the saddle, Calard watched as the longship splintered. Men continued to fall, bones breaking as they hit the ground. He saw that the long chasm-like corridor of water behind them was closing, and in another moment it claimed the shattered Norscan vessel, which was crushed by the pressure of the water rushing in upon it.

That frantic ride through the valley of water was the strangest experience of Calard's life thus far, and as they galloped up the causeway and onto the mainland itself, he marvelled at the power that was his sister's to command. Parting the ocean itself – he would never have believed such a things was possible.

The fog above continued to obscure their progress, so that the Norse had no warning of the attack they were about to face. With Reolus riding at the fore, the lance of Bretonnian knights galloped out of the ocean, angling their ride across the hard packed sandy beach that led around the bay towards the emplaced, infernal war machine of the enemy on the hillock protruding into the ocean half a mile to the north.

The enemy were completely unprepared for such an assault, and before they had even registered the presence of the enemy in their midst, the Bretonnians were cutting a swathe through them, galloping along the hard packed wet sand around the edge of the bay. They passed scores of longships, many of which were being pushed into the sea by warriors. Some of these marauders saw the Bretonnians behind them, and their voices rose in shock and alarm.

Calard's lance took a surprised Norscan in the face, the tip of his weapon punching through the man's eye-socket and smashing out the back of his skull. Releasing his hold on the weapon, he drew the blade of Garamont in a smooth motion and hacked down another enemy warrior, cleaving deep into flesh.

Horns of warning sounded, and Reolus pushed the knights on. They were not far from the war machine's emplacement now, but Calard knew that there were tens of thousands of Norscans all around – it was only a matter of time until they were surrounded and overwhelmed.

A sound like the roaring of a thousand lions echoed out across the land, and an immense ball of red flame shot into the air from up ahead, arcing above the strait towards Castle Lyonesse. Flames dripped like molten rock from the immense, deep red missile as it hurtled though the air, and the heat that came off it was intense. Choking black smoke blanketed the area where the shot had come from, upon the hillock jutting into the bay up ahead, and Reolus guided them towards it.

Norscans ran into their path, screaming in fury, but the Bretonnians carved through them like a scythe through wheat. Reolus fought with incomparable skill, killing with every strike. Dozens had already fallen beneath his blade and lance, and no enemy had even looked like landing a blow upon him.

They swung westward, hugging the sweeping bay and rising out of the fog that blanketed the water and beachhead, closing in on the enemy artillery.

They could see more clearly now, but as they climbed out above the fog they were themselves revealed to the enemy. Countless fires dotted the darkness in the east, and thousands of Norscan warriors yet to take part in the siege snatched up their weapons and began racing through their camp towards them.

The desolation of the mainland could be seen clearly. The burnt-out husks of buildings stood like blackened skeletons. It would take many years to rebuild the town back to what it was, for the taint of the Norscans to pass and for the scars of this destruction to fade.

At a curt gesture from Reolus, half the knights riding behind him peeled off to the east. If the Norse overwhelmed them from the rear before they had a chance to destroy the enemy artillery then this whole gamble would be for nought, and so those knights that wheeled off from the main formation would hold them off as best they could.

Calard felt a pang of sadness and pride as the formation split. Those knights peeling away were forming a long line to protect their rear, and every last one of them must have known that he would likely not survive, yet not one of them baulked in the face of their duty. Part of Calard wished that he was riding at their side, for their names would surely be remembered in the pages of history, their noble sacrifice honoured for all time. It was only by chance that he was positioned on the left side of the lance formation, and so was not part of that group riding off towards certain death and eternal glory.

Calard snorted. There was no certainty that *any* of them would make it back to Castle Lyonesse from this risky sortie, and he realised that the sacrifice of those knights would be meaningless if they did not succeed in destroying the enemy artillery.

They were climbing steadily now, rising off the hard packed sand lining the bay and joining a rough roadway leading up towards the headland, where the emplaced war machine was located. A low, crumbling wall separated the promontory from the town, and as the knights rode through a shattered gate, he realised what this area was set aside for; it was a cemetery, a sacred garden of Morr.

Of course no noble would ever have been buried here; this was a graveyard reserved for the peasant dead. As such there were few individual gravestones scattered across the snow-covered hill, for the vast majority of those buried here would have been packed into mass pits, their graves unmarked. Only the wealthiest peasant merchants could have afforded their own plots. Clumps of skeletal rose bushes protruded from the snow, though few of the trademark black roses that could be seen in the gardens of Morr all across the Old World were in flower.

Calard focused his gaze upon their target, squinting towards the infernal war machine that was smashing apart Castle Lyonesse with its relentless barrage. Hulking, ape-like creatures attached to each other by chain could be seen hard at work around the machine, being whipped by squat, barrel-chested figures, but he paid them little thought, his eyes widening as he looked upon the hulking metal construction.

It was partially obscured by steam and acrid black smoke exhaled by the hellish machine as if it were alive and breathing. It was something akin to the cannons of the Empire that Dieter had described to him, but he had never imagined one to be this size. Its huge barrel must have been twenty feet in diameter, and it squatted upon huge bronze wheels filled with clockwork mechanisms. Glowing runes were engraved upon its brazen body, and Calard felt his eyes sting just looking upon them. The bulk of the creation shuddered, swelled and contracted, as if its hide was organic, not unliving bronze and black iron. Curiously, the machine was staked down, with giant chains hooked to its form and hammered into the ground, as if it were a wild beast its captors feared and not an inanimate cannon.

The image of the war machine seemed to shimmer as if in a heat haze, and he saw the squat figures tending it shovelling what looked like body parts and coal into a gaping metal funnel upon its back as they rode closer. In disgust, Calard realised that many of the mass graves of the peasants were even now being dug up, with scores of what must have been slaves working to exhume the bodies of the dead. For a moment Calard had the impression of a huge, insatiable beast being fed by its caretakers, but he discarded the thought as the product of an overactive imagination.

He realised that the slave-creatures were orcs, though they were larger and darker-skinned than the ones he had fought in Bordeleaux. Their heads hung low beneath their massive shoulders, and their flesh was covered in scars and burns. They cringed as their squat captors whipped them, each lash of the barbed leather lengths flaying skin from muscle.

None of them registered the Bretonnians' presence until they were almost upon them, so intent were they on their work. A hulking orc worker looked up at the knights bearing down on them as it dragged a frozen corpse up from one of the pits, and it blinked at them dumbly with beady red eyes.

Then the creature bellowed, its massive tusked jaw opening wide, and its comrades lifted their heavy heads towards the knights.

Calard saw what he presumed to be the leader of the war machine's crewmen swing towards them, and growl something in a strange, grating tongue. The creature – it was certainly not a human, but neither was it a greenskin – was a stunted thing, wearing an outlandish high helm and clad from head to toe in heavy plates of overlapping armour.

Its broad chest was covered by a thick black beard tied into tight coils, and stubby tusks protruded from its mouth. Calard realised it was one of the dwarfen-kin said to inhabit the mountainous reaches of the Old World. He had always been led to believe that they were honourable and doughty allies, even if they were greedy and stubborn, but there was nothing good in this warped creature; it had clearly been twisted by the malignant forces of Chaos. It shouted something in its strange, deeply resonant language, and the black-skinned orc slaves were whipped into the path of the Bretonnians.

The slaves needed no encouragement, scrambling out of the grave pit, hefting their tools and launching themselves towards the knights. Behind them the stunted worker-creatures continued to toil away at 'feeding' the monstrous war machine. The slavemaster itself lifted a weapon from a stand at its side. That weapon vaguely resembled Dieter's repeater handgun, but where the Empire ambassador's weapon had five thin barrels, this arcane construction had just one barrel, though it was flaring and wide at its end.

The black orcs were hampered by the chains welded around their necks, but they attacked the knights without fear. Perhaps they longed for death, Calard thought. Each of the beasts was huge, with densely muscled arms twice as thick as a man's thigh. Reolus took the head off the first of the beasts with a sweep of his dimly glowing sword and ran another through with his lance. Two other orcs were raised into the air, half-strangled by the chains around their necks as Reolus lifted the spitted orc high, before hurling it away from him with a flick.

Several of the hulking beasts used the chains binding them as a weapon to take out the legs of the horses, showing a glimmer of bestial intelligence. Several steeds were felled as the black orcs pulled the chains taut, muscles straining, and the knights riding these unfortunate horses were catapulted from their saddles.

Calard slammed the blade of Garamont down onto the head of another of the dark-hued greenskins. It was like striking rock, sending a jarring shudder up his arm, but his blow shattered its skull and hacked deep into its miniscule brain, blood spurting. The creature didn't register it was dead right away, and it snarled and swung a wild blow, forcing him to sway to the side to avoid it.

Calard saw the dwarf slavemaster heft his heavy weapon to its shoulder, and he gave a shout of warning. There was a tremendous boom, and fire billowed from the widely flared barrel of the blunderbuss. A swath of death ripped through the Bretonnians and four knights were killed instantly, flesh and armour shredded.

There was a sound like some infernal giant beast sucking in a great intake of breath, making the air reverberate, and then the war machine fired again, sending a roaring fireball skyward.

At this range, the heat was nigh on unbearable, and Calard's vision wavered before him. A black orc made a grab at him but he severed the creature's arm at the wrist, leaving its immense hand locked around the reins. Another knight was thrown from the saddle as one of the greenskins wrapped its ape-like arms around the forelegs of his steed, getting trampled in the process but managing to drag the destrier down to the ground. The knight directly behind tried vainly to haul his steed out of the way, but there was not enough time or room, and the legs of his horse were broken as it slammed into the fallen steed in front.

Calard struck another orc a glancing blow, his sword rebounding off its thick skull, making it reel. It stumbled and disappeared under the flashing hooves of another knight, and they were through.

Reolus galloped hard, steering them towards the snarling, stunted dwarf slavemaster. The heavily armoured creature had discarded its blunderbuss in favour of a heavy axe, its blade gleaming black obsidian. Its companions had joined it now, hefting heavy spiked tools in their thick, gloved hands.

Each of the dwarfs was no more than four foot high, but built like oxen. Each had a thick beard that fell down over their leather and iron aprons, and their arms were almost as thick as their bodies.

Behind them the immense enemy war machine lurched, seemingly moving under its own impetus, and Calard recoiled in the saddle as he saw clawed legs of living bronze at the front of the war machine's carriage ripping up the ground as they dragged its weight around to face the knights.

Choking black smoke was exhaled from the barrel of the infernal machine, and Calard saw the entire thing writhe as it turned, metal flexing like living flesh. Daemonic faces appeared in the brazen sides of the giant weapon, pressing outwards from within, snarling and hissing. He saw that the rim of the gaping barrel was lined with tusks and fangs. The inside of the barrel was lined with concentric circles of teeth, thousands of them, and volcanic fire raged deep within, making Calard's eyes water and his armour heat up unbearably.

The barrel snapped shut as the living war machine lunged forward, straining like a wild bull at its restraints. Hellish runes glowed white-hot as it pulled against the chains. The steeds of the knights, as well trained as they were, refused to continue the charge towards the infernal daemon engine, baulking and fighting against their riders.

The knightly formation fractured, some horses rearing and bucking while others came to a dead halt. Others swung to the side, flattening their ears and galloping at full speed, while some tried to throw their riders.

Calard's steed reared, pulling against him, and he fought to regain control.

The dwarfen slavemaster stepped forward and hacked his obsidian axe into the chest of one bolting horse, and it screamed in a disturbingly human manner as it collapsed to the ground, throwing its rider. The knight was instantly set upon by a pair of brutish black orcs, who slammed his head into a rock, crumpling his helmet like paper with a sickly, metallic squeal.

Only Reolus continued the charge, and he cut down two of the Chaos dwarfs with slashes of his blade. The immense daemon engine ripped free of several of its chains, tearing the links apart in its fury, and it lurched towards Reolus, brazen fore-claws ripping up great sods of earth in its eagerness.

Calard cried out as the immense, sentient engine lunged for the grail knight. With masterful control, Reolus forced his steed to back up, and the huge maw of the hellish cannon snapped shut just feet in front of him. He drove his silver lance into the machine, and smoke rose from where its point entered the beast, as if it were a heated poker being plunged into water.

Reolus ripped his lance free as the daemon engine thrashed in pain or anger, and red fire spouted from the puncture wound.

Calard was thrown from the saddle of his steed as his destrier bucked again, and he landed hard. He heard again a deep sucking intake of breath, and gasping for breath he pushed himself to his knees, turning towards Reolus.

The grail knight was seated defiantly in the saddle before the immense daemon engine, a glowing aura surrounding him. Calard shouted in denial as the machine belched volcanic red fire towards the grail knight.

Reolus was completely hidden from view, lost within the hazy inferno that consumed him, and Calard pushed himself to his feet. The blade of Garamont was in his hand, and bellowing in outrage, horror and despair, he charged towards the hellcannon.

The dwarf slavemaster was suddenly before him, snarling hatefully as it swung its black-bladed axe in a murderous arc. Calard managed to get his shield in the path of the blow, but the axe sheared through it, knocking Calard to the side but saving him from harm. He slashed with his own blade, but the dwarf turned it aside easily. This was a foe of considerable skill, Calard realised.

The hellfire spewing from the maw of the daemon engine ceased, and the young lord of Garamont risked a quick glance towards Reolus, expecting to see nothing but a charred corpse. Miraculously, the grail knight appeared unharmed, sat aback his night-black steed, and the aura around him glowing almost painfully bright. The Chaos dwarf's axe almost took off one of Calard's legs as he gaped at the holy knight, but he managed to step back at the last second, though the axe grazed his armour, cutting through it with contemptuous ease.

The glow surrounding Reolus began to fade, and he urged his steed towards the giant hellcannon, brandishing his weapons. The infernal daemon engine snapped at him, but he ducked beneath its gaping maw and drove his blade into its side, tearing a gaping rent in it as he rode by. The machine thrashed, and flames the colour of blood roared from within its body.

It rounded on the grail knight, clockwork wheels grinding and bronze forelimbs scrabbling, and dozens of reaching talons extended from the machine's sides, grabbing for him. He evaded their grasp with ease, severing several of them with cuts of his blade. They fell to the ground, hunks of lifeless, inert metal, the life infusing them gone, and he plunged his lance into the beast again.

It was clearly in pain now, and the runes binding it blazed with heat. Another slash of his sword carved through one of the binding hoops of iron that ringed the engine's barrel, and its runes disappeared with a hiss.

Pegasus knights suddenly descended from the low clouds. A lance sliced towards the dwarf that Calard was frantically defending against, and the stunted creature swatted the weapon aside with a sweep of his axe.

Laudethaire himself swooped down low and struck the hellcannon with his own blade. It did little real harm, his sword merely ringing off its barrel with a hollow metallic ring, but it distracted the daemon engine, which swung at him, jaw snapping. That was all the opening that Reolus needed, and he leapt from his saddle, driving his sword down into the hellcannon like a dagger, using both hands to push it home.

Again the metal hide of the beast parted like yielding flesh beneath his sword, tearing a gaping hole in its side. The grail knight leapt backwards as lava and red fire spewed from the horrendous wound. The runes binding the daemon hissed and disappeared, and the entire engine began to melt beneath the heat contained within it. Its metal-cogged wheels began to sag, and its brazen forelimbs dripped like syrup.

Calard saw the surge of rage in the dwarf slavemaster's eyes, and he smiled.

Then, there was a primal scream of victory as the daemons that had been bound within the machine were released from their imprisonment. For a second Calard saw their true form, standing amidst the fiery destruction of their hellcannon prison. They were black-skinned creatures three times the height of a man, with shadowy bat-like wings extending from their shoulders. Fire burnt in the cluster of eyes set into their foreheads, but their screams of victory turned to one of outrage and fury as their bodies began to turn to smoke. With a final bellow of pure hatred that echoed for a hundred miles in every direction, the daemons were sent roaring back to the infernal plane from whence they had came as the material form that had bound them to the real world was destroyed.

A blast of superheated air exploded outwards, knocking everyone within fifty yards to the ground, and Calard closed his eyes against the furious light that surged into the heavens as the daemons were banished.

It was perhaps thirty seconds later when Calard's senses returned to him and he registered the shape of Reolus, once again in the saddle, looming over him.

'Take my hand, Calard,' ordered the holy paladin.

In awe, Calard accepted the proffered hand, and he swung up behind the grail knight. Then, together with the last of the knights that had accompanied them, they turned back towards Castle Lyonesse.

High Jarl Egil Styrbjorn stood motionless, his face unreadable as he surveyed the carnage unleashed as Zumarah's hellcannon was destroyed. Bjarki paced back and forth like a caged animal, snarling, his hands clenching and unclenching.

'Why is it that the enemy seer is able to part the sea, and yet you are not?' said Styrbjorn mildly, though there was a dangerous edge to his voice.

Bjarki spat a curse in response, and continued his restless pacing.

'Is her power so much greater than your own?' continued Styrbjorn.

'I'll rip her heart from her chest before this siege is done,' snarled Bjarki.

'You say the bitch goddess of this land is weak, so why is it that her seer continues to shame me?' said Styrbjorn. 'Is their goddess stronger than you say? Or is it my seer that is the weak one?'

'Insult me and you insult the gods themselves,' snarled Bjarki in a warning tone.

'The gods reward those who are strong and fearless, and punish those who are useless and weak. I have long been in the gods' favour.'

'Things change, *mighty jarl*,' said Bjarki, his tone mocking and derisive. 'The favour of the gods waxes and wanes like the green eye in the night sky.'

The seer began pacing again.

'Calm yourself, little bear,' said Styrbjorn in a steady voice. The unnatural fog blanketing the turbulent strait was dissipating, blown clear by the icy gale, and he saw the ocean closing behind the enemy. He watched as a handful of knights rode towards the distant gatehouse, and dimly heard the cheers that welcomed their return.

'That hellcannon was our best chance of breaching the cursed fortress,' said Bjarki.

'It is a setback, nothing more,' said Styrbjorn. 'And the enemy has revealed something to us this day.'

Bjarki looked to his jarl questioningly.

'The waters of this strait are not so deep,' said Styrbjorn. 'The roadway is perhaps thirty feet beneath the waves at most.'

'Thirty feet or three hundred feet, what difference does it make?' said Bjarki.

'Your eagerness for blood is clouding your mind, little bear,' said Styrbjorn. 'Think!'

The seer's face twisted in outrage, and his hand flashed for the dagger at his side. For a moment it looked as though he would draw it and stab his jarl, but the moment passed, and his expression changed to one of introspection.

'Thirty feet,' he said, his hand rising from the hilt of his dagger to the braided goatee beard hanging from his chin, which he scratched at absently. In the distance, the heavy gates leading inside the enemy fortress slammed shut behind the handful of knights that had managed to escape the Skaelings' wrath, and the heavy portcullis crashed to the ground, sealing the entrance way.

Realisation dawned, and Bjarki flashed a smile at his jarl. Styrbjorn grinned savagely in return.

'Thirty feet is not so deep,' said Bjarki.

CHAPTER SIXTEEN

Elisabet's arms and legs were bound to the four corners of the bedposts and her mouth gagged. She fought against these restraints with possessed fury, muscles straining, and blood flowed from her wrists and ankles. Her flesh was lathered in sweat and her long dark hair plastered against her skin. Her eyes were completely black, and she thrashed wildly as Anara continued to speak the words of banishment, standing at the foot of the bed.

Calard watched on in horror as the thing inhabiting Elisabet's body struggled to maintain its hold. The air was chill in the room despite the roaring flames of the fireplace, and shadows danced at the edges of his vision.

Elisabet's heavily pregnant body went into spasms, her back arching and lifting her off the bed as Anara's voice rose in intensity. The shadows all around seemed agitated, and Calard could hear a faint whispering in his ears, and his hand closed around the hilt of his sword.

Anara had assured him that the daemon-shades were unable to manifest within the room – she had sanctified and blessed it in the name of the Lady – but Calard was still uneasy.

With a shout, Anara completed her ritual, and Elisabet went into a final, shocking paroxysm, her eyes rolling back in her head and her limbs going rigid. Spasms wracked her frame, throwing her around on the bed, which shuddered under her exertions. Then, the girl was suddenly still.

Calard moved to Elisabet's bedside. She was breathing shallowly, for which he was grateful – he had thought for a moment that her heart might have given out altogether.

Anara slumped backwards into a padded chair. She was pale and drawn, with dark rings around her eyes as if she had not slept for a week. The exorcism had clearly drained her.

The young castellan of Garamont was exhausted as well, though his was a physical tiredness. It had been two days since the enemy daemon-engine had been destroyed, and the Norscans had been attacking the walls since then non-stop. Calard had managed to snatch a few hours of rest between attacks, but even then his sleep had been haunted by visions of the Green Knight, and he had awoken feeling more tired than before. His armour was dented and splattered with gore, and his once pristine blue and red tabard was torn and smeared with blood and mud.

'Well?' he said. 'Is Elisabet herself?'

Anara opened her eyes and looked at him with exhausted eyes. The damsel nodded her head.

'When will she wake?' he said. 'Will she recover?'

Anara merely shrugged in response. In the distance, Calard heard horns sound. Another assault was about to commence. He swore, and gave Elisabet one final look. Her breathing seemed regular, if shallow. Anara curled her legs up beneath her like a little girl, and was instantly fast asleep.

More horns blared, and Calard turned and walked wearily from the room. He closed the door softly behind him.

Calard's cousins were waiting for him outside, but they did not immediately register that he had emerged from Elisabet's room.

'You know what must be done, Tassilo!' Baldemund was saying, his voice low and threatening.

'I'm just not sure any more that this is the right path,' said Tassilo, shaking his head.

'It is too late for second thoughts now, cousin,' said Huebald fiercely. 'We gave our oath to Folcard. He is relying upon us.'

'Why are you arguing? Folcard is relying on you for what?' said Calard, frowning. His cousins froze, then turned slowly to face him. Tassilo dropped his eyes to the floor.

'Nothing that need concern you, cousin,' said Baldemund. 'You have enough on your plate already.'

Calard wanted to press the point, but found he simply did not have the strength. He was so tired.

'Is Elisabet...' said Huebald in concern. 'Is it done?'

Calard nodded, too weary to speak.

'Are you all right, cousin?' Baldemund asked him in a quiet voice.

'Let us get back to the walls,' said Calard, ignoring the question.

HAEGTESSE JOLTED, FEELING a horrible sense of vertigo as her spirit slammed back into her aged, decrepit and cancer-ridden body.

The witch tried to scream in outrage and denial, but a leather gag ensured that nothing but a weak, gargled cry passed her lips. Opening her eyes, she could see little. Once again she was practically blind, cataracts filling her milky orbs, and her heart fluttered weakly within the fragile cage that was her ribs. Her hands were tied tightly behind her back. Rats squeaked and rustled through the mouldy straw that littered the dank ground.

In the deepest oubliette beneath Castle Garamont, with her hands bound and her mouth gagged, there was nothing for the witch Haegtesse to do but wait for death.

Chlod was ripped from his restless, haunted sleep as a heavy boot kicked him hard in the side. Horns were sounding from the towers all around, and he groaned. The enemy had been coming at them relentlessly for almost three days now. The defenders had repelled wave after wave of attacks.

Everything hurt. His body was a mass of bruises upon bruises, and his limbs ached. Breathing in deeply was painful, and he was certain that at least one of his ribs was broken. He'd twisted his left leg badly the day before, and throbbing pain emanated from his knee. The little finger of his right hand had been severed by an enemy axe, and while he knew that he had been lucky – had he not slipped on a pool of blood and fallen on his arse, then the axe would have taken his head off – that thought did little to alleviate the pain.

Chlod had thought he would have been able to slink away from the front line at some point during the battle, or in the lapses between assaults, but so far he had been allowed no such opportunity. The yeomen wardens were as watchful as eagles, and they guarded all the stairways leading from off the walls. He had already seen them kill half a dozen would-be deserters, the screams of the dying men ringing out sharply as they were hurled over the battlements. He had considered leaping off, but his legs had begun to shake even just looking down towards the courtyard inside the curtain wall. It was perhaps thirty feet to the ground, and he was certain that he would break both his legs upon landing on the unforgiving stones below, if he survived the fall at all.

So exhausted had he been after the last assault that he had just slumped down in a heap where he had been fighting, huddling up against the battlements to escape the penetrating winds. He had fallen into a dreamless, exhausted sleep almost immediately.

It seemed as though he had only just closed his eyes, but already the next assault was about to begin.

'Get up, you dogs,' barked a grizzled man-at-arms, jabbing the butt of his halberd into peasants still lying on the ground. One of them didn't move, and Chlod realised the man had died in the interim between the last assault, having either frozen to death or succumbed to injury. He didn't look older than fifteen.

'Get rid of him,' snarled the man-at-arms, and Chlod was pushed roughly from behind. Together with two other peasants, he manhandled the already ice-cold corpse over the crenulations, pushing it over the edge to join the growing pile of bodies at the base of the wall.

Snow was falling once again, blanketing everything in an ever-deepening layer, and Chlod stamped his feet in an attempt to get some feeling back into them. He had cheered as he saw the holy paladin Reolus riding back into the castle, jumping up and down and hollering loudly, hoping that the grail knight would acknowledge him as one of his pilgrims. He had hoped that if Reolus saw him, he might be allowed off the walls in order to go to the grail knight, but if he was heard, the knight gave no indication.

Chlod had tried to convince the yeomen guarding the stairways that his master needed him, but they had laughed in his face. One of them pushed him backwards hard with his polearm, and Chlod had fallen on his backside, staring up at the man hatefully.

In truth, Chlod *had* felt considerable joy that Reolus still lived. Though he cared not a jot for the nobility, he found himself pleased that the grail knight was not yet numbered among the casualties. There was something special about him, that much was obvious, and Chlod felt somehow that while the knight lived they still had hope. It mattered not that he was just one man. While the grail knight lived, Chlod felt confident that the enemy would be repelled.

He pulled off his helmet and scratched his head. A peasant nearby was staring slack-mouthed at the shaved circle on the crown of his head.

'What are you staring at, gimp?' said Chlod.

'Are you really his pilgrim?' asked the man. He was a solidly built simpleton with one shoulder hanging half a foot lower than the other.

'Yeah,' he said.

'You an abbot or something?' said the man.

'That's right,' said Chlod, puffing out his chest. He looked around him as if checking to see if anyone else was within earshot, then beckoned the big man towards him.

'Tell you what,' said Chlod. 'You guard my back in the next attack, and if we are both livin' at the end of it, I'll make you my novice.'

'Would you?' said the man, his eyes widening. Chlod nodded gravely.

'What's your name?' he asked.

'Otho, father abbot.'

'Brother Otho. It sounds good, dunnit?' said Chlod. The big man nodded his head. Chlod produced a small bone from his tunic pocket with a flourish, and held it out to the man, who took it in his hands reverently.

'What is it?' he said breathlessly, staring at it as if it were made of solid gold. 'The finger of a saint?'

'Better,' said Chlod in a hushed voice. 'It's a chicken bone.'

'A chicken bone,' said Otho with reverence in his voice.

'A chicken bone gnawed on by none other than Reolus the... the Oh So Mighty and Grand,' said Chlod, affecting a dramatic voice that elicited an exhalation of wonder from the big peasant. 'It will protect you. But only – *only* – if you make sure that I, his holy abbot, am kept from harm. If even one heathen lays a hand upon me, the bearer of that sacred bone will be struck down. You understand?'

The big man nodded his head solemnly.

Other horns blared, and warning shouts announced that the enemy longships were drawing near. Trebuchets began firing, and Chlod pulled the broken sword from the loop of leather around his waist, feeling quietly smug at having tricked the big peasant into protecting his back. Perhaps he would survive a little longer than he expected.

Otho dropped to his knees before Chlod, bowing his head. After a moment of staring at the man in incomprehension, Chlod chuckled to himself and stepped towards him. What matter did it do to push the charade a little further?

He made a warding sign in the air, imitating a benediction that he had once seen a priest make, and placed his hand on the man's head.

'Bless me too, father abbot!' shouted another peasant, dropping to his knees.

Other men pressed in, reaching for Chlod with outstretched hands. Others pushed themselves to the ground before him, heads bowed to receive his benediction. They were not just peasant archers and men like he, drafted hastily into service, either; a number of men-at-arms wearing the duke's white and red tabards were among their number. Chlod shook his head at the absurdity of the situation.

His pet rat squirmed under his shirt, and he patted it absently, a gormless smile on his face.

'Here they come again!' came a shout.

'Bless you all, sons of Reolus!' shouted Chlod.

The peasants gathered around him roared their approval, and hefted their weapons in their hands as the first arrows began to fire upon the enemy storming up the beach.

CALARD PLUNGED HIS sword into the neck of another Norscan as he tried to clamber over the battlements. Blood spluttered from the barbarian's lips, yet the dying warrior gripped Calard's blade with one hand, trapping it.

As Calard struggled to free his weapon, a man-at-arms to his right fell backwards, a spear jutting from his chest, and a white-bearded, heavily muscled Norscan leapt over the wall, howling like a blood-maddened wolf. The veteran enemy warrior swung to his left, slamming his axe into a knight's neck, shearing through metal. As the knight fell, the Norscan ripped his axe free and swung towards Calard, who was still struggling frantically to free his trapped sword. Seeing Calard's predicament, the warrior who had a hold of his sword grinned, blood dribbling from his mouth.

Calard growled in frustration, using all his strength trying to rip his sword loose, but to no avail. Still, he had no intention of releasing his grip on the Garamont heirloom, for he knew that as soon as he let go the Norscan would fall backwards to his death, taking the sword with him.

Bertelis slammed into the white-bearded Norscan from the side, driving him into the battlements. Losing his grip on his axe, the old warrior hammered his elbow into Bertelis's helmet, snapping his head backwards. Bertelis reeled, and Calard saw his brother's blade embedded to the hilt in the Norscan's gut.

Huebald and Baldemund stepped protectively in front of Bertelis as the Norscan pulled the bloody sword from his flesh and hurled it away from him. Blood was gushing from the mortal wound, but the Norscan merely roared in fury and hurled himself at Calard's cousins.

Calard placed one foot upon the edge of the crenulations and heaved with all his might, and finally tore his sword free, severing the Norscan's fingers in the process. The man dropped backwards, still grinning, and was gone.

The young lord of Garamont swung around to see white-beard with his paw-like hands wrapped around Huebald's neck, throttling the life out of him even as Baldemund stabbed him repeatedly.

Calard bellowed wordlessly as he launched himself to the aid of his cousins, and the Norscan looked up at him, still howling, just a fraction of a second before the blade of Garamont carved into his skull. Blood and brain matter splattered over Calard's face and chest, and the Norscan finally fell.

'Breach!' shouted Tassilo, leaping past Calard as giant, black-armoured warriors heaved themselves onto the battlements behind them. A knight fell, hacked from collarbone to sternum by a sickeningly powerful axe blow, and his companion butchered a pair of men-at-arms, black-bladed twin swords flashing.

Tassilo barged into the first of them with his shield. The Norscan was a head taller than the young Bretonnian nobleman, but the icy stonework was slippery underfoot, and he lost his balance. The Norscan barked a curse and dropped his axe, black-armoured fingers scrabbling for a handhold as he fell back over the battlements.

The second Chaos warrior took a step towards the wall's defenders, pale eyes burning with cold intensity within the shadowy depths of his helmet. Almost as an afterthought he lashed out with one of his swords, and Tassilo fell with a gasp of pain as the tainted weapon carved through the plate armour encasing his forearm. Tassilo dropped to his knees, grasping his wounded arm, and Calard saw his cousin's vambrace blacken and corrode.

The Chaos warrior's broad shoulders were hung with wolf pelts, and he towered over Calard and his companions. Black smoke rose from the deadly, jagged blades of his weapons, and Calard knew that this must have been one of the enemy chieftains. More enemy warriors leapt over the walls behind him, but Calard's gaze was fixed on the giant warrior closing towards him. This was a worthy foe, he knew, and he relished the opportunity to prove himself before the Lady and his comrades – and to himself.

'This one's mine,' he said, though Baldemund and Huebald were already stepping away, leaving him at the fore, alone and exposed, though Calard noticed not at all.

Tassilo managed to scramble back before the chieftain's advance, still clutching at his wounded arm in obvious agony.

Calard gripped the hilt of the sword of Garamont tightly, and whispered a swift prayer to the Lady of the

Lake as he stepped forward to meet this enemy champion.

A shadow fell over him and he ducked involuntarily as a winged shape swooped low over his head.

The enemy champion took a step back, raising his swords up before him, but before he could ward off the blow, a lance was driven into his chest, punching though his armour and impaling him on its length. The lance tip burst out through the back of his body, transfixing him, and then the pegasus mounted knight was past, banking sharply off to the right.

A cheer rose up from the defenders as Laudethaire flew over their heads, drawing his sword and brandishing it in salute. Calard realised that scores of men had seen the Parravonian strike down the enemy chieftain, and he had no doubt that all those who had not would know of it before the day was out.

'Bastard,' said Calard. Once again Laudethaire had claimed the glory, and Calard and his ilk were left to clean up the remnants.

The Norscans came at them in a rush, and Calard only just managed to get his shield up in time to turn aside a swinging axe. He was knocked to his knees by the force behind the blow, and he slashed desperately with his sword. The blade sank deep into his attacker's calf. The Norscan fell with a curse and was finished off by a peasant, who hammered the spiked tip of his polearm down into the man's face.

As Calard rose back to his feet his shield was knocked aside by a heavy hammer, the blow designed to leave him unprotected. A boot struck him full in the chest, sending him crashing backwards, his breastplate groaning under the force and the wind driven from his lungs.

He hit the ground hard, flat on his back, and his head struck the stone. Had he not been wearing his helmet he might have been killed. As it was he was merely stunned, though he would have a headache for a few days if he survived this latest assault.

Winded, he struggled to rise, though he saw that the Norse who had managed to storm onto the ramparts had been killed, their ladders pushed from the walls.

The Norse champion, impaled upon the length of Laudethaire's lance, was still alive, though he was clearly mortally wounded. The blood that dripped from his wound was black and hissed as it struck the stonework, melting shallow pits in the rock where it fell.

He stared up hatefully at Calard as he stepped forward to finish the warrior. Calard's blow shattered the Norscan's helmet and took half his head away, but still he did not die. The shattered pieces of the warrior's helmet fell away from his face, exposing a mass of skinless flesh. Maggots writhed through the fibrous muscles of the champion's face, and his lipless mouth was studded with rotting fangs. A single large horn protruded from the Norscan's forehead. Calard had thought that horn but part of the brutal ornamentation of the Norscan's helmet, but he saw now that it was part of the champion's own flesh and bone.

The chieftain spat a gobbet of phlegm up at Calard, which splattered against his helmet, just below his eye-slit. He could hear the foul acidic sputum eating through metal, and he ripped his helmet off his head, dropping it at his feet.

The enemy chieftain chuckled, his ice-white eyes filled with dark humour, and Calard struck him again, this time hacking his putrid head from his shoulders. A rancid stink rose from the corpse, and Calard gagged.

Several men-at-arms were with Tassilo, helping remove the armour from his arm, and Calard saw that the wound was already festering with poison. Calard barked an order, demanding that the champion's fell, black-bladed swords be wrapped in blankets and hurled from the walls. He ordered the rancid corpse of the Norscan thrown over the battlements, and half a dozen men lost the contents of their stomach at the repulsive stink of the rapidly decomposing body.

Bowmen stepped lightly through the knights and men-at-arms at a shout from a yeoman warden, and they began firing between the crenulations once again; another enemy assault was about to hit home.

Bone tired, Calard leant against the wall, his back to the battlements and closed his eyes, breathing hard.

It seemed like only moments passed before he heard ladders slam up against the walls as the next enemy assault struck. Weary beyond words, he opened his eyes and pushed away from the battlements, turning to wait for the enemy to appear.

As weary as he was, Chlod was starting to enjoy the level of respect and deference he was receiving from the soldiers fighting around him. In truth, he had begun to believe his own rhetoric; he had started to believe that he *was* the prophet of Reolus's glory, and that in his exalted position he was afforded a certain amount of holy protection.

So it came as a considerable shock when a hulking Norscan berserker, his red hair and beard a tangle of braids and dreadlocks, tore through his fanatical devotees like a maelstrom of death and grabbed him by the shirtfront. Chlod's eyes bulged and he scrabbled to free himself from the man's grip.

A mailed fist smashed into his face. Then he was lifted off his feet and tossed over the battlements. He was unconscious before he hit the ground.

ELISABET AWOKE TO sharp pain, gasping. It took her a moment to realise that she could see clearly and that she was no longer curled upon the rotting pallet in the dank dungeon cell. She was lying in a soft bed, and she stared up at the rich velvet draped above the four-poster bed, not knowing if she was dreaming, or if this was reality and being trapped in the body of the old crone had been the delusion. The sheets under which she lay were drenched in sweat and she doubled over in agony, groaning, as shooting pain again lanced through her.

Her hands clutched at her belly, and horror rose within her as she felt the swelling there. She threw off the covers and stared in incomprehension at her heavily pregnant young body.

Had she escaped one horrific nightmare only to find herself in another?

'Your contractions are close,' said a voice from nearby, and she turned her head to see a slight, waifish young woman with a distant expression on her face. She recognised her as Calard's sister Anara, and she gaped at her in horror as she digested the damsel's words.

'Contractions?' she breathed.

'The child is ready to enter the world,' confirmed Anara.

'Tell me this is a nightmare,' said Elisabet in desperation. 'Tell me this is not real!'

Anara held a wet cloth to Elisabet's forehead as fresh pain made her double up in agony. She called for water and towels over her shoulder, and as she shook her head in the negative, Elisabet cried, wailing in fear, incomprehension and pain.

'How?' she managed. Then another thought struck her, and she leant towards Anara, clutching at her in desperation. 'Who is the father?'

'The enemy,' said Anara.

CHAPTER SEVENTEEN

Chlod awoke to darkness. He could hear shouts and screams in the distance, but they were muffled and faint. I am dead, he thought, and I am hearing the echoes of the living seeping down into Morr's underworld.

He realised dimly that the reason he could not see was because he was lying under something. Another thought struck him then; maybe he was *not* dead, but rather was buried alive.

The thought was horrifying, and with a strangled cry he fought to wriggle and squirm to the surface. His eyes registered firelight, and he saw that he was half buried beneath a pile of corpses. He panicked. In desperation and terror he struggled to escape the morass of dead bodies, fighting to free himself. The stink of death, a vile mixture of blood and excrement from loosed bowels, was heavy in his nostrils.

His head spinning, Chlod crawled out from under the bodies beneath which he was pinned, stumbling over the uneven mound of corpses as he pushed himself to his feet. He tried not to look at their blood-smeared faces or their hideous wounds. His eyes were wild and slightly unfocused, and he could feel that the left half of his face was slick with blood. His helmet was gone, and his body was aching all over.

A body slammed down next to Chlod, and he stared at it in mute incomprehension. The man was a powerfully built Norscan and he wasn't dead yet, though blood was pumping from a horrible throat wound. The bodies had cushioned his fall, as they had doubtless done for him. He was trying to scream, but all that came from his mouth was a gargle of blood. The Norscan reached a hand towards Chlod, though he could not tell if it was a silent appeal for aid or a threatening gesture.

Chlod lifted his gaze, following the direction from where the man had come, and only then did he register that he was at the base of immense castle walls. He was confused for a moment and he stared up stupidly. Wasn't he meant to be up there? Had he fallen?

Sound came crashing in on him suddenly, as if stoppers had just been removed from his ears, and he staggered under the aural assault.

Men were roaring in pain, anger and challenge, and the sounds of weapons clashing rang out sharply. He heard the unmistakeable sound of steel hacking into flesh and bone, and heard the snap of timber and leather as trebuchets fired. Arrows sliced downwards, loosed from the ramparts as well as from slits in the walls and towers, and one of them grazed his wrist, eliciting a gasp of pain and shock from his lips. Ladders crashed against parapets, and war cries were belted out at the top of warriors' lungs. Feral drums echoed across the battlefield, bouncing back off the castle walls, and horns rang out.

Chlod pressed his hands to his ears and stumbled backwards, his eyes wild as he saw the carnage and mayhem unfolding all around him. There was movement everywhere, and hundreds of enemy warriors were pushing and shoving as they climbed the ladders nearby or hauled themselves up thick ropes. No one seemed to register his presence, though there were hundreds of Norscans only yards away.

Then war horns were sounding the retreat, and the enemy began streaming back towards the longships half hidden in the blinding gale of wind and snow.

A Norscan leaped off the ladder he was climbing, landing heavily in front of Chlod. He staggered back away from the blood-smeared warrior. The man snarled at him and lunged forwards, grabbing him by the front of his tunic. He raised his axe for the killing blow, and Chlod cringed, whimpering like a babe as he waited for death.

Another Norscan barked something in their crude language, and Chlod saw his would-be killer scowl and lower his axe. He was shoved backwards, and he tripped over a headless corpse. The Norscan gestured angrily with his axe, shouting at Chlod. He stared up at the brutal warrior, not understanding his meaning, and received a boot to the head that sent him sprawling backwards.

Spitting out a couple of teeth, Chlod pushed himself to his feet as the Norscan shouted again, gesturing towards the ocean with his axe. Chlod turned his head to look where the warrior was pointing. He could see Norscans pushing longships back into the ocean. The Norscan stepped forward to strike him again, and like a dutiful dog, Chlod began scurrying towards the ocean.

Hundreds of enemy warriors were running down the beach and throwing their weight against the ships, pushing them into the furious ocean. Chlod staggered down the sand in their midst, being shoved along by his Norscan captor.

Arrows cut down dozens of men as shafts struck them in the back and in the legs. Bodies were floating face down in the ocean, being tossed to and fro by the surf and banging up against the sides of the longship. Their comrades ignored those that fell, or who were already dead. Breathing hard, Chlod was pushed towards one of the longships, which was already putting to sea.

Chlod splashed into the ocean. The water was freezing, instantly numbing his feet. He sucked in a breath and stepped back sharply as he saw black fins cutting through the water only ten yards out. A boot in the small of his back shoved him forward, and he fell to his knees in the icy waters. A breaker crashed over him, and he came up spluttering.

Arrows sliced into the water around him, striking several Norscans wading out to the departing longships. He saw a shark lurch out of nowhere and clamp its jaws around the leg of one warrior as he hauled himself over the side one of the ships, taking it off at the hip. Screaming and with blood pumping from the stump, he was kicked into the sea by his comrades, who clearly had no mercy or time for a warrior unable to stand.

A spinning hunk of masonry hurled by a trebuchet came crashing down through the hull of another longship a dozen yards out into the strait, instantly killing several men. The others were forced into the shark-infested waters as the ship was split in two, and the ocean turned red and turbulent as the voracious carnivores feasted.

Chlod floundered in the whitewash as a wave hit him. He jerked as the frantic rat hidden inside his shirt front bit his chest in its fear. He swung around, desperate to put as much distance between himself and the cold-blooded killers circling nearby, but was met with a solid fist to the jaw. The blow laid him out cold. He didn't feel a thing as his lifeless body was hefted onto the Norscan's shoulder, nor when he was thrown over the side of the longship like a sack of wheat and kicked into the iron cage, alongside a score of other prisoners.

He came awake instantly as strange, pungent herbs were shoved under his nose. A savage tattooed face framed by matted dreadlocks and braids was just inches from his own. The figure squatting over him grinned down at him, exposing teeth that had been filed to points, and a hand slapped him hard across the side of the head. Chlod found that his hands were bound behind his back, and he was dragged to his feet by a pair of unseen figures. Then the flat of a blade smacked across the back of his knees, forcing him to kneel.

Chlod's eyes flickered around him, taking in his surroundings. He was in the middle of what he guessed was the Norscans' encampment. Two pyramids of severed heads, each easily twenty feet high, were behind the barbarian holding Chlod immobile. Crows and ravens hopped over the grisly shrines, pecking at eyeballs and tearing tongues from mouths, and as he looked upon them, he began to shake uncontrollably.

'It is good you are awake,' said the barbaric figure, and it took Chlod a moment to realise that the man was speaking Breton, though it was with a brutal accent. The man clamped a hand around Chlod's jaw, holding his head steady. 'Gods hear you scream when you awake.'

He registered the wooden block that was before him. He saw the marks where an axe had bitten into the wood repeatedly, and he saw blood – some fresh, some dry and old – that had stained the chopping block almost black. He started blubbering like a teething babe, tears and snot running down his bloody, dirt-smeared face.

'No, please, no, no,' he said, closing his eyes tightly against the foul image.

Chlod was grabbed by the hair from behind, and forced forward. His arms were reefed up behind his back painfully, and the side of his face slammed into the wood of the chopping block. He could taste fresh blood on his lips.

'You will not die just yet. I'm going to cut you first,' said the Norscan seer, whispering in Chlod's ear. 'Just enough to make you scream. Your cries will get the attention of the gods – only then will your death come.'

Chlod was crying like a bairn, his eyes clamped tightly shut. He felt the cold touch of a blade upon the back of his ear and he screamed. Hands held him immobile, pressing his head hard into the chopping block.

BJARKI GRINNED AS the prisoner screamed beneath him. He could feel the presence of daemons nearby, just beyond the veil separating the real world from the blessed madness beyond, and knew that they were savouring the pain he would unleash upon this one.

'Wait!' screamed the Bretonnian. 'I can help you!'

Bjarki ignored him.

'I... I know a way into the keep!' screamed the Bretonnian. 'A secret way! Unguarded! Please don't kill me!'

'Stop,' ordered a voice. Bjarki swore. The Bretonnian continued to scream, wailing like a beaten dog.

'I said stop, little bear,' growled the voice again, more forcefully this time, and Bjarki's head snapped up. He glared angrily at his jarl, who was standing flanked by his two daughters. Each of them had their hands on the hilts of their blades. The jarl had his arms crossed over his broad chest.

'Why?' said Bjarki.

'What did he say, just then?' demanded the jarl.

'He's pleading for his life,' said the seer. 'Pathetic, really.'

'Did he not say anything else,' said Styrbjorn, eyes narrowed.

Bjarki licked his lips, wondering if he could get away with lying to his jarl. He dismissed the idea; he would not risk further distancing himself from Styrbjorn over the life of one Bretonnian dog.

'He claims to know a way into the keep. An unguarded way, he says.'

'Let him up,' said Styrbjorn.

'He's lying!' stormed Bjarki. 'He'd say anything if he thought it would give him a few more seconds of life!'

'Let him up, I said,' growled the Skaeling jarl.

'They are offerings to the gods, my jarl,' snarled Bjarki. 'You risk offending the great powers by intervening.'

Styrbjorn levelled a finger threateningly at the seer, and Bjarki shook his head, muttering under his breath.

He glanced down at the pitiful wretch still held immobile beneath his knife. The Bretonnian had stopped screaming now, and was merely whimpering, tears mixing with blood and mucous. Then in one sharp, angry movement, he sliced away the Bretonnian's ear. The wretch screamed in agony, and his squeals increased as alcohol was splashed onto the wound.

'Fine,' said Bjarki, and he shoved the bleeding wretch to the ground at Styrbjorn's feet. He tossed the man's ear to one of the warhounds lurking nearby, which caught it deftly in its mouth and swallowed it in one gulp.

It did not take long to wrangle the information out of the wretched Bretonnian. Bjarki found it disgusting at how quickly the man betrayed his comrades. Still, he was a cunning one – he kept the exact location of this supposed secret entrance into the keep to himself, clearly trying to keep himself alive. In truth, had he coughed up the location of the entrance, he would already be dead, so perhaps he was not as stupid as Bjarki first thought.

'He will not keep it from us for long,' said Bjarki with not a small amount of relish, brandishing his serpent dagger.

'No,' said Styrbjorn. 'I don't want to hear any more of his pathetic screams. He'll lead us to it.'

'You will accompany this raid yourself?' said Bjarki.

'Gods no,' said Styrbjorn with a laugh, shaking his head, and his daughters smirked. Sensing there was something he was missing, Bjarki bristled, narrowing his eyes.

'It would take a week to get the smell out of my nostrils,' said Styrbjorn, and an evil grin appeared on his face. 'No, dear Bjarki, *you* will lead it.'

'What do you mean about the smell?' said Bjarki, still wary. Styrbjorn laughed again, as did his daughters.

'I think I already know what this "secret entrance" is. You'll see,' said the jarl with a mischievous glint in his eyes.

BJARKI SCOWLED UP at the latrine chute some twenty feet up the north side of the keep's wall.

It had taken the better part of two hours to navigate their way around the rocks to this position unseen, and Bjarki was in no mood to see the humorous side of the plan.

Half a dozen men had been chosen to accompany him. All were slightly built warriors, smaller than their brethren. At first Bjarki had thought this was some implicit insult, but now he understood. The latrine chimney was narrow; only the slimmest Norscan would have any hope of fitting inside.

They had waited until the white moon had slunk over the horizon before setting off, moving stealthily and keeping to the shadows. Weapons had been wrapped in furs, and jangling buckles and armour stripped off them so that they could move in silence. For most of the way they had been forced to wade through waist-deep water, always keeping a wary eye out for sharks, and trying to keep their bodies low, so as to ensure that wherever possible the rocks were between them and anyone who may have been looking down from above.

The wall beneath the chute was slick with excrement, and it coated the rocks at the foot of the wall. At any time other than extreme low tide the waves would be lapping up against the base of the wall, washing away the foulness. Already the tide was beginning to turn, and Bjarki realised that there was no chance of getting back around to the east of the island before the rising waters forced them to swim. He did not relish the idea of that, giving the dark fins of the ever-present sharks a glare. They were true beasts of Kharnath; fearless, indiscriminate killers, and driven mad by the merest whiff of blood in the water. He knew they would take him as willingly as any other Norscan or Bretonnian that fell into their domain – that he was a seer of the gods mattered not at all.

Bjarki still didn't see the need for this far-fetched ploy, and he suspected that Styrbjorn insisted on it merely because it amused him to think of his seer climbing a filth-smeared chute. He was certain that the direct attack Styrbjorn planned would be enough to take the castle walls, but seeing that there was no turning back now, he sighed and nodded to one of the warriors accompanying him, Eilif.

Eilif was Styrbjorn's nephew, and the slender young warrior had his blond hair pulled back in a single thick plait that hung down past his waist. He nodded back at Bjarki and began picking his way over the rocks to the base of the wall. He had a length of rope looped over his shoulders, knotted every couple of feet, and after pausing to look up for a few moments to pick out his route and memorise the location of handholds, he began his ascent.

Eilif climbed swiftly and surely, and Bjarki cast a look up towards the battlements atop the keep. If anyone looked down now, they would see the Norscan clearly, but thankfully the arrogant Bretonnians seemed not to expect any attack from this quarter – there was no room to land a ship, and the keep was too high for ladders or grappling hooks. The Norscan continued climbing hand over hand, digging his fingers and toes into the gaps between the stones.

At last the young Skaeling reached the toilet chute and he jammed his feet into crevices and pulled a hammer and a six-inch iron spike from where they had been tucked into his belt. Waiting until a wave crashed against the rocks to help disguise the sound, Eilif struck the spike sharply, driving it into the mortar between two stones, before pressing himself hard up against the wall and freezing. He was concealed from above by the jutting chimney of the latrine shaft itself, and Bjarki and the others ducked back behind the rocks, lowering themselves into the black waters as the heads of several sentries up above peered over the edge.

After a minute or so, Bjarki risked a glance upwards, and saw that the sentries were no longer visible. He signalled to Eilif, who quickly unlooped his rope and tied its end to the piton. He let the rope unfurl, and Bjarki grabbed it as it fell down to the base of the wall.

The iron bars that blocked the latrine chute were corroded and crumbling, and it took little effort for Eilif to rip the latticework free, though Bjarki winced at the sound, ducking back behind the rocks. When no sentry seemed to have heard the sound, the bars were dropped from above and deftly caught by a warrior below. The young warrior climbed swiftly back down the rope.

'Bring him,' said Bjarki in a low voice, and the Bretonnian prisoner was shoved forward. His head was bound in cloth, and blood soaked the area where his left ear had been. His mouth was gagged so that he did not shout out and alert the guards. His eyes were wide with fright and pain, and filled with tears. Still, having someone that knew their way around the inside of the castle would be useful.

'You first,' growled Bjarki.

He was a hunchbacked wretch, and the seer looked at him critically for a moment. Though he was certainly stronger than he looked, the malformed Bretonnian peasant might have trouble climbing the rope, let alone the vertical latrine chimney. And if he slipped and fell while half-way up, he might ensure those behind him fell as well.

'No,' said Bjarki, changing his mind. 'I am first.'

The Bretonnian nodded his head, clearly just grateful to be alive. Still, Bjarki knew that given the briefest opportunity, he would try to run. He dipped a finger into a pouch, and leant towards the wretch, who drew back away from him in fear.

'Give me your hand,' said Bjarki, imparting a portion of his power into his voice. Unable to resist the seer's order, the Bretonnian held out his hand, palm up. Had Bjarki told him to slit his own throat he would have done so, and the terror in the man's eyes showed that he understood that.

Bjarki took the man's hand in his and closed his eyes, muttering arcane phrases. After a moment he opened his eyes and turned the peasant's hand over. There was a black mark upon his wrist, and the wretch's eyes widened as he looked upon it.

'This is the mark of *Drazh'la'gha* the flesh-eater,' said Bjarki in a low, menacing voice that made the peasant wince. 'It is a curse, and I am the only one that can remove it. Attempt to escape, shout a warning to any defender, or try to trick me in any way, and *Drazh'la'gha* will consume you from the inside out. Do as I say, and I will remove it. You understand?'

The peasant clenched his eyes tightly shut, and tears were once again running down his face. It was disgusting and shaming, and Bjarki felt nothing but loathing for this pathetic creature.

'You understand?' he said again, and the man nodded his head. 'And do not think that death is an escape. If you die while the curse is still in place, your soul shall never have rest. It shall be the plaything of *Drazh'la'gha* for all eternity. You do *not* want to fall to your death while climbing, Bretonnian filth.'

Satisfied, Bjarki nodded to the young Skaeling warrior, Eilif.

'See that he follows close behind me,' the seer ordered. Then giving the latrine chimney one last, sour look, he began the climb.

'WHAT WAS IT?' said Duke Adalhard, speaking to one of his knights who had gone to look over the edge of the keep, having heard a metallic sound from below.

'Nothing, lord,' said the knight. 'Perhaps a trick of the wind.'

Adalhard nodded vaguely, turning his mind back to the task at hand. From atop his towering keep, Duke Adalhard was organising the defence of his castle, communicating with those below with flags and runners. He saw hundreds of longships ploughing through the seas towards the western battlements, the longest stretch of wall within the castle, and the least heavily defended. It would be difficult for the enemy to gain a foothold upon the narrow strip of land beneath the western walls, and the approach was treacherous, with many hidden rocks and the surging waves.

Still, a foothold *was* possible, and he could ill afford to leave those walls undefended. With some reluctance he ordered them bolstered, sending the last reserve companies of men-at-arms and knights towards them. The eastern walls had taken the brunt of the assault and were in desperate need of reinforcement, but there were no more men to spare. Ideally, the defenders would be rotated on shifts, in order that weary men were able to get some decent rest and food, but that was a luxury that the duke was unable to afford.

The Norse assault was now hitting Castle Lyonesse from all angles. The heaviest concentration of enemy forces came at the eastern walls, but longships were being rowed at speed towards the island from every quarter in an effort to ensure that the Bretonnian's defences were spread as thinly as possible; and it was working. Only the north was not suffering attack – the keep took up most of the northern tip of the island, and it was simply too tall, and the ocean's currents north of the island too fierce, for an attack to have any attempt of success from that quarter.

Thankfully the enemy artillery had been silenced. Adalhard was under no illusions as to what would have happened had it not; he would have gone down in history as the only duke to allow Castle Lyonesse to fall to the enemy.

Damaged crenulations and battlements had been barricaded with sacks of grain, barrels filled with water and hastily nailed together planks of wood. One wall section fifty feet wide had collapsed, killing three knights and scores of peasants, leaving the wall only half its original height.

That was the biggest chink in the castle's armour, and the enemy had hurled themselves against it, clambering eagerly up the loose stones and chunks of masonry, screaming war cries and bellowing praise to their infernal gods. It was only because the grail knight Reolus had taken it upon himself to stand there, atop the crumbling wall, defying the enemy, that the section had not yet been overrun. His presence inspired those around him to great heights of bravery and courage, and it was there that the fighting had been the fiercest.

Between attacks the duke ordered wine, bread and cheese distributed amongst the defenders, and he had opened up his storehouses, seeing to it that even the lowliest peasants drafted into service – those of them that were left alive at any rate– were supplied with blankets, replacement weapons, adequate arrows and shields.

Had this been any other enemy, Duke Adalhard would have felt confident that he would be able to hold almost indefinitely, or at least long enough for aid to come from Couronne, if not from his eastern neighbour, the bastard Duke of L'Anguille. His greed-sick rival was doubtless enjoying hearing of his misfortune, already plotting how he could move against Lyonesse and extend the borders of L'Anguille.

With all the reserve companies committed to action, there was little more that Adalhard could do. He ordered a manservant to bring him his shield and helm.

'You cannot be considering fighting on the walls, my duke?' said one of his nobles, the stick thin Baron Broussard, aghast at the notion.

'I am. And *you* will be fighting alongside me, my dear baron,' Adalhard said with some relish. 'Every man able to wield a sword is to fight.'

The man blanched. Inwardly, Adalhard was pleased to see the man squirm. He had little time for those willing to send honourable men to their deaths but who would not face the same dangers themselves. Broussard was a political animal – Adalhard had always been sure to keep the man onside for he would have made a deadly political opponent – but in truth he loathed the man, and he was certainly no warrior.

'But if you were to fall, my lord, surely that would be a terrible blow to morale?' said Broussard smoothly, though Adalhard noted that a sheen of sweat glistened on his brow.

'And what does it say to the men if I were *not* to fight? It will give heart to the men to see me face the same dangers as they,' replied Adalhard dismissively.

'It is foolishness, my lord!' protested Broussard. He turned towards his companion, the porcine Marquis of Carabas, looking for support, but the man avoided his gaze. 'We must hand the young woman over to the Norscans! Any other path is folly, my lord duke!'

'I have already made my mind up, baron. See that your man brings your weapons and armour. I expect to see you garbed for war in ten minutes time. A second late and I will have you branded a coward and turncoat, and I will see you swing. Am I understood?'

'I always knew that you were a fool,' said Broussard bitterly.

'If I am to die,' said Adalhard, 'then I will do so with honour, defending the realm I was sworn to protect. I will not cow to the demands of any Norscan whoreson, even if it *does* mean certain death.'

'There is no honour in death, however it comes,' said Broussard. 'The notion of honour is a convenient fiction, and every Bretonnian with half a brain knows it. It means nothing!'

'You are wrong, baron,' said Adalhard.

'I should have allied myself with L'Anguille long ago,' said Broussard. 'At least then I would still be alive on the morn.'

The duke said nothing, merely regarding Broussard with the expression of one who unwittingly steps on a slug while walking barefoot.

'None of us are going to survive this!' said Broussard, an edge of hysteria entering his voice. 'We are all going to die here if you don't hand the witch over to them! What does she matter to you, anyway? She's just some Bastonnian whore! Can you not see that?'

'What I see,' said Adalhard, 'is a man willing to hand a woman of noble birth over to blood-drenched savages in an attempt to save his own pathetic, worthless, honourless life. What I see is a man unwilling to take up a sword and fight the enemies of his lord. You disgust me, Broussard. I should have disposed of your services long ago.'

Broussard's face twisted in fury, and he scrabbled for the dagger sheathed at his waist. Before any of Adalhard's bodyguards could react, he pulled the blade clear and lunged at the duke.

Adalhard swatted the dagger aside with the flat of his hand and backhanded the baron in the side of the head. Broussard was knocked to the ground, and before he could rise the duke's men were upon him, pinning him down.

The Duke of Lyonesse drew his sword. Elven runes engraved upon the blade glittered, and he took a menacing step forwards. The baron struggled, his eyes wide with terror, but he was held firmly.

'You condemn every man in this castle to death if you do not hand her over,' Broussard said, breathing hard.

'And I condemn every man to live in shame if I do,' said the duke.

Broussard licked his lips, and a spark of hope appeared in his eyes as the duke sheathed his ancestral sword.

'You are not worthy of dying a warrior's death by this sword,' said Adalhard, shattering that fleeting hope. 'It would be a dishonour to the memory of my forefathers to stain its blade with your blood. Hurl him over the battlements.'

The baron began screaming and fighting, and Duke Adalhard turned away as Broussard was manhandled towards the crenulations atop the keep. The man was bustled over the edge, and his screams grew faint. A moment later they stopped altogether.

The duke's manservant returned, bearing Adalhard's gleaming, golden helmet and white shield, with its red lion's head heraldry protruding in relief from its surface.

'What of you, Carabas?' said the duke as he pulled his helmet onto his head. He looked towards the overweight noble.

'I'm no warrior,' said the marquis, 'but I would be honoured to stand at your side and do my part.'

There was fire in his voice, and Adalhard believed him. As porcine and gluttonous as Carabas was, he had always known there was a certain strength in the man, and he felt admiration for him at his words. For a warrior, his body and mind trained for war, it still took great courage to walk onto the battlefield. To walk onto the field of war knowing that you were unskilled, unfit, and that the first enemy you met would most likely kill you took courage beyond what Adalhard believed he himself possessed.

'The honour would be mine, Carabas,' he said, with feeling.

'Can't say I ever liked that bastard,' said the fat marquis, gesturing over the ramparts with his thumb. 'About time, I'd say. But I fear I will make you wait longer than the ten minutes you gave him. It will take me that long to get to the bottom of the stairs, let alone have my man stuff me into my armour.'

Adalhard smiled.

'I'll wait,' he said.

In the distance there came a horrible trumpeting sound that Adalhard had heard before, and the smile dropped from his face.

'What in the Lady's name was that?' said Carabas.

THERE WAS LITTLE room inside the latrine chute, yet Bjarki climbed steadily and easily, using his back, knees and elbows to wedge himself in the shaft and shimmy his way up. He slipped once or twice on the faeces-slick walls of the chimney, but did not panic, and caught himself each time before he had fallen more than a yard or two. A little light filtered down from the various latrines that joined the chute; just enough to see by.

The progress of the Bretonnian captive below him, however, was painfully slow and halting, and Bjarki snarled in frustration as he looked down at the shadow of the man, willing him to hurry up. The noise the man made as he climbed made him cringe, and with every passing moment he was certain that they would be discovered. The peasant's breathing was heavy and laboured, and he had wedged himself inside the shaft as he tried to catch his breath. Bjarki could just make out the wretch's arms and legs shaking with fatigue, and he cursed again.

'You fall, and eternal torment awaits,' Bjarki said in a hoarse, low whisper, his voice ghosting down to the Bretonnian's one good ear. He heard the man swallow thickly, and start climbing again, and Bjarki smiled grimly in the darkness.

It had been such a simple thing to trick the peasant into believing he had placed a curse on him. Curses were tricky things, requiring considerable preparation and not a small amount of risk – much more trouble than one ignorant wretch was worth. He smirked again as he thought of the black 'mark of *Drazh'la'gha*' upon the man's wrist; nothing more diabolical than powdered charcoal mixed with spit.

Hearing the man coming up behind him, Bjarki recommenced climbing, shimmying easily up the chimney until he came to an angled pit that entered the shaft. Flickering candlelight could be seen between the cracks in the planks that sat on top of the latrine, and Bjarki manoeuvred himself so that he could push himself up towards it with his feet against the far wall.

Praying that the Changer of Fates was smiling upon him, Bjarki pushed the cover up an inch and hooked his fingers around the rim of the latrine. Then, hearing nothing in the room beyond, he pulled himself up, pushing the cover back with his head.

The room was small and square, with a slit window set in its back wall. Its door was pulled closed, and seeing no one, Bjarki hauled himself fully out of the latrine chute.

He had left his thick fur back at the camp, and his sinewy bare arms and tattooed torso was smeared with stinking effluent. His dreadlocked hair had been pulled back into a ponytail and it too was covered with the noisome filth.

Turning, he could see that the Bretonnian was struggling. Reaching down, Bjarki grabbed the man by the scruff of his tunic, and hauled him up and into the room.

Chlod flopped, stinking, onto the floor and Bjarki curled his lip in disgust.

'Where are we?' he said. The Bretonnian looked at him stupidly, and Bjarki tore the gag from the man's mouth.

'Where are we?' he repeated.

'In the keep?' said the Bretonnian slowly.

Bjarki swore in the Skaeling dialect, shaking his head at the man's staggering stupidity.

'*Where* in the keep?' When no answer was forthcoming, Bjarki narrowed his eyes. 'You've never been in the keep, have you?'

'Please don't kill me, lord,' wailed the man, throwing himself to the floor before Bjarki.

'Quiet, fool!' hissed Bjarki, hearing footsteps outside the door, but there was no placating the bubbling peasant. Bjarki drew his dagger, its blade undulating like a serpent's body, and he tensed himself as he heard the footsteps halt beyond the door.

The door was pushed inwards and Bjarki saw a man bedecked in a white and red tabard, his face framed by a chain coif. His eyes registered his surprise as Bjarki leapt forwards and rammed his dagger up under his chin, the blade sinking to the hilt. Seeing another figure in the hallway stiffen in shock, Bjarki sidestepped the first man, dragging him inside the small room as he did so.

Bjarki reached out towards the man that was about to raise the alarm, his fingers stabbing forward like claws and he barked a single guttural word in the Dark Tongue. Swirling ribbons of energy leaped from his fingertips and struck the Bretonnian in the head. Blood burst from his ears, nose and eyes and he fell to the ground without a sound.

Moving to the body, Bjarki cast a quick glance along the corridor to ensure he was unseen. Thankfully, it seemed that the two soldiers had been alone. He grabbed the body by its shirtfront and dragged it out of the hallway.

Eilif had emerged from the latrine, his face and hair smeared with foulness. He was crouching over the body of the first man that Bjarki had killed, blood pooling beneath him. The Bretonnian peasant was pressed back against the wall, shaking in fear and exhaustion from the climb. Bjarki retrieved his serpentine dagger and cleaned its blade upon the quaking peasant's shirt front before re-sheathing it at his waist.

The Norscan seer stepped back out into the corridor, checking for guards. He gestured, and Eilif joined him, dragging the Bretonnian peasant along with him, and the other Skaelings began emerging from the latrine.

When they were all out, Bjarki led them silently down the western corridor, judging that one way was as good as another. They all moved quietly, hugging the shadows. He signalled that he, Eilif and the Bretonnian would take the lead, while the others were to keep some distance back.

They moved forward warily. Bjarki cautiously tried the first few doors they came across, which opened into rooms filled with rich furnishings – tables, couches and sumptuous carpets. Moving on, they came to a staircase, and Bjarki led his companions down four flights, at last coming to the ground floor of the keep. Two other staircases also descended from the upper levels here, all three of them emptying into a broad hall lined with ancient suits of armour. Torches burnt in dozens of sconces, lighting up the cavernous expanse.

Bjarki, Eilif and the Bretonnian peasant were cautiously descending the stairs when the sound of voices and marching feet reached their ears. Bjarki waved a warning to those behind, who melted into the shadows without a sound. He and Eilif backed up, dragging the Bretonnian with them, and they dropped behind a thick stone balustrade.

Peering around the corner, Bjarki saw a middle-aged man in golden armour appear, descending the grandest of the three staircases alongside a grossly overweight man who looked vaguely comical in his oversized armour. Twenty knights marched behind them.

There were too many of them to be taken by force, and Bjarki and his comrades remained motionless, all but invisible in the gloom as the enemy knights marched across hall. A huge pair of doors was thrown open, and the sound of battle beyond entered the hall. Then the enemy were gone, and the doors slammed shut behind them.

Moving swiftly, Bjarki moved towards those same doors, accompanied by the other Skaeling warriors. Opening the doors, he peered outside, looking across the small inner courtyard of the keep, towards its gatehouse that led out into the castle proper.

There were few soldiers outside – they were all defending the outer walls. Pockets of archers patrolled the keep's walls but none of them were looking down into the courtyard – none of them expected an enemy from within.

'Eilif and I will make for the harbour as planned. We raise that gate and this siege is as good as over,' snarled Bjarki. 'We'll take the Bretonnian with us – he may prove useful.'

Bjarki's gaze passed over the gathered warriors.

'Raising the portcullis is all that matters,' he said. 'Once the enemy sees us, it is your role to draw the attention away from us.'

Each of the warriors understood what it was he was asking, and their chests puffed out in pride.

'We go,' Bjarki said 'Now!'

The Norscans slipped out into the courtyard and made a dash for the keep's gatehouse, Bjarki in the lead. Eilif was a step behind him, half dragging the Bretonnian along with him, and the other warriors moved swiftly behind them. There were no cries of alarm, and they managed to move into the cover of the gatehouse unseen. Silently, they padded beneath a hanging portcullis as they proceeded through the tunnel-like corridor towards the other side of the gatehouse. Murderholes and arrow slits glared at them, and Bjarki knew that taking this gate by force would have been costly indeed. He was thankful it was open. They passed beneath another portcullis, and then they were out into the square beyond the keep.

Enemy soldiers ran to and fro, reinforcements streaming towards breaches in the walls. At first, no one seemed to register that the enemy were amongst them, and Bjarki darted towards a side-alley.

The Norscans were halfway across the square when there was a shout, and Bjarki saw a shaven-headed Bretonnian pointing in their direction. A group of warriors began running towards them.

'Take them!' the seer shouted, and the Skaeling warriors, bellowing war cries at the top of their lungs, threw themselves into the path of the enemy. Bjarki darted towards a side-alley, Eilif and the Bretonnian peasant at his heels.

They ducked into the shadows of the alley, and Bjarki paused, looking back to see if they were being pursued.

It appeared that they were not. The Skaeling warriors that had accompanied him were carving into the enemy, axes and swords hacking into flesh, but already they were being surrounded.

'Die well, warriors of Norsca,' said Bjarki, and he turned away, continuing south towards the island fortress's harbour.

It took them the better part of five minutes to wind their way down to the harbour unseen, and a further five to pick their way around its edge to the immense gatehouse that spanned the harbour entrance.

The only entrance they found was locked and barred.

'Might I try, my lord?' ventured the peasant. Bjarki raised an eyebrow, and gestured for him to go ahead.

The Bretonnian peasant stepped forward and rapped on the heavy door. Bjarki stepped to the side, and pulled Eilif with him. He heard a wooden panel slide aside a moment later.

'What?' demanded a voice.

'Rations,' said the peasant. 'Bread and wine.'

'We've already got ours,' said the voice, with a hint of suspicion and wariness.

'I'm just followin' orders. But if you don't want 'em…'

'I didn't say I don't want 'em. Hold on a minute,' said the voice, and Bjarki heard the sound of bars being removed, then a heavy key turning in a lock. Eilif readied his knife.

The door was thrown wide.

'Where are these rations then?' said the voice. Eilif stepped around the corner and plunged his knife into the speaker's throat.

They bustled inside, and Eilif finished off the warden with half a dozen stabs to the chest, before lowering him in a corner and covering him with empty sacks. Then they began to climb the stairs of the gatehouse.

Moving as quickly as possible, they climbed a steep staircase that spiralled up and up, and at last came upon a landing. A heavy, locked door barred their progress. The peasant grinned at Bjarki and lifted his eyebrows questioningly, but the seer doubted the charade would work a second time, and he knew that his time was drawing short.

Bjarki gathered himself, closing his eyes and sucking in a deep breath. He gestured sharply, and the door was smashed inwards as if struck by a battering ram.

Eilif was through in an instant, and by the time Bjarki had entered the room, two of its occupants were already dead. Eilif tackled the last to the ground and slit his throat.

The room was large, with arrow slits in the southern wall looking out to sea and large arched stained glass windows in the north wall looking down over the harbour and across the castle itself. They were located directly above the harbour entrance itself, Bjarki realised.

In the centre of the room there was an immense circular wheel embedded in the floor, with a number of wooden spokes protruding from its sides. A pair of mules were hitched to these spokes, and the stone under their hooves was covered in sand and hay. They stood immobile, disinterested in the killing that had occurred around them.

Bjarki studied the wheel for a moment. It was not dissimilar to a millwheel, and he guessed that it was connected to gears and turning mechanisms underneath the floor. He reached out and pulled down a lever, and nodded in satisfaction as he heard disengaged gears clamp together beneath the floor.

'Bar the doors,' he ordered. The Bretonnian backed away into a far corner, out of the way, and Bjarki ordered him to stay put. Eilif positioned himself atop the staircase that they had just climbed, weapon in hand.

Bjarki moved to one of the arrow slits looking southward. He could not see the longships lurking out there in the gloom and the snow, but he knew they were there, waiting for his signal. With a muttered incantation his left hand erupted into blue fire. He saw a single torch flare briefly in response out there in the darkness, eight hundred yards out.

Bjarki watched closely, biting his lip as he waited for the ships to appear. The minutes dragged by, but then he saw them, a score of dragonships ploughing swiftly through the ocean swell on a direct course for the gatehouse. Judging by the shouts he heard from atop the gatehouse, he guessed that the enemy too had sighted them, and he could hear grinding as the giant trebuchets above were levered around into position to target them.

Gauging the distance and speed of the dragonships, Bjarki left it another thirty seconds before running back from the window and slapping the rump of one of the mules. It dutifully began trudging around in a circle, as did its companion, and the sound of grinding gears could be heard. A rumbling could be discerned underneath the floor, and the sound of chains tightening around pulleys. Then those pulleys began to turn, and the chains began to be reeled in, locking around the teeth of immense cogs concealed within the walls, and the dual portcullis began to open; one latticework descending into a slot carved into the rocks twenty feet beneath the water, and the other lifting up into the gatehouse itself. From the outside, it must have looked like the mouth of some giant beast opening.

The mules continued to trudge around in their monotonous circle, and the grinding of gears and chains echoed loudly, making the whole gatehouse shudder.

There were shouts of alarm and shock from outside, and there came a pounding at the doors. A moment later, heavy weights began slamming into those doors, making the wooden braces barring them groan.

Moving back to the south-facing wall, Bjarki looked out to see the dragonships no more than fifty yards out. This was going to work, he thought, with a grin. Then one of the doors gave way, its timbers splintering inwards, and enemy soldiers bundled inside.

Still grinning, Bjarki turned towards them, the power of the gods flaring in his eyes. Blue flames sprang up over both hands as he called upon great Tchar. With a roar, he thrust his hands towards the enemy, and they were instantly consumed in a roaring conflagration. The faces of daemons could be seen in that billowing blue fire, and those caught within the inferno screamed in torment as their bodies were twisted out of shape, remoulded into a form more pleasing to the Great Changer.

Fifty feet below, a score of Skaeling dragonships ploughed beneath the open portcullis and into the harbour. Each of the ships was packed with blood-hungry berserkers, the most rabid, unhinged warriors in the entire Skaeling war host.

In the distance to the east came the sound of deafening trumpeting.

CALARD WAS STARING in mute horror towards the south as he saw the enemy ships slipping into the harbour inside the curtain walls.

'How?' he breathed, feeling all hope fade.

The flagging spirits of the defenders had lifted as the Duke of Lyonesse joined the fray. The lord of Lyonesse had moved along the walls, speaking to the knights, offering words of praise and encouragement, and to have him amongst the fighting had made morale soar.

Much to Calard's surprise, the duke had even spared a few words for the peasants defending his walls, praising their efforts and promising them a feast worthy of the king himself once the enemy had been seen off. Calard saw the effect such a simple gesture had on the defenders, knight and peasant alike. He saw shoulders that had been slumped in defeat and despair straighten, and chests puff out as the duke rekindled their sense of pride. These were the actions of a true leader, Calard recognised, and as lord of Garamont, he pledged to remember these lessons. Whether he lived long enough to put them into practice was another thing completely however – and all the good that the duke's presence had done was now shattered. Every Bretonnian fighting on the walls saw that all their dogged resistance had come to naught, for the enemy was now sailing right into the heart of the fortress so many of them had already died to defend.

Calard saw the duke in the distance shouting orders and barking commands as he attempted to redirect defenders from the walls towards this new threat. He was sending one out of every three men down to face the enemies within the castle, and although Calard saw this risked losing the walls to the enemy, it would not matter if the enemy took the castle from within. More enemy longships were ploughing through the gatehouse into the harbour, and Calard knew that if the great portcullis was not closed, then the castle was lost. He saw the duke gesturing towards the arched gatehouse that spanned the entrance to the harbour, and saw a trio of white winged shapes begin hurtling towards it; Laudethaire and the last of his companions.

Swearing, Calard chopped his sword into the neck of a Norscan as he scrambled over the ramparts, and he kicked the man's body off the walls as he slumped forward.

'Let's get off these damned walls,' he called to his brother, who nodded. They made to move towards the stairs, but a deafening trumpeting sounded, painfully loud, and Calard froze. Turning, he peered out through the driving snow and wind beyond the castle wall.

He saw a giant shape in the ocean that he at first mistook for just another longship, packed with warriors. It was moving inexorably towards the island, though it was rolling steadily from side to side, and for a moment Calard stared at it, uncomprehending, as he saw it had no sail.

Feeling a sense of rising dread, Calard moved to the battlements and narrowed his eyes, shielding them from the biting wind with one hand. His breath caught in his throat as he realised that it was not a ship at all; it was the wooden fortress strapped atop one of the giant, hateful mammoths that had wreaked such havoc three weeks earlier. The beast was fording the strait, battling against the pounding surf as it trudged along the same causeway that Calard had himself ridden two days earlier. It was no more than fifty yards from the beach.

The water washed over the beast's shoulders, so that only the top half of its dome-like head could be seen. Its trunk was lifted up out of the water, and the great wooden fortress chained upon its back heaved from side to side as the behemoth strode through the heavy swell. Waves crashed over the top of the battlements of the mobile fortress, but the berserkers clinging there merely howled in defiance, their cries sounding barely human at all. Calard caught sight of the other two giant beasts wading through the swell behind it.

Horror filled Calard as he realised that if the mammoths were large enough to walk along the causeway then they were large enough to allow those riding upon their howdahs to leap directly onto the walls, as if they were living siege engines.

Behind him, blood curdling roars echoed throughout the castle as the enemy longships inside the harbour were driven up against the shore, and the merciless warriors within leaped over their gunwales, intent on the slaughter.

Calard felt utterly torn, not knowing where his sword was most needed.

'Lady protect us,' he breathed.

CHAPTER EIGHTEEN

Calard and the other defenders upon the eastern walls stared in mute horror as the first of the mountainous war mammoths rose from the ocean like some infernal beast emerging from the depths. Its matted, thick fur hung in sea-drenched ropes and steam rose from its flanks. Its massive head was protected by plates of black iron hammered into its skull, and giant bands of metal studded with spikes as long as a man's arm encircled its four sweeping tusks. Overlapping links of black iron protected its trunk, forming a flexible carapace like the shell of a beetle, and its large, flapping ears were pierced with dozens of hooks and rings each as large as a man's head.

The beast lifted its heavy head as it trudged out of the ocean, and it trumpeted deafeningly, the sound making Calard's ears reverberate painfully. The waves crashed around its tree-trunk legs, and the ground shook as it strode out of the breakers and onto the beach.

The warriors riding within the fortress upon the giant beast's back roared in eagerness and bloodlust, driving themselves into a berserk fury. They clashed their weapons against their shields and the sides of the great howdah holding them, and a hugely muscled Norscan pounded upon a pair of huge drums, human skin pulled taut across their tops.

Banners of flayed flesh covered in Norscan runes and symbols of infernal deities hung from twisted icons of dark metal, flapping in the fierce gale. Easily a hundred Bretonnian heads were impaled upon spears and metal spikes protruding from the sides of the wooden howdah. The bodies of a score of knights had been pushed onto lances, and they rose in a grisly fan from the back of the howdah.

The second and third mammoths following behind the first could be seen clearer now, battling through the fury of the breakers amid the driving snow and wind, and Calard saw that the enemy warlord himself was accompanying this latest assault. He rode upon the back of the second war tusker, seated in a high-backed wooden throne, arrogantly prominent upon the forecastle of his howdah, clearly disdainful of the Bretonnians' arrows.

A spinning hunk of masonry hurled high into the air by a trebuchet crashed down onto the head of the third mammoth, striking it a glancing blow, and it bellowed in rage and pain, shaking its head from side to side. The heavy iron champron hammered into its skull was dented inwards by the blow, and hot blood began to stain the waters around it as it floundered in the surf. It stumbled, and Calard could see the fins of fifty or more sharks circling wildly, the taste of the blood in the water driving them into a frenzy that mirrored that of the Norscans themselves.

A larger shape scythed through the breakers suddenly, scattering the sharks before its bow wave. It powered into the shallow water with powerful flicks of its tail, and Calard saw that its hide was black and white. Its mouth gaped wide, exposing hundreds of razor-like teeth, and it hit the mammoth hard, knocking it sideward and ripping a great chunk of flesh from its body.

The mammoth bellowed again, and the warriors upon its back jabbed downwards with spears, trying to fight off the monstrous attacker. Calard saw several of the fearless warriors leap over the sides of the howdah, dropping onto the back of the thrashing black and white beast and driving spears deep into its body.

The mammoth swung around and struck its attacker with its tusks, lifting it out of the water and hurling it away, sending the foolhardy Norscans upon its back flying. The killer whale plunged back into the water thirty feet away, only to be turned upon by the sharks and other killer whales lurking in the deeper water. The Norse warriors that had been sent flying were ripped apart by the voracious ocean predators, shredded in an orgy of bloodlust.

The mammoth regained its footing and charged up onto the beach, blood streaming from its wounds. A huge chunk of flesh was missing from its shoulder, and the flesh within was pink and wet.

'Shoot them!' screamed Calard in desperation, seeing that the peasant bowmen all around were frozen, staring in gormless horror at the three mammoths that were now charging towards the castle walls. With those monstrous beasts outside the walls, and the enemy inside the walls, Calard knew that the resolve of the peasants was about to snap. All it would take was for one of them to turn and run and the whole stinking rabble would throw down their weapons and stampede from the walls.

The rising panic and desperation was palpable as the courage of the defenders faltered, and he knew that the next few moments were critical to forestall a complete rout. His old weapon master, Gunthar, had taught him that in moments of indecision it was the nature of men, particularly peasant inbreds, to want someone to step to the fore and give them direction. If no one did so, then they would become a mindless rabble.

'In the name of the king, hold!' Calard roared in his loudest and most authoritative voice. He registered that men, even knights, were turning towards him, looking to him for direction and perhaps reassurance.

'Aim for their eyes!' he shouted. 'Now!'

Generations of enforced servitude ensured that the peasants responded to Calard's order without question, and as one they lifted their bows and launched a shower of arrows towards the charging mammoths.

Countless shafts rained down upon the titanic creatures. Many ricocheted off the thick armour plating of the beasts, but hundreds more embedded themselves in flesh and muscle, until the lead creature's forelegs resembled pin cushions. The warriors upon the back of the beasts ducked behind their wooden battlements and held their shields high, and hundreds of arrows sank into the woodwork, but some were struck, screaming in pain as arrows thudded home into their flesh.

A pair of arrows struck the lead beast in its left eye simultaneously, sinking deep into the rage-filled orb and instantly flooding it with blood. It bellowed in agony and reared up onto its hind legs, ceasing its thunderous charge. Men fell from the howdah as it tipped precariously backwards, while others clung on desperately.

More arrows thudded into the mammoth's underbelly as it reared up, and as its forelegs came crashing back down to ground, it turned away from the castle walls.

Enraged and in pain, it struck out at the Norscans racing up the beach alongside it, smashing them aside with a sweep of its tusks.

Scattered cheering rose from the defenders, but it sounded strained and weak, for the other two mammoths came on at full speed, lowering their heads like charging bulls. The handler of the enemy warlord's mammoth tugged on his crude reins, dragging on the vicious barbed hooks driven though the tusker's sensitive ears, turning it directly towards the wall section only thirty yards from Calard's position. The other beast thundered headlong towards the immense gate leading into the castle itself.

It struck with the elemental power of an avalanche and the metal lattice-work of the first portcullis buckled inwards with a sickening shriek. The heavy reinforced gates beyond were smashed apart, and the sound of wood splintering echoed sharply as the dozen immense bars that sealed the gate, each as thick as a tree trunk and bound in iron loops, were sundered.

The other beast struck the wall like a living battering ram, and hundreds of men staggered as the whole wall section shook. Large hooks of black iron attached to chains were hurled over the battlements, and then the first of the enemy were over, leaping onto the walls and laying about them with huge, jagged axes and swords, killing with every stroke.

These warriors were the enemy warlord's elite bodyguards, each of them a mighty champion in their own right, massive warriors clad in black plate festooned with unholy fetishes and icons. They were unlike anything that the Bretonnians had yet encountered, men whose lives had been extended by the Dark Gods; they were faster, stronger and more deadly than any mortal man.

With contemptuous ease they killed everything that stood before them, hacking through armour, flesh and bone, but they were as children next to the enemy warlord who stepped onto the walls in their wake, hefting a massive axe in each hand. Red gems embedded in the axe blades blazed with fiery power each time the fell weapons claimed a life, as if pleased with the slaughter they enacted.

Scores of knights roared war cries and ran forward to stem this breach, only to be hacked apart by the enemy warlord and his unholy bodyguard. More ladders slammed against the castle walls and scores of grappling hooks were hurled over the battlements. Calard and his kin tried to fight their way towards the enemy warlord, but it was like trying to battle against a raging flood. For each step they took towards the brutal giant of a man, they were forced back three paces by the sheer weight of the enemy. Norscans were streaming over the now undermanned walls, hacking down men-at-arms and knights left and right, and Calard roared in fury as he and his kin were driven back.

The enemy warlord fought like a bloody demigod, his twin axes wailing as they sliced through the air, hacking limbs and heads from bodies with every swing. He laughed as he killed, revelling in the screams of the dying, the geysers of blood fountaining from neck stumps and the sound of bones shattering beneath his axe blades.

Seeing the brutal warlord carving effortlessly through the defenders upon the wall, Reolus moved to intercept him, but there were a score of enemies between them. The grail knight fought with a burning intensity that was terrifying to behold, killing with every strike of his holy blade, Durendyal. Norscans fell before him as he rampaged along the wall. He carved his sword through the neck of one enemy and lopped off the arm of another with the return blow as the Norscans came at him. He spun, avoiding a sword thrust and rammed his blade into the guts of his would-be killer, before ripping the blade clear in a spray of blood and decapitating another man as he continued to turn.

The grail knight swayed to the side and a massive spiked mace missed his skull by scant inches, and he kicked the legs from beneath the off-balance Norscan before smashing his blade down into his head, splitting it to the neck. A jagged sword stabbed towards his unprotected back but he sensed it coming and whipped around, deflecting the blade with his armoured forearm, and punched the man square in the face with the hilt of his sword, his whole body weight behind the blow as he turned. The man fell back with a cry, spraying blood and teeth, and Reolus lashed out with his blade, the tip nicking the Norscan's neck with all the precision of a surgeon, and arterial blood spurted from the wound.

The black-armoured elite bodyguard of the enemy warlord came at Reolus, and he ran forward to meet them head-on.

He traded blows with the first, glittering silver-steel clashing with tainted black-steel, and he was forced back a step by the sheer brutal power of the Chaos warrior. The fully armoured Norscan was taller than Reolus, and his shoulders a foot wider, but as fast as he was he could not match the grail knight's sublime grace.

Reolus ducked in beneath the Chaos warrior's defences as an axe sliced through the air where his head had been a fraction of a second earlier and slammed his blade into the Norscan's side. The blow sundered his heavy armour, buckling it inwards and carving a bloody rent that shattered a dozen ribs. Before the Chaos warrior could react, Reolus had whipped his sword back for a blinding return blow that struck the Norscan in the side of the head, carving through his helmet and skull. With a heavy clatter of armour the enemy warrior fell.

The next died in a heartbeat. Hefting an immense, double-handed spiked hammer as he charged towards the grail knight, the Chaos warrior did not even have a chance to bring it crashing down before Reolus's blade had penetrated the eye slit of his helmet, sinking deep.

The holy paladin of the Lady killed another two of the huskarls, sustaining only a few scratches himself, drawing ever closer to the enemy warlord. Perhaps recognising the presence of one worthy of facing him, the Norscan turned towards Reolus, and their eyes met across the mayhem of the brutal melee.

The two began moving towards each other.

'Lady of grace, grant me, your servant, the strength to defeat this enemy,' breathed Reolus. He clenched Durendyal tightly in both hands, and the fury of the goddess infused him.

THE INSIDE OF the gatehouse spanning the entrance to the castle harbour had been transformed into a scene out of a nightmare, and Chlod stared around him in abject terror.

Men whose bodies had been remoulded into obscene, unrecognisable forms by the Norscan seer's dark magic flopped upon the ground, bellowing in agony and torment, the sound torn from bloody throats that opened up at random across their bloated flesh.

Their bodies were in constant flux and they continued to mutate wildly, bones cracking and reforming in random and bizarre forms, their flesh rippling and bulging with new, unholy life. Spines burst from the backbones of some, while gibbering, mouthed tentacles burst from the flesh of others, cackling and waving wildly. Human skin changed texture and colour, becoming scaled and dark on some, while others sprouted thick, brightly coloured fur and feathers. Worm-like appendages appeared within the flesh of others, making skin bulge grotesquely as it struggled to contain these new growths, and blood splattered as they burst forth.

Useless flaps of membrane-skin with a glistening sheen grew between the random, gristly protuberances that sprouted from one man's arms, while the head of another was ripped apart from crown to chin, exposing hundreds of savage teeth. A revolting, fleshy tongue emerged from within the exposed skull, and it began probing the ground until it was severed by the gaping skull-mouth slamming shut. Chlod stared in horror at the severed tongue as it flopped back and forth on the ground. Its tip peeled back to reveal a snapping mouth, and it proceeded to devour itself, even as it bulged and mutated into a new and wild form, sprouting legs and wings.

Several of the men had merged together, and this vile amalgamation of flesh and muscle screamed incoherently as its body mass bulged and grew, and turned upon its horrified companions. Limbs of glistening, wet muscle sprung from its body, spikes of bone protruding from club-like appendages, and the monster dragged itself towards its erstwhile allies, half a dozen once-human faces screaming insanely. It lashed out with its ever-changing limbs, smashing knights and men-at-arms into the walls, pulping their flesh.

One knight was speared through the midsection by three lengths of bone that had grown from what was once a human leg, and as he bellowed in agony, he was dragged in close to the hideous creature that the seer's magic had spawned. Ribs cracked as the creature's chest tore open in a vertical slit, flesh and muscle ripping apart. The broken stubs of ribs resembled vile teeth, and the knight was pressed into this newly formed, mouth-like cavity. The creature's chest slammed shut, locking the knight within its body, and his flesh became one with the growing beast.

A thick appendage of blood-slick muscle shot from within the chaotic creature's body and wrapped around the arm of another knight, who struggled to free himself. A circular lamprey mouth appeared upon the tip of this rope of muscle, and it burrowed up into the knight's armpit, squeezing through a gap in his armour and biting through his chainmail. The knight began to scream as it burrowed into his flesh, consuming the man from the inside out.

The two mules that were hitched to the wheel mechanism used to raise and lower the portcullis were whinnying in fear and straining to escape their traces. The monstrous spawn tore one of them loose, lifting it up into the air before ripping it in two. One half it devoured, while the other half it hurled at the knights who were bringing their swords to bear on it, smashing several of them backwards as the bloody corpse struck them.

Behind all this, the Norscan sorcerer was striking down more Bretonnian warriors, clearly revelling in his power.

Chlod backed away from the horrors being unleashed, his sanity fraying, and found himself up against the large stained glass windows in the north wall that looked out over the harbour and island.

Seeing a bloody knife that a dead Lyonessian soldier had used lying on the floor nearby, Chlod half-considered grabbing it and plunging it into his own breast; better to die than be consumed by that hulking spawn creature and become part of it. Then he recalled the sorcerer's words: *If you die while the curse is still in place, your soul shall never have rest. It shall be the plaything of Drazh'la'gha for all eternity.*

Chlod looked down at his wrist again, staring at the daemonic black mark there, and began to weep.

Then there was an ear-splitting crash as the stained glass windows exploded inwards.

Chlod fell forward to his knees as shards of coloured glass rained down around him, cutting his hands and face, and he felt strong winds buffet him.

Something large and white hurtled over the top of him, and there was a clatter of hooves on stone.

Gaping up from the ground, Chlod saw a knight riding upon a pristine white pegasus plunge his lance into the heavy mass of flesh that was the Chaos spawn. Black blood spewed from the wound, hissing and burning, and a dozen mouths opened and screamed in pain.

Two other pegasus knights crashed through the stained glass windows, and Chlod pressed himself flat to the floor, making himself as small as possible, praying that he would not be trampled.

Through his fingers Chlod saw the first knight, Laudethaire, plunge his lance into the spawn again, and for a moment he thought the Beloved of Parravon was going to slay the beast, adding to his already impressive tally of heroic feats.

Then the throat of Laudethaire's pegasus was torn out by ripping teeth, thick bloody cords of muscle, ligaments, arteries and flesh torn free in a torrent of blood. Its virginal white fur was splattered with gore, and the noble beast reared and fell, throwing Laudethaire from the saddle.

One of Laudethaire's companions was killed, the Chaos spawn impaling him and tearing him from his saddle. His steed reared, kicking out with its hooves, but whipping tentacles studded with barbs wrapped around its neck and bore it to the ground.

The thrashing beast had its noble flesh subsumed into the spawn's bulging mass, before the creature consumed Laudethaire's dying pegasus noisily. Twisted, befouled wings sprouted from the beast's back in mockery of the pristine white wings of the noble creature. The Parravonian noble himself staggered to his feet but was struck bodily by the young blond-haired Norscan who had accompanied Chlod and the seer.

The Norscan strained to ram his knife into the knight's throat. Laudethaire managed to catch hold of the warrior's wrist before the knife plunged home, and the pair struggled, locked together, shards of coloured glass crunching beneath them. They reeled around, almost as if they were locked in some macabre dance, and then toppled out through the smashed window.

There was a horrible screech as the third knight rammed his lance into the monstrosity's head – or at least one of them. A large flipper-like appendage slammed into the knight that had wounded it, breaking his steed's wings like twigs and sending nobleman and pegasus smashing back through the stained glass windows, falling to their deaths.

Chlod backed further away from the thrashing monster. It might have been in its death throws, but he could not be sure. A lance still protruded from it and black blood was oozing from the wound. The Norscan sorcerer was nowhere to be seen. Backing up against the smashed window, Chlod looked down and saw Laudethaire clinging desperately to the ledge just below, hanging by one hand. If he fell, his plate mail would certainly drag him to the ocean floor.

Hundreds of black crows and ravens were circling around the gatehouse outside, filling the air with their ugly cries, sensing death.

'Help me!' urged Laudethaire, his voice filled with panic. 'For the love of the goddess, help me, damn you!'

Chlod licked his lips. He didn't want to risk getting pulled out of the window himself; even if he survived the fall, which was doubtful, he was a poor swimmer. Still, having the vaunted Beloved of Parravon in his debt was a tempting proposition.

'I'll make it worth your while, damn it!' begged Laudethaire. His fingers were beginning to slip on the stonework.

Greed outweighing self-preservation, Chlod went to reach for the knight. Laudethaire slipped suddenly, his finger losing their hold, but he managed to catch himself just before he plunged to his death, grabbing another ledge just below the first.

Chlod swore. There was no chance of him reaching the knight from his position now and so, trying not to look down, he climbed out onto the first ledge. Keeping one hand holding tightly to the windowsill, he stretched his hand down towards the Parravonian knight, tongue sticking out the side of his mouth in concentration.

'Quickly, you foetid little peasant bastard!' snarled Laudethaire from between clenched teeth.

Chlod's expression darkened and he froze, just inches from grabbing hold of the knight's forearm.

'What are you doing?' gasped Laudethaire, his eyes filled with fear and indignant outrage. 'Help me, damn you!'

Chlod snorted, and stood upright.

'I'll see you hang for this!' snapped Laudethaire. 'Don't you know who I am?'

'You're dead,' retorted Chlod, and slammed his heel down into the knight's face.

Laudethaire lost his hold on the ledge and he was gone, dropping like a stone towards the ocean, falling to his death. Chlod watched the knight plummet, arms and legs flailing wildly, until he hit the water. Then he was gone, disappearing into the black ocean waters, the weight of his armour dragging him down. Chlod spat after him derisively.

Something fleshy and stinging touched his neck, and Chlod almost fell himself as he swung around to see a pinkish, lumped tentacle squirming over the windowsill from inside. He gave a girlish screech of shock, and brushed it away with the back of his hand, shimmying along the ledge as he did so to escape its touch.

More tentacles appeared, flowing over the windowsill like a living waterfall, and Chlod knew that there was no escape from their numbing touch.

Without giving himself time to rethink the idea, Chlod closed his eyes and let go, falling backwards off the ledge.

Duke Adalhard deflected an overhead blow with his shield and slashed open his attacker's throat. Blood fountained from the fatal wound, and Adalhard stepped back, his blade flashing down to deflect a spear that was stabbing towards his groin, and with a roll of his wrist he struck upwards, the tip of his sword crunching up into the chin of another Norscan, shattering bone and teeth.

At his side, the corpulent figure of the Marquis of Carabas stabbed another berserker in the belly. The baron's wide eyes betrayed his fear, but the duke was proud of the fighting spirit of the man. An axe blade sliced through the air to take the baron in the neck, but

Adalhard struck out, knocking aside the killing blow and plunged his sword into the Norscan's chest, sliding the blade between the ribs to pierce the heart.

There was a moment's break in the fighting and Adalhard gazed down towards the harbour. The cobbled road he stood upon was slick with the blood of the dead and dying, and from the top of the hill leading down to sea level he could see hundreds more Norscans leaping ashore. He had seen Laudethaire's noble attempt to retake the ocean gatehouse, and the Parravonian might yet succeed in closing the portcullis, but the damage was already done.

'We can take them, my lord,' urged one of his knights, but Adalhard shook his head.

Behind him, the enemy were streaming through the shattered main gates, while a black wedge of enemy warriors had taken up position upon the east wall, where hundreds of Norscans were pouring in over the breach. The eastern gatehouse too was lost to the enemy, the entrance smashed asunder by one of the Norscans' immense tuskers. Thousands of enemies were streaming through the gap.

The castle was lost.

Adalhard was so tired. A part of him wanted nothing more than to charge down into the enemies before him, to go down fighting, here and now; get it over with. But he knew what had to be done. He would make the enemy bleed for every inch of ground they took, to make their progress as painful as possible. That was his duty; to the Lady, to the king and to himself.

'Back!' roared the Duke of Lyonesse, though it left a bitter taste in his mouth. 'Fall back to the keep!'

* * *

REOLUS PAUSED AS frantic horns sounded the retreat. He glanced down and saw hundreds of knights and men-at-arms streaming back towards the keep.

The grail knight pulled his gaze back towards the enemy warlord, who was moving purposefully towards him, spinning his twin axes. Every instinct screamed for him to engage the enemy leader, to smite him in the name of the Lady, for his presence in this holy land of his ancestors was an affront, a cancer that needed to be cut out, a boil that needed to be lanced.

He glanced down again and saw the Duke of Lyonesse in the centre of a block of knights, prominent in his golden armour and helmet. They were falling back in steady order, the duke hollering orders over the din of battle. The enemy were surging up the streets from the harbour like a dark tide, and Reolus knew that his place was down there, protecting the duke's retreat.

He turned back towards the still advancing enemy warlord, and gritted his teeth in frustration.

He knew it was only his pride that made him want to defeat this enemy rather than aid the fallback of the duke and his men. As if sensing his decision, the enemy warlord ceased his advance.

'As the Lady is my witness, we shall face each other soon,' promised Reolus, though he doubted whether the enemy could understand his words. The Norscan said something in reply, a guttural utterance that might have been acknowledgement.

Reluctantly, Reolus backed away, moving towards the stairs descending down the inside of the wall. Enemies moved to intercept him, but they were waved back by the enemy warlord, and he realised that the Norscan had understood his intent, if not his words.

Eyes blazing with the white heat of righteous fury and frustration, Reolus nodded his head towards the towering enemy leader. It was not a gesture of respect, merely an acknowledgement that they would meet again. The Norscan inclined his head in response.

Yes, they would meet again, Reolus thought. And when they did, one of them would die.

CHAPTER NINETEEN

The keep at the heart of Castle Lyonesse, its *donjon*, was a strongly defensible structure built of the same gleaming white stone as the outer walls. It was in essence a fortress in its own right, with five tall, cylindrical towers at its corners and walls almost eight feet thick, topped with crenulations and dotted with arrow slits. An impressive gatehouse was the sole entrance into the keep, complete with a pair of portcullises and massive, barred iron-bound doors.

The castle now belonged fully to the enemy, and they swarmed over the abandoned walls and up the streets from the harbour. So many longships had by now passed beneath the still-open arched gatehouse and entered the harbour that there was no room for them to beach; the Norscans merely lashed them together and clambered from ship to ship onto the land, streaming up to surround the keep. They ransacked, smashed and torched every building within the curtain walls, and choking black smoke filled the air.

The main gatehouse in the eastern wall was a shattered ruin, having been smashed almost to the ground by one of the war mammoths, and thousands of Norscans surged through the breach now that there was no one to stem the tide.

Cheers had risen from the keep as one of the giant war mammoths was felled. Barrels had been fired by the great trebuchets atop the keep, and a handful had smashed down upon one of the great beasts, dousing its matted fur and howdah with oil. Hundred of arrows lit in flaming braziers had been fired from the tops of the towers, and the beast had roared in pain and fear as it was consumed by fire. It had rampaged through the enemy ranks, killing hundreds as it smashed them out of its way with its spiked tusks. Nevertheless, it was but a small victory amid the darkness, and the cheers quickly died away.

In the distance, a handful of hermit knights had defended the temple of Manann upon the south-western island headland until the last, and the Bretonnians within the keep had watched mournfully as the last of them had been cut down in the distance. With their protectors slain, the old priests of the sea god had been dragged outside and sacrificed, their heads hacked from their shoulders and impaled on spears. Ropes were tied around the mighty bronze statue of Manann atop the temple, and it was brought crashing to the ground. Peasant archers and men at-arms upon the walls of the keep moaned in horror and whispered prayers of appeasement at this sacrilege.

Untold thousands now surrounded the keep, and there was not a knight or lowborn within with any doubt that it would fall. It was not a matter of *if* the keep fell, but of *when*.

Thousands of crude skin drums pounded a relentless tattoo, and the enemy warlord strode through the ranks of his horde, an unmistakeable figure that towered over his minions. He was surrounded by a coterie of black-armour elites, and Calard stared down at him in hatred from the crenulated keep walls.

The enemy gave the defenders no chance to rest or recoup their strength, and Calard knew that every one of the Bretonnians was as exhausted as he. He'd never felt as tired in all his life. He felt numb, and yet sore all over, and his thinking was vague and hazy, as if his head was stuffed with wool. Every movement was an effort. Still, there was no opportunity to close his eyes and fall into the sleep he so desired.

With a gesture from the warlord, thousands of screaming Norscans launched themselves at the keep, streaming past their black-armoured leader, who stood with arms crossed, an implacable rock amidst the dark tide of chaos. Hundreds were cut down by wave after wave of arrow fire.

Under the cover of shields, the Norscans reached the foot of the gatehouse, attaching thick chains to the portcullis by hooks. These chains had been hitched around the shoulders of the largest of the enemy war mammoths, the one that had borne the enemy chieftain onto the walls just hours earlier, and its handlers urged it forward, striking it with barbed switches. The immense long-furred beast bellowed and lurched forward, chains snapping taut behind it. The portcullis groaned and held for a moment. The mammoth bellowed again and its titanic muscles strained. With a tortured groan of protesting metal, the portcullis was ripped free, and it was dragged fifty yards across the ground, carving a furrow through the snow before the mammoth was halted.

More Norscans were killed as they charged through the now open, arched gateway towards the second portcullis. Scores were killed in the arched passageway leading through the gatehouse as arrows were fired at close range through narrow slits, and the tortured screams of hundreds more echoed loudly within the enclosed space as boiling oil poured from murder holes in the walls and ceiling. Men screamed in agonising torment as their flesh was scalded red raw, eyeballs hissed and smoked as they boiled in sockets, and the Norscans fought each other in their desperation to escape.

Those that did manage to reach the portcullis at the end of the murderous passage were met by polearms and spears thrust through the latticework, and dozens were impaled as they ran headlong into the wall of steel. More archers stood on the other side of the portcullis with the men-at-arms and knights, and they fired their deadly shafts into the Norscans straining to hook their immense chains onto this second barrier. No armour was protection against fully drawn longbows at such close range, and arrows punched through helmets and solid iron breastplates with ease.

Still, the Norscan warlord sent wave after wave of his warriors into the deadly passage, uncaring of the mounting casualties, so intent on taking the keep was he. When the oil ran out, the Bretonnians pumped boiling water through the murder holes and dropped rocks down upon them, while their arrows continued to cut down the Norscans in their scores.

More than a thousand men must have died within the space of some fifteen minutes, and the scale of slaughter was awesome and terrible to behold. Still the enemy came on, charging into the corpse-filled passageway, clambering over the dead and dying in their desperation to reach the portcullis at the far end and earn the approval of their lord and gods.

For more than an hour the enemy continued to storm the gatehouse, with little success. Even when the great chains were secured upon the portcullis, the Bretonnians on the other side were able to unhook them, dislodging them and slaughtering the Norscans beneath their withering hail of arrows.

The enemy chieftain paced back and forth. He seemed determined to take Lyonesse in the shortest time possible regardless of the cost, and the Bretonnians were shocked and horrified at how much the barbarian had achieved in such a short space of time.

Everything Calard had ever learned of siege warfare from Gunthar and his tutors spoke of how they were generally long, drawn out affairs that might last half a year or more. The great siege of Carcassone, some two hundred years earlier, had lasted over three years. Generally, he had been taught, an adequately manned castle facing odds of ten to one or less would fall only when the defenders were starved out, had succumbed to disease, or were betrayed from within. Walls sometimes collapsed when tunnels were dug to undermine them, or fire used to destabilise supports and make stone crack, but such tactics were slow and plagued by failure.

When a siege reached a point of stalemate between rival noble houses of Bretonnia, the outcome was often decided by a duel. That was often preferable to a long, protracted siege, which was costly both monetarily and in manpower.

This, however, was not a war being waged between honourable Bretonnian families. Nor was there a stalemate here; the enemy was winning this war, swiftly and surely, and Calard was still staggered that an ignorant savage, a bloodthirsty raider of the northern seas, had been able to take Lyonesse where so many had failed before, and at a speed that was almost unfathomable. And once the second portcullis was torn down, the keep had an hour, perhaps two, before it was overwhelmed.

From within the keep, Calard heard the cry of a woman in pain – Elisabet, in the midst of labour.

'This is no natural pregnancy,' Anara had told him that morning, stating the obvious.

'Of course not. A month from conception to birth? It is an abomination,' Calard had said, shaking his head in horror.

'There is no guarantee what the child will be,' Anara had said.

'What do you mean?'

'There is power in it,' Anara had said, ominously. 'It is no normal offspring of man and woman.'

I truly am cursed, thought Calard bitterly. And perhaps my curse is such that it lays low all those that I care for.

Unbidden, a vision of the Green Knight flashed into his mind, staggering in its intensity.

'*Face me!*' the vision boomed, its voice hollow and full of potency. Once again Calard's terror overwhelmed him. He fell back from the supernatural apparition that was bearing down on him, blade drawn. The Green Knight towered above him, eyes blazing with iridescent light.

'I cannot!' he whimpered.

'What?' said Bertelis, standing alongside him on the wall, and Calard snapped back into reality. His brother was looking at him in concern.

'Nothing,' he said with a forced smile.

Elisabet groaned in agony, her teeth tightly clenched. She was lying back upon the four-poster bed, her body lathered in sweat. Basins of water were nearby, blood-soaked cloths lying over their edges.

'The child is close,' said the Damsel Anara, her voice vague and distant even at such a time. Elisabet cried out, tears running down her red, sweat-streaked face.

'I can't do it,' she sobbed. 'I don't want it!'

Anara shrugged. 'The child will come whether you want it or not.'

Elisabet screamed in agony, exhaustion and anger.

BJARKI WAS STANDING alongside his jarl when the new-born's birth scream echoed out over the din of battle. The sheer, unfocused power contained in that scream made him stagger, intense pain stabbing into his mind. The sound was excruciating, tearing through both the real world and the insubstantial realm of Chaos, existing in both realms simultaneously.

Even as he winced, a trickle of blood running from his left nostril, the Skaeling seer grinned fiercely; never in his life had he felt such pure, raw power as was present in that scream. The daemon-child was even more puissant than his divinations had foretold. Even those with no affinity for the winds of magic, blissfully unaware of the ever-present and potent energies swirling around them, felt an uncomfortable wrench in the pit of their stomach as the daemon-child announced its arrival.

Warriors on both sides that had been battling furiously a moment before backed away from each other, knowing that something momentous had happened but unsure as to what. The sound of swords clashing grew more sporadic, then stopped altogether. An unnatural silence descended over the entire castle.

'My son,' said Styrbjorn in awe. 'My son!'

The jarl took a few steps towards the enemy held keep, pushing his black-armoured huskarls out of his way.

'Make them understand my words, seer,' ordered Styrbjorn over his shoulder.

'What?' said Bjarki, recovering himself and wiping the blood from his nose.

'Make them understand my words,' said Styrbjorn, flashing his seer a glare. 'Or is such a thing also beyond your power, little bear?'

Bjarki glowered at his jarl.

'Fine,' he said at last, and centring himself, he began muttering an incantation. Drawing his knife, he cut a slash across the palm of one hand. With a flicking motion, splatters of blood struck the ground before him, and as he completed his rite, he nodded to Styrbjorn.

Waving his huskarls back, Styrbjorn strode forward into the open killing ground before the keep, with Bjarki at his heel. The strings of hundreds of bows were drawn as he moved into range, but no arrow was loosed. Fifty paces from the keep, Styrbjorn came to halt, staring dismissively at the defenders.

Styrbjorn's eyes, as pale as the frozen pack ice that ringed his homeland in the winter months, searched the faces of the keep's defenders. He picked out the one bedecked in gold that he had judged to be the jarl of this stone fort, but his eyes continued scanning the ramparts.

At last he found the one he sought: the swordsman in white and blue; the one that he had hoped to cross blades with upon the castle walls. That one was perhaps the only worthy opponent amongst the enemy, and he could not understand why he was not the jarl of this stone fort, for he was clearly more deadly than the one armoured in gold.

'I am Egil Styrbjorn, High Jarl of the Skaelings, slayer of souls and butcher of immortals,' roared Styrbjorn, his booming voice infused with the power of the gods. 'Hear my words!'

Calard jolted with shock as, a fraction of a second after hearing the warlord's indecipherable challenge, a second voice whispered in his mind, translating his words. That voice spoke Breton with a thick, Norse accent, but it was understandable.

The knights around him glanced around them in shock, muttering, shuffling their feet, and invoking the protection of the Lady, and Calard knew that they too heard this unholy voice. His eyes drifted towards the smaller figure at the warlord's side, and he realised that the whispering was issuing from his lips and being projected through some diabolic sorcerous means into the minds of all the defenders.

'The blood of ten-thousand slaughtered enemies stain my blades,' roared Styrbjorn, hefting his twin axes, Garmr and Gormr, into the air. 'I have bested nameless horrors in the northern wastes and walked free to speak the tale. Alone, I speared a great wyrm of the undersea, battling it for a day and a night before dragging it ashore and cutting its head from its neck. I have walked the smoking paths of the nightshades and emerged unharmed. I have strangled ice trolls with my bare hands. I have run with the ulfwerener, hunted with the ymgir and feasted with the bloodbeast. I have stood upon the Knife Peaks as the gods threw jagged bolts of lightning down upon me, and defeated one of the great dragon-kin wakened by the storm, cutting its still beating heart from its chest.

'This and more have I done, I, Egil Styrbjorn of the Skaelings! Never have I asked for quarter from an enemy, and never have I offered it. Until now.'

Bjarki's voice faltered as he completed the translation, and his jaw dropped. What madness was this? Muttering rippled through the Skaeling war horde.

'My jarl?' Bjarki questioned.

'They have my son, little bear,' said Styrbjorn.

'The keep will be ours within the hour!' said Bjarki. 'We do not need to debase ourselves by seeking terms with these weaklings!'

'They have my son!' hissed Styrbjorn. 'Who is to say they will not smother him before the fort falls? That they will not hurl him from the ramparts as soon as we take it by force? It is what *I* would do in their position.'

'If they were intending to kill the child, they would have done so by now,' reasoned Bjarki, his voice angry.

'This is *my son*!' bellowed Styrbjorn, and Bjarki took an involuntary step back from his jarl's rage. The power of the gods radiated from Styrbjorn as his fury rose to the surface, making Bjarki's skin tingle. 'I have waited this long for one to carry my name; I will not risk losing him now!'

'Honourless dog! Lickspittle! Coward!' bellowed a voice that sounded like rocks grinding against each other and Styrbjorn swung towards his own lines, eyes blazing with fury.

The Chaos dwarf, Zumarah, stepped forward, pushing Norscans out of his way.

'Oath breaker!' roared Zumarah, his tusks quivering in rage.

Bjarki could feel the Chaos dwarf's words resonate with the Skaeling horde, and he saw many of the Norscan warriors shifting uneasily. They had come this far, and had lost many of their sword-brothers in taking this castle. Not a one of them would be content to walk away now, with the destruction of the enemy within their grasp, and the fiery words of the dwarf were striking a chord with them.

Styrbjorn pointed one of his axes at the bristling dwarf.

'You dare insult me, Zumarah?' he roared in outrage.

'I do and I do so again. I call you coward and oath breaker, Styrbjorn. I will not be cheated of my dues!'

'You mouth is still flapping, stunted wretch,' Styrbjorn bellowed back. 'Quiet your yapping, or I'll beat you like the dog you are.'

'You're welcome to try, oath breaker,' snarled Zumarah, unshouldering his obsidian greataxe. 'I'll carve your flesh and grind your bones.'

Bjarki licked his lips. Styrbjorn had no choice but to face this challenge or risk losing face in front of the entire horde.

Styrbjorn brandished his twin axes, and began marching towards the dwarf, his face a mask of fury. Zumarah leered at him and set his feet wide, hefting his double-bladed axe. The Skaeling jarl broke into a loping run, and with one quick glance up at the Bretonnians, wondering what they must be thinking, Bjarki turned to watch the outcome of the challenge.

Ensorcelled obsidian met hellforged steel, and the two warriors traded a score of blows within the space of a few heartbeats. Nearly seven feet tall, the Norscan towered over Zumarah, but the dwarf was like a rock, unyielding and immovable. Zumarah fought with a rabid fury, spitting and growling like a beast as he hacked and chopped.

Zumarah turned his shoulder into a swinging axe blade, taking the force of the blow without flinching, and met a strike from the Norscan's other blade head-on with one of his own. The Norscan hammered the flat of his foot into Zumarah's chest, but it was like striking a mountain and the dwarf remained unmoved.

Zumarah swatted aside a blow that arced towards his thick, bull-like neck, and hammered his greataxe into Styrbjorn's side.

The blade tore through the Skaeling's black armour and bit deep into his flesh, breaking ribs. Growling in pain, Styrbjorn dropped his axes and grabbed the haft of the dwarf's weapon, locking it in place. The blazing red wolf eyes of Styrbjorn's axes faded to darkness now that they were separated from their master's touch.

Zumarah hissed and spat as he tried to free his greataxe from the grasp of the Skaeling. Keeping hold of the axe shaft with his left hand, Styrbjorn slammed his gauntleted right fist into the dwarf's face.

The black armour that encased his fist was spiked and barbed, and the Skaeling struck with enough force to crack stone. Indeed it was like striking stone, but Zumarah merely laughed maniacally even as blood began to stream down his broad face.

Again and again Styrbjorn pounded his fist into the Chaos dwarf's face. One of Zumarah's tusks snapped under the onslaught, but the dwarf did not weaken, and continued to fight to free his weapon. Styrbjorn struck the dwarf another half dozen blows around the head, each more powerful than the last, but they seemed to be having little effect other than breaking the skin. The dwarf's skull was like iron. Perhaps it *was* iron, thought Bjarki.

With a surge, Zumarah threw Styrbjorn off, who spun and stumbled to one knee, facing away from the Chaos dwarf. Zumarah grimaced in victory and stepped forward to finish the jarl. The Skaeling war horde stood immobile and silent, the only sound the whip of banners and the howling of the wind.

One of Styrbjorn's axes, Garmr, was lying in the snow before him and Styrbjorn launched himself at it even as

Zumarah came at him, swinging his greataxe back for the killing blow. Styrbjorn's fingers closed around the haft of his axe and its blood-ruby eye flared into life.

Rolling onto his back and with a grunt of effort, Styrbjorn hurled his hellforged axe at the Chaos dwarf. It spun end over end and took the dwarf square in the face. Zumarah's charge faltered, and the dwarf stood there for a moment, the axe buried deep in his skull, before he fell to the ground, dead.

The blood ceased streaming from Styrbjorn's wounded side as his god-touched body began to heal, and he rose to his feet. Growing stronger with every passing heartbeat, the Skaeling jarl retrieved his weapons and swung towards his warriors, his face angry. Behind him, a host of crows and ravens descended on the dwarf, almost completely obscuring him.

'Is there anyone else?' he roared, his voice infused with the power of the gods, echoing painfully loudly around the castle. 'Is there anyone else that would dispute my will?'

There was no movement and no sound from the Skaeling war host, and Styrbjorn continued to stare challengingly across their ranks for long moments. Satisfied at last, he turned back towards the Bretonnian keep.

The figure in gold was standing atop the ramparts, his cloak flying behind him.

'I am Duke Adalhard of Lyonesse,' he shouted, his voice echoing out over the silent Norscan hordes. 'Speak your terms, Norscan.'

Silence greeted the Norscan's demand.

Duke Adalhard turned to look along the ramparts, and his eyes met those of Reolus. The grail knight nodded his head almost imperceptibly, and the duke turned back towards the enemy.

'It shall be so,' hollered Duke Adalhard. 'One hour's time.'

Reolus was kneeling in silent communion within the duke's private grail shrine when the door slammed open. The grail knight recognised the distinctive perfume of the Damsel Anara; a mixture of rose petals, lilies and pine needles.

'What do you think you are doing?' Anara said, coldly.

Reolus finished his prayer and opened his eyes. The pristine features of the Lady gazed down upon him, the statue's eyes full of love and sympathy. Kissing the golden chalice icon he held in his hands, he rose to his feet and turned to face his lover.

'My duty,' he replied in a soft voice.

'The child is not yours to barter,' said Anara, her eyes full of anger. 'And yet you offer it to the Norscan butcher?'

'The Norscan challenged me,' said Reolus. 'I was honour bound to accept.'

'You did not need to accept his terms,' said Anara.

'You would have preferred to see Lyonesse reduced to a smoking ruin?' said Reolus, more sharply than he intended. 'For every man here to be offered to the Dark Gods as sacrifice? The duke, your brother, the Lady Elisabet? Yourself? Me? Everyone would have been butchered. You know that as well as I.'

'The child is important,' said Anara.

'And the enemy will take it only if I fall beneath the Norscan's axe. I do not intend to do so,' retorted Reolus.

'The child is not yours to use as a bargaining tool like some prized sow,' said Anara.

'The child is a Norscan half-breed!' said Reolus, his voice rising in pitch.

'That child is promised to the Enchantress!' shot back Anara. Reolus stared at her in silence, his anger fading.

'Of what do you speak, my love?' he said, his voice soft.

'The reason I am here. The reason *we* are here. I am to deliver the child to the Enchantress. She sensed the power in it as soon as it was conceived. It cannot be allowed to remain in the world. The Enchantress shall take it into the realm of the fey, where its power can be controlled.'

Reolus's shoulders slumped, a haunted look appearing in his eyes as he contemplated this new information. He fell to his knees before Anara, his head hung low.

He knew that he had wanted to test himself against the Norscan warlord. He wanted the glory of defeating him. Had he allowed his pride to blind him? Had he angered the goddess by his actions?

'I did not know,' he said finally. Anara regarded him coldly.

'You did not need to know,' she replied. The only sound was the howling wind outside, which beat upon the small shuttered window high in the shrine's back wall. Hundreds of candles flickered as a slight breeze managed to creep through the cracks in the window.

'It is foolish to think that the enemy will depart after you kill the Norscan. They have no honour,' said Anara.

'But I do,' said Reolus. 'It would have been beneath me to refuse the challenge just because I believe they will not honour their promise.'

The damsel sighed, her cold mask slipping. She embraced him, pulling his head to her bosom.

'You are a fool, Reolus,' she said.

'I cannot go back on my word, Anara,' said the grail knight.

'I know,' she said, and a single tear ran down her cheek.

THE COUSINS, BALDEMUND and Huebald, stood at Tassilo's bedside, their faces grim. The injured knight's sickness was worsening. Wounded by the tainted blade of the corrupt enemy champion, Tassilo's body was lathered in sweat, and he was shivering violently. The flesh around the wound had turned black and stank like rotten meat, and all the ministrations of the duke's overworked surgeons had been for naught; the sickness continued to spread.

'We must do it tonight,' said Baldemund fiercely. 'Before the duel. While his guard is down.'

'I had hoped that he would fall in battle,' said Tassilo weakly. 'At least then he would have had an honourable death. And our hands would not be stained with blood.'

'But he did not,' said Baldemund. 'And this war is all but over. What we do is for the good of the Garamont line. Remember that.'

'We would be betraying Garamont if we did *not* act,' said Huebald.

'I just don't know anymore,' said Tassilo miserably. 'What if Folcard was wrong?'

'Folcard is not wrong. None of us takes pleasure in what must be done,' Baldemund hissed. 'But it is our *duty*. Calard's blood is unclean. His mother was fey-touched. His sister's a freak, and his brother was... well, we all saw what his brother was. We cannot risk the Garamont bloodline being forever tainted.'

'Calard must die,' said Huebald. 'We do it, *now*.'

CHAPTER TWENTY

CALARD WAS SLOUCHED on a simple bench in one of the keep's kitchens, weary beyond words but unwilling to allow himself to fall asleep. The kitchens were not an area often frequented by nobles and the furniture in the room was simple and functional, with little thought for comfort or aesthetics. Still, just to be sitting down felt like luxury, even garbed in full armour as Calard was.

His sword was upon the thick wooden table in front of him, and he was chewing on some salted meat that Bertelis had discovered in one of the clay pots in the adjoining walk-in larder. He, his brother and the Empire ambassador, Dieter Weschler, were sharing a jug, and even though it was just cheap cooking wine – all the good vintages would be stored in the no-doubt cavernous cellar beneath the keep – no wine had ever tasted finer to Calard.

They sat in silence. Calard's mind was a jumble of turbulent emotions. He replayed his vision of the Green

Knight over in his head, trying to decipher its meaning, but the thought of Elisabet, nursing her Norscan-fathered child upstairs, kept intruding. He was also excited by the prospect of seeing Reolus meet the barbarian warlord in challenge. He was certain that the duel would be recounted all across Bretonnia in years to come, and he felt privileged to be present at such an august event.

'He will win, won't he?' said Bertelis.

'The Lady is with him,' replied Calard by way of answer.

'I have never seen a better swordsman,' said Dieter, 'except my Emperor's personal champion, Ludwig Shwarzhelm. And even then, it would be a close thing.'

'You think your Emperor's man could beat Reolus?' said Bertelis, doubtfully.

'I would not wager my entire fortune on it,' said Dieter. 'Perhaps just a portion.'

'I'd happily wager my fortune on Reolus,' said Bertelis. 'Had I a fortune to wager.'

'By Sigmar's grace, such a wager will only ever remain theoretical,' replied Dieter. 'Long have the bonds between our realms been strong, and long may that continue.'

'I'll drink to that,' said Calard. 'We have plenty enough enemies around us than to draw weapons against friends.'

The door to the kitchen was pushed open as Calard and Dieter clunked their goblets together in salute, and Huebald and Baldemund walked in, looking grim and tense.

Calard's brow creased in concern.

'Tassilo?' he said.

'Worsening,' said Huebald, coming to stand opposite Calard. Baldemund sat down at the table, sliding the sword of Garamont aside.

Calard and Bertelis stood instantly, intending to go to their cousin's side, but Baldemund held up a hand to forestall them.

'He is weak. The surgeon says he should only receive one visitor at a time,' he said. 'And he has asked to see Bertelis first.'

'Really?' said Calard, who had always been closer to Tassilo than his brother. Baldemund nodded.

Calard looked at Bertelis, who shrugged.

'Well, he has asked for you, so go,' said Calard, and Bertelis left the room.

Huebald, sharing a glance with his conspirator, cleared his throat and turned towards Dieter.

'Could you give us the room, ambassador? There is a family matter that my cousin and I would like to discuss with Lord Garamont.'

'Of course,' said Dieter, who stood up and gave a curt bow of the head to Calard before taking his leave.

Huebald and Baldemund were left alone in the kitchen with Calard, who offered them the jug of wine. They made no reaction to his offer, and he frowned as he placed the jug back onto the table.

'What is it?' he said, a feeling of dread descending over him. Was Tassilo dead? Had something happened to Elisabet?

'You know that we are loyal to Garamont, don't you cousin?' said Huebald.

'What are you talking about?' said Calard in confusion. 'Of course I know that.'

'And you know that if anything were to threaten the Garamont line, we would do whatever it took to preserve its integrity, yes?' said Huebald.

'What is your point?' said Calard.

Baldemund stood. Calard stared up at his two grim-faced, silent cousins.

'By the love of the goddess, spit it out,' Calard said.

'I'm sorry that it has to go this way, cousin,' said Baldemund. Then he and Huebald slid their swords from their scabbards.

'What is this?' said Calard, suddenly conscious of the fact that his own sword was beyond his reach.

'Something that should have been done a long time ago,' said Huebald, moving around the table towards Calard, blade drawn.

'I'm sorry, Calard,' said Baldemund, circling around his other side. 'The purity of the Garamont line must be preserved.'

Calard stood up sharply, knocking over the bench on which he sat. Huebald picked up the sword of Garamont and hurled it across the room. It clattered on the stone floor and slide to a far corner, beneath the great arched oven built into the wall.

'Your bloodline is cursed; you know that as well as we do. It cannot be allowed to bring Garamont to ruin.'

'This is madness,' snarled Calard, still backing away from the two armed knights.

'No,' said Huebald. 'It would be madness for us to ignore the oath we swore to your father and stand by and allow his house to fall to damnation.'

'You swore the same oath to me,' snapped Calard. 'Where is your honour?'

'You should have stood aside and let your brother rule, Calard,' said Baldemund. 'You could have avoided all this.'

'Enough talk,' snapped Huebald. 'It is time the taint that besmirches Garamont's honour was removed once and for all.'

Calard backed up against the wall. There was nowhere to run.

* * *

'PLEASE DON'T HATE me for my part in it,' said Tassilo, his eyes feverish.

'Hush,' said Bertelis. 'Calm yourself. You need your rest, cousin. Lie back.'

'You don't understand,' said Tassilo, fighting off Bertelis's mothering attentions. 'It had to be done! For the good of the Garamont line!'

'Sleep, cousin,' said Bertelis. 'You'll feel better once you have had some rest.'

Tassilo was burning up, sweat pouring off his body and his skin radiating heat. He reached out and grabbed Bertelis by the arm.

'Listen to me! His blood is tainted,' said Tassilo. 'It had to be done. Do not hate me.'

'What are you talking about, cousin?' Bertelis said warily, wondering if Tassilo was delirious.

'You will do Garamont proud, Bertelis.'

Bertelis felt a sense of foreboding descend over him, and he stared at Tassilo with haunted eyes, fearing the answer to his next question.

'What have you done, Tassilo?' he said.

'Do not hate me,' said the feverish knight. He coughed, splattering blood and mucous down his shirt front.

'You are talking about Calard, aren't you?' said Bertelis with some urgency. 'What have you done, cousin?'

'For the good of Garamont,' Tassilo managed, in-between wracking coughs.

Bertelis stared at him in horror. Could this merely be some fevered delusion? In his heart he knew that it was not.

'Oh mother, no,' he breathed. Long had his mother, the Lady Calisse, hated Calard; long had she desired to see her own son take up the rulership of Garamont. Bertelis had been convinced that she had been behind the attempts on Calard's life six months ago, before the death of their father, but his mother had vehemently denied that.

Bertelis had even gone so far as to keep the identity of one of Calard's would-be killers from his brother, in an attempt to save his mother from shame and retaliation. It had been Tanebourc, a favourite of his mother's, that had tried to kill Calard on the field of battle in Bordeleaux, and had his identity been made known, then the finger of blame would surely have settled upon Bertelis's mother, the Lady Calisse.

Still, his mother had denied it so vociferously that he had almost believed her, for all that he knew she was capable of such a thing. Almost.

'Lady of grace, let it not be so,' breathed Bertelis, and he spun to leave.

He paused in the doorway and looked back towards the sick man, who was staring at him with dark ringed eyes.

'If any harm has befallen my brother, I will return here and kill you myself,' promised Bertelis. Then he drew his blade, and ran from the room.

'Forgive me,' breathed Tassilo.

MALORIC YAWNED AS he strode along the corridor, heading towards stairs that would lead up to the ramparts atop the keep. He came to a fork, and glanced down the shadowy side-passage. He did a double-take when he saw a pair of men-at-arms dressed in the red and blue livery of Garamont standing guard outside a door halfway down the corridor. At a whim he changed his course, turning to walk towards them.

The pair of guards were talking in low voices, but they fell silent as they saw him approach. They stared resolutely ahead as he stopped in front of them, wisely not looking him in the eye. Their polearms were crossed over the door, barring the way.

'What is in there, peasant?' Maloric demanded of one of the men.

The man-at-arms stuck out his unshaved chin.

'Kitchen, my lord.'

'Very important duty, guarding a kitchen,' said Maloric. 'Stand aside.'

'We cannot do that, my lord,' said the man-at-arms.

'The lord of Garamont is having his way with a serving girl inside, is he?' sneered Maloric.

'I wouldn't know, my lord,' said the peasant, shifting his feet awkwardly.

'Of course not,' said Maloric. 'Stand aside.'

'We cannot do that, my lord,'

Maloric stepped in close, staring into the peasant's eyes. He could smell the cat's piss stink of the man's sweat, and his lip curled in disgust.

'I am going through that door, *peasant*,' said Maloric in a low voice. 'And if you attempt to stop me I shall see you both hang.'

Maloric put a finger upon the blade of the man's polearm and pushed it out of his way, staring at the man the whole while, daring him to resist. Cowed, the man shifted his feet and looked down, but did not make a move to stop him. Maloric turned to stare at the other man, who, after glancing at his companion, moved his own weapon out of Maloric's way.

'That wasn't so hard, was it?' he said, and pushed through the doors, a half-smile on his face.

Unarmed, Calard knew that he had no chance against both Huebald and Baldemund. Both were skilful swordsmen and he had no more room to back away from them, nor was there any form of weapon nearby.

'The Lady curse you,' he snarled.

'You are the cursed one here,' returned Huebald.

The door to the kitchen opened inwards suddenly, and the traitorous cousins were momentarily distracted.

Calard moved swiftly, stepping in close to Huebald and slamming his fist into his cousin's face.

Huebald managed to turn his head, so that Calard's gauntlet glanced off his cheek rather than breaking his nose. Still, the blow was a powerful one, and Huebald's head snapped back.

Before Calard could wrest the sword from Huebald's grasp, however, the tip of Baldemund's sword was at his throat, and he froze. More pressure was applied to the sword tip, and Calard was backed up against the wall. Only then did he notice who the intruder was.

'What in the name of the Lady is going on here?' said Maloric in amusement, a sardonic half-smile on his face.

'This is none of your concern, Sangasse,' snapped Huebald. 'Walk away. *Now.*'

'I don't take orders from the likes of you, Garamont lapdog,' replied Maloric, casually walking further into the kitchen. 'Think I'll stay awhile.'

'I'm telling you, Sangasse; turn around and walk out of here,' growled Huebald. 'This is nothing to do with you.'

In response, Maloric turned a chair around so that its back was facing the Garamont knights. He sat down, straddling it, an amused expression on his face.

'Two armed knights against one, unarmed. Not very sporting,' he commented. 'But please, don't let me stop you.'

Calard tensed himself, about to risk trying to overpower Baldemund, who still had him pinned to the wall, a sword at his throat.

'Don't,' warned Baldemund, sensing his intention. The sword tip pressed harder against his neck, breaking the skin.

'Do as he says, Maloric,' said Calard. 'Get out of here. This is a family matter.'

'Your family really is not normal, Garamont, you know that?' replied Maloric, smirking. 'Inbred lunatics, all of you.'

'I told you to leave, Sangasse,' Huebald said, taking a threatening step towards Maloric.

'Take one more step towards me with that drawn sword,' said Maloric, still looking at Calard and still smiling, 'and it will be your last.'

'Kill the Sangasse bastard!' shouted Baldemund, and Huebald stepped forward, his blade flashing for Maloric's head.

The Sangasse noble stood quickly, stepping back, drawing his blade and kicking the chair he had been sitting on into Huebald in one smooth motion. Huebald stumbled as the chair struck him in the mid-section, and Maloric's blade slashed through the air.

Huebald dropped his sword, which fell with a clatter to the floor, and lifted a hand to his throat, which had been neatly sliced open from left to right. He lifted his hand, covered in blood, up before him, and his eyes goggled in shock and his mouth gaped open soundlessly. Then Huebald fell, first to his knees, then face first onto the floor.

Calard felt Baldemund tense for the killing thrust, and he grabbed the blade in his hands, dragging it to the side. The tip of the blade sliced across his throat and blood began to run freely from the wound, but it was just a shallow cut, and he managed to wrest the blade to the side. Throwing himself forwards, he smashed into Baldemund, knocking them both off balance.

Of the pair, it was Baldemund who recovered the quickest, and he thundered an elbow into the side of Calard's head. The young lord of Garamont hit the ground hard. He tried to rise but fell back onto the floor, struggling to maintain consciousness.

Baldemund stood over him, blade poised to finish him off, but he turned warily towards Maloric as the Sangasse noble stalked towards him, blood dripping from his sword.

'I have no argument with you, Maloric,' said Baldemund, but the Sangasse noble snorted in derision.

'I believe your words were *"kill the Sangasse bastard"*. That's good enough justification for me. It's not every day I get to kill lackeys of Garamont,' said Maloric, and their blades came together.

It lasted no more than a few heartbeats. After trading several blows, Maloric parried a desperate attack and sent a lightning riposte that clipped Baldemund in the temple. The knight staggered as blood welled up from the scalp wound, and he fell to one knee. Maloric stepped forwards and ran Baldemund through.

Bertelis came crashing through the kitchen door, blade in hand. Seeing Maloric standing over his brother, bloody sword in hand, he let out a roar and charged towards him.

Maloric twirled his blade in his hand, the half-smile returning to his face, and he stepped forward to meet Bertelis head-on.

'No,' said Calard, pulling himself shakily to his feet.

Bertelis's and Maloric's blades came together, their deeply ingrained enmity lending their attacks venom. Bertelis's blows were swift and powerful, but they were all turned aside by Maloric's flashing blade, which seemed to twist through the air like a silver-scaled serpent, awaiting the perfect moment for a fatal strike.

'Stop!' bellowed Calard.

'Why?' growled Bertelis, keeping his eyes on his opponent.

'Don't stop on my account,' sneered Maloric.

'If he had not arrived, I would now be dead,' said Calard.

'Don't flatter yourself that it was intentional,' retorted Maloric.

Bertelis lowered his sword, glancing down at the lifeless bodies of his cousins, Baldemund and Huebald. He shook his head in disbelief.

At that moment a horn sounded, joined instantly by the brutal pounding of human-skinned drums. A great roar erupted from beyond the keep's walls, and thousands of weapons began clashing against shields in time with the drums, a deafening, barbarous din.

'Reolus,' said Calard.

The outcome of the war was about to be determined.

CHAPTER TWENTY-ONE

CALARD, BERTELIS AND Maloric burst out onto the top of the keep. The ramparts looking down over the square were packed, with the majority of the surviving defenders crowding in to get a clear vantage. The battlements and towers were thronged with men, and peasants clung to flagpoles and took up precarious positions atop the crenulations in order to get a clear view down below.

Maloric spun to leave them, to find his own way through the press of bodies. He turned and looked back over his shoulder, as if feeling the looks of hatred he was receiving from the brothers. He stared hard at Bertelis.

'We have unfinished business, you and I,' said Maloric, before shoving a path through the heaving pack of humanity away from the brothers.

Bertelis spat upon the ground in the Sangasse noble's direction.

'Our own cousins,' Bertelis said bitterly, shaking his head. 'I can still not believe it.'

Calard grunted in response. In truth, he was still in shock himself, and gnawing doubt was churning his insides. What if Huebald and Baldemund were right?

'Out of the way, peasants!' said Bertelis in a large voice, barging his way through the press in a different direction. Calard shook his head, trying to dispel his anxiety.

The Garamont nobles pushed their way through the unwashed masses, bustled from side to side as the crowd surged. The knights towered over the vast majority of men-at-arms and bowmen, hundreds of generations of malnutrition and inbreeding ensuring that few of low birth stood even to a knight's shoulder.

'Get out of the way, damn you,' snarled Bertelis, brutally shoving men out of his path. Those he deemed too slow received a hard clip over the back of the head for their troubles, despite the fact that there was nowhere for them *to* go.

They barged their way through the stifling crowd, both of them turning their noses up at the ungodly stink of the peasants, until they finally stepped up onto the battlements. With much cursing and shoving, they finally neared the crenulations. A pair of Lyonessian knights errant turned as they were jostled from behind. Their harsh words died on their lips as they saw that Calard and Bertelis were of higher status, and grumblingly vacated their position in deference.

Their position gave them an unrestricted view of the square below. They could see the vast sea of Norscans arrayed in a semicircle around the keep, a seething mass of barbarians. They maintained a distance of some two hundred paces from the base of the keep's walls, leaving the square below – the agreed location for the forthcoming duel – clear.

A roar rose from the throats of every Norscan as the enemy warlord stepped out of the ranks of his barbaric countrymen, and Calard squinted as he took in his appearance.

The Norscan was an absolute beast of a man. By his silver-streaked beard and craggy, weather-beaten face, Calard judged that he was in his middling years, but he was no less impressive for that, and he looked to be in the prime of his strength.

Bedecked in heavy armour of dark metal, the barbarian wore a thick white fur of some unknown beast over his massive shoulders. Curving horns emerged from his dark helmet, their tips encased in beaten bronze. His thickly muscled upper arms were tattooed and encircled with iron torcs; his forearms and hands encased in black plate gauntlets.

An immense pair of twin axes, blades fashioned to resemble wolf heads were strung over the Norscan's back, and a smaller pair of single-headed axes were strapped to his armoured thighs. Threaded onto strings of sinew, the teeth of sharks, wolves and other larger and more unfamiliar predators hung alongside engraved bone-fetishes around his neck.

In the centre of the Norscan's breastplate was a large jewel of pale blue that resembled a great, unblinking eye, and it made Calard feel vaguely uneasy even to look upon it.

The barbarian chieftain's face, framed by his helmet and its vertical nose-guard, had been daubed with blood or paint, every inch of exposed skin coloured a bright red, giving him a daemonic appearance. Charcoal had been rubbed into his eye sockets, making his eyes stand out dramatically.

Turning towards his own lines, the Norscan lifted his clenched fists, encased in black, segmented armour, above his head and the cheering intensified. Then the warlord began striding out into the open area between his lines and the Bretonnian keep. His head was held high, and his walk was of one supremely confident in his own ability.

Half way to the keep he came to a halt and stood there, gazing contemptuously at the defenders. Then he bellowed a challenge, his voice deep and reverberating, and though the Bretonnians could not understand his words, his tone was an unmistakeable challenge.

In answer, the great oaken doors of the keep's gatehouse groaned open, and its one remaining portcullis rose. Reolus walked out, alone, to face the Norscan warrior, and the gates sealed behind him, echoing with finality.

The Bretonnians' voices rose as one as they cheered their champion, who was striding in a direct line towards the towering Norscan, his head held high. He was fully bedecked in his ancient, ornate plate mail, and the unicorn crest atop his helmet was surrounded by candles. His pristine regal blue cloak rippled out behind him, and the silver edging of his tabard seemed to glow with reflected moonlight, for all that it was daytime, and the noon sun hidden behind the mass of clouds overhead.

The revered grail knight seemed calm and relaxed as he marched forward to meet his enemy. His weapon was sheathed and he carried no shield – indeed Calard had never seen the paladin use one.

When Reolus was forty paces from his enemy, the Norscan unhooked one of the handaxes strapped to his thighs. The grail knight's holy blade, Durendyal, was instantly in his hands, the movement so fast that Calard had not even seen it drawn, and Reolus broke into a run towards the Norscan.

The black-armoured warlord hurled the axe at his closing attacker, eliciting an angry murmur from the

Bretonnians. Duels were meant to be fought hand to hand, face to face; it was dishonourable to utilise missile weapons on the field of battle, let alone in a formal challenge. Peasants were allowed to use bows and man trebuchets, for they had no honour to lose, but no knight of noble birth would ever sully himself by using a ranged weapon outside of the hunt.

The axe was hurled with incredible power, and it spun through the air, end over end, towards Reolus's head. He swayed to the side as he increased the speed of his run, and the throwing axe hissed by him, missing him by scant inches.

Less than twenty paces now separated the two paragons of war, and the Norscan had his other throwing axe in his hand. He waited for the grail knight to draw closer – fifteen paces, ten – then hurled the missile at Reolus with even more power than the first.

The grail knight swatted the axe aside with his sword and sprinted towards the Norscan, his blade clenched in both hands. The enemy warlord drew his twin battleaxes and stalked forward to meet Reolus head on. With a roar they came together.

Reolus ducked beneath a swinging axe and sliced his blade across his opponent's side as he surged by him, his gleaming sword carving through armour and flesh. Still, there was no great cheer from the Bretonnians as their hero took first blood – the onlookers watched on in tense silence. The blood on Reolus's blade danced and spat, like fat on a hot skillet, leaving its surface spotless.

The wound did not appear to slow the Norscan, however, and he swung towards the grail knight, twin axes carving murderous arcs through the air, forcing Reolus to duck backwards and sway his body to the side to avoid their touch.

The Norscan went after him, axes cutting left and right, and Reolus was forced to his knees as he blocked a heavy overhead strike. The barbarian warlord kicked the grail knight hard in the chest, sending him crashing onto his back, eliciting a deafening roar of approval from the Norscan host.

Reolus was back on his feet in an instant, and again the combatants hurled themselves at each other. Reolus's blade was a blur of silver that weaved a deadly pattern through the air as the grail knight ducked and spun, in constant motion, as he avoided the Norscan's brutal attacks.

He could not match the Chaos lord's sheer power and risked having his sword knocked from his hands by meeting the Norscan's blows head-on. Nevertheless, his sword mastery was beyond compare. With the most delicate of touches, he ensured that blows that would have shorn his head clear of his shoulders and severed limbs were deflected, just missing their mark and leaving him unscathed. He deftly turned aside axe blows that, had they connected, would have hacked him in half, and his blindingly fast ripostes sliced through the Norscan's armour, scoring several wounds within the first minute of the duel, splattering the snow underfoot with blood.

The spectacle of the two champions doing battle, both displaying skill and strength far beyond normal men, was breathtaking. Several times Calard felt certain that Reolus would be caught by the Norscan's devastatingly powerful strikes and slain, only for the grail knight to sway out of the way at the last moment, or knock the axe head off target, before spinning away and launching a series of attacks that had the warlord frantically defending. More than once a cheer lifted in Calard's throat as he was certain that Reolus was about to land the killing blow, but each time the cheer died away before it sounded, with the Norscan battering the Bretonnian's sword aside just before it plunged into his throat, or forcing the grail knight to pull the blow before it landed by launching a deadly attack of his own.

Axe and sword came together with a clash that echoed through the castle, neither warrior backing down. Reolus ducked under his enemy's guard, even as the Norscan sought to drive his knee up into the Bretonnian's midsection, and the grail knight carved his sword into the warlord's side as he moved smoothly past the bigger man. The wound was deeper this time, and blood began to run down over the Norscan's hip and leg, staining the ground underfoot.

The Norscan turned, roaring in anger, swinging his axes in a pair of lethal arcs. Reolus stepped forward and dropped to one knee, the axes slicing the air above his head, and thrust his blade into the warlord's stomach.

The gleaming silver blade of Durendyal drove through his foe's gut, melting through the thick plate armour smoothly. Lunging forward, Reolus wrenched the blade sideward in a disembowelling cut. Blood erupted from the terrible wound, and a deafening roar erupted from the Bretonnians. Calard punched the air victoriously, screaming at the top of his lungs, ignoring the pain in his neck, and Bertelis howled in approval.

However, the Norscan was not yet done. He backhanded Reolus, putting all his strength and bodyweight behind the blow. His armoured fist caught the grail knight under the chin and snapped his head back. Reolus was lifted off his feet and thrown backwards, his back arching, and came crashing down onto the hard packed snow ten yards away.

The Norscan swayed and dropped to one knee, grimacing in pain, blood streaming from his stomach like a waterfall. His twin axes dropped from limp fingers. Blood pooled beneath him, melting the snow, and his head drooped.

Reolus's gleaming sword was still protruding from the Norscan's gut, impaling him, and blood spat from the wound as if the blade was white-hot. Calard held his breath, willing the barbarian to fall, aware that he was watching the death of a mighty foe.

Reolus picked himself groggily up from the ground, visibly unsteady on his feet, and turned to watch the Norscan die. His helmet had been wrenched out of shape by the Norscan's fist. He pulled it off and hurled it away from him, shaking his head to clear it. Blood was on his lips, and he wiped it away with the back of his hand.

The sight of that blood filled Calard with disquiet. It seemed to bring the revered grail knight down to earth, emphasising his mortality, making him seem vulnerable and human. Calard had always regarded Reolus as some eternal saint of the Lady, ageless, immortal. He had never considered that he was a man of flesh and blood, a man that could be killed, just like any other.

Still, he had bested this mighty enemy, and Calard wondered if there was any living being that could possibly defeat the holy paladin. At this moment, he believed not. Surely, only a god would have any chance.

Calard's eyes widened in horror suddenly, and a hushed silence fell across the ramparts.

In defiance of death, the Norscan dragged the hissing blade slowly from his body, and dropped it to the ground.

The torrent of blood flowing from the Norscan's gut wound had slowed to a trickle, and then it stopped altogether. Calard shook his head in horrified wonder as the towering barbarian pushed himself to his feet, in defiance of Morr's claim upon him, in defiance of rational thinking.

No man should have still been standing after such a dismembering cut, nor after losing so much blood.

The Norscan picked up his axes as he rose, and he rolled his shoulders and stretched his neck from side to side, as if he were merely warming up rather than having just received what should have been a mortal wound. He sucked in a deep breath, and Calard felt his skin prickle, as if there were unholy forces at play here that he could not perceive. Then the Norscan breathed out, and a cloud of black smoke emerged from his lungs. The barbarian's eyes locked onto Reolus with icy intensity. He flashed the grail knight a predatory smile, white teeth contrasting sharply with his red painted face, and Calard felt his blood run cold.

Was the Norscan not a man at all, but rather some immortal daemon in human form? Had Reolus been tricked into fighting a being incapable of being killed?

The Norscan spun his axes in front of him, rolling his wrists. The blades wailed as they cut glittering arcs before him, as if the air itself cried out in pain as they sliced through it.

'He can't lose,' said Calard. 'He *can't*.'

'He won't,' said Bertelis, though Calard thought he could detect a hint of doubt in his brother's voice.

Grail knight and hellspawned Norscan warlord stood staring at each other in hatred, one armed, one not. Reolus's sword, Durendyal, lay upon the ground in front of the barbarian lord. The blade of the hallowed weapon was glowing fiercely, as if reacting to the proximity of this ancient, ancestral enemy.

Surprised murmurs rippled along the battlements as the Norscan kicked Reolus's weapon over to him. Bertelis smiled in wonder and Calard blinked in disbelief. He was shocked to see such an honourable move from an accursed Norscan child-murderer.

The immense warrior gestured for Reolus to pick up his sword and continue the battle. Reolus stared at his sacred blade for a moment, then knelt to retrieve it. He turned it around in his hands, so that he held its blade point downwards like a dagger. He leant his head against its crosspiece, eyes closed as he prayed to the Lady. The Norscan began to pace back and forth like a caged beast, clearly impatient but graciously allowing his opponent to finish his entreaty to the goddess.

After a moment, Reolus opened his eyes, and white holy fire burnt there, furious and intense. He saluted, his sword leaving a faint glowing after-image hanging in the air for a moment, and nodded to the Norscan. The barbarian warlord ceased his restless pacing and strode towards the grail knight, axes bobbing up and down in his hands in eagerness.

They came together with a brutal clash of weapons, trading blows back and forth with such speed and skill that it was impossible for the eye to follow.

Calard found himself virtually unable to breathe, so focused was he on the struggle between these two awesome warriors. Never would he see their like again, he knew. Each was a champion that rose but once a century, and both would doubtless be remembered long into the future, their deeds recounted for generations to come.

Reolus stepped around his larger opponent, every movement in perfect balance, his glowing blade flashing back and forth to turn aside the Norscan's furious attacks. For long minutes the two battled, each straining to land a killing blow, yet they were so evenly matched that few hits found their mark at all, and none of those were fatal.

They stepped apart after a brutal passage of attacks, and both men were breathing hard. The Norscan was bleeding from a dozen wounds, and parts of his armour were hanging loose from his body. Reolus was bleeding from a cut to his head where he had suffered a glancing blow, and his armour was rent in two places, with blood seeping from wounds to his thigh and shoulder.

Still, neither warrior was about to relent, and after no more than a few heartbeats rest, they closed the distance separating them, grunting with effort as their blades came together.

The Norscan snarled and brought one axe crashing down in a powerful blow, intending to cut Reolus from crown to sternum. The grail knight whipped his sword around in a circular double-handed parry, and the axe blade slid down his sword to slam into the ice-hard ground. The Norscan's second axe wailed as it hammered around in a vicious arc, slicing towards Reolus's hip, and Calard tensed.

Rolling his wrists deftly, Reolus continued the movement of his circular parry and his blade flashed up, slicing cleanly through the Norscan's wrist even as the axe screamed towards him. The Chaos warlord's hand was completely severed, and it fell to the ground, axe still clutched in its grasp. The move had been so perfectly executed, so perfectly timed, that it took Calard a moment to register what had just occurred.

The barbarian bellowed in pain and rage, blood pumping from the stump of his arm, but still managed to get his other axe blade in the way of a savage strike from Reolus that was arcing in towards his groin. The Norscan deflected another two lightning attacks, staggering backwards in an effort to put some room between him and his furious attacker.

A wild swing forced Reolus to jump backwards, giving the Norscan some much needed breathing space. The bloody stump at the end of his left arm was dripping into the snow, and he was hissing in pain and rage.

Reolus circled the Norscan warily, the blood that had splattered his silver and blue tabard sliding off it like water off oiled leather, leaving it pristine and unspoiled. The Norse were chanting a word – a name? – over and over, stamping their feet and clashing weapons against shields in time to the pounding rhythm.

'Styr-bjorn! Styr-bjorn! Styr-bjorn!'

The sound echoed relentlessly around the castle, rebounding back off the curtain walls, reverberating maddeningly. The sound drowned out the shouts and cheers of the heavily outnumbered Bretonnians, and the Norscan warlord seemed to find strength in the sound.

'Styr-bjorn! Styr-bjorn! Styr-bjorn!'

With a roar, the Norscan launched himself towards Reolus, slashing his axe towards the grail knight's neck. Reolus turned the blow aside and struck for the throat, but the Norscan caught the blow on his armoured forearm, knocking it aside. The grail knight deflected two more slashing axe blows, each one knocking him back three paces, and the Norscan kept coming after him, roaring in fury.

Reolus swayed aside from one of the frenzied attacks and the Norscan's arm flicked out as they came close together, bloody stump hooking around the back of the grail knight's neck. Before he could slip free, Reolus was pulled into a rising knee, the blow striking him in the sternum with sickening force. His breastplate buckled inwards, and the Norscan drove his knee up into the smaller man again, wrenching his armour further out of shape.

The grail knight managed to twist free of the Norscan's grasp, his blade slashing a bloody gash across his enemy's face.

Reolus ducked beneath a hate-fuelled strike, the axe slicing a hair's breadth past his face, and stepping to the side, the grail knight slashed his blade across the barbarian's thigh. The blade sliced through armour and iron-hard muscle and struck bone. The Bretonnian paladin tore his sword free, and as the Norscan swung at him with his bloody stump, he impaled the limb on its length. The sword passed through the warlord's forearm and slid clear though the other side.

With a twist of his arm, the Norscan disarmed Reolus, leaving the fiercely glowing blade Durendyal jutting from his arm, and with astonishing speed, the warlord backhanded his opponent, the hallowed sword plunging into Reolus's neck.

The grail knight staggered back a step, gasping in shock as blood sprayed from the fatal wound. Using his body's momentum, the Norscan's axe wailed through the air and hacked Reolus's head from his shoulders.

Calard reeled as he saw the grail knight's head sail into the air, blood spraying out in fountain as it spun. It hit the ground and bounced and rolled, finally coming to rest staring up at the keep, eyes wide and staring and mouth fixed open in an expression of surprise. The fey white flames in Reolus's eyes spluttered and died.

His body was on its knees, blood pumping from his neck like a geyser, then it fell forwards into the snow, lifeless.

The Bretonnians had fallen into deathly silence, staring in disbelief and shock at the headless corpse of their defeated champion. Calard groaned in horror, shaking his head in denial, his eyes wide with shock.

'Lady of grace, no,' breathed Bertelis.

'Styr-bjorn! Styr-bjorn! Styr-bjorn!' came the relentless pounding chant of the Norscans, the sound increasing in volume.

The Norscan warlord turned and struck the grail knight's corpse, leaving the blade embedded deep in his flesh in the manner of a woodsman leaving his axe embedded in a log. Then the towering warrior limped over to Reolus's head, and bent to retrieve it. He hefted it into the air by its hair, and Calard groaned again as the warlord raised it high for all to see. Throwing his head back, the Norscan roared his victory to the heavens.

As if in response, lightning crackled through the dark clouds overhead, lighting them from within, followed a moment later by rolling thunder.

For a fraction of a second Calard saw a second image superimposed over the body of the Norscan, a black-fleshed daemon of incalculable power. It was larger than the Norscan by a good four feet, cloven hoofed, and its eyes blazed with hellfire. Shadowy wings were furled behind its back, and black smoke billowed from its fanged mouth. Two pairs of horns curled from its head, and its pitch-black muscles rippled with power. Before the image flickered and disappeared, Calard saw that it had but one hand, and in its other it held a familiar, wolf-headed axe, its ruby eye burning red. The image was gone in an instant, and he blinked, unsure if he had truly seen it or not. Was it a glimpse of what the Norscan was becoming? Was it the Norscan's true form?

'Styr-bjorn! Styr-bjorn! Styr-bjorn!'

Calard swayed as the sound pounded against the keep, and he saw the enemy warlord turn and bark an order, beckoning with his bloody stump of an arm.

The Norscan sorcerer strode forward, a grin on his savage face, and rammed a spear into the snow, its tip pointing towards the sky. Then the savage warlord rammed Reolus's head onto the spear, and fresh roars erupted from the barbarian horde as thunder rolled ominously across the heavens.

The sorcerer slashed his hand and began to chant, and the warlord turned back towards the keep.

'Bring me my son,' he boomed, his voice stabbing into the mind of every man present.

'CALARD!' SAID ELISABET as the doors to her chambers were thrown open. Her haunted face lit up momentarily to see him, but the young lord of Garamont's face was a grim mask and he avoided looking at her. The Duke of Lyonesse entered behind him, accompanied by the sweating, fat Marquis of Carabas.

The young lady of Marlemont was propped up in her bed, with her swaddled babe asleep in her arms. Her face was flushed, and the Damsel Anara sat in a high-backed plush chair nearby, her tiny frame dwarfed by the massive chair.

'He is dead, then,' said Anara flatly.

Calard nodded curtly in reply, and he saw tears in his sister's eyes before she dropped her head.

'I felt it when he passed over,' she said, 'but I hoped that I had been mistaken.'

'He fought bravely,' said Calard, his voice cracked. He still could not believe Reolus was dead.

'You have come for the child, then,' said Anara, and Elisabet glanced sharply at the damsel.

'I do,' said Calard coldly, answering his sister.

'The babe was promised to the Enchantress,' said Anara, rising to her feet.

'Of what do you speak?' Elisabet breathed, clutching her child protectively to her chest.

'It is nothing but a Norscan bastard,' snapped Calard, looking at Elisabet for the first time since entering the room. She recoiled from his anger and hurt, tears coming unbidden to her eyes. The baby was woken by Calard's sharp tone, and it began to cry.

Calard swore, and his gaze quickly shifted, moving back towards his sister. Anara had a determined look upon her face, chin jutting forward. He remembered her wearing the exact same stubborn expression as a child. His expression hardened.

'We *have* to give them the child,' he said coldly.

'You cannot take him,' said Elisabet. Calard saw that her face was unnaturally pale and drawn, and there was a feverish light in her eyes. She was rocking back and forth, her son bawling in her arms. 'He speaks to me, speaks right into my head. He doesn't want to go with you. You cannot have him.'

'She is not in her right mind,' said Anara. 'She has been through much.'

Calard stared at Elisabet in horror and pity.

'Will she recover?' he said.

'Perhaps,' said Anara. 'Given time.'

'Reolus gave his word,' Calard said in a low voice. 'I have to take that child.'

'It was already promised to the Enchantress,' replied Anara.

'It would besmirch Reolus's honour if we did not give it to the Norscans,' hissed Calard, not taking his eyes off Elisabet, who was still rocking back and forth, muttering to herself.

Calard realised that if his sister decided to put her foot down and refuse to hand the child over to the Norse, there was nothing that he, or the duke for that matter, would be able to do to contradict her. As all damsels, Anara operated outside of the structured, hierarchy of order in Bretonnia, having the power to overrule knights and dukes alike, though they rarely chose to enact that power in practice. Only the king held more sway than they, and even he could be overruled by the Enchantress.

'The young castellan of Garamont speaks the truth, Lady Anara,' said Duke Adalhard. 'As much as it pains me, we must. It would make a mockery of Reolus's memory if we did otherwise.'

Anara continued to stare at Calard, and he could see that she was divided. Her eyes filled with tears once again, and she dropped her gaze.

'Why did you leave me?' she whispered. 'Foolish man.'

She blinked away her tears and lifted her head.

'The consequences of this act will lie upon you two, and you two alone,' she said finally, staring first at Calard, then at the Duke of Lyonesse. 'Whatever evil befalls Bretonnia as a consequence of this child living – and evil *will* befall Bretonnia because of this child – *you* will be the blame and cause of it.'

'Agreed,' said Calard.

'Agreed,' said Duke Adalhard after a moment of thought.

Anara stepped aside, shaking her head, and Calard hardened his heart as he walked to Elisabet's bedside.

'He doesn't want to go with you,' said Elisabet. She screwed her eyes shut tightly, and began shaking her head from side to side. 'He's hurting me! He says he will stop hurting me if you all go away! Go away! Don't take him from me. He needs me!'

Elisabet was in obvious pain, and she clutched her wailing child tightly to her body.

'Give me the child,' he said in a low voice.

Elisabet continued to cry, shaking her head.

'Elisabet,' said Calard, his voice cracking as he reached for the swaddled babe. 'Elisabet, you have to give him to me.'

She wailed, crying out in denial and pain as her child was taken from her. Calard turned his back on her, head bowed, holding the child in his arms. Elisabet screamed and sobbed, clawing at him as he walked away.

Calard looked down into the bawling child's face. He looked like any other babe, with nothing to hint at any inherent evil lurking within. A tuft of pale hair topped his head, and his eyes were a startling silver-grey. He was a big baby, strong and healthy, and his cries came from powerful lungs. Calard tried to shut out Elisabet's frantic cries as he walked from the room.

Bertelis and Maloric stood outside, and the passageway was lined with knights, their faces uniformly sombre.

Down the grand marble staircase he descended, the only sound his own footsteps echoing sharply, the cries of the child in his arms and the ever more frantic screams of Elisabet, echoing through the passages behind him.

Reaching the bottom of the stairs, he began to cross the broad chamber towards the keep's inner courtyard, flanked by Duke Adalhard and the Marquis of Carabas. Scores of knights were gathered as witness in the great hall, as silent and respectful as if they were attending a funeral procession. The Empire ambassador, Dieter Weschler, bowed curtly as they passed.

Halfway across the hall, Calard heard a strangled cry and turned to see Elisabet, dressed in her nightclothes, struggling to chase after him. She was being held back by Bertelis at the top of the stairs, and Anara hovered in the shadows behind her.

'Please, Calard, don't!' Elisabet wailed. 'He is scared, my love, and he is hurting me! He doesn't mean to. Give him back to me and the pain will stop. He needs me!'

Elisabet struggled against Bertelis, and her nails dug into the younger Garamont noble's face. He cursed, and released her. Bertelis pushed her away from him, positioning himself to block her progress.

'Calard, please!' begged Lady Elisabet.

'Quiet, woman!' barked Bertelis. 'Poisoner! Deceitful slattern! Murderess! All of this is your fault! Every knight that died here is on your head! Every one! Reolus died because of you!'

Lady Elisabet slapped Bertelis across the face, the sharp sound echoing throughout the hall.

Blood was seeping from the corner of his mouth, and Bertelis's eyes blazed in anger. He slapped Elisabet back, striking her with the back of his hand, perhaps harder than he had intended. The young Bastonnian noblewoman reeled back from the blow, losing her balance as her bare feet slipped on the smooth marble surface at the top of the stairs.

Calard sucked in a breath as he saw Elisabet fall. Bertelis reached for her in desperation, trying to grab her, but he was too slow, and Elisabet tumbled backwards down the staircase. Her head cracked sharply on the corner of one of the steps, and she came to rest half way down, broken, lifeless.

Bertelis took a few steps down towards her, his eyes wide in horror. Anara pushed by Bertelis and descended swiftly, kneeling besides the fallen girl. She felt for a pulse, and looked Calard in the eyes. She shook her head.

Calard halted, a wracking sob making his body shake. The child in his arms continued to bawl, his cries echoing through the expanse of the hall. Bertelis looked down at his brother, his eyes filled with despair and horror.

'I... I...' said Bertelis, shaking his head in denial.

'Come, lad,' said Duke Adalhard, placing a hand upon Calard's shoulder. Calard stared at his brother for a second, then turned and strode from the hall.

He exited the great doors and walked down the steps into the small courtyard beyond. Snow crunched underfoot, and the sky above was filled with the ugly cries of carrion birds. Calard walked across the courtyard, his expression hardening with every step.

As he walked towards it, the great doors of the keep's gatehouse were swung wide, and the one remaining portcullis lifted with the clanking of chains. Only half an hour earlier, Reolus himself had walked out through those same gates.

The duke was a reassuring presence at his shoulder, and he kept his head held high as he walked through the devastation of the killing ground. Untold hundreds of bodies were strewn within the passage passing through the gatehouse, killed by arrow and scalding hot oil. They lay, contorted in their twisted death throes, many of them with their skin blistered and peeling from their bodies. The stench was repulsive.

Calard's eyes fixed onto the figure waiting beyond the gatehouse; the enemy sorcerer. The wiry man grinned like a fox, peering hungrily towards the child held in his arms, and Calard felt his hatred swell within him.

The immense figure of the enemy warlord stood twenty paces back from the keep, arms folded across his broad chest. He looked even larger than Calard had remembered, and he clenched his jaw together tightly, wanting nothing more than to see the Norscan dead. A young woman stood at his side, garbed for war in the manner of a man, and the resemblance between her and the warlord was so strong that there could be no doubting that she was his daughter.

A black-armoured Norscan was dragging Reolus's body through the snow by one foot, and he dumped the holy knight unceremoniously before the gatehouse.

The Norscan warlord bellowed something in his indecipherable tongue, the words sounding harsh and mocking to Calard's ears.

The sorcerer translated, speaking Breton with a heavy accent.

'The High Jarl of the Skaelings says that you may keep the body,' said the sorcerer, grinning, exposing teeth that had been filed to points. 'The head he will keep, so that his enemy's power will be his, now and forever.'

Calard bristled but bit his lip to keep quiet.

'Take the child and be gone, Norscan filth,' said Duke Adalhard.

'Yes, the child,' said the sorcerer, eyes lighting up covetously. 'Give it to me.'

Calard's jaw twitched, and he looked to the duke. Adalhard nodded, somewhat reluctantly, and Calard stepped warily towards the sorcerer.

As he drew near, he realised he could smell the man. It was the smell of a predator's den – a mixture of rotting meat, wet fur and sweat – though there was something else there as well, an oddly metallic tang that made his skin crawl.

Every instinct screamed to draw his sword and run this foul creature through, but Calard pushed the urge back. His eyes flashing with the desire to do violence, he held out the wailing boy-child to the enemy.

The sorcerer snatched the babe from him, sneering at Calard victoriously. Then the sorcerer spat, and Calard felt the Norscan's hot saliva strike him in the face. He snarled and reached for his sword, taking an aggressive step towards the sorcerer, but Duke Adalhard was at his side in an instant, a hand on his arm. Cursing under his breath, Calard slid the half-drawn sword of Garamont back into its scabbard.

The enemy sorcerer snorted derisively and barked something in the Norscan tongue that was clearly an insult, then turned his back on Calard, striding towards the towering warlord.

The barbarian lord took his child in his arms, and its crying ceased instantly. The brutal Norscan, his face still painted a terrifying, daemonic red tone, smiled down at his son and the babe gurgled and smiled back.

Then the Norscan lifted the child in one hand, and turned to face his army. He roared two words at the top of his lungs, words that could only have been 'my son', and the Norscan army roared.

'WE HAVE THE child,' gloated Bjarki. 'Let us finish the horsemen bastards off. Great Kharnath will rejoice as their blood flows and his throne is garnered with their skulls.'

'I agree,' snarled Hrefna. 'Let us bleed them all for the death of my sister.'

Styrbjorn's elder daughter, Fraygerd, had died beneath the blade of the gold-armoured enemy jarl, and Hrefna was still feeling the loss keenly.

'No,' said Styrbjorn, smiling down at the gleeful face of his son.

'No?' said Bjarki. 'Why in the name of the true gods not?'

'I defeated a worthy foe this day,' replied Styrbjorn, 'a mighty champion the equal of any that I have ever battled. I gave my word that if I defeated him I would leave these shores once my son was delivered to me. I would honour his memory by holding to my word.'

'Honour his memory?' spat Bjarki. 'He was a soft, southern whoreson! He deserves no such honour!'

'I said no, Bjarki. For now.'

Styrbjorn turned towards the gatehouse of the enemy stone fort, seeing the enemy jarl, armoured in gold. Another man stood at his side. This one had dark hair, and wore a tabard of blue and red over his armour. A silver dragon was emblazoned on his chest. A good symbol that, he thought. To the Norse it represented power, martial strength and passion. That warrior was young, he saw, and bristled with hatred. That was an emotion Styrbjorn understood, and knew that had this angry young knight been born of a Skaeling woman he would have been blessed by great Kharnath and become a mighty warrior indeed.

'Translate for me,' he ordered, and began to speak.

'I shall honour your dead champion, and hold to my promise. I leave these shores, but I shall return. On that day my son will stand at my side. Together we shall lay waste to your lands. We shall kill every man, woman and child that we find, and shatter every last one of your stone forts to rubble. There shall be no quarter given then. There shall be no bargaining for your lives.'

The young, angry knight dressed in red and blue snapped something in reply as Bjarki completed his translation.

'What did he say?' he asked.

'He said "I will be waiting", my lord,' replied Bjarki.

Styrbjorn smiled, nodding his head towards the young knight.

'I believe that he will,' he said. Then he turned and walked away, barking orders.

Within two hours the Norscans were gone, dragonships heading back out to sea, turning northward once at the horizon. They left their dead where they lay, thousands upon thousands of corpses left to rot, and the shores of Lyonesse were littered with shattered ships.

'I will be waiting,' repeated Calard.

CHLOD WOKE WITH a start as his rat bit him hard on his one remaining ear. He cried out, feeling constricted, unable to see, and shivering uncontrollably. He was soaked to the skin and half frozen, and bizarrely, the smell of apples was strong in his nostrils.

It took a moment to remember what was going on. He was not dead; not yet, at any rate. He was inside a barrel in the storeroom at the bottom of the harbour gatehouse. He'd spent almost an hour and half in the freezing waters feigning death, trying to appear as nothing more than another floating corpse, before an opportunity to escape had arisen. He had slunk out of the harbour like a half-drowned rat, his limbs numb with cold, and had managed to evade detection as he crawled his way into the storeroom. Once there, he stowed himself inside a half-empty barrel, climbing in and pulling his legs up to his chest, sitting on top of a pile of rotting apples, before pulling the lid over its top.

He pushed up that lid now and peered out, his tongue sticking out the side of his crooked mouth. Seeing no one, and hearing nothing, he climbed warily out, and stretched his aching back.

He moved to the entrance of the tower, keeping to the shadows and ready to duck back into his hiding place at the slightest sign of trouble, and looked out across Lyonesse harbour. There was not an enemy in sight; even their longships were gone. He saw figures moving through the streets, and ducked back until he realised they were men-at-arms, sorting through the dead.

The Norscans were gone. It was a miracle!

He was alive!

Chlod looked down at the scrap of regal blue cloak still clutched his hands. He rubbed the inside of the scrap against his face, liking the sensation of the mink-fur against his skin. Placing it on his lips, he kissed it. Did it truly have protective powers? Had his prayer to Reolus truly been answered?

He pondered the notion for a moment, and came to the conclusion that Reolus must have protected him; there was no other explanation.

'I truly am his pilgrim,' he said in wonder.

It took him the better part of an hour to make his way up to the keep, and by the time he got there his stomach was full of food looted from abandoned houses, and he was dressed in clothes that were almost completely free of bloodstains that he had stripped from a corpse. He wore a pouch bulging with coin, and upon his fat, sausage-like fingers he had pushed several copper and bronze rings, which he had hacked from the bloated fingers of the dead.

All in all, Chlod was feeling mightily pleased with himself, but that newfound sense of well-being was shattered when he came upon the corpse of Reolus. The headless body of the grail knight lay atop a stone altar in the middle of the square before the keep, surrounded by flowers and candles. Hundreds of mourning nobles were trailing past the body, paying their last respects, and Chlod wordlessly joined the peasant queue.

For six hours he waited, kept twenty paces back by stern-faced wardens, but at last the queue began to move. No lowborn was allowed within a dozen yards of the holy paladin's body however, and Chlod stamped his foot in frustration – he had been hoping to garner a holy keepsake from the grail knight's corpse, just in case the protective magic of his scrap of Reolus's cape ran out. He had a knife in his hand, hidden in a deep pocket, ready and everything; he had thought to perhaps get himself a finger.

Chlod stuck his lip out in a pout as he stood on tiptoes to see the corpse. There were too many guards around for him to have any hope of sneaking past them to get his relic; he'd just have to wait until the knight was interred. He'd been a grave robber before, and had no qualms about desecrating one of Morr's gardens again.

He was about to turn away when he heard a voice.

'Stop that peasant! Yes, that one!'

A hand grabbed Chlod by the scruff of his neck, and he was dragged backwards, wincing.

'The wretch stole something from you, did he?' said the warden who had a hold of him, and Chlod squinted up to see a young knight walking towards him.

He recognised him as the lord of Garamont, and he swore under his breath. He'd run into the man several times over the last year; he'd narrowly escaped a hanging after poaching on Garamont lands, and had even been employed to kill the knight once. That had been a narrow escape. He tried to keep his head down, praying to Reolus that he wasn't recognised, else he would hang for sure.

'Release him,' ordered the knight, and the warden did so. The man-at-arms gave him a cuff over the head for good measure, and Chlod glared at him.

'I know you, don't I?' said the lord of Garamont, eyes narrowed.

'I don't think so, my lord,' said Chlod, his eyes downcast.

'No, I do know you. You were one of Reolus's pilgrims, weren't you?'

'Um,' said Chlod, not sure the best way to answer.

'Answer the question, scum,' snapped the warden, cuffing him hard over the head once again.

'Enough of that, warden,' said the knight sharply, his tone icy.

'Sorry, my lord,' said the soldier, glaring at Chlod as if the rebuke was somehow *his* fault.

'Were you or were you not one of Reolus's grail pilgrims?' asked the noble once again.

'Yes?' ventured Chlod finally.

'What will you do now?' said the noble, and Chlod tensed.

This was a dangerous question, and he licked his lips as he tried to concoct an answer that would not condemn him. All peasants within Bretonnia owed fealty to a lord or landowner; they were bonded to them as serfs, and they could not as much as pass wind without their say-so. Those engaged in holy pilgrimages were sometimes allowed a modicum of freedom, but since Chlod's benefactor was now nothing more than food for worms, he had no right to claim being on a pilgrimage any longer. If it was made known that Chlod had run away from his lord's service he would be flogged, castrated and left to rot in a cage hanging from the castle walls.

'I, ah…' he said.

'I think he's an imbecile, my lord,' offered the warden, but he promptly shut his mouth when the knight glared at him.

Before Chlod could fashion a plausible story, the noble spoke again.

'Can you cook?' he said. Chlod blinked, surprised by the question, and then nodded his head vigorously.

'Clean?'

Again he nodded his head.

'Good. If you are no longer bonded to any lord, I offer you employment,' said the lord of Garamont. 'Out of respect for your former, now deceased benefactor, may the Lady bless his soul, you will be my manservant. Is that agreeable?'

Chlod nodded his head enthusiastically once again. He clutched the scrap of Reolus's cloak tightly in his hand. Once again, the grail knight had smiled upon him. Things were looking up.

'CALARD,' SAID BERTELIS, pushing through the crowd to reach his brother's side. The younger son of Garamont's eyes were red-rimmed, and his lip was trembling.

'I... I'm so sorry,' he said, unable to look Calard in the eyes. 'It was an accident. I didn't mean...'

Calard stared at him coldly.

'You killed her,' he said, accusingly.

'Brother, please...' breathed Bertelis, a pained expression on his face. Calard's voice, devoid of emotion, interrupted him.

'From this day forth I have no brother,' said Calard. He turned his back on Bertelis, and walked away, a hunchbacked peasant loping along behind him.

EPILOGUE

CALARD STARED GRIMLY at the two bodies hanging from the walls of Castle Garamont; a traitor and a witch.

After the death of Reolus back in Lyonesse, three months earlier, he had gone to his cousin Tassilo's side. He had been horrified and disappointed to learn that the dying knight had been a party to the plot against him, and the young noble begged for forgiveness. With his dying breath he had confessed to Calard from whom the order had originated.

He stared coldly at the corpse of the old chamberlain, Folcard, as it swung in the breeze.

In truth, he had been surprised that the plot had originated from Folcard, for he had suspected that the Lady Calisse, Bertelis's mother, had been responsible. Calard felt a momentary twinge of guilt for how he had treated Bertelis, but hardened his heart against it. Since he had returned to Garamont, the Lady Calisse had confined herself to her quarters, which suited Calard just fine.

Even if she was no murderess, she was a still a viperous serpent and he had no wish to look upon her.

The witch had been a surprise. Left to rot in the deepest oubliette of Castle Garamont's dungeon, she had been dragged out on Calard's order, and with a shock he realised that he recognised her. Not her physical appearance – he was certain that he had never clapped eyes on the hideous crone before – no, it was by her hate-filled eyes that he had recognised her.

He had ordered her tongue cut from her mouth on the spot, and had not felt happy until he had seen her last twitch of life as she was hung.

'Cut the hag down,' Calard ordered. 'Have the body burnt.'

The hunchbacked manservant nodded his head.

'The other one?' the peasant said.

'It can serve as a warning to all traitors,' said Calard. 'Leave it where it is.'

With a bow, the hunchback limped off and Calard, castellan of Garamont turned on his heel and strode through his castle. Servants and bondsmen curtsied and bowed as he passed them by. He climbed a staircase, his footfalls ringing out sharply, and marched down corridors lined with portraits of previous lords of Garamont.

He stepped out onto an east-facing balcony. The early morning sunshine was bright, and there was not a cloud in the sky.

A table was set for breakfast here in the sun, and his guests sat there, dining.

Baron Montcadas, a strip of folded silk covering his empty eye sockets, was snorting into his food at some jest made, no doubt, by Calard's young cousin, Orlando. Opposite the boy sat Montcadas's niece, Lady Josephine. She smiled warmly at Calard as he approached the table.

Montcadas turned his head in Calard's direction, hearing his approach.

'That you, boy?' boomed the baron, and Calard shook his head slightly, a ghost of a smile on his lips.

'I'm no more a boy than you are the Fay Enchantress,' replied Calard.

'Bah,' said Montcadas, waving a hand dismissively. 'When you get to my age, everyone is young. Will you join us for breakfast?'

'No,' said Calard, and he saw the disappointment on Josephine's face. He felt a certain amount of regret; he had come to truly care for the girl, and he believed that had his heart not been so damaged, he would have come to love her. She would have made a fine wife, but his path was set.

'You intend to go through with this, then?' said the baron, all levity gone from his voice.

'I do,' said Calard.

The castellan of Garamont turned towards his young cousin, who was sulking. The boy didn't want him to go, he realised.

Calard placed the scabbarded sword of Garamont upon the table before the seven year-old Orlando.

'Until the day comes that I should return, victorious, you are now the castellan of Garamont, young master knight,' Calard said.

No one said anything, and with nothing more to be said, Calard bowed and walked away.

Calard's heart felt lighter than it had done for what seemed like an age, he realised. It was as if a burden had been lifted from his shoulders. He knew that he left his realm in good hands. Baron Montcadas had promised to stay with the boy, to govern in his stead until such a time came as Calard returned to claim his position, or Orlando came of age – whichever came first.

He had a spring in his step as he strode through Castle Garamont, the home that he was about to leave behind for the Lady knew how long. It was highly likely that he would never live to see its halls again, but even that thought did not dampen his spirit.

Quickening his pace, Calard hurried to the small shrine to the Lady on the ground floor of his castle. Outside its entrance was his lance, and he took it his hands, bearing it before him as he entered his family's humble chapel, where countless Garamont lords before him had prayed.

Once inside, he placed the lance reverently upon the altar. Hundreds of candles lit the chapel, lending the space a serene glow. Kneeling, Calard bowed his head.

'Lady of grace and beauty,' he began, speaking the ritualistic vow in a hushed, reverential tone, 'I set down my lance, symbol of duty, upon your shrine. I spurn those whom I love. I relinquish all, and take up the tools of my journey. No obstacle will stand before me. No plea for help shall find me wanting. No moon will look upon me twice lest I be judged idle. I give my body, heart and soul to you, oh Lady, and I shall seek wherever thou might be found. This is my questing vow, and I swear it before you, mistress of mercy, and beg that you shall strike me down should I falter.'

He felt the spirit of the Lady infuse him, warming him from within, and he knew that he had made the right decision.

This was the only way that he was ever going to prove his purity, to his knights and to himself. This was the only way that he was going to be free of the recurring nightmare of the Green Knight. It was time for him to face his fear, to stand and defy it.

It was time for Calard to take up the quest, never to rest until he was visited by a vision of the Lady of the

Lake herself and offered a draught of her sacred grail. For many knights such a journey took decades, though most were slain long before their goal was fulfilled.

Many of those knights who succeeded in their search and drank from the holy grail died as a result, found unworthy; only those pure of heart, with not a hint of taint within them, survived imbibing that divine nectar.

Calard smiled. He was now embarked on the Long Journey; he was now a Questing Knight of Bretonnia.

IT WAS NEARING midnight and Bertelis was huddled before a spluttering fire, miserable and soaked to the skin. He sat in the lee of a dark ruin. Once it had been a sacred grail chapel, but it had long been abandoned to nature and the weather, its crumbling walls overrun with ivy and moss.

The younger son of Garamont raised his head as he heard the sound of horse's hooves on the road, and watched as a knight garbed in white plodded through the rain towards him. As he got closer, Bertelis recognised the knight's heraldry; a distinctive black fleur-de-lys. His jaw dropped in wonder. This was none other than Merovech of Arlons, the albino knight who had bested him in the tournament before word of the Norscan invasion had come. He stood to welcome the swordsman to his camp, suddenly embarrassed at his pitiful fire.

'Ho the camp,' called Merovech from twenty paces distance. 'May I approach your fire?'

'Please do, my lord,' called Bertelis.

The knight reined in and looked down at the youngest son of Garamont. He raised the visor of his helmet, exposing his face, as pale as winter snow.

'Bertelis, isn't it?' said Merovech, taking in his host's heraldry.

'I am honoured that you remembered me, my lord Merovech,' said Bertelis with a bow.

'I said that we would meet again,' replied Merovech. 'I was impressed with your swordsmanship. It showed potential.'

'I fear that my humble skills pale in comparison to yours, my lord,' said Bertelis.

'Ah, but skills can be learnt,' said Merovech, exposing sharp canines as he smiled. 'And I am a very good teacher.'

ABOUT THE AUTHOR

After finishing university Anthony Reynolds set sail from his homeland and ventured forth to foreign climes. He ended up settling in the UK, and managed to blag his way into Games Workshop's hallowed Design Studio. There he worked for four years as a Games Developer and two years as part of the Management team. He now resides back in his hometown of Sydney, overlooking the beach and enjoying the sun and the surf, though he finds that to capture the true darkness and horror of Warhammer and Warhammer 40,000 he has taken to writing in what could be described as a darkened cave.

ISBN 978-1-84416-551-3

ISBN 978-1-84416-396-0

ISBN 978-1-84416-527-8

BESTSELLING WARHAMMER SERIES

The First Omnibus contains the novels *Trollslayer, Skavenslayer* and *Daemonslayer*

The Second Omnibus contains the novels *Dragonslayer, Beastslayer* and *Vampireslayer*

ISBN 978-1-84416-391-5

ISBN 978-1-84416-509-4

UK ISBN 978-1-84416-663-3 US ISBN 978-1-84416-575-9